LIBERTY FOR PAUL

ROSE GORDON

D1525712

LIBERTY FOR PAUL

© 2011 C. Rose Gordon
Cover image copyright © 2013 Liberty Digital Graphics Designs
All rights reserved.

Published by Parchment & Plume, LLC
www.parchmentandplume.com

Other Titles Available by Rose Gordon

SCANDALOUS SISTERS SERIES
Intentions of the Earl
Liberty for Paul
To Win His Wayward Wife

GROOM SERIES
Her Sudden Groom
Her Reluctant Groom
Her Secondhand Groom
Her Imperfect Groom

COMING 2012-2013

BANKS BROTHERS BRIDES SERIES
His Contract Bride
His Yankee Bride
His Jilted Bride
His Brother's Bride

OFFICER SERIES (AMERICAN SET)
The Officer and the Bostoner
The Officer and the Southerner
The Officer and the Traveler

For my oldest son who spent most of his fourth year referring to himself in the third person.

And to my husband, who reminds me every day that chivalry is still alive by coming home from work, offering me his arm and escorting me to the mailbox; then opening it and saying, "Your mail, Mrs. Gordon."

Chapter 1

Early December 1812
London

Liberty Banks had two loves in her life. One of which her entire family (and most of London Society) knew about: propriety. Her other love she went about hiding a little better. Not perfectly, but well enough that for the most part she was able to keep her second love a secret, and that, was her love for revenge.

Sure, when she and her sisters were young girls, Brooke, her oldest sister, knew it was Liberty who had tied her slippers together with some white string just long enough that Brooke didn't notice it before she started to walk. After only three steps, Brooke fell on her face because she'd taken too large a step and the string caused her to trip. Both Liberty and their other sister, Madison, laughed, but neither owned up to the prank; nor placed the blame on the other. But Brooke didn't need a confession. She knew it was Liberty. Not two days later, Liberty opened up one of her drawers to grab a pair of stockings and a toad jumped out at her causing her to nearly leap out of her skin!

When she confronted Brooke, who was the only Banks sister who would dare touch a toad, Brooke simply told her it was what she deserved for tying her slippers together. Liberty just shook her head and didn't disclose that the reason for tying Brooke's slippers together in the first place was because Brooke had stolen them from her at the milliner's shop. Well, maybe not stolen exactly. Liberty had seen them first and was about to grab them and claim how wonderful they would go with her new green velvet gown. Just then, Brooke accidentally knocked them from where they'd been sitting on the shelf because she wasn't used to how puffy her new stays made her dress. Then, when Brooke leaned down to pick them up, she'd cried with delight about how perfectly they'd match *her* new green silk dress and wouldn't part with them. This infuriated Liberty who decided then and there to get her revenge. And quite honestly, she'd been rather pleased to see Brooke fall on her face, even if it were only in front of her family.

The toad was a different matter altogether. It took her a while to get revenge for the toad, but when she did, she was able to escape notice and nothing happened to her in return. It was a good thing she hadn't been discovered, because she'd done something that really upset Brooke. She'd cut all the heads off her roses. Had Brooke known it was her; she'd probably be missing her own head. Brooke had always put a lot of time into her roses; they were her pride and joy. However, from listening to Brooke drone on spring after spring about her roses, Liberty knew that pruning them, or cutting the tops off, if one was being precise, actually helped the rosebush. So in a way, she did Brooke a favor.

Liberty didn't always do these things to be spiteful, mind you. On the other hand, some of it was pure, unadulterated spite, but she had a good reason to be a little spiteful. She was the youngest of three daughters and that came with a lot of vexation.

When she was younger, her older sisters would leave her out, saying she wasn't old enough to join in their games. With her sisters being only a year apart, and the younger of the two, Madison, being three years older than Liberty, it was easy for them to get away with leaving her out.

And, *if* they were made to include her, she always got the terrible part in whatever game they were playing. Sometimes she had to be the person standing in the middle while her sisters threw a ball back and forth over her head, or sometimes when they'd play Pioneers and Indians, she'd be the Indian who was given the inferior weapon. In short, she always had the unacceptable role.

When she and her sisters got older they were able to enjoy each other's company more. Perhaps "enjoy" wasn't the right word, but they were able to do activities together and be civil to each other. However, by then, the damage was done and Liberty made up her mind to pay her sisters back in kind for the way they'd treated her when she was younger.

At first, her newfound love for vengeance involved doing harmless, good-natured things to her sisters—either for their past or present sins. But a few months ago she started seeking revenge on someone outside of her family, and it wasn't exactly harmless or good-natured.

It had only happened a few times seven months ago. But today, she'd decided she was once again going to seek revenge against a man named Mr. Paul Grimes.

Mr. Grimes was a devilishly handsome vicar who lived near Bath. He had a flawless face with high, distinguished cheekbones, a wide mouth that could make a girl swoon when he grinned, and beautiful emerald eyes that rested behind a pair of silver rimmed spectacles. His hair was a sandy blond color and was kept an inch or two longer than was fashionable. They'd been introduced at a house party that was being hosted by her uncle, Edward Banks, Baron Watson. Mr. Grimes had come to the house party to seek out Liberty's father—who also happened to be a minister. Upon meeting, Paul had told her father he had some problems in his vicarage and had asked her father to mentor him. Of course her father had agreed, because one, he liked to help people, no matter who they were or how awful their personalities; and two, because while spending some time in England, the man needed a hobby—desperately.

John, her father, grew up in England and went on his Grand Tour at nineteen. He was twenty when he reached America and met a woman named Carolina. In no time at all, he made her his wife and they moved to New York where he began work as a minister. It wasn't long after that the family grew and less than five years later they had three young daughters: Brooke, Madison, and Liberty.

This was the first time in twenty-five years that John had set foot on English soil. He'd said he loved his wife, daughters, and America and saw no reason to return to England. But when Brooke had reached her twenty-second year without any prospects and Madison fell into a state of melancholy after ending a courtship,

John packed them up and decided to see if the girls could make matches with English gentlemen.

Liberty had been so excited at the prospect, but knew she lacked the beauty her sisters possessed in abundance, therefore, she'd taken it upon herself to learn all the rules and execute them to perfection as her way of finding a husband. So far it hadn't worked, but she hadn't given up hope. Not yet anyway. Following the rules of society always had a way of helping a woman find a husband—she had numerous books to prove it. A man would not wish to be embarrassed by his wife, even if he did hold her in high esteem.

It was Liberty's love of propriety that led to her complete and utter dislike—and dare she admit, hatred?—for Mr. Grimes.

When they were first introduced, he'd immediately told her his wish for her to call him Paul instead of Mr. Grimes. There was no way she was going to be so informal with a man she'd just met; so she'd insisted he refer to her as Miss Liberty and she would call him Mr. Grimes. Just as she finished explaining her wish to remain formal, dinner was announced, and because no other unmatched lady or gentleman was nearby, they were paired up. So she ended up having to suffer his dreadful personality through the entire dinner.

The whole time he sat there looking angry. His jaw was clamped shut and his face appeared hard and as impassive as stone. When she spoke to him, he'd nod or give monosyllabic answers. He asked no questions and offered no conversation. It took her less than two minutes to conclude he was a bore.

If that had been the end of their acquaintance, she would have merely disliked him. But no, they had four other unfortunate encounters.

The next meeting happened when she was having a private conversation with Madison; which unbeknownst to her, he was eavesdropping on. In the middle of their conversation, he cleared his throat and proceeded to volunteer his unflattering opinion of Liberty. He'd told her she'd never find a husband and had said she was cold and callous. After such remarks, he'd had the nerve to *act* polite by seeking her out and apologizing; which she'd known he'd only done to save his newfound friendship with her father.

The second encounter had been only days later when he'd purposely let someone roll a lawn bowl over her toe. When he'd shown no real remorse, she'd elbowed him in his midsection; which had then led to the end of their second encounter, but had produced the need for a third.

After she'd elbowed him, he had made a yelping noise and had hobbled away. Not ten minutes later she'd been summoned to the room where he'd been waiting with her parents. Her uncle, the baron and host of the house party, had born witness to the events on the lawn and had told her father what had happened. Papa had demanded she do whatever Mr. Grimes thought was necessary for her to make amends. Then Papa and Mama had left, leaving her alone with Mr. Grimes.

Not two minutes after they left, Mr. Grimes started to remove his clothing! Come hell or high water, there was no way she was going to give her virtue to that beast. So she did the first thing that came to mind: picked up the closest thing to her and hurled it at his head.

She ran to her sister Brooke for help, and then went to the library to hide from Papa. He'd always been kind and gentle before, giving her no cause to be afraid of him, but after what had just happened, she'd be lying if she didn't admit she was terrified.

When he found her, he told her to stay away from the man, and that's exactly what she had done—until now.

She'd intended to avoid him forever, but then the most embarrassing accident she could imagine happened; and made it necessary for a fourth encounter.

In late November, winter hit with a vengeance. Snow and ice covered the streets of London and much to everyone's surprise, by early December the Thames had frozen over. When a large enough patch of ice covered the river, a Frost Fair opened.

Liberty wanted desperately to go, but neither Madison nor their parents wanted to go with her. She was certain Brooke would have gone with her, but Brooke was busy at Rockhurst with her new husband, Andrew Black, Earl of Townson. So when the highly annoying and always ill Lady Olivia Sinclair claimed she had a desire to go skating, Liberty could not agree to accompany her fast enough. She may not enjoy the company overmuch, but it might be the only way she could ever go, she reminded herself as she accepted the invitation.

They were there only a half hour when Lady Olivia took a brutal fall and brought Liberty down with her. Though Liberty had skated many times before, Lady Olivia had not, and she'd been hanging onto Liberty so tightly that when she fell, Liberty had no way to remain on her skates.

They fell on a thin sheet of ice and the weight from their bodies caused it to crack. When Lady Olivia started to roll around kicking and screaming like a banshee, the ice cracked more. Alex, Liberty's cousin, who just happened to be there, came to the rescue and helped Lady Olivia to her feet first—probably just to stop the ear piercing screams. He was too late in turning back to help Liberty before the ice broke completely, and down she went into the icy Thames.

She remembered splashing and trying to keep her head above water, but her wet skirts were making that impossible, and when she wasn't able to get a grip on Alex's hand, she went under. That's the last thing she remembered.

A week later she woke up to see Madison sitting by her bedside, telling her that her fever had finally broken. Now that the fever had passed, she was able to remain awake for longer periods and conduct a small conversation. But she still had to remain in bed, so Mama or Madison would come and entertain her all day.

Almost fully recovered, Liberty decided it was time to ask Madison what had happened. She told Madison she remembered going skating and her accident, but had no idea what happened afterward.

Madison's clear blue eyes looked out the window for a few moments before she took a deep breath. "Liberty, you're not going to want to hear this, but there are two unlikely heroes in your tale."

"Two? Unlikely? Whatever do you mean? I remember Alex

being there, but he's not an unlikely hero, is he?" Liberty asked, perplexed.

"Yes, Alex was there. However, he fell in, too. The Duke of Gateway pulled you both out," Madison said evenly, tucking one of her blonde curls behind her ear.

Liberty couldn't believe it. The duke hardly knew she existed. They had barely ever spoken. What she did know about him though was he was the worst kind of man there ever could be. He never did anything to be nice, and some—most—considered him to be very dangerous and not a man you'd want to be indebted to. Liberty shivered.

"Who was the other?" she asked curiously. If Gateway was one of her unlikely heroes, who else could it possibly be? Nobody was more unlikely than Gateway.

"Mr. Grimes," Madison said quietly.

"That's impossible," Liberty snapped, crossing her arms across her chest. "He wasn't even there. He was at his weekly visit with Papa. And anyway, he wouldn't help me unless his very life depended on it."

"That's not true," Madison said softly. "I know you don't like him, but there's no reason for you not to like him. He's actually very nice once you get to know him."

Liberty scowled. "You can get to know him all you like. My opinion of him hasn't changed. He is a filthy scoundrel who wants my virtue." Liberty inclined her chin an inch. "But he shall not get it."

Madison shook her head. "He doesn't want your virtue. I know you think he was undressing in order to ravish you; but Papa says he was angry and got overheated, and after everything that had just happened, I'm inclined to believe him."

"Oh Madison, you may be three years older than me, but you are far more naïve. No man starts to take off his neck cloth and shirt just because he's hot." Liberty had heard that explanation, too, and about died of embarrassment when she later thought about it—especially because it made sense. She may be a virginal nineteen almost twenty, but she knew if he meant to have her virtue, he probably wouldn't have started with his cravat. However, she couldn't put her finger on if she was embarrassed because of her silly assumption and hasty actions or if it was because he didn't want her that way. Her cheeks still burned whenever she thought about it.

"Liberty," Madison said as she idly played with the fringe of Liberty's counterpane and stared out the window again. Moving her eyes back to Liberty's face, she swallowed. "I think if he wanted your virtue, he would've already taken it."

Outraged, Liberty balled her hands into fists. "What's that supposed to mean?"

That's when Liberty heard about her life's most humiliating moment, a moment she wasn't even awake for.

After Gateway had loaded both her and Alex into his carriage (Lady Olivia had gone into hysterics and her maid had taken her home already), he took Liberty to her residence and dropped her off. He didn't stay, however, because he needed to deliver Alex to his house. The only person at home at the time was Mr. Grimes, who just happened to be there waiting for his weekly meeting with Papa. It was a Wednesday afternoon and all the servants were gone for their time off, so she'd been left completely in the hands of Mr. Grimes.

Madison told her that he had gathered her in his arms and carried her up to her bedroom. Once inside, he stripped off *all* of her clothes and wrapped her in a blanket. Then, he carried warm water up and filled the copper tub that was in her dressing room. After the tub was full, and he had word that the doctor was on his way, Mr. Grimes took her naked, unconscious body and placed her in the water. Then he sat beside her and waited with her there until Papa and Mama arrived.

Liberty thought she was going to die! Mr. Grimes had seen her naked! She closed her eyes to block the tears of embarrassment that were threatening to spill.

Madison claimed she was in the room when Mr. Grimes explained all of this to Mama and Papa. "He was so uncomfortable and embarrassed talking about it," she said calmly, as if that would make Liberty feel better about everything. "I have never seen anyone turn that shade of red, except perhaps you. Right now, you are just as red as he was when he recounted the events to Mama and Papa."

Liberty didn't respond. She couldn't respond. She was too busy wishing he had just let her die, rather than take off her clothes and look at her naked. The man was a monster who knew no bounds when it came to decency!

"Liberty, it's not that bad. As it is, you never even see him. You've made yourself scarce whenever he's been around since that house party. This changes nothing," she assured her. "You're not going to see him again, so it shouldn't matter."

"You wouldn't know," Liberty said between the sobs that were wracking her body. "You've never had a man see you naked before."

Madison looked like she'd been struck. Liberty thought she should say something, she hadn't meant for it to come out like it sounded. But she wasn't given the chance to make amends, before Madison quietly stood and departed. That was the last time she saw Madison for the rest of the day.

Sitting alone in silence, she thought of the apology she owed Madison. After she'd worked out the perfect words to express her remorse for her heartless comment, she started to form her plan of how she was going to get revenge on Mr. Grimes. He had no business seeing her naked, which was bad enough, but he'd taken it one step further by carrying her around and bathing her.

Madison said he'd *claimed* not to have taken her virtue, but he was the only one who really knew for sure. Even she couldn't be certain she was still intact down there. She suppressed *that* thought immediately.

There was no denying it, Mr. Grimes had gone over the line this time, and she was going to make sure he never did it again. After she was done with him, he would never show his face in England again. Well, perhaps it wouldn't be so bad that he'd be exiled, but, at the very least, he would not be going anywhere near any member of the Banks family. She was going to make sure of it.

Chapter 2

With a sigh, Paul sank further into the steaming hot water that filled the copper tub. He'd had a long day of travel and the hot water felt good on his aching muscles.

He still wasn't sure what had possessed him to accept the invitation to spend Christmas with the Banks family, but he had, and the least he could do was attempt to have a good time starting with a soothing bath.

When he'd first arrived, Turner, the Bankses' unusually unusual butler, told him the family had gone to the oldest daughter's townhouse for dinner and a night's entertainment.

Feeling relieved he wouldn't be forced to endure an uncomfortable dinner so soon after his arrival, he asked the butler to order him a tray and send for a bath.

Dinner was good. The bath was better.

Paul grabbed the cake of soap that was resting by the tub, dunked it in the water and spun it with his hands, creating a foamy lather. Paul ran the soap up his arm and shook his head. The irony was too much, he thought, transferring the soap to the other hand. The last time he'd been to this house, he'd been giving someone else a bath.

He scowled. That was a day he longed to forget. The whole situation had been awkward, but necessary. What else could he have done, let her catch her death from the ague? No. No matter how much he disliked Liberty, he couldn't have allowed harm to come to her.

When he saw how badly she needed help, he did the only

thing he could think to do: take care of her.

When the duke first brought her in, her lips were blue and her skin was so pale it was almost translucent. Coupled with her shallow breathing and low pulse rate, he knew instantly she required immediate care. Since it was Wednesday, the day of his weekly meeting with John and the servants' day off, he realized it was up to him to provide the care she required.

Leaving all rational thought behind, he scooped her up, took her upstairs and without much thought or emotion, removed her wet garments. Wrapping her in a warm blanket, he set out to boil some water and summon a doctor.

When the water was ready, the doctor still wasn't there, so he did what any person with a shred of humanity would: he bathed her.

At the time, it seemed the best course of action. She was literally freezing; she needed a hot bath to warm her. But half an hour later, it seemed like the worst idea he could've ever come up with.

Paul was kneeling down by the tub. He'd rested one arm on the back of the tub, supporting her head. The other hand held a warm, wet cloth and he was running it over the parts of Liberty that were not submerged in water—namely, the top of her chest. Suddenly, the door flew open, revealing a very shocked John and Carolina Banks.

Paul froze. "This isn't what it looks like," he said lamely, squeezing the cloth tightly in his hand and wishing he were invisible. It was bad enough to be caught giving their youngest daughter a bath, but to compound it with a lame excuse made it seem even worse. With a loud *Ker plunk,* the cloth he'd been holding hit the water, and Paul stood. "Sir, I…I…" Paul trailed off. There really wasn't anything to say. It didn't matter that he'd only been trying to help. He'd just been found bathing a naked young woman, and *nothing* he could say would justify that.

"Paul," John said roughly. "My study. Five minutes."

Paul's moss green eyes went wide behind his spectacles. He nodded his agreement and wordlessly left the room as fast as he could, studying the tops of his boots as he went.

The walk downstairs was what he imagined the walk to the guillotine must feel like: time suspended as your weary muscles force your heavy limbs to keep moving forward, all the while being alone with nothing but your thoughts, knowing the end of your life was right around the corner. The only difference was, at least the people who were slated to go to the guillotine would die very quickly, and in a humane way at that.

However, unlike a guillotine victim, he was about to be made to suffer in an inhumane way and for who knew how long. Surely John wanted to see him, so he could demand he marry that hoyden, which was actually worse than death in his opinion.

Too anxious to take a seat, he went to the window and looked out at the street. It was only one floor down to the street, too short of a fall to kill him if he jumped, he thought grimly. In light of being forced to marry Liberty, it wouldn't be perceived as cowardly at all to do oneself in; it would probably be thought to be heroic.

With a deep exhalation that fogged up the window, Paul resigned himself to his intolerable fate and plopped down into an empty, uncomfortable chair. Thoughts of what he *should* have done came flooding into his head: go get a lady from next door to care for her, send for the doctor sooner, keep her in her wet clothes and stick her in the tub. Any of those would have been a preferable course of action and would have eliminated the position he was currently in.

No use in wallowing in self-pity, he told himself, deciding that when John entered, he'd just tell the truth and beg for mercy. And if that didn't work, he'd marry her.

Paul reached into his coat pocket and took out his pocket watch. It wasn't anything of value to anyone but him. His maternal grandfather had given it to him when he was nine and his mother had died; for that reason alone, it had become his most valuable possession. Running his finger over the engraving, he popped it open to see how much longer he was going to be left alone with his thoughts. John had said five minutes, but after spending seven months in his company, Paul had learned John spoke in prophetic time, and five minutes really meant thirty. It had only been twenty. He closed the watch with a snap and shoved it back into his pocket, reminding himself for the hundredth time he needed to get a chain for it.

The last ten minutes ticked away slowly, and just as he'd predicted, when exactly thirty minutes had passed, John came into his study.

Paul jumped up from his chair. "Sir, please let me explain," he said before John could make his demands.

"There is no need to explain anything," John said quietly, coming over to stand beside him.

His eyes searched John's face. While John had always been extremely kind to him, this was a situation over which even the most composed person could find himself in a temper. "Pardon?"

"I said there's no need to explain anything. I heard about her fall on, or perhaps I should say *in*, the river," John said unevenly.

They both stared at each other for a minute. If John knew everything, did that mean he wasn't going to insist Paul marry Liberty? Or did that mean he was going to insist on it, but wasn't sure how to say it? His hopes soared, He dismissed his latter thought almost instantly when he remembered that, only seven months earlier, John had insisted a man marry one of his other daughters for a far lesser offense. If John hadn't demanded it yet, Paul was certain he wouldn't. Sighing with relief, he wasn't prepared when two arms wrapped around him and gave him a tight squeeze.

Paul awkwardly brought his hand up to pat John on the back.

"Thank you," John said after a minute then released him. A lone tear rolled down his face. "I cannot thank you enough for what you've done. If not for you…"

Paul nodded. "You're welcome, sir," he said tentatively.

"I know you two cannot abide each other. Why, I have no idea, but in any case, thank you for saving her."

Paul knew why they didn't like each other, and John should know it, too, but he wasn't going to say anything. "Once again, you're welcome." Was this it? Was the only reason John wanted to see him to give him an awkward hug and thank him?

Indeed, that had been it. The two went about their weekly meeting talking about his church. He had stayed for dinner that night and afterward Carolina asked him to join them in the drawing room. Afraid it would be then that he would be told they expected him to marry Liberty, he tried to beg off, but they wouldn't have it and he found himself in a room with gold wallpaper, sitting on a pink settee being interrogated about the events of the afternoon.

If he'd thought he'd experienced his most uncomfortable moment in life when he'd been found bathing Liberty in her room, he'd been wrong. Retelling the story to her parents and sister had been far worse. With each retelling, he'd been fearful it would be during that recount, they'd find fault with his actions and his world would end.

But thankfully, that never happened. In fact, by the end of the evening, he'd been praised as a hero. Not wanting to push his good luck, he slipped out before their opinion could change.

During the subsequent few weeks he'd avoided going to their London residence, because he knew Liberty would be upset with him when she recovered and heard the story. He'd experienced her wrath enough in the form of her sharp tongue, a well-placed elbow in his privates, and being knocked unconscious by a book she'd thrown for no apparent reason; he had no desire to experience what she might find fitting for retaliation this time.

But he couldn't avoid the family forever. Only a week ago, John practically begged him to come spend Christmas with them, knowing Paul had no ready excuse to refuse. Paul's brother and his brother's wife were having a large party at their estate, but he wasn't one for parties—not that he'd even been invited. Using his church as an excuse was futile. John knew as well as Paul that most of the members didn't get along and would prefer to gossip about each other—and their minister—rather than try to peacefully coexist for an attempted Christmas service. He was still hesitant though, and to further persuade him, John promised Paul he wouldn't be alone with Liberty even for a minute.

Thus, he'd agreed to spend the holidays with the Banks family in London.

Paul rubbed his fingers over his face. Pulling his hands back, he stared at his fingers. They had more wrinkles than a ninety-year-old woman. It was definitely time to get out of the tub.

Standing up, he twisted his body and reached for the towel he knew was on the stool behind him. But instead of landing on a fluffy towel, his hand was met with the hard wooden surface of the stool. Fully turning his body around to better see the offending piece of furniture, Paul discovered the stool did not hold a towel at all. All he saw on top of the wooden seat were his wire rimmed spectacles.

Stepping out of the tub, he put on his spectacles and looked under and on both sides of the stool. There was not a towel in sight. He frowned. He remembered specifically asking the maid for a towel and taking it from her when she came back. Then he'd gone behind the screen and placed it on the stool before disrobing. Where had it gone?

Paul sighed. It wasn't a problem; he'd just stand there a few minutes to let the air dry his body, then he'd put on his clean clothes.

When his skin felt dry enough to drag his clothes over it, Paul stepped out from behind the screen and walked over to where he'd laid his clothes out on the bed.

Reaching the bed, Paul groaned with deep irritation. Had the maid accidentally taken his clean clothes? He'd heard her come in during the middle of his bath and assumed she was trying to please her employer by being efficient. Not used to a lot of servants, he hadn't questioned her activities. It did make sense if she'd taken the wrong clothes, since they were the only clothes on this side of the screen. The clothes he'd worn earlier were in a pile on the other side of the screen. Shaking his head, Paul padded over to the corner to dig out different clothes from his trunk.

Leaning over at the waist, he slowly opened his trunk. With one hand holding up the lid, he bent over and extended his fingers to snatch up whatever clothes were on top. Not being bent over far enough to reach anything, he bent farther and farther until his bare arse was straight up in the air and his fingers collided with the hard bottom of his empty trunk.

Straightening himself up and abruptly letting go of the lid, causing it to crash down on the box with an echoing thud, Paul grabbed a match off the bottom of the wall sconce that was directly above his trunk and lit the lamp. Surely his mind was playing tricks on him, or perhaps his vision—even with spectacles—was so bad he'd been reaching beside the chest. Those were the only explanations he was willing to entertain for his recent discovery.

Lamp lit and glowing, Paul yanked open the lid of his trunk with more force than necessary only to reveal what he already knew: there was nothing inside.

Slamming down the lid, Paul made a noise of irritation. This was the work of one person: Liberty. He'd been told the family was out visiting the earl and countess, but that didn't mean she hadn't given orders to the maid before she left. Now it made sense why the maid came in while he was bathing. And why his towel had gone missing.

Angrily, Paul stalked across the room. No matter how much John tried to convince him otherwise, he wasn't staying. Having his clothes stolen was not his idea of an enjoyable visit. And this was only the first night. Who knew what other treats she had planned for him! He'd just have to put on the clothes he'd worn earlier, even if they were wrinkled and slightly wet from the snow. He knew these clothes were still in the room. He'd taken them off and thrown them in a heap at the far end of the tub. The maid hadn't come behind the screen. Well, she'd had to in order to grab his towel from behind his back; but she hadn't gone to the end of his tub and collected his dirty clothes.

Rounding the screen, Paul swiftly walked to the end of the tub and leaned down to retrieve his clothes.

"Looking for something?"

Chapter 3

Paul's hands instinctively flew to his privates and his head snapped up so fast he was left with a dizzy feeling—or maybe the dizzy feeling was caused by the sight in front of him, he wasn't sure.

Not three feet away, standing by the fireplace was his nemesis, Liberty Banks; and she was holding his clothes—directly over the roaring fire.

They weren't actually on fire. Yet. He considered that fortunate, indeed. "Would you kindly give me back my clothes?" Paul asked irritably, glancing down at his hands to make sure he was covered properly. She might have the illusion that he owed her the privilege of viewing his body because he'd seen hers. Unfortunately for her, he wasn't in the mood to become a source of virgin entertainment.

Liberty laughed. "You don't need to cover up. I already saw your…" She trailed off and sent a pointed look to where his hands were doing their best to shield at least part of his body from her view. She smiled up at him with a crooked smile. Her dull brown hair was coming loose from the hideous bun she always wore on the top of her head and a lock was falling into her face, partially covering one of her hazel eyes.

"Nonetheless," he said stiffly, twisting his body to offer more protection from her gaze. "Your game is up. And unless you want to see it again, you'll give me my clothes back."

"Are you threatening me, Mr. Grimes?" Liberty asked archly, lowering her hand an inch and bringing his clothes that much closer to the flames. "It seems to me that I hold all the cards, or clothes, as the case may be."

"Indeed." Did she *want* to see him naked? A chill ran down his spine. There was only one way to find out. Turning back to face her, he said, "Well, if you've already seen it, and you're still holding my clothes, then I guess you didn't get a good enough look. Do you want another peek?" He took delight as her eyes widened when he moved one of his hands away, still leaving him somewhat covered.

Under normal circumstances, he'd never be so bold as to issue such a challenge or follow through with it, but his irritation with her, coupled with his strong desire to have his clothes back and be on his way, was impacting his brain and turning him into someone he didn't recognize.

Outstretching his free hand, Paul asked, "May I please have my clothes back now, or do I need to remove my other hand and get them myself?"

"Why should I give you your clothes back?"

"Because now we're even," Paul snapped.

"We're not even," she responded sharply, her gaze at his waist, absorbing what was exposed to her curious eyes.

"No? Would you like to bathe me, is that it?" he countered, slowly reaching for the clothes she held hostage above the fire.

"No," she snapped, her eyes flying to his. She took the small bundle of his clothes and brought them to her chest, wrapping both arms around them and clutching them tightly to her chest.

"All right; then give me back my clothes." He reached out farther, attempting to grab them from her arms, but she was holding them with all her might and he knew that in order for him to get them back, he'd have to use both hands.

Liberty smiled at him again. If he weren't so infuriated with her at the moment, he'd almost think she looked pretty. Of course nobody else, including Liberty, he'd bet, actually thought she was. She had plain brown hair combined with hazel eyes and a long nose. Her mouth was wide with slightly crooked teeth and she was nearly as thin as a scarecrow. Her looks would be considered plain at best, not pretty or ugly really, just plain. But when she smiled, it lit up her face and transformed it in a way that he found rather attractive. The trouble was, she barely ever smiled, and never specifically at him—until just now.

"You'll get your clothes back when I'm satisfied I'll never have to clap eyes on you again," Liberty said tartly, still smiling.

"I agree," Paul said heartily, more than happy to oblige her. "Give me my clothes and I'll be gone in less than ten minutes."

Liberty shook her head. "No, that's not good enough. I need insurance. I need to know you'll not be coming back into this house, or my presence, ever again."

"And taking my clothes is going to accomplish that?" Paul could feel his irritation growing again. Why didn't she just give them back to him already?

"Don't worry, you'll get them back—eventually," Liberty said, scooting along the wall away from the fireplace and to the shadowed corner.

"Listen here," Paul hissed. "If you think that you're going to continue to hold my clothes while I stand here naked, you're greatly mistaken. I'll get my clothes back one way or the other; and if you don't give them back of your own accord, you'll wish you had."

"How so?" she queried from the dark corner.

Paul slowly walked closer to her. He could hear the rustle of fabric and knew she was about to do something with his clothes. He just didn't know what. "I'm not keeping myself covered because of my own modesty."

"I've already told you that you could move your hands, I already saw your thing," she said nonchalantly, a ripping noise following her words.

Paul didn't believe her the first time she'd told him she'd seen his tool, and he certainly didn't believe it when he moved his first hand and her eyes were drawn to his waist like a moth to a flame. But he'd had enough, and if he had to wrestle her to the ground naked in order to get his clothes back, so be it. Removing his other hand from his privates, he raced to the corner, bent on grabbing his clothes from her evil clutches.

Liberty squealed and ran in the opposite direction, causing him to nearly collide with the wall. Throwing caution—and pride —to the wind, Paul ran after her. He chased her around the furniture, going over the bed, around the wardrobe, behind the screen, around the tub, to the vanity, and back to the tub, knocking over the screen with a loud crash as they zipped by. Paul reached out and stopped her by taking hold of the loosened ribbon on the back of her gown.

"I've got you now," he breathed in her ear, after he'd tugged her back to rest against his chest.

"No, you don't," she said, moving in such a way that made the ribbon he held slide through the loops, freeing her from his hold. She immediately scurried to resume her former position by the fireplace.

Paul looked down at his hand where the ribbon that had once been a bow on the back of her gown now lay across his palm in a wrinkled mess. Looking back up, he saw Liberty over by the fireplace with her gown in complete disarray. Most of the buttons going down the front were undone, showing the tops of her breasts and about three inches of her corset. There was a tear in her gown along the stitching of her sleeve and the skirts were crumpled beyond repair. Her hair, for the most part, had fallen down and looked to be in an awful tangle. There was no way she could look like that after briefly running around the room, could she?

Throwing the ribbon down to the floor in disgust, Paul stared at her. She had a blank expression on her face and her gaze was leveled on his waist. But he didn't even care. He was beyond caring. "See something you like?" he teased, hoping to distract her, so he could grab his clothes.

Her face turned crimson and she pulled her eyes up to his face, not quite meeting his eyes. "Actually, no, I didn't. I think I would've liked what I saw much better if that scar," she pointed to a jagged scar he had on his left hip that ran from his hipbone to half an inch from another part of his anatomy, "went just a little farther over."

"You're a bloodthirsty one, aren't you," Paul said easily. Leave it to her to want him emasculated, as if this whole situation weren't bad enough already.

"I'm not bloodthirsty," she said hotly. "It's just a shame, that's

4

all."

"A shame I was not unmanned?" he asked in disbelief. "I think that part of my anatomy has suffered at your hands enough already, thank you." What had he ever done to her to make her harbor this hatred for him?

"How did it happen?" she asked quietly, ignoring his remark.

Paul was in awe. Her voice had been so quiet it was hard to be certain, but he could have sworn her tone had held a hint of sympathy. "When I was twelve, my brother Sam and I found my uncle's old fencing rapiers. Never having had a fencing lesson, we started wildly swinging them around at each other. Neither of us realized the protective tip wasn't securely attached to Sam's until, in one undisciplined swing, Sam's tip flew off and his rapier cut me." Paul saw her wince and added ruefully, "Although you've expressed disappointment that his rapier did not travel farther, I'm rather glad it stopped where it did."

"I'm sorry for my earlier remark, it was most unkind of me," Liberty said softly, still looking at his scar.

"It's all right," he assured her. Compared to all the other things she'd said or done, that was nothing. "May I have my clothes now?"

His words pulled Liberty out of her trance. Looking down at the clothes in her arms and her own gown, she bit her lip before she looked up and met his eyes again. "I...I..."

It didn't matter what she was going to say or do next, because just then the door to his bedchamber swung open and was followed by a shriek of surprise.

Though Paul had his back to the door, he deduced who it was; and for further confirmation, he knew with certainty he'd guessed correctly when Liberty turned as white as chalk.

Chapter 4

"What's the meaning of this?" roared Papa.

Neither Mr. Grimes nor Liberty said anything.

Mr. Grimes swallowed hard and his face turned bright red, but he didn't say anything. Drat the man. Couldn't he say something and get them out of this mess? Isn't that what gentlemen were good for? They helped damsels in distress, didn't they? Granted she had never really considered him a gentleman; and she was the one who took his clothes; and he was standing in front of both of her parents and their butler naked—covering what he felt was important, of course—but couldn't he do *something*? This was *not* how she'd envisioned the evening concluding when she'd cried off early at Brooke's and crept into his room to take his clothes.

She'd slipped in during his bath with all the stealth and silence of a cat and removed all his clothes from his trunk and off the bed. Who in the world laid their clothes on their bed? Why he didn't drape them over the screen like everyone else, she'd never know. But she'd always thought him unusual, so she hadn't dwelt on it while collecting his clothes.

Standing in the shadows by the screen, she'd waited for him to dunk his head into the bath. That's when she'd grabbed his towel. Getting his dirty clothes, the ones she still had clutched to her chest, had been harder to accomplish. She'd stood in the shadows while he'd dried off; when he'd walked across the room to get his other clothes, she'd tiptoed behind his screen and grabbed them up in a bundle. Then she'd waited.

Just as she'd predicted, when he hadn't found any clean clothes, he'd come back to retrieve his dirty ones. The look on his face when he'd seen her holding his clothes over the fire was worth any unpleasant consequences she might be forced to face if this ended badly—all except the one she was now facing, that is.

She hadn't expected her parents to appear upon the scene so early. Her plan could have still been salvaged, if they hadn't knocked over the screen while running around the room. But since they had, she now found herself in the only situation that wasn't worth seeing the shocked look on Mr. Grimes' face when he saw her holding his clothes over the fire.

"John," Mr. Grimes said softly, "there is an explanation for this."

"Good," Papa said roughly. "I'm rather interested in hearing it."

"Do you think we could talk about this in your study?" Mr. Grimes asked hopefully.

"No."

Mr. Grimes nodded slowly and all of the blood drained from Liberty's face. He was about to tell Papa what she'd done. Then, not only would her plan be ruined, but who knew what sort of punishment Papa would mete out for this. The last time she'd done something he'd considered "inappropriate" to Mr. Grimes, Papa had threatened to ship her off to America if she so much as looked at him wrong in the future. She shivered. He wouldn't send her home all alone in the dead of winter, would he?

"As it happens, there was a misunderstanding regarding my clothing," Paul said evasively, his face turning even redder, if such a thing were possible.

"Do not worry about your clothing, sir," said the butler helpfully. "I saw Miss Liberty heap them outside the door earlier. Not to worry, I took them all down to Mary. She will have them all pressed and returned within the hour."

Liberty repressed a groan. Their butler was the most unprofessional butler in all of England. If there had been any means to escape this scrape, they were definitely gone now.

"Thank you. I look forward to having them back more than you know," Mr. Grimes said dryly.

Ignoring Mr. Grimes, Papa cast a probing glance at Liberty. "Explain yourself," he thundered.

Liberty thought she was going to swoon. But fate had never

been that kind to her. She swallowed past the lump in her throat and flickered a glance at Mr. Grimes; he looked just as interested in her answer as Papa. "I...I...I don't know," she stammered weakly.

"Yes, you do," Papa barked.

Liberty's body shook of its own accord as her father's gaze pierced her. Her eyes started to fill with tears, and she found that her lips were trembling, and she was powerless to stop them.

The tension in the room was so thick, she thought she might choke to death on it, but of course that wouldn't happen, either. She wasn't that lucky.

A delicate cough broke the silence, and Liberty's eyes shifted to where Mama was standing next to Papa in the doorway. She'd forgotten Mama was there and sent her a pleading glance. But Mama just shook her head as if to say: "Sorry, my dear, I can't save you this time."

"Do you have something to say?" Papa asked in clipped tones.

Liberty thought he was talking to her, but Mama must have thought he was addressing her. "Actually, I do," Mama said; her cheeks turning pink. "Liberty, would you kindly give Paul back his clothing, please?"

Liberty flushed. At least now the blood was flowing back into her head, she thought wryly. With a tight grip on the bundle of clothes, she weakly extended her hands toward him. But Mr. Grimes didn't take them from her.

"Liberty, spare the man anymore embarrassment and throw them on the bed," Papa said irritably.

Knowing Papa like she did, she knew he'd meant "throw" in a general sense, not a literal one. But truly how could she resist such an opportunity? "Yes, sir," she said smugly, sending him a tentative smile. Then hefting the bundle of clothes over her head, she used all her strength—which wasn't *that* much since she was a lady, after all—and hurled his clothes across the room to fall into a graceless heap. Of course, they didn't land on the bed, not that she'd expected them to.

Proud of her defiant demonstration achieved by literally

following his orders, Liberty turned to face Papa and was about to make an inane comment when her words died on her tongue as she heard Mama gasp and saw Papa's eyes almost pop out of his head. For a moment, she'd forgotten the state of her gown. However, their responses quickly reminded her of her own state of undress.

She'd purposely destroyed her gown by ripping the sleeves, undoing half the buttons and somewhat crumpling her skirts, all before he'd chased her around the room, which had only added to the dishevelment. Her plan had been to be caught with her gown this way and accuse him of trying to ravish her. Of course, she hadn't planned to take this so far as to make it public. She just wanted to convince her father to end his friendship with Mr. Grimes. That plan wasn't going to work now.

"Sir, may I please have a few minutes to dress?" Mr. Grimes asked evenly.

"Fine," Papa barked. "Both of you. My study. Five minutes."

Leaving the room in haste, Liberty ran as fast as her slippers could take her. But no matter how fast she ran, or how many times she looked over her shoulder, Mama was still right on her heels.

"Liberty Ellis Banks, what were you thinking?" Mama demanded, grabbing hold of the back of Liberty's dress to keep her from entering her room without Mama.

Liberty cringed. She hated her name. Liberty was all right, but she hated being called Ellis. She'd let people think it was because it was more commonly a boy's name. However, the truth was, it was her mother's grandmother's maiden name, and to be quite frank, she'd never liked her great-grandmother very much. Great-Grandma Ellis had been a crotchety ancient biddy who was always spewing vile insults and darning something. On Liberty's eighth birthday, she'd told her she'd never live up to the Ellis name, then in front of all the friends and family that had gathered to celebrate, she'd pointed out all of Liberty's flaws. She'd made sure to mention how plain Liberty had been compared to her sisters and had declared she'd never catch a husband with her hideous smile.

Unconsciously, Liberty ran her tongue along her crooked top teeth. They weren't *so* bad, she admitted to herself. In fact, they were better than most; yet compared to the rest of her family, hers looked awful. One of her front teeth was straight, but the other was at a slight angle. It sat a bit in front of the straight one, not a lot, but enough to catch notice. Thankfully, her bottom teeth could be more easily concealed, because they were a jumbled mess. None of them could be considered straight—except the larger ones, but those were in the back, blast it all.

"I don't know," Liberty admitted solemnly after a minute, unfastening the rest of her buttons. She knew what she *had* been thinking up until the time that Pa...er...Mr. Grimes had told her the story about his scar. That's when she'd grown a conscience, or perhaps it was a brain. Either way, it was then she'd realized she couldn't go through with her heartless plan. Not only was it a stupid thing to do, but she'd discovered she didn't have the heart to do it. Of course, she still didn't like him. But, to sentence him to the kind of life he'd have been forced into had she followed her plan and the story had leaked out, she shuddered just to think of it.

"You do too know," Mama snapped.

Liberty's fingers froze. She'd never heard Mama be sharp, ever. Nothing she'd done in the past had brought about this amount of anger from Mama. "I'm sorry."

"Sorry?" Mama repeated angrily. "Sorry. You're sorry? No, that's not good enough, Liberty."

Liberty swallowed. She didn't know what to say, or how to even start.

"I demand to know exactly what happened in that room tonight."

"I took his clothes," she admitted quietly.

"Why?" Mama demanded, coming over to help her out of her gown.

Liberty had always been one to own up to her mistakes when confronted, no matter how awful they were. This one just happened to be of gigantic proportions. "As you know, I detest Mr. Grimes. I had planned to make it look like he had forced himself upon me," she said meekly, swallowing harder this time. "I thought if Papa believed he'd done something to harm me, his youngest daughter, he'd end his friendship with Mr. Grimes."

Mama stared at her as if she didn't recognize her. Liberty knew it had been a bad idea, and saying it aloud only made it sound worse, but there it was. "That is the *stupidest* thing I have ever heard," Mama declared. Her emphasis on the word "stupidest" made Liberty flinch. "Do you not realize what trouble you could have caused him?" Mama's voice echoed off the walls in the small bedchamber.

Liberty gulped. "I'm sorry, Mama."

Mama shook her head in disgust. "Liberty, you're my daughter and I love you. But this time, you've gone too far. If the circumstances had been anything else, I would have taken up in your defense and tried to talk Papa out of whatever punishment he had in mind for you, but not this time."

"It's all right, Mama. I'll accept whatever Papa has in mind." Her words came out even, belying the turmoil she was fighting inside. What if he sent her back to America? What if he never spoke to her again? It was a foolish notion that he'd never speak to her again, but after the foolish thing she'd done, it could happen.

"You do realize," Mama said, breaking into her thoughts, "that Papa might demand you marry Mr. Grimes?"

Liberty thought she might swoon. Marriage? Marriage to Mr. Grimes? *That* possibility hadn't entered her mind. "Oh," she said, her voice sounded like a sharp staccato.

"If that happens," Mama continued, seeming oblivious to Liberty's distress, "you will accept Mr. Grimes' suit and be the perfect wife. Am I understood?"

Still numb to the idea she might be forced to marry her archenemy, Liberty nodded her understanding.

Neither of them said another word as Mama helped Liberty change and they descended the stairs together.

Walking down to Papa's study had never been so daunting. She would have had more bravado if not for the worry of having to be Mrs. Paul Grimes niggling in the back of her mind.

"It's about time," Papa said sharply when she and Mama came into the room.

Liberty's eyes scanned the room and landed on Mr. Grimes sitting in the corner. Of course the man was sitting, he wasn't a gentleman. A gentleman would have stood when she'd entered the room. Apparently, it was too much effort for Mr. Grimes to force himself to stand.

Papa directed her to take a seat. With a wary glance from Papa to Mr. Grimes, she did as she was directed.

Mr. Grimes' face was rigid, and if she were any judge, she'd say he looked like he would like to strangle her. His hair looked like he hadn't bothered to brush it after his bath, and his clothes were slightly askew, probably because he had hastily dressed. Her eyes slid down his body. Now that she'd seen him without his clothes, she knew exactly what he concealed under those clothes. A heated blush crept up her face and she hastily jerked her gaze away.

"While you two were upstairs taking your time getting yourselves down to this meeting, Mr. Grimes and I had a very enlightening conversation," Papa said with a pointed glance at Liberty.

Liberty sprang off her settee. "Please, Papa, don't make me marry him!" she pleaded, pointing at Mr. Grimes.

Papa chuckled. "My dear, do you think I would subject him to that life of torment?"

Deflated, Liberty sat down. Save *him* from a life of torment? He was her father; he should be taking her side and saying he was keeping *her* from that life of torment he spoke of. "So you're not going to force me to marry him, then?" she asked, trying to keep excitement from creeping into her voice.

"No," Papa said flatly. "Now you two quit looking so excited at the prospect of not being shackled to one another. Any idiot can see that the two of you cannot stand each other. One of you clearly has a better reason to despise the other." Papa shot an apologetic glance at Mr. Grimes. "Nonetheless, I have no desire to find out what would happen if you two were forced to share a house."

Liberty could have sworn her father shuddered after his last sentence, but she was too offended by his apologetic glance at Mr.

Grimes to care.

"What will happen now?" Mama asked quietly.

"It's simple: nothing" Papa said easily. "Nobody but us, save the butler, knows about what happened. We'll just keep it to ourselves. Additionally, Mr. Grimes and I have decided to put an end to our professional acquaintance."

Mama nodded her understanding and sent a sad and somewhat worried glance over to Mr. Grimes. A week or two before Papa and Mr. Grimes had started meeting, or about seven months earlier, Papa had told the family they'd be going back home in about six months. But, then Brooke married and soon after announced she was increasing. Not wanting to miss the birth of their first grandchild, her parents had decided to stay in England until the baby was born. Subsequently, much to Liberty's dismay, Papa's relationship with Mr. Grimes had continued.

During the past seven months, Liberty tried to ferret out Mr. Grimes' secrets, but never learned what problems compelled him to seek Papa's advice. Oh well, that was a small price to pay to not have to see him again. It looked like she got what she wanted after all.

"Well, now that that's been settled, I should be off to bed," Liberty chirped, getting off the settee.

"Not so fast," Papa snapped. "You may think this has all resolved itself, but there is still the matter of your punishment to discuss."

Liberty resumed her seat on the settee.

"You didn't think that was the end of it, did you, my dear girl?" Papa asked way too sweetly.

"No, of course not."

During the next five minutes, Liberty sat quietly with her hands in her lap as she watched Mr. Grimes and Papa mumble words of goodbye. Then, Mr. Grimes shook Papa's hand and gave Mama a hug before walking out the door without a backwards glance in her direction. Not that she blamed him for his easy dismissal of her, she'd deserved it. Her treatment of him, today and in the past, had not exactly been endearing. And yet, his easy dismissal of her struck her differently than she'd thought it would.

The five minutes that followed that were not nearly as pleasant. It took only five minutes for her entire world to change.

First, she heard her father, who was a minister, mind you, use a phrase that no gentleman should say in the presence of a lady. "What in the bloody hell are you about, Liberty?" he demanded, as soon as Mr. Grimes was out of his study.

So shocked he'd said "bloody hell", she squeaked and looked at Papa as if she expected him to be struck by lightning.

"Close your gaping mouth and answer me, girl," he barked sharply, seeming as oblivious to the impossibility of his statement as Liberty was.

"You just said 'bloody' *and* 'hell'," Liberty said softly in reply.

"Yes, I did. And I'll say it again, if you don't answer me," he snapped.

Liberty sent an imploring glance to Mama. But Mama just shook her head, offering her no help.

The following three minutes, Liberty did her best to explain what had happened, taking care to pick her words carefully in order not to make the situation worse than it already was.

Then came the final minute. The one that had actually changed her life. For the first forty-five seconds, Papa yelled all sorts of vile things, most of which made his earlier use of bloody hell seem like children's talk. She'd never even heard half the words he used this time. Then, he turned to Mama who'd been standing rigid and pale by the door. "I'm sorry, Carolina, please forgive me for talking that way in front of you," he said sheepishly. His eyes snapped back to Liberty. "As for you," he'd said with a sneer of disgust. "I thought I'd raised you better than this. I've been bewildered by some of the things you've done. I've been embarrassed by some of the things you've done. But until today, I couldn't say I'd ever been disappointed. See to it that you never act in such a disappointing way again, now go!"

Each of his words was like a blow to her heart. She hated the idea of disappointing someone she'd always admired, especially when she'd tried so hard to follow the rules to perfection.

Fighting tears, she stood up. "I'm sorry," she said quickly and fled the room, vowing then and there she'd never be termed a disappointment again.

Chapter 5

Paul got into his carriage and directed his coachman to take him to the nearest boarding house. It might be unfashionable to stay in one, but as usual, fashion was the furthest thing from his mind.

Tonight had been a disaster, to say the least. He had no idea what she'd been trying to accomplish with her scheme, and he'd long ago decided it didn't matter. At least now he wouldn't have to encounter her ever again, and for that, he was truly thankful.

Unfortunately, that also meant he'd lost his friendship with John and Carolina. Over the past seven months, he'd come to value their friendship a great deal. He'd known since the day they'd met that one day their friendship would end. Too bad it had to be in such a dramatic way, he thought wryly, shaking his head.

That night Paul slept in a strange place and in a strange bed; and the next day, he rode to his empty house and slept in his equally empty bed.

The next few weeks ran into each other with the passing of Christmas and the mark of the New Year. Following tradition, he spent the holidays alone. Sam had little need for him since he'd inherited his title seven years ago.

In the middle of January, Paul decided it might be time to think of marriage. He'd thought about it two years ago when things were going well. Then when his life had crumbled, he'd been too focused on that to think about women. Not that it would have mattered anyway. As things stood, none of the unmarried girls within fifty miles of him were allowed to be courted by him. That only left widows, to whom he didn't even speak for fear of what might circulate if he were seen speaking to one.

Now his only choice was London.

London had never held much appeal to him, but now it did.

Although, he wasn't sure if he felt London was beckoning him to search for a bride or if it had to do with the odd missive he'd received from John Banks the day before.

Paul picked up the evasive note again. He'd read it about a dozen times already the night before and hadn't made any sense of it. Paul looked down and scanned it again.

Paul,
I need to speak to you post haste. Please meet me at my London residence day after tomorrow. This is a matter of great importance.
John

Paul frowned. What did John want with him? It had been well over a month since his last debacle with Liberty. Surely, he hadn't changed his mind after all this time, had he? No matter. John had helped him when he needed it, and he'd be damned if he didn't help John when he was in need.

***

Paul arrived at the Bankses' house in London around midday.

He'd just opened the door to his carriage and was about to hop down, when the front door to the townhouse John was staying at burst open.

Paul brought his head up and blinked, when he saw it was not Turner at the door, but John. "Hello, John," Paul said cheerfully.

"Paul," John said stiffly, making a hand gesture that staid Paul. "Let's go for a ride."

Paul had never seen John so rigid before. And considering all the uncomfortable conversations the two of them had shared in the past, something must be very wrong indeed for John to have such a stiff demeanor.

"How can I help you?" Paul asked without ceremony after John shut the carriage door.

"Marry Liberty," John said with the same frankness as Paul.

Paul coughed. "Excuse me?" If John had said, "Marry my daughter," Paul could have pretended he meant Madison, and might have seriously considered the request. But he could have sworn John had said, "Marry Liberty," and that was a request he hoped he'd misheard.

"That rapscallion of a butler—the one we used to have--went to the press with details of last month's—" He broke off, trying to think of a good word. But when he decided no word fit, he shoved a well-worn newspaper into Paul's hands.

Paul flipped open the paper and his eyes flew to the headline: *A Botched Seduction, Butler Tells All.* Quickly he read the article.

It has come to my attention that last month a young lady by the initials LB set out to seduce a country vicar. Her anonymous butler claims she invited him to her family's London residence and while he was in the bath, rinsing off the traveling dust one would assume, the young lady went into his room and began to undress. The young lady's plans for seduction were brought to a screeching halt when her parents arrived home early from visiting a certain noble relation.

When the young lady's parents opened the door to the bedchamber the two were occupying, they found a naked vicar and a half dressed young lady. When asked why this had not come to the public's attention until now, my source informed me the family pretended it never happened and paid money to keep it hushed up.

Now, I ask you, dear reader, is this the kind of young lady we want patronizing our events, mingling with our daughters, and marrying our sons? I think not.

The paper slipped from Paul's hands and fluttered to the floor. He'd heard of Lady Algen's weekly gossip column, appropriately named *Tattle and Prattle,* but he'd never read it before. His life was filled with enough gossip without having to read about it.

"Paul, I wouldn't ask it of you if there was any other way," John said solemnly. "I know you don't like her, but her reputation is beyond repair."

Paul looked at him skeptically; resisting the urge to ask how it was his problem her reputation was in shreds. "Are you sure people know it was Liberty?"

"They know," John said flatly. His normally laughing clear blue eyes looked old and worried. "Every day this week we've had more callers than usual."

"That doesn't mean—"

"Yes, it does," John snapped. "Sorry," he said in a softer tone. "They have to know. Nobody has brought it up directly, but the only people who have come by are either the old gossip hungry harpies or the biggest rakes within a hundred mile radius."

"They know," Paul agreed grimly.

John nodded.

"What about going back to New York early?" Paul suggested, ignoring the little voice in the back of his head that was chastising him for denying John's request.

"I thought of that already," John conceded. "The problem is that with the weather being what it is, there are no passenger ships."

That was a valid excuse, Paul thought with a sigh. The Thames was still frozen over; the ocean was bound to be full of ice, too. Biting his tongue so he wouldn't suggest the family try walking across the ocean on the stretches of ice, he stared at the floor in silence.

"You do need a wife," John said helpfully. "You never know, it might help your situation."

Paul's head snapped up. He knew he needed a wife and he'd even come to the conclusion that a wife might be beneficial in battling the gossip; but with Liberty as his wife, the gossip was likely to spread and multiply. She didn't seem the sort to stand by her husband when things got hard, and no doubt at the beginning of their marriage, things would definitely be hard.

"I'm sorry, John, but I don't think Liberty is the solution to my problems," Paul said truthfully.

John nodded and scrubbed his fingers up and down his face before threading them through his hair. "All right, then," John said, sighing loudly.

Paul felt bad for John and Carolina, he truly did, but not

enough that he'd marry their hellion of a daughter to help them out. A man had to draw the line somewhere.

"How's your den of iniquity?" John asked suddenly, breaking the silence.

"Fine," Paul ground out.

John cocked his head and twisted his lips in the way Paul had seen him do many times when he was in deep contemplation. "You know, my boy, I do believe you are in need of a wife," John said thoughtfully.

"Yes, I've been thinking the same," Paul agreed. What was John up to?

"Tell me, do you have someone in mind?"

Paul pursed his lips. "No."

"I see." John nodded slowly. "Hmm, if I remember correctly your prospects at home are not so grand. I suppose that means you'll be coming to London for the Season to find a bride," he mused aloud.

"That's the most likely possibility," Paul allowed, trying to keep his curiosity from his tone or face.

"You do know the Season is still a few months off, don't you? Do you suppose there is enough time between now and the start of the Season for quiet country rumors to spread all the way here?"

Paul's eyes narrowed. The Mr. John Banks he'd met more than eight months ago would never even allude to gossip, let alone spread it. "Are you threatening me, sir?"

"No. I was merely pointing out how quickly rumors spread and how damaging they can be, that's all."

Paul ground his teeth. "I'll think about it."

"You will?" John asked jovially, a smile transforming his rigid face. "How can I help you make up your mind?"

"You can't," Paul returned flatly. Why had he just agreed to think about marrying Liberty? Did he want to spend his life in misery?

"Oh, there must be something I can say to help."

"There's not."

John shook his head. "Hmm, what if I increase her dowry? I

gave Townson five thousand pounds. What if I give you six?"

"Sir, do you remember that you once told me you only had twelve thousand pounds with which to dower all three girls? If you've already given Townson five, and you're planning to give me—or whoever is crazy enough to chain themselves to Liberty for life—six, then that leaves only one thousand for Madison?"

"I know that," John retorted. "There's nothing wrong with my arithmetic, young man. But as you pointed out, there is an extra thousand pounds. How about I bump Liberty's dowry up to seven? That's the highest I can go though."

Paul rolled his eyes. "Then that leaves nothing for Madison."

"As I said already, there is nothing wrong with my arithmetic," John said sharply. "The fact is, Madison has no desire to marry, and if she changes her mind, her looks will be enough to snag the richest in the land. A lack of dowry won't be a problem where she is concerned."

"Are you saying you don't believe Liberty is as attractive as Madison?" Paul asked coolly, interested in John's answer. It had to be hard for Liberty to grow up in the shadows of her older, more attractive sisters.

"As their father, I think they're both equally attractive. Just in different ways, of course," John said smoothly. "But it matters not what I think, when it comes down to it. It's the opinion of the gentlemen who wish to court them that matters."

"So why the extra two thousand pounds?"

John shrugged, then slumped back in his seat. "Think of it as compensation for anything of yours she might destroy."

"Anything, but my pride," Paul muttered, folding his arms. "It's not important anyway; I have no desperate need of funds."

"All right," John conceded. "Think about this: if you marry Liberty, you will not have to spend a Season in London going to exhausting balls, boring soirees, ear piercing musicales or dull garden parties. Not to mention, you won't spend a shilling on flowers, candies and other token gifts gentlemen bring when they call upon young ladies."

"As I said earlier, money is not a concern for me. Anyway, I might enjoy an outing or two," Paul pointed out with a shrug.

"What about all that other sentimental rubbish? Do you enjoy writing ridiculous poetry and spouting it in front of a room full of people in hopes of gaining the girl's affections?"

Paul blinked. Spout poetry? No, thank you. "Not all men do that. My brother didn't."

"Your brother had a title."

"Thank you for reminding me," Paul said with a grimace.

"Come now, Paul, why chase a woman when there is one who is already perfectly willing?" John asked encouragingly.

"Willing?" Paul echoed. To his memory, Liberty was willing to yell at him. Or willing to unman him. And perhaps even willing to make him look a fool. Not, willing to marry him.

"Yes, willing," John assured him. "I know your past few encounters with her weren't very positive, but trust me when I tell you, Liberty does have a heart of gold somewhere in there."

A heart of gold? He didn't even think she had one made of flesh buried in her chest. "John, I'm sorry. If there were any other way I could help you, I would, but as you said yourself, who knows what might ensue if we have to share a house."

John sighed and leaned against the squabs, a look of defeat on his face. "Do you happen to have the time, Paul?"

Paul's fingers ran over his gold pocket watch that was sitting in his coat pocket. "No, I'm sorry I don't."

"I thought you always had a pocket watch with you?" John said skeptically, favoring him with a questing glance.

"I do. I did. What I mean to say is, I have the watch with me, but unfortunately it no longer works," Paul said evenly.

"Take it to Philip Michaels on Bond Street. He's the best jeweler in town."

Paul shook his head. "I already have. He said it was irreparable and offered to buy it to sell the gemstones and melt the gold."

John chuckled. "I can imagine what you told him to do with his suggestion."

"You bet I did," Paul said with a rueful grin. He had no desire to even think about the jeweler's suggestion. The watch held too much sentimental value for him. As for him still carrying it around, well, old habits were hard to break, and every morning he found himself shoving the old, busted thing into his pocket, nonetheless.

"Sorry to hear that," John said casually. "It was a mighty fine watch. Had a crest on the outside, did it not?"

"Yes, sir."

"An earl?"

"Duke," Paul said tightly. "My mother's father was the Duke of Charlton."

"Fascinating," John said passively. "I suppose the time is of no importance. Surely it cannot be too late. Do you mind if we run an errand?"

Paul shook his head.

"Good, because I already told your coachman where to take me before I climbed inside."

Paul smiled. It was typical for John to do something underhanded like that. "Where are we going?"

"The office for the *Daily News*. I have an article for them."

"You do?" Since when did John start writing articles for the paper?

"Yes." John pulled out a piece of vellum from inside his breast pocket. "I wanted to drop this off for Lady Algen to run in her next prattling and tattling column," he said excitedly.

Paul laughed. "I believe it's called *Tattle and Prattle*. But I like your description better. Why are you giving that woman gossip? Don't you think she finds enough on her own?"

John shrugged. "I just thought to give her the follow up to last week's article."

"The follow up? Last week's article? Do you make it a habit to read that column every week?"

"No, no. I just thought to amuse the readers of London with another juicy story, that's all. Would you like to know the title?" John asked with a teasing smile.

"Not particularly," Paul muttered.

"Too bad. I'm going to tell you anyway. It's called, *A Vicar's*

Seduction, A Father's Tale. Does that sound catchy or what?"

"Or what!" Paul exclaimed. "What did you write," he demanded, reaching for the paper.

John quickly shoved the paper under his bottom and shot a smug smile at Paul. "Now, I have another article here," he reached into his coat pocket and pulled out another piece of vellum, "this one is an announcement of the marriage of Mr. Paul Grimes to Miss Liberty Banks." He willingly gave the sheet to Paul before looking out the window and asking, "It appears we're only a block away. Which paper shall I bring inside with me?"

Paul exhaled deeply. And unfortunately, it hadn't done a thing for his anger. "This one," he said tersely, handing John back the wedding announcement. "I'll marry her. But I have two conditions for you."

"I'm listening," John said with a happy smile.

"First, I want the seven thousand pounds you mentioned earlier."

"Done."

"I want it in cash, John," he said with a hard stare.

"Fine," he agreed heartily. "I'll give it to you in cash. I'll even bring it to the wedding if you'd like. I'll even put it in a bag and set it on the floor right next to Liberty so you can glance at it periodically throughout the service," he joked with an easy smile.

Paul chuckled. It seemed now that he'd agreed to take that hoyden off his hands, John's normal personality had returned. "That will not be necessary," he assured him. "However, for my second condition, I want your promise that if things are miserable between Liberty and me, you'll take her back to America with you and Carolina after Brooke has her baby."

John's smile slipped. "Take her back to America?" he repeated, his tone full of disappointment.

"Yes."

"That won't be for at least six months. What if she is with child by then?" John asked, his head cocked and eyes full of interest.

"Sir, if she finds herself with child, then you'll be taking her back with you for sure," Paul said tonelessly.

John's body stiffened and his face looked as impassive as marble. "Perhaps, I misjudged your character."

"No, you didn't." Paul took a deep breath. "If it were my child, I wouldn't let a stream separate us. However, if there's a child, it won't be mine. I don't plan to have that sort of marriage with Liberty. This is not a love match, it's a business arrangement," he explained in his defense.

"I see," John's blue eyes lit with humor. "You do realize that the majority of marriages are not love matches, and yet they still seem to produce children?"

"I'm aware of that. I even know how babies are made, so please do not feel the need to have that talk with me. My father took care of that many years ago," Paul quipped. "The fact is, I have no desire to take my clothes off in her presence."

"Shy?" John teased.

If he and John hadn't known each other for so long, Paul would have taken offense or been irritated, at the very least. But as it was, they knew each other well, so well in fact, they could talk to each other about almost anything, and probably already had. "No. I'm not shy. I have nothing to be shy about," Paul said proudly. When John laughed at his declaration, he added, "She's already attempted to decrease my chance of procreation with her elbow, taken my clothes and made me chase her naked around a room, as well as expressed an interest in seeing a rapier remove what I consider to be a vital piece of my anatomy. I have no desire to find out what might happen if I willingly take my clothes off in her presence."

John laughed softly. "You might change your mind, you know?"

"I doubt it," Paul muttered.

John didn't respond. He was out of the carriage and running up the stairs in a flash. Paul shook his head. John was probably just trying to ensure Paul would go through with it. Once the announcement ran in the paper, there would be no chance to change his mind. Paul removed his spectacles and rubbed his green eyes until he saw stars.

If his watch worked, he'd know how long John had stayed inside the building, but if he had to hazard a guess, he'd say it had been about thirty minutes already. More than enough time to drop off the marriage announcement, he thought.

Leaning over and drawing back the curtains to see if the footsteps he heard were John's, his eyes fell on the piece of vellum John had shoved under himself, after he'd wisely judged that Paul wouldn't reach under another man to retrieve a piece of paper. A part of him wanted to snatch up the paper and read what John had written. He knew it had to be about the day Liberty fell into the ice and Paul was caught bathing her.

Finally, curiosity got the better of him, and he picked it up. Quickly, he had it unfolded and he read the paper so fast his brain barely comprehended what his eyes were seeing.

Paul,

I imagine by now you're done seething about what you've agreed to do, only to be seething again, now that you've unfolded what you thought to be an article bound for the gossip column and, instead, found a letter to you from me. However, you must know that I would never have spread gossip about you around town either by speaking it or having it printed. I'm merely a concerned father who is willing to go to great lengths to save my daughter from a life of ridicule, even if it's her own fault. Please forgive me.

I honestly do believe the two of you are a good match. You and Liberty both might not see it now (and to be honest, nobody else may, either), but I do. Just be patient and give her time. I'm certain you'll soon develop a great esteem for her.

You need not wait for my return from inside the Daily News *office. I shall take a hack home. I should hate for you to disappoint Liberty by having to cry off the wedding due to being locked up in the London Tower for murdering your soon-to-be father-in-law in your carriage.*

Oh, and if it helps, you're not the first unsuspecting soul I've trapped. Ask Townson about his fruitless three hour wait in my

brother's study.
    John

Paul should be furious. But for some bizarre reason, he wasn't. He'd already resigned himself to the fact he'd be marrying Liberty. And because of that, her father's schemes didn't really bother him. In fact, he almost found it humorous. Almost.

Chapter 6

It was too late in the day to travel back home. And for obvious reasons, he wasn't going to accept an invitation to stay with the Banks family, not that one had been issued. However, he was certain one would be if he were to stop by their house. He knew that's what John expected him to do after reading that infuriating scrap of paper. Instead, Paul decided to make a quick stop at the Earl of Townson's townhouse.

The earl, Andrew Black, was a great gentleman in Paul's opinion. At first glance he appeared intimidating with his unusual height and a body similar to a tree trunk. He wasn't an overly attractive man on the whole. His nose was a bit off and, like Paul's, his skin was darker than most which made his deep blue eyes only stand out more. But it wasn't merely his looks that made him intimidating. He had a tendency to raise his brow as a way of asking a question, and Paul had witnessed more than one man squirm in his seat at the gesture.

Andrew made a mistake eight months earlier by purposely getting caught in a scandalous situation with the beautiful Brooke Banks, Liberty's eldest sister. Since then, he'd done whatever necessary to prove himself worthy of Brooke. As for the love and devotion those two shared—it was enough to make a man sick.

"Good afternoon, Paul," the earl said, coming into the drawing room.

"Townson," Paul greeted.

"Andrew," he corrected, taking a seat behind his huge oak desk.

"Andrew," Paul repeated.

"I hear congratulations are in order," Andrew said jovially.

"Good news travels fast, I see," Paul muttered as he

unceremoniously plopped into one of Andrew's plush chairs.

Andrew looked slightly bewildered. "Pardon me?"

Paul waved a hand dismissively. "I'm just rather surprised you've already heard the news, that's all."

"Already heard? Whatever do you mean? All of London has been in shock for days about it."

Andrew must have assumed that Paul knew of Lady Algen's article sooner than today and had agreed to marry Liberty earlier in the week. It was of no account now. "The paper was inaccurate in their report," Paul said lamely. "Of course you already knew that, since you know neither of us would wish to seduce the other."

"Oh, I wasn't talking about that. I knew that was false. I was congratulating you on the announcement in the paper about your engagement," Andrew said, shuffling through a pile of old newspapers on his desk. When he found what he was looking for, he pulled it out of the stack and handed it to Paul. "See?" He jabbed a finger at a little paragraph in the newspaper that declared for all and sundry that Mr. Paul Grimes and Miss Liberty Banks were engaged.

"Well, I'll be," Paul muttered. "He tricked me twice, that rascal. I'll get him for this."

Andrew chucked. "Welcome to the family. It happens to all of us, I'm afraid."

"Yes, I hear he left you waiting for his nonexistent return," Paul teased.

"Exactly so," Andrew said, shaking his head. "I was so furious with him, I vowed the whole ride back to London I'd tear his head off with my bare hands for that."

"I see that you didn't," Paul remarked, setting the paper down.

"No. It's probably best that I didn't anyway. It certainly wouldn't have helped me in my fight to win my wife back."

"No, I imagine killing your father-in-law is not a good way to get into your wife's good graces," Paul mused. "However, I think you got off easy, Andrew."

"How so?"

"You just had to sit in a room for three hours. I have to spend a lifetime married to someone who, for some unknown reason, hates me."

Andrew laughed. "It'll be all right, just give it time."

"That's what John thinks, too," Paul said grumpily. "I just wish I knew why she detests me so much."

"That, my friend, I don't know. But I do know that given time, she'll grow on you," Andrew said, leaning back in his chair.

"You make her sound like a fungus," Paul said dryly, twisting his lips in distaste.

"You speak of her like she's one," Andrew countered, raising his brow in a dare.

"No, I don't," Paul argued, slightly offended.

"Yes, you do. You sneer every time you talk about her, which isn't often, I'll grant you, but still. Perhaps if you try to think of her as someone you could come to care for, you'll see things differently. You'll see *her* differently," he emphasized.

"I do see her differently. I believe I'm the only one who does."

"Oh?"

Paul twisted his lips. "What I mean is that I don't see the drab mousy woman she projects to the rest of the world," he said with a hint of disgust.

Andrew folded his hands in his lap. "And how do you see her?"

Paul shifted in his seat. This conversation was swiftly becoming more uncomfortable than the one he'd had with John in the carriage. "I see the woman she can be, I suppose. I've seen her smile a handful of times and I know how attractive she looks when she does so. But the problem is, she smiles very rarely, and never in my direction."

"Then make her smile."

Paul scowled. "You make it sound as if it's as simple as breathing; when quite frankly, the only way I could make her smile is if I were to stop breathing."

"You're clever," Andrew said, shrugging. "You'll think of something."

Paul wished he shared Andrew's confidence. He shook his

head. "I'm not so sure of that. Apparently, I'm nothing if not predictable," he muttered, tapping the toe of his boot on the floor.

"What has that to do with anything?"

"It has nothing to do with our recent topic. But it has everything to do with why John ran that announcement in the paper earlier in the week." Paul looked out the window and watched water drip off the end of a melting icicle. "I do wonder what John did when he ran into that building earlier," Paul mused aloud.

"Perhaps he'll tell you when you see him next," Andrew suggested, taking to his feet.

Thinking he was about to be dismissed, Paul stood, too. "Thank you for the talk, Andrew. I may not have a great relationship with my future wife, but I do believe I enjoy the family she's bringing me into."

"Are you leaving, then?"

"I was about to."

"Oh, then I guess you'll have to wait for another time to ask John about his activities this afternoon," Andrew whispered, pointing to a door on the side of the room.

"Is he in there?" Paul mouthed to Andrew.

Andrew nodded quickly. With a hint of a smile, Paul stalked across the room, called a casual farewell to Andrew and opened the door of his study. Standing by the door, he pressed one finger to his lips and stomped his feet a few times, each step a little softer than the one before it.

Andrew must have caught on to what he was doing because he sent Paul a waving signal. Paul interpreted that to mean "shut the door", which he did, then slipped behind a tall potted plant by the door. After the door was firmly shut, Andrew sat down in his chair again and said, "All right, John, you can come out now."

"Thank goodness," John said, stepping out of the closet. "Did you know you have a little spider problem in that closet? I do believe my right leg has not suffered so many insect bites since my older brother was experimenting with spiders when we were boys." He shook his head and brushed a cobweb off of his sleeve. "No matter. I'd gladly take a hundred spider bites in a dark closet rather than suffer Paul's anger at the moment. The man is nearly impossible to deal with when he's in a temper. It's not often I've seen him that way, I admit. But I've seen enough to know Liberty had better behave herself or a wolf will look like her best friend compared to him."

"I must commend you, John. I have underestimated you yet again. You always seem to surprise me," Andrew said, shaking his head.

"Yes, well, you're not the only one," John said, smiling. He leaned down and started dusting off the rest of his clothes.

"Do you like surprises, then?" Paul drawled, walking out from behind the plant.

John spun around so fast, he almost fell over. "Paul," he said breathlessly. His blue eyes had become as big as two tea saucers. His suit was crumpled and covered in dust, and there was a large cobweb stuck to the front part of his bright blond hair, hanging over onto his forehead. If not for his irritation, Paul would have laughed at the sight.

"Just tell me this," Paul said, taking a menacing step toward John. "On our wedding day—whenever that may be—my bride will not find it a surprise that I am to be her groom, will she?"

"No," John gulped, shaking his head violently. "Liberty is well aware she will be marrying you."

"All right," Paul said quietly. There was no point in asking her reaction to learning she would have to marry him, he knew it already. He was more interested in making sure she wasn't going to learn for the first time that she was to become Mrs. Paul Grimes when she reached the church. He tried to convince himself he was only concerned about this so that she wouldn't make a scene at the chapel, but if he were honest, the real reason was he didn't think anyone deserved that kind of a surprise.

"Care to stay for dinner, Paul?" Andrew asked, walking to the door.

***

"These two seats are for the happy couple," Mama chirped,

pointing to two chairs in Andrew's dining room that were at the end of the small table and positioned unusually close together.

Liberty fought the urge to groan as she started to walk over to where her mother stood by the two chairs, beckoning her with her finger. To her good fortune, just before she reached her spot, she caught sight of a smiling Brooke who was coming from the other direction and plopped herself down into one of the chairs. "Andrew dearest," Brooke called to her husband. "Come sit. It's time to eat."

Liberty flashed a grateful smile to Brooke. She'd resigned herself to the fact that she was going to have to marry Mr. Grimes, but that did not mean she wanted to sit so close to him that anytime either of them moved, they'd brush against the other. Nor did she think anyone could possibly confuse them for a happy couple.

"Brooke," Mama said with a speaking glance.

"Sorry, Mama," Brooke said innocently. "I thought you were referring to Andrew and me."

"Well, I wasn't," Mama said tightly.

"It's of no account, Carolina," Mr. Grimes broke in, "Liberty and I will have the rest of our lives to sit together. Besides, I should hate to inconvenience Lady Townson."

"See, Mama, nobody minds," Brooke said blithely. "Anyway, you can stop your matchmaking tricks; they've already agreed to marry."

"Yes, I know," Mama acquiesced. "All right then, for the rest of the seating arrangements, how about if—"

"Why doesn't everyone just take a seat wherever they wish," Andrew cut in smoothly, sitting down next to his wife.

For the first time in Liberty's life, she agreed wholeheartedly with throwing propriety to the wind and sat in the end seat on the other side of Brooke, the chair typically reserved for the hostess. It didn't matter if she sat there since the hostess was sitting in one of the chairs that Mama had tried to get her to occupy. Madison shot her a curious look, but shrugged and plopped in the seat across the table from Brooke.

Mama looked disapprovingly at the trio that was sitting

huddled together at the end of the table, but thankfully said nothing. Instead, she quietly took a seat on the other side of Andrew, with Papa on the end and Mr. Grimes filling the vacant seat next to Madison.

"Thank you," Liberty whispered to Brooke after everyone had started to eat.

"You're welcome," Brooke told her. "But Mr. Grimes was right, you know. You will have to sit next to him for the rest of your life. I won't always be there to save you."

Liberty swallowed. "I know."

"And sitting next to him won't be the only thing you'll soon be expected to do," Madison said with a wink.

Liberty's face heated up as the blood rushed to her head. The blood roaring in her ears was so loud she almost didn't hear Brooke's burble of laughter.

"Shhh," Liberty hissed at them both. "That is not appropriate dinner conversation." Although she dearly loved her sisters, neither one of them seemed to care one whit for propriety. Brooke was always doing outrageous things. As for Madison, well, as sweet as she was, she had a few of her own rude behaviors that were quite unbecoming.

"Oh, nobody can hear us," Brooke assured her quietly, tucking one of her stray raven curls behind her ear.

"I can," Andrew chimed in, smiling. "But not to worry, those three," he sent a pointed glance toward their parents and Mr. Grimes, "cannot hear you. Your parents are too busy asking Paul questions about the wedding."

Liberty's eyes snapped to the end of table. Mama had a happy smile on her face. One which would suggest she was planning the wedding of the century, when in truth, neither the bride nor groom gave a fig about the wedding. Both of them cared about the marriage—being forced to live with the other until death do they part, that part they cared about—but the wedding itself was a different matter. Papa looked like he normally did, except for his ruddy cheeks and the fact that he couldn't stop coughing and patting his chest after every sentence Mama said.

She imagined that was due to more and more of his secrets being revealed. Papa had gone so far as to put the betrothal announcement in the paper, arranged for the special license *and* contacted a local minister—all before trapping the reluctant Mr. Grimes into agreeing to marry her.

Speaking of the reluctant Mr. Grimes, his face was as grim as she'd ever seen it. She'd seen the man unhappy many times, but just now, he looked angrier than she'd ever seen him.

Liberty grabbed her drink and guzzled it down in the most unladylike fashion imaginable, inadvertently drawing attention to herself.

"You have some on your face," Brooke murmured to her, handing her a napkin.

"Thank you," Liberty whispered uneasily. "He looks so angry. What am I to do?"

"I can suggest a thing or two that will improve his mood instantly," Andrew offered with a teasing smile.

Liberty didn't know exactly what he meant, but knew it had to do with something that should only be done in the dead of night in a locked bedchamber. Her suspicions were confirmed when Brooke gave him a swat on the arm. "Don't listen to him," she told her sister. "Mr. Grimes won't be angry forever. And if it becomes too unbearable, you can always do what I do and use quotes from the Bible to point out the error of his ways."

"That's true," Liberty conceded. After spending nearly twenty years watching Brooke quote Bible scripture to their father as a means to extricate herself from trouble, there was little doubt in Liberty's mind that such a tactic would work.

"Perhaps you should just see how it goes and give him a chance," Madison put in. "I may not know him well, but I do know that he has not given me a reason to dislike him."

"Would you like to marry him in my stead?" Liberty asked Madison and laughed when Madison's eyes bulged and she shook her head with so much vigor her coiffure started to slip.

"I agree with Madison," Brooke said, nodding slightly. "I'll admit when we were first introduced, I thought he was a bit odd;

but now that I've gotten to know him, I don't think so anymore."

"That or you've just gotten used to it," Liberty suggested. "Perhaps you've been around him and have become so accustomed to his oddness, you think he's normal."

Brooke rolled her eyes. "Does it matter?"

"I suppose not," Liberty answered dully.

They ate in silence for a few more minutes before Madison whispered. "Well, if it helps, he's already seen you naked and has still agreed to marry you."

"Madison," Liberty gasped. She shot a sharp glance at Brooke who was giggling outright, and caught sight of Andrew's lips twitching.

"She has a point," Brooke said a moment later when she got her giggles under control. "It will make your wedding night a bit easier."

"Brooke," Liberty said through clenched teeth. Did these two know no bounds? They were eating dinner, for goodness' sake.

"By the bye," Brooke continued, ignoring the scathing glance she was receiving, "after dinner come to my room. I want to have a little talk with you and this might be my last chance."

Liberty had a good idea what kind of a talk Brooke wanted to have with her. "That won't be necessary," she said quickly.

"Yes, it will," Brooke assured her. "If you're counting on Mama, you may not be properly informed."

She looked skeptically at Brooke. Mama had been married for more than twenty-five years and had three daughters. She obviously knew *something*.

"Just come see me," Brooke repeated.

Liberty fought the urge to tell her there was no need since she had no plans to do whatever activity necessary to have children with Mr. Grimes. Not that she didn't love children, because she did, she adored them in fact; but she just didn't want to become that intimate with Mr. Grimes. Swallowing past the lump that had formed in her throat, she said, "All right."

"Good," Brooke said with a simple smile. "This way you'll know what to expect."

"If you're going to describe that thing that dangles between his legs, don't bother," Liberty said, throwing good manners to the wind like the rest of the Heathens she was seated with. "I've already seen it."

"You have?" Brooke squealed.

All three of them, who had been huddled together talking like nobody else was in the room, suddenly felt the questioning gazes of their parents and Mr. Grimes.

"Excuse my wife," Andrew cut in evenly, sending the trio a laughing smile. "She was merely shocked when Madison said she'd already decided on the gown she was going to wear to the wedding."

Mama shot Brooke a sympathetic look; then resumed her conversation at the other end of the table.

"Sweetheart," Andrew said to Brooke. "Do try not to squeal again. I don't think I can make up another viable excuse."

"Thank you," Brooke said, giving him a quick kiss on the cheek before turning back to Liberty. "Now, you'll definitely need to come to my room for a talk."

"Fine," Liberty ground out. "But only if Madison comes with me."

Madison, who usually liked to be a silent member of the sisters' conversations, put her drink down with an indelicate clang. "No, thank you. I think I'll pass on having to hear any more about Mr. Grimes' love musket."

Brooke erupted with laughter; Liberty gasped; and Andrew choked on his bite of meat at her coarse and slightly unusual words. Madison, however, looked rather pleased with herself, Liberty noted when she recovered from her shock.

"Are you all right?" Mama asked Andrew.

He continued to cough and smack his chest while his face grew red.

"I think he's choking," Papa said, jumping up.

Brooke's laughter dissolved instantly and she pulled her arm back as far as she could before she used the heel of her hand to hit her husband with an echoing *thwack* squarely in the middle of his back.

Brooke's smack must have dislodged whatever it was that was stuck in Andrew's throat, because Andrew brought his napkin to his mouth for a moment, then turned to her and said, "Thank you, darling, I don't know what I would do without you."

"Think nothing of it," Brooke answered, a sweet smile curving her lips.

"Perhaps you should cut your bites a bit smaller," Mama suggested in an overly helpful, motherly sort of way.

"Perhaps you're right," he agreed, looking at Madison and trying not to laugh.

Their dishes were cleared away and dessert was served, before anyone spoke again. "Ladies," Andrew said in low tone, catching the attention of Liberty and her two sisters. "I believe for the rest of the meal, the conversation shouldn't stray from clothing and whatnot. However, Madison, I must commend you, even I had not heard that term before."

"Thank you," Madison said graciously, acting not the least bit embarrassed. But then again, why should she bother to act embarrassed when she wasn't? The whole family knew she was wont to use a coarse word or a shocking phrase every now and again. Where else would Liberty have learned the ones she knew? It wasn't until recently she'd ever heard her father use one.

When the dessert dishes had been cleared away, Mama was the first to get up from the table. Actually, from where Liberty was sitting, it looked like she literally sprang to her feet. "Shall we retire to the drawing room?" she suggested.

Andrew stiffened. Liberty could tell he wanted to say something. Perhaps something that most would not consider nice. After a little incident with a game of charades last year, he wasn't nearly as tolerable of Mama's parlor games.

"Actually, I must be going," Mr. Grimes said, taking to his feet. "It appears I have a busy day tomorrow."

Liberty knew what he was alluding to. It would seem that tomorrow was to be their Big Day. Poor man, he had no idea when he was summoned to London that his entire life was going to change so drastically before he returned home.

Shifting her gaze to Papa, she noticed he had a hesitant smile on his face, probably because he had just done a great wrong to someone he'd come to care about. Her heart sank. Papa would never have done the things he had if it weren't for her. This was just another way she was a disappointment. Well, starting tomorrow that would all change. She would become Mrs. Paul Grimes and do her best to be an exemplary wife. She may not be happy about it, but she'd do whatever she needed to.

Chapter 7

Paul had never had such a restless night. Part of him was angry—nay, furious—with John. He understood John's desire to protect his daughter, but he'd gone too far this time.

Pushing past his anger over John's tricks, he found himself infuriated anew by the fact he'd just agreed to die a virgin. Though he was a minister, he was not a monk, and he'd be lying if he didn't acknowledge his disappointment at the prospect of never being with a woman. Of course, he could tell Liberty it was his husbandly right to make her share his bed, but that wouldn't be very satisfying. Well, in a way it would be, he thought wryly. He had seen her naked once and, despite his best efforts, every now and then the image popped into his head. At the time, he had only been doing his best to get her warm and had no other motives, but his brain must have absorbed more of her naked image than he'd originally thought.

The first time he'd woken up in a cold sweat with a throbbing erection after having a dream about her, he'd lain awake for hours trying to make sense of it. Finally, just as the sun was rising, the simple—and obvious—solution presented itself. It was because he'd never seen a naked lady before. Actually, that wasn't exactly true, he'd seen one once, but she was no lady.

When he was eighteen, his father died and his brother inherited the title. That's when Paul had started to seriously pursue his life in the ministry and had come to terms with the knowledge that he would be just as inexperienced as his future wife. It really hadn't bothered him so much. First, she'd be a virgin and wouldn't know the difference. Second, as a minister he couldn't have a reputation for sleeping with unmarried—or married—women. And third, at least this way he would avoid getting a bawdyhouse disease.

That reason alone seemed good enough for Paul to keep it in his pants. However, two years past when he was sixteen, he'd questioned if he would go into the ministry like his father had before inheriting the title due to his brother's lack of male issue. He knew that in living a minister's lifestyle, he'd never get to experience many of the same things his brother and his friends would.

After a month's contemplation, he asked his older brother to take him to a brothel the next time he went. Sam readily agreed and the next night Paul found himself at Lady Bird's, a local brothel. Sam introduced him to the Madam, and together the two of them decided Ginger should be the one to introduce Paul to the alluring world of bed sport.

Nervously, Paul took a seat in the front room and waited while Ginger "freshened up". His brother sat next to him and informed him Ginger wasn't the best looking, but she was the most patient. And if he should have any trouble, he should just close his eyes and imagine Lucy. Paul nodded with great enthusiasm. Lucy was their dairymaid, and a very fine looking girl. He'd had no doubt that thinking about her would solve a problem, should one arise, or lack thereof, as the case may be.

A few minutes later, a woman dressed in a tattered chemise walked up and grabbed Paul's hand. Resisting the urge to pull from her clasp, he got up and followed her back to the room.

"I hear yer a virgin," Ginger purred, clucking her tongue.

Paul nodded.

"Ginger'll take care o' that right away," she said, as if virginity were some pesky little thing he needed to be divested of post haste.

Paul smiled tentatively. Perhaps this was not such a good idea, he thought once he was inside the room. His eyes swept his surroundings, causing his stomach to clench. In the middle of the room was a mattress with rumpled and stained sheets. Next to that was a half full chamber pot and half a dozen different articles of clothing were scattered across the floor, most of which belonged to men.

Paul took a deep breath and immediately regretted breathing

through his nose. The room smelled of sex. Not that he was an expert, but he did know what semen smelled like, and this room reeked of it.

"Come here, you big boy," Ginger called suggestively.

Paul's eyes flew to where she was lying on the mattress, rubbing her hand in a circle next to her. He swallowed and closed his eyes. Squeezing them tighter, he tried to picture Lucy, but had no luck. His brain could not summon her sweet face.

His eyes were still shut when he heard Ginger get off the mattress and walk toward him. Her hands grabbed onto the front of his shirt. "Yer a shy one, huh?" she mused with a husky laugh.

He opened his eyes, but could do nothing more than stare at her rouged face and nasty teeth.

"Let's try sumthin' else," Ginger said, trailing her hand down his front.

He jumped back instinctively when she grabbed for the buttons of his pants.

"Yer gonna have to git it out, ye know," she said, her voice becoming slightly impatient. "It don't matter if yer small, I'll teach ye how to please a woman. But I gots to know wot yer working with."

Paul stared at her unblinkingly. She thought he was hesitating because he was small? She could think that if she liked, he decided. He had no desire to prove her wrong at this point. He may not have had much personal experience in seducing women, but he'd accidentally walked in on more romantic trysts than he cared to count, and he knew without a doubt "small" was not an accurate adjective to describe him.

Ginger laughed again. "Hmm, pr'aps tis will help wit yer problem," she said, slipping the straps of her chemise off her shoulders and letting the dirty, ragged garment drop to the floor.

Just like spotting an overturned carriage, Paul couldn't stop himself from looking at her body. A quick, yet thorough, sweep of her body told Paul everything he needed to know: he could not sleep with this woman. Her pale skin was covered with bruises and scars. She was so thin, the outline of almost every bone she possessed was visible. Her small, misshapen breasts were covered in harsh looking red marks, and he wasn't positive, but it appeared one was slightly larger than the other.

He watched in silence as she walked backwards to the mattress and reclined on it, rubbing her hands up and down her body seductively as she went. Slowly, she opened her legs to his gaze. Naturally, being sixteen and curious, he didn't even try to stop his gaze from dropping to what she'd just freely exposed to him. Just as quickly as he looked, he fled the room.

Breathlessly, he ran from the room and dashed out of the brothel, yelling to the Madam that his brother would take care of his bill.

When a furious Sam confronted him later about why he'd stiffed the wench, Paul claimed it was because he had an attack of morals and couldn't go through with it. Since their father had been a minister, and it was well-known that Paul would be one, too, Sam didn't question him. Paul was eternally thankful that he hadn't, because he would have hated to admit he'd gotten a view of what the pox looked like, and the sight made his stomach revolt.

After that night, he'd never seen another naked lady until Liberty. Instead, he'd settled for the occasional peek at the books of naughty drawings some of his friends had taken from their fathers' libraries. Then at eighteen, he'd put all that behind him and gladly accepted that he'd just have to wait until marriage where there would be a mutual attraction and both parties would care a great deal for each other.

But presently at four and twenty, he found himself only hours away from taking vows that would make him the equivalent of a monk. He would never use force to get Liberty into bed, and judging by the way she detested him, it would take nothing less than force—most likely the physical kind—to get her into his bed. Now that he thought about it, it was better he didn't sleep with Ginger, or any woman for that matter, because at least now he wouldn't know what he was missing.

Shaking his head to rid himself of the images of Ginger, Paul stood up and went to the window of his rented room. John had tried to convince him to stay at his house overnight. But Paul refused and assured him nearly a hundred times not to worry; he'd arrive at ten o'clock and marry Liberty.

Paul quickly shaved the scruff off his face and threw on his clothes. He hadn't come to London yesterday with the intention of getting married today, so he'd need to run by a tailor shop and pray they had something nice already made that he could buy. He doubted anyone would care or notice, but he thought it would be outright disrespectful to show up in his wrinkled clothes from yesterday.

Two hours and three tailor shops later, Paul finally had a new suit of clothes and was traveling to the Banks residence when he called for the coachman to stop. He knew time was running short, but he needed to get one last thing before he went to Watson Townhouse. A quick glance down both sides of Bond Street and he found what he'd been looking for. Telling his coachman to wait there, he ran across the street and returned quickly with a small bundle. After a quick word, he was on his way to his wedding.

"It's about time," a disgruntled John Banks said as soon as Paul opened the carriage door.

"Sorry, sir. It took a bit longer than I expected this morning," Paul said, not sure why he was bothering to apologize, since he wasn't actually late.

John made a dismissive hand gesture in the air. "It's of no import now. You're here. I'll go tell Liberty to dry her eyes and get downstairs."

That sounds like a positive start to our marriage, Paul thought, climbing the front steps to the townhouse. She was already in tears and they hadn't even said I do yet.

In more than five years of being a vicar, Paul had officiated at many weddings. Most at churches, some in gardens, some in fields, a few in drawing rooms, but this was the first wedding he'd ever attended that took place in the entry hall. He understood why: there was no decent looking room in the Watson Townhouse. They were all hideously decorated and had stuffed game mounted on every wall or resting on any flat surface that was bigger than two square feet.

There were no chairs brought in and, with it being only a small family affair, nobody complained. Everyone was assembled and waiting when John cleared his throat from the top of the stairs, catching the attention of the group.

All eyes fell on Liberty as John escorted her down the stairs and brought her to stand beside Paul.

Her pale pink dress brushed his legs as she took her spot next to him. She cast him an apologetic glance as she righted her gown. One of the corners of his mouth tipped up and he took her hand, giving it a squeeze to assure her everything would be all right. He wasn't sure when he'd come to that conclusion, but somewhere in the last thirty seconds, he had.

The ceremony lasted a whole three minutes and it was now time to kiss his bride. Paul leaned forward to kiss her and when he caught sight of Liberty's panic-stricken eyes, he realized this must be her first kiss and she looked terrified that it was to be made public. Quickly, he changed his course of action and settled for brushing a light kiss on her forehead.

"Thank goodness," Brooke said with a sigh after the kiss. "I was afraid Andrew and I were going to have to demonstrate," she teased, making the little group laugh and breaking the proverbial ice.

As was custom, a breakfast followed the ceremony. Thankfully, it was over quickly enough, followed by Liberty saying a tearful farewell to her family.

Paul tried to act patient while he waited by the carriage for her to finish hugging everyone for the third time. When she was done, he helped her inside and climbed in before any more words could be exchanged. With a sharp rap on the roof, they were on their way.

***

The carriage ride was very uneventful. Neither of them said a word for the first hour. With the exception of an occasional sniffle, utter silence filled the carriage. During the second hour, Liberty gained control of her emotions and settled for just staring out the window. Now she knew why Madison did it so often, it was actually rather entertaining.

She didn't know how long she stared out the window before the carriage came to an abrupt stop and her husband asked if she was hungry or needed to get out and stretch. She declined both offers and waited for him to do whatever he was doing inside the inn.

She fidgeted when he got back into the carriage and he brushed her knee with his leg. "Sorry," he murmured, taking a seat.

"It's all right," she mumbled. After the things Mama and Brooke told her last night, she'd gladly settle for his leg brushing hers. Suddenly she felt over warm. "I fear I may be in need of some air after all. Do you mind?"

"Not at all," Mr. Grimes said, opening the door to the carriage for her.

After he helped her down, she walked around the courtyard, taking deep breaths. What if he expected her to do *that* when they reached his home? Last night she'd been trying to convince Brooke that she didn't need to hear the details because she would not be engaging in marital activities with Mr. Grimes, then all of the sudden, Mama barged into the room. Mama and Brooke had a stare down before Mama finally relented and said Brooke could stay, but only if she added something productive to the conversation, strongly stressing the word productive.

Mama put her arm around Liberty and sat next to her on the bed. "Tomorrow night…uh…Paul is going to…um…come to your bed and…" She trailed off and fanned her red face.

"Oh, for goodness' sake," Brooke muttered, sitting down on the other side of Liberty. "Liberty, you remember that thing you saw dangling between Mr. Grimes' legs?"

"Brooklyn," Mama snapped.

Brooke waved her off. "When he sees you naked, that thing will get hard—"

"Brooklyn, I demand you stop right this instant," Mama all but shouted.

Brooke's eyes left Liberty's face and snapped to Mama's. "Is it true?"

"Yes," Mama admitted sheepishly.

"What's he going to do with it?" Liberty asked, unable to keep the terror she felt from creeping into her voice. Was he going to touch her with it? She needed to know, desperately.

Neither Brooke nor Mama answered, they both looked to the other one, each expecting the other to answer her.

"He's going to touch me with it, isn't he?" she exclaimed, seeing the answer on their faces.

"Perhaps you were right," Brooke said, looking at Mama. "I believe this is a conversation better had between a mother and daughter," she added, getting off the bed.

"Oh, no you don't," Mama said, grabbing her hand and pulling her back to the bed. "You wanted to be a part of this conversation; you're going to see it through."

"I only wanted to be a part of it because I wasn't properly informed. I wanted to spare her the uncertainty I faced," Brooke said evenly, looking from Mama to Liberty then back to Mama.

"Forgive me," Mama said a bit irritably. "Like everyone else, I was under the assumption you no longer required the information on your wedding day."

Brooke mumbled something Liberty couldn't quite make out. Not that she even cared about their conversation; she was too busy thinking about what was going to happen to her.

"Yes, he's going to touch you with it," Brooke said uncomfortably. "At first it will hurt, but then it won't..." She trailed off and her face went as red as Mama's.

"Then what?"

"She already told you, then it won't," Mama said somewhat sharply, not meeting Liberty's eyes.

Liberty looked back and forth between the scarlet faces of her sister and mother. "Well, it doesn't matter," she finally declared.

"Yes, it will," Mama told her softly. "Liberty, you may not want to, but Mr. Grimes might, and if he does, as his wife, it's your duty to be willing."

Liberty swallowed but nodded her understanding. Earlier

she'd made up her mind to do whatever necessary to be a good wife, and if that meant letting him touch her that way, she'd allow it.

Biting her lip and swiping at the tears on her cheeks, she looked around the outside of the inn. Mr. Grimes was probably waiting on her, she'd better hurry up and get back so they could be on their way.

"Are you feeling better now?" Mr. Grimes inquired from beside the carriage.

"Yes, thank you," she replied, accepting his help getting into the carriage.

"I have something for you," he said, after he'd sat back down. "I apologize I didn't give it to you earlier, I nearly forgot about it until just a moment ago."

What could he have for her? All of her things were in trunks on the top of the carriage. Had something fallen off?

"Here." He handed her a small, wrapped bundle that she immediately recognized as a book from Bronson's Books, a little bookshop on Bond Street.

"Thank you." She ran her fingers along the twine that was holding on the paper.

"What are you waiting for? Open it," he said with a lopsided smile.

"I have nothing for you," she whispered, horrified.

Mr. Grimes reached his hand over and patted the back of hers. "That's all right. You didn't need to get me anything," he said evenly. When she glanced at him like she wasn't convinced, he added, "Besides, it's nothing too terribly extravagant, just something to occupy you until we can fetch your library."

Liberty fought to keep the smile from her lips. All the books she had could easily fill half a library. Papa had promised he'd bring them to her in the next few weeks. He must have mentioned it to Mr. Grimes last night at dinner. "Thank you," she repeated, pulling one of the ends of the twine, causing the bow to release and the twine to loosen. Tossing the string on the floor, she made quick work of the paper and flipped the book over to read the title.

"The man at the bookshop said this was the newest book he had, so I'm certain you haven't read it," Mr. Grimes told her.

Liberty nodded. The book was titled *Loving Her Gentleman*, obviously it was a romance novel. "The man was correct, I haven't read this one," she murmured. Truth be known, she'd never even read a novel before. She'd bought a couple the first time she'd been in Bath, but had been unable to stay interested past the first fifty pages. Perhaps this time it would be different. "Why did you buy me a book?" she blurted out.

Mr. Grimes shrugged. "I don't know. Perhaps because I thought you might be bored waiting for your books. Unless you have plans to join the local sewing circle and start baking goods for the needy, that is."

Again she almost smiled, but didn't. It was obvious he was trying very diligently to be nice. "Well, whatever your reasons, thank you very much. Though I must say, I'm rather surprised to see you bought me a romance novel," she said curiously.

"What did you expect me to do? Give you a copy of the Bible and tell you to read Ruth, Esther and snippets of the Song of Solomon?"

Despite her best efforts, she couldn't stop herself from smiling. "Actually, that is exactly what I expected of you."

He grinned at her. "We still have a while before we arrive. If you'd like, you can begin to read now," he suggested.

Liberty nodded and flipped open her book. The old Liberty would have tried to annoy him by reading it out loud, but she'd turned over a new leaf and didn't want to start things off on the wrong foot, so to speak.

In no time at all they pulled up to a little brown bricked two story cottage she would now call home. The cottage belonged to the church and as part of his compensation, the current vicar was allowed to live in the little cottage.

There were only a handful of rooms inside and it took only a few minutes for Liberty to realize that this cottage was built with the intent that the husband and wife were expected to share a room.

Standing in the doorway of the only room she'd seen with a

bed, Liberty trembled as her eyes stared at the bed.

Fighting the urge to run, she took a step inside when she suddenly felt a staying hand on her upper arm. "There's another room upstairs," Mr. Grimes said softly in her ear.

"I didn't see that one," she whispered, relaxing.

"You may sleep in whichever you prefer."

Liberty nervously licked her lips. "Where do you want me to sleep?"

"I don't care," he said hastily. "I've just been using this one since it was more convenient. But if you want it, I'll move my things upstairs."

Liberty was confused. Did that mean he wasn't planning to share her bed, or that he would just visit her there, then leave to go sleep in his own room? She had to know. Stiffening her spine and willing herself not to blush, she asked, "Are you planning to leave?"

"Leave?" he echoed, piercing her with his gaze.

Liberty blushed violently. "Yes, leave after you touch me with your...your....love musket,"

"Excuse me? My what?" Mr. Grimes asked, his lips twitching.

Liberty closed her eyes and fisted her hands into her skirt, trying in vain not to faint from mortification. She should have known he would have no idea what she was talking about. Even Andrew had admitted to never having heard that stupid term. Obviously Mr. Grimes hadn't heard the term, either. But she had no idea what it was called. Nobody had seen fit to tell her and now she was making a fool out of herself. "You know, that thing," she said, vaguely pointing in the direction of his waist.

"Is that what your mother called it?" Mr. Grimes asked; his tone and eyes full of laughter.

"No," Liberty snapped, her mortification deepening. "She did not. She didn't call it anything. I have no idea what it's called, that's just what I heard Madison call it."

Paul howled with laughter. "Madison said that?"

"Yes," Liberty answered testily. "Are you planning to visit my bed tonight or not?" she demanded angrily, bringing his laughter to an abrupt end.

He stopped laughing and blinked at her. "No," he said finally, shaking his head.

"In that case, I'll take the room upstairs," Liberty said stiffly, running up the stairs.

Chapter 8

Liberty didn't know why she was irritated that he didn't want to share her bed, she just was. Not that she was looking forward to it, in fact, she'd actually been dreading it. At the same time though, she couldn't help but feel unwanted by his easy rejection.

The whole conversation had been humiliating enough already and when he'd said "no" so casually, emphasized by shaking his head wildly, that was enough to send her into complete mortification.

Shedding her clothes, she crawled into bed, heedless of needing a bath. She was so tired she feared she might fall asleep in the tub and drown. With her luck, *he'd* be the one to find her dead, naked body.

Today wasn't all bad, she thought, pulling the covers up. He'd been rather nice in the carriage. Perhaps Madison and Brooke were right and he was nice, or perhaps, it was all a ruse and his real personality would reappear the next day. It didn't really matter, she told herself. No matter what atrocious thing he did, she was determined to be as sweet as sugar in return, even if she seethed on the inside like she was doing just now.

After what felt like an extended blink, Liberty opened her eyes to see the sun shining through her uncovered window. Rubbing her sleepy eyes, Liberty gained her feet and looked around for her clothes.

Selecting a green day gown out of the one trunk that had been brought up, she draped it over the dressing screen, then went to where she thought the bell pull was located only to find it had been disconnected. "Now what?" she muttered. How was she supposed to get hot water for her bath?

She searched through her trunk again and found there wasn't a single dressing gown. Deciding it wasn't worth trying to stuff herself back into yesterday's gown, Liberty left her room in only her chemise and tiptoed to the stairs. "Hello?" she called.

Nobody answered.

Last night she'd been introduced to Mrs. Siddons, their only fulltime house servant who worked as their cook and housekeeper. Perhaps she was in the kitchen and couldn't hear her calling. She wasn't worried about Mr. Grimes seeing her, he wouldn't be home at this hour. He'd be out teaching Latin or doing whatever it was that vicars did during the day. Her own Papa had never been home during the day, so why would Pa—Mr. Grimes?

Liberty carefully walked down the stairs and to the kitchen where she found a large copper tub full of steaming water. This wasn't where she would have liked to take a bath, but it seemed she had no choice in the matter since she couldn't carry the large tub full of water upstairs.

With a sigh, she pulled her chemise over her head and stepped into the tub. Letting her feet and legs get used to the heat, she slowly sank into the warm tub. Not terribly comfortable with the idea of bathing in the kitchen, Liberty made short work of getting clean.

Right next to where she'd placed her chemise on the towel rack was a clean towel. Gripping the end of it with her fingertips, she gave it a gentle tug. With ease, the towel slid off the rack and she wrapped the fluffy cloth around herself and was drying off when she heard footsteps outside the door.

Worried she wasn't going to be able to escape without being seen, she spotted a halfway opened pantry door and quickly dashed behind it.

The kitchen door creaked open and Liberty heard heavy footfalls walk across the room. Her chest constricted. What would happen if he opened the door to the pantry and saw her? She shivered, and not necessarily because she was cold.

Inside the pantry was darker than night, and there was absolutely no room to move about. She stood there for what seemed like forever listening as her husband splashed around in the tub like a child, humming the tunes to popular American songs. He must have realized she was in here, she thought, leaning against the shelves. There was no other explanation for why he was now singing the chorus to Yankee Doodle.

Shaking her head in irritation, she considered going out there and giving him a set down for playing with her this way. That's when she realized two things: one, she couldn't go out there and give him a piece of her mind because she was hardly any better dressed than he was, because two, she'd left her chemise on the towel rack.

Agitation welled up inside her. It was her own fault he knew she was here. If only she'd snatched her chemise on the way to the pantry, he'd have been none the wiser and probably would have been long gone by now.

Silence finally filled the air and Liberty opened the door to the pantry as slowly as she could so it wouldn't creak. Relieved to find the room empty, Liberty stepped out of the pantry and darted over to the towel rack to get her chemise. Surely he wasn't such a cad that he'd take it with him, was he?

He was.

***

Paul went to bed the night before with a lot on his mind. Though he'd only been married for twelve hours, he'd already drawn two major conclusions. First, something was different about Liberty. For the majority of the day, she hadn't been herself. Part of that could be chalked up to the fact they didn't know each other, but that didn't account for all of it. The woman he'd met last year was fiery and somewhat quick tempered. The woman he spent most of the day with was as docile as a newborn kitten. Something was definitely wrong. It seemed her spirit was broken, and he wasn't sure why, but for some reason that unsettled him.

The second thing, which actually was closely linked to the first, was that he had realized it was possible for them to create an enjoyable life together—but only if they both worked at it.

The few times they'd spoken, Paul had actually enjoyed the conversation. He'd wanted to talk more while they were in the carriage and found himself rather disappointed when she took his suggestion and started to read her book. As much as he hated to admit it, he would have even enjoyed it if she had read the book to him. It wasn't that he had any great interest in romance novels; he just would have liked to have heard her read.

Their conversation outside his room had reminded him a little of the old Liberty especially when she'd gotten angry and snapped at him. He hadn't meant to laugh at her. He'd known what she'd been talking about the whole time, but every time she'd said something, he couldn't help but want to hear more. As much as it pained him to even think it, he would have rather fought with her all day than sat there in silence.

Before he extinguished the last candle on his nightstand, he vowed that come tomorrow he'd try to get another glimpse of the old Liberty, even if he had to purposely agitate her. He'd never done it on purpose before; it seemed his mere presence had been enough in the past. The difference was, in the past, she hadn't been trying so hard not to get her feathers ruffled.

Without any effort on his part, an opportunity presented itself first thing in the morning.

He'd gotten into the routine of taking a bath in the kitchen before breaking his fast. At first, it had seemed odd bathing there, but Mrs. Siddons couldn't carry the pails of water and since it was only him, he soon grew accustomed to it.

Paul had no idea Liberty was there before he'd strolled into the kitchen, and if she had been in the open, he would have apologized and looked for a different opportunity to provoke her. But since she had gone through the trouble of abandoning her chemise and hiding in the pantry, he decided to take full advantage of the situation.

At first he just thought to take a long time and act childishly by splashing around loudly. When that didn't seem to work, he upped the ante by humming tunes he knew she had to be familiar with. Though his knowledge was lacking on the subject of her homeland, he did know the melodies to a few of their songs. He hummed through two of them, not sure he'd gotten the tune right. But there was one song he knew the chorus to and most of the verses, Yankee Doodle.

Of course he knew that song because he'd grown up hearing people sing it in a manner aimed at taunting the Americans. The verses he'd heard were about them being cowards and getting devoured. Whereas she was likely to only be familiar with the ones praising George Washington and his stallion as he commanded a million. Judging it best only to spike her ire, not go to war, he stuck to just singing the chorus.

Five times he sang the chorus. Each time he sang it, he got just a bit louder. After the fifth time, he frowned and decided to get out of the tub. He'd have to do something else. Mrs. Siddons would soon be back and she'd need the kitchen to cook breakfast.

Drying off, his eyes kept straying to her chemise. She'd be furious if he swiped it. That wasn't exactly what he wanted. He wanted to get her dander up, not give her a reason to scalp him.

One step away from the door, he turned around and, against his better judgment, he swiped her chemise and stalked out the door before he could change his mind.

***

Liberty pulled the towel around her as tightly as she could. There was nothing for it, she was going to have to dash to her room and run by Mr. Grimes wearing only her towel in the process.

She scowled. She'd never been more convinced he was a jackanapes than she was at this moment. Lifting her head with pride she didn't feel, she opened the door quietly, falsely hoping if she were quiet he wouldn't realize she'd left the kitchen.

Padding down the hallway, she couldn't help but smile when she reached the first step without seeing or hearing him. Surely she would have encountered him already, if he planned to taunt her. Just as her foot landed on the third step, she glanced to the right and saw him standing in an open doorframe across the hall. "Missing something?" he drawled, shaking her chemise in front of him.

Startled, she froze momentarily before tightening her grip on her towel. She should run up the stairs like she'd originally planned, but seeing his face-splitting grin while he shook her chemise only infuriated her more. "Give it back," she said in a low, fierce tone.

"Come and get it," he drawled, extending it in her direction only enough to taunt her, not enough for her to actually be able to reach it.

Though anger burned inside her, she wasn't going to give him the satisfaction of seeing her beg or play a silly game in order to get her clothing back. "Keep it," she said casually, giving him an insincere smile.

Paul's hand lowered. "Care to know a secret? You have a beautiful smile, but only when it's genuine," he said softly, tossing her chemise on the banister before walking away.

Liberty's body froze. Her eyes drifted back and forth from her chemise to his retreating back. Had he meant what he'd said, or had he been only mocking her? Sticking to her original opinion that he was an awful villain, she quickly decided he'd been mocking her. With a sharp exhale, she grabbed her chemise and escaped to her room.

Chapter 9

Throughout the rest of Paul's day he couldn't quit thinking about the events of the morning. He'd tried so hard to provoke her and had thought he'd finally broken through her barrier when she'd demanded her chemise back. But once she'd flashed him that false smile, he'd known he was no closer than when he'd started. Aggravated, he gave up the battle and went for a ride.

The ride hadn't helped and all during his Latin lessons and home visits, thoughts of his wife kept niggling in the back of his head.

Dismounting, he decided tonight he'd apologize for his rude behavior and any future attempts he made to break down her defenses would be more tasteful. He could only imagine what a fool he'd looked like shaking her chemise and grinning like an idiot.

Dinner that night was served in the kitchen. Since he had always eaten alone, he'd seen no reason to use the dining room. Perhaps now that he was married he ought to ask Liberty where she preferred to eat.

"Good evening, my dear," Paul drawled when Liberty walked into the kitchen. "Care to join me?"

She nodded her acceptance, but said nothing.

"Mrs. Siddons, why don't you go home early? We'll worry about the dishes," Paul said to the housekeeper.

Mrs. Siddons bobbed a quick thank you and was out the door before Liberty could object.

"Why did you send her home?" Liberty asked, clearly uncomfortable being completely trapped alone with him.

"Because I wanted to talk to you," Paul said earnestly, spearing a piece of chicken.

"You could have just asked her to leave the room."

Paul smiled at her. "If you're worried about being alone with me, don't be. I have no intention of ravishing you."

Color crept up Liberty's face. "Good, because I'd put up the biggest fight you've ever seen."

Ah, now they were getting somewhere. "Would you now?" he drawled.

She bit her lip and looked away. He could tell she had a hot retort waiting on the tip of her tongue, but for some reason she wasn't going to put voice to it. No matter. His intention tonight was to apologize. He'd find another way to bait her tomorrow. "Liberty," he began softly, catching sight of how she bristled when he spoke to her. "I would like to apologize for what I did this morning."

"It's of no account," she said stiffly, her eyes belying her statement.

Obviously it was of some account or she wouldn't be blinking so rapidly. "Yes, it is. I went too far when I took your—"

"Don't say it," she cut in, the words delivered from between clenched teeth.

"I was going to say clothing," Paul said honestly.

"Sorry," she muttered, picking up a dinner roll.

"Let me guess, you thought I was going to say chemise," Paul said, ducking so she wouldn't hit him if she threw her roll.

But the roll didn't fly like he expected. Instead, her hands squeezed it so tightly that within three seconds it was unrecognizable. "Mr. Grimes," she began in a brittle, if not somewhat starchy tone, "it's highly inappropriate to speak of such things."

"Clothing?" he asked cocking his head. "Hmm, I may not go to London that much, but I believe that many young ladies talk to gentlemen about clothing." Paul heard a noise of vexation that would almost pass as a grunt emerge from somewhere within Liberty's throat.

"Some do," she said flatly, still clutching her used-to-be dinner roll.

"So then what's the problem?" he asked, his lips twitching at the sight of her reddening face.

She glared at him.

"Oh, is it because the young ladies talk about gowns, bonnets, ribbons and the like and I was speaking of undergarments?" he asked innocently, taking delight in the way she bristled again. She wouldn't be able to hold her resolve much longer if he kept this up. At some point those walls she'd erected were going to come down, and not only was he counting on it, he was going to enjoy watching it.

"Mr. Grimes," she said in steely tones. "It's bad enough you had your filthy hands on it; please refrain from reminding me of the tragedy my chemise suffered this morning."

Paul grinned at her. "I do believe Joshua has just marched around the city seven times."

"What is that supposed to mean?" she demanded, her eyes shooting daggers at him.

"Nothing, my dear; nothing at all." He picked up his dinner roll and bit off half of it.

Shaking her head, Liberty ignored him and focused on her dinner.

"Liberty dearest," Paul said sweetly causing her angry eyes to snap to his. "Perhaps since you've ruined your roll," he gestured to the mangled piece of bread in her hand, "you should use your fork to stab the beans instead of just chasing them around the plate like that." He watched in quiet amusement as her fingers tightened their hold on her fork until her knuckles were completely white. "You can pretend the beans are my head if you'd like," he suggested with a lopsided smile.

For the first time in what seemed like ages, a true smile took hold of her lips. The image caused a tendril of heat and desire to coil in his stomach.

"Thank you for the suggestion. I will do just that," she said sweetly, changing the position of the fork in her hand so that she was holding it with a fist and the tines were pointed down toward her plate. Then, with more force than necessary, she started stabbing at the beans. Loud screeching and scraping noises where her fork was hitting the plate along with the beans echoed throughout the room.

"See, sweetheart, it's much easier to eat that way," Paul told her while trying to keep a straight face. She was absolutely obliterating some of those beans with how much force she was using. She must truly hate him, he thought somberly, his smile rapidly fading.

"Stop that," she said tightly, stabbing at her plate.

"Stop what?" he asked with sincere innocence. What was he doing now that was irritating her?

"Stop calling me that," she said through clenched teeth.

"What? Sweetheart? I only called you that once, it's not as if I've made a habit of it. Yet."

"Well, stop. I don't like it."

"All right, you don't like sweetheart. How about when I called you 'my dear' or 'dearest'?" he asked just to tease her.

She pursed her lips. "Mr. Grimes, I feel you are deliberately trying to anger me. Let's get one thing straight. We only got married because of my stupidity and my father's anger. This is not a love match. Therefore, I would prefer if you did not call me any of those endearments."

"All right." He'd called her those things only to help fuel the fire of her vexation. Until now, he doubted they were working. Apparently they were. Good.

"Thank you," she said semi-cordially.

"You're welcome, Liberty," Paul said softy.

She slammed her fork down on the table. "Do not, and I repeat do not, call me that."

"What by your name?" Paul asked, bewildered.

Her eyes flashed fire. "You may call me Mrs. Grimes."

One of the corners of his mouth tipped up. She would rather he call her by the name he'd given her than her own name. That was rather amusing. "Why would I do that?"

"Why wouldn't you?" she countered.

Of course the majority of married couples addressed each other formally, he knew that. But just because he knew it, didn't mean he agreed with it. "Because you're my wife," he returned simply.

Liberty rolled her eyes heavenward for a moment before meeting his again. "Just because I'm your wife does not give you the right to take such liberties," she blustered then exhaled sharply when she realized her own blunder. "Mr. Grimes, take that smile off your face before I wipe it off for you."

Paul raised his hands in mock innocence. "Forgive me," he said, his voice uneven from trying not to laugh. "I did not mean to take such liberties, Liberty."

She twisted her lips and contorted her face in such a way that she looked like she was suffering from a digestive complaint. He couldn't hold it in any longer and let out the howls of laughter he'd been trying to keep inside.

She scowled at him. "Don't think for one moment if you choke on your dinner that I'll whack you on the back and save you the way Brooke did for Andrew."

"Not to worry," he said in between bursts of laughter, "I didn't have any food in my mouth."

"What a pity," she muttered.

When Paul got his laughter under control, he stared at his wife across the table. Her face still had the pinched-up, constipated look, but she was still there, which was a good sign in his opinion. "Hmm. What was that you said last spring? Oh yes, liberty means freedom from external rule. I do believe your parents named you well. I don't believe anyone could rule you."

"I know," she said pertly and smirked.

Paul got up from his spot at the table and walked to Liberty's side. "Liberty," he said, deliberately using her name to irritate her, "I believe I shall retire for the evening. But before I go, I would like to inform you that I am granting you the liberty to call me Paul."

Chuckling at her angry face, he walked out the door and didn't even stop when her crushed dinner roll hit him squarely in the back of the head.

Chapter 10

The next morning Liberty was awakened by a *rap, rap, rap* on her door. Thinking it was her annoying husband, she pulled the covers over her head and ignored the second, louder round of raps that followed.

She groaned a few minutes later when she heard the door open.

"Ma'am, are you awake?" the housekeeper asked.

Immediately, Liberty pulled the blankets down. "I'm sorry. I thought you were my annoying husband."

"Sorry to disappoint, but he couldn't knock," called her infuriating husband from the hallway, "because he was standing out in the hall holding two very heavy buckets of hot water."

Mrs. Siddons looked like she was trying not to laugh. "He insisted you have a bath in your room this morning," she explained, pulling a copper tub into the middle of the floor.

"He insisted?" Liberty repeated hollowly. What was he up to now? Her eyes narrowed on the housekeeper. Surely she was not in on whatever his plans were.

"Yes," she said, nodding. "I told him I was unable to carry the water up, bad back, wouldn't you know," she ran the knuckles of her left hand up and down her spine a bit. "He said that was fine and carried the pails up himself."

There must be more to this story, she thought.

"Are you ready for me yet?" Mr. Grimes asked from the hall.

"Almost," the housekeeper hollered back then looked to Liberty for her to confirm she was ready.

Liberty pulled the blankets up to her chin. "You can come in now."

"Good," he said, walking into the room. Wordlessly, he poured the steaming water into the tub. Then went to leave, pausing at the door to flash her a quick smile and softly say, "Enjoy your bath, Liberty."

She nodded and he left.

Mrs. Siddons asked if she needed any assistance, and Liberty shook her head no.

Once she was alone, Liberty slipped into the tub and enjoyed herself for so long that by the time she got out, the water had become lukewarm.

Liberty didn't know what to do with her day. Yesterday she'd read the entire novel Pau—Mr. Grimes had given her. She hadn't meant to read it all at one time, but she'd enjoyed it so much, she hadn't been able to make herself put it down. They lived only a thirty minute ride from Bath. Perhaps she'd go to a bookshop there and get another.

She frowned. She had very little pin money left, and Papa had told her that he and Pa—Mr. Grimes hadn't discussed her allowance. She swallowed. She doubted she'd ever be getting one with how much her husband seemed to dislike her. And she certainly didn't feel comfortable enough with him to ask him about it.

Liberty went down the stairs and in search of the library. Mr. Grimes had mentioned she would likely fill their library up with her books; but surely he had to have some of his own already there.

Scanning the shelves, a tidal wave of disappointment swept over her. All he had were books that were either written in Latin, therefore, rendering them unreadable to her, or they were about Theology.

Marching upstairs, she ran into Mrs. Siddons carrying down her dirty linens. "Mrs. Siddons, do you know when Mr. Grimes will return?"

"Just before dinner," the housekeeper said.

"Oh," Liberty said, deflated. Even if he were unpleasant to be around, it beat being by herself all day.

"Not to worry, he'll get that old bathwater out as soon as he gets here," the housekeeper said with a cheery smile.

Liberty started. "Oh yes, my bathwater."

"I best be about my duties," Mrs. Siddons said, hurrying off.

"Wait," Liberty called. "What is there to do around here?" She knew it probably seemed selfish to ask a servant what there was to do, but boredom made a person say things they usually wouldn't.

"You can go to Bath."

"I'm not the best rider," Liberty admitted truthfully. She'd never even ridden. Anyway, she'd rather admit she didn't have good skills on the back of a horse than admit she had no money.

"Take the carriage," Mrs. Siddons said simply. "The master left it here for you."

"Brilliant." She may not be able to buy anything, but at least she'd get out of the house.

Less than an hour later, she stood in the same bookshop she'd browsed the last time she'd been to Bath.

She walked around the room and found the romance novel section. Running her finger across the shelf, she scanned all the titles. She dared not pick any of them up for fear she might actually want to read it. She'd seen several that the title alone made her want to read. Then she'd sternly remind herself she was just looking and would swiftly pull her hand back to her side.

"Have you already read all of these?" a voice behind her asked, startling her.

Liberty turned around and saw a petite woman who somehow looked familiar. She wasn't sure how or why, but she'd swear she knew this woman. "No," she said hesitantly.

"That's too bad. Some of them are very good. And others, well, they're not."

Liberty nodded.

"Which one are you thinking of getting?" the woman continued, favoring her with a sweet smile.

"I'm not." When the woman blinked at her, she elaborated. "I didn't bring enough money with me today," she said evenly. It was the truth. She'd left what little money she had at home.

"Oh, well then, just have them put it on your husband's credit," the woman suggested easily.

What an excellent idea! Liberty tried not to smile as she

thought of all the things she was going to be able to buy on Mr. Grimes' credit. The man may think to control her by not giving her an allowance; well, she was going to see that she got what was hers, one way or the other.

Grabbing a few volumes off the shelf, she flashed the woman a grateful smile and walked to the counter. "I want to purchase these on Mr. Paul Grimes' credit, please," she told the clerk with a cheeky smile.

The clerk's eyes traveled up and down her form and he licked his lips. "I'm sorry, but he doesn't have credit in this store. However, I'd be happy to let you buy them on your own credit."

Liberty blinked. "All r—"

"There's no need for that," the other woman cut in sharply, glaring at the cashier. "You can put them on my son's credit."

"Yes, milady," the clerk said with an audible gulp.

"That's not necessary," Liberty protested. Who was this woman? And what had caused her to react so severely to the clerk's suggestion?

"Yes, it is." The woman paid for the books she had in her hand and signed the ledger for Liberty's.

"No, it's really not. I'll just put these back and return when I have more money," Liberty said, grabbing the books off the counter.

"Nonsense. My son will pay for them."

"I cannot accept that," Liberty choked out. "I must pay for them myself."

"You can work it off," the lady told her airily, waving her hand.

"Work it off?" Liberty breathed, her lips quivered. What did this woman mean by that? She knew there were many women who worked off gifts by doing what some called "favors" for gentlemen. She didn't know exactly what these "favors" entailed, and to be honest, she didn't want to know. "No!" Liberty shouted.

The other woman jumped nearly a foot in the air at Liberty's outburst. Putting her books down, the woman put her hand on Liberty's wrist in a comforting gesture. "Calm down, dear. This man might expect you do to that for the books," she cast a scathing glare at the clerk, "but my son won't. He's quite in love with your sister."

Mortification like she'd never known before washed over Liberty. No wonder this woman looked familiar, she was Andrew's mother. They certainly weren't identical, in fact, Andrew resembled his father in many ways, but he had a few of his mother's traits, especially her eyes. She could see that now. "How did you know who I was?" she asked uncomfortably.

"Brooke," the countess said simply, as if that explained everything.

"Oh dear." If Brooke had been talking about her to Andrew's mother, who knows what might have been said.

"It's not so bad," she assured her. "She says only the nicest things about you. Anyway, when I walked in, I recognized you right away from a miniature Brooke has of you. She shows those things off *all* the time."

Liberty giggled. "That doesn't sound like something she'd do."

The countess snorted. "I assure you, she does. One would think she's older than I am, the way she talks of her family and wants to show anyone and everyone miniatures of them."

"You two must get along quite well," Liberty mused.

"We do," the countess agreed. "Would you care to walk with me?"

"That would be lovely," Liberty agreed, shooting her own scowl at the clerk before they departed.

"He's scum," Andrew's mother said when they got outside.

"Pardon me?"

"I said that clerk is scum. But that's of no consequence now. He won't give you any trouble now that he knows your relation to Andrew."

Liberty nodded. "Lady Townson," she began.

The dowager countess stopped and turned to look directly at Liberty. "Don't call me that," she said sharply. "You may address me as Elizabeth or Lizzie, that's it."

"A…all right," Liberty said, swallowing a nervous laugh that was lodged in her throat.

"Now then, dear," Elizabeth said sweetly, "what was it you wanted to ask?" Her dark blue eyes softened and her smile had returned in full force.

"I was just wondering what you meant by me paying Andrew back for the books," Liberty said uncomfortably. "I mean, you already knew who I was."

"Yes, I knew," Elizabeth acknowledged. "I have a proposition for you," she said with a twinkle in her eye.

"You do?"

"How would you like to be a lady's companion?" Elizabeth asked, shocking Liberty to her toes.

"I would love to," she exclaimed. "Wait, whose lady's companion?"

"Mine, of course," Elizabeth said, laughing.

"That would be delightful." As long as she didn't slip and call her "Lady Townson" again, they'd get along famously.

"Excellent, you may start tomorrow."

Liberty and Elizabeth walked around the block to iron out the details before Liberty got back into her carriage. Her new post as Elizabeth's lady's companion was just the thing she needed. Elizabeth explained she didn't need her company every day, and they decided three days a week would be plenty. That settled what she'd be doing three of the days each week. Now she just needed to decide what to do for the other days.

Chapter 11

The next week breezed by. Liberty spent three days being a lady's companion, one day acting as the perfect vicar's wife, and, to fill the other three days, she'd decided to join some of the local organizations.

The decision to join the local sewing circle had come about when Mrs. Jenkins, the director, had come to her home unannounced and had seen her hemming one of her gowns. Liberty didn't think she was very handy with a needle, but the stubborn Mrs. Jenkins claimed her work was acceptable and wouldn't take no for an answer.

She also joined an organization that helped a group of local illiterates learn to read after seeing a flyer for it posted outside the local tavern, of all places. She loved to read and could think of nothing better to do with her Tuesday mornings than to help others learn.

Finally, she'd decided she'd spend her last free day doing light shopping for herself and the household. However, that plan fell apart when she very quickly realized that Mr. Grimes had no lines of credit in any store in Bath. Therefore, with nothing else to do, she decided it would be a good thing to bring baskets of food to the less fortunate. She'd started with the sick and elderly first and had asked around to see if others needed it, as well.

Her husband acted excited when she told him about her chosen activities. She'd conveniently left off that she was getting paid to act as a companion to Andrew's mother. She didn't want Mr. Greedy to confiscate her wages like he had her dowry. Elizabeth had insisted on paying Liberty's wages herself claiming she didn't like to take money from Andrew. Liberty didn't understand that, since the man had buckets of it now that he'd literally struck gold. Last summer he'd built mines on his land to dig for silver and, instead, he'd found gold.

Brooke liked to tease him by saying it was because of her that his life turned to gold. Oddly enough, he'd usually just kiss her and say, "I know."

Liberty sighed. Oh, how wonderful it must be to love your spouse, she thought with a wistful smile. Unfortunately, she'd never know that feeling with Paul...er...Mr. Grimes. Drat. She was having a harder time now than before remembering even to *think* of him Mr. Grimes.

The man was absolutely determined to get her to call him Paul. The problem was that she already had a hard enough time thinking of him as 'Mr. Grimes' before his latest campaign. But now, it was nearly impossible. And she knew if she started to think of him as 'Paul', she'd slip and call him that. Then, no doubt, he'd gloat.

Earlier, at dinner, he'd been absolutely infuriating. She had just taken her seat at their little kitchen table. Although it was intimate, she didn't mind for some reason. Anyway, he'd come into the kitchen with the two pails of her bathwater from that morning and announced, "Paul's hungry, is Liberty?"

"Excuse me?" she said, flabbergasted. Here she'd been thinking how sweet he'd been all week by bringing hot water up to her everyday so she could bathe in her room, and he had to go and ruin it with that ridiculous statement.

"Paul said, 'Paul's hungry, is Liberty?'" he repeated as if she were the idiot of the pair.

"I heard what you said."

He smiled at her and silently took a seat across the table.

Unable to take his teasing smile another second, she demanded, "What are you doing?"

Shrugging his shoulders, he glanced down to where his hand was on the serving piece. "Paul's just about to serve you your lamb. Scoot your plate over here a bit closer, Liberty."

Resisting the urge to whack him upside the head with her plate, she pushed it closer to him and watched as he put the better piece of lamb on her plate. "Thank you," she said when he pushed her plate back to her.

"You're welcome," he said, fixing his own plate.

"What did you do today?" she asked, becoming startled when she realized those words had actually passed through her lips. She jumped again when she realized she was actually interested in his answer.

"Paul had a very productive day," he said, nodding enthusiastically. "Paul taught lessons to a group of boys. Paul thinks they're actually beginning to understand it. Then Paul visited a sick man, and Paul was asked to pray for him because the family thinks his time is near. Then Paul came home and emptied Liberty's bathwater, and now Paul is about to eat."

"Stop that," she ground out, irritated with herself that she'd even bothered to listen to all that nonsense.

He set his fork down, wiped his mouth and glumly said, "Paul's sorry if Paul's eating offends Liberty. Paul will wait until Liberty's done."

She wanted to laugh at him. He knew what she was talking about. She'd bet her life on it. Yet, he was playing the idiot just to get to her. Fighting the smile that was tugging on her lips, she forced herself to scowl and ask, "What are you about?"

He blinked. "Nothing."

"Well, stop it."

"Stop what?" His face had the look of pure innocence. If she didn't know better, she'd believe him innocent of just about anything with a face like that.

"Stop talking about yourself in the third person," she ground out.

"Oh, Paul's sorry," he said, smiling when she pursed her lips. "Paul decided since Liberty cannot seem to remember Paul's name, Paul should remind Liberty of it as often as possible."

"I know your name. I just choose not to use it," she said airily.

"And why is that?" he asked, cocking his head.

"Because it's not proper," she ground out, stabbing a leaf of lettuce with her fork.

"Proper? You won't call me by my name because it's not proper?" The amusement left his face and a cold impassive stare took its place.

"Correct," she said pertly. "Most couples address each other formally."

"I see," he said, though he looked like he didn't understand at all. "Not your parents. Not your sister," he said in a defensive tone. "Why do you insist upon it?"

"They're different."

"You mean because the circumstances of their marriages are different?" he asked flatly.

"Well, yes. Good point. Both couples you mentioned clearly love each other," she agreed before taking a swig of her drink.

"I see," he repeated. His voice turned gravely serious almost like he was about to impart some bad news. "Liberty, may I ask you one question? Then, I'll leave you be for the rest of the evening, I promise."

"All right," she said hesitantly, uncertain how she felt at the prospect of being asked a serious question by him or the prospect of being left to her own devices all evening.

"When you think about me in private, how do you think of me?"

She nearly choked on her drink. "Pardon me?" she asked more harshly than she meant to.

"I mean in your head. When you hear me coming, what do you call me in your mind?" he elaborated.

"Oh, in that case, 'Mr. Grimes'," Liberty said quickly, ducking her head to cover the red creeping up her face. She'd been aware that on a few occasions she'd accidentally thought of him as Paul, or at least started to, before she'd corrected herself.

"I'm sorry to hear that," he said quietly.

For the rest of the meal, the only noises heard were created by the occasional scrape of silverware on plate.

Chapter 12

Unable to lie abed a moment longer, Paul got up before dawn the following morning. He felt like such a fool for his idiotic behavior the night before at dinner. Or perhaps he felt the fool because Liberty had as much as told him she'd never come to care for him.

Because he knew she'd grown to expect it, he considered taking her water to her room before dismissing the thought with the excuse that she'd survive one day without a warm bath.

Today, her family was coming to see them and bringing Liberty's five hundred plus volume library with them. He scowled. He had no problem that she liked to read. It was *what* she liked to read that was the problem. He'd heard many indirect—and direct —references to Liberty's love of reading etiquette books. That was the reason for his scowl. He'd bet everything he had, even his life, these books were where she'd gotten the absurd notion into her head that even in private she could not address her husband by his first name.

After scratching out a few words telling Liberty he'd meet her at her uncle's this afternoon, he set out to run a few errands, or at least he'd intended to.

Instead of running the errands on his list, he went fishing. It was one of his only pastimes he could do all year long. It may be a little more difficult in winter with the ice and such, but it was still possible.

He fished and caught absolutely nothing until the sun was directly overhead. Studying the sun's position, he decided it was time to call it quits and go to the baron's house.

A quick change of clothes and he was on the road.

No need to ride too fast. Watson Estate was fairly close. Anyway, it's not like they'd be waiting for him. There'd be more than enough people there for everyone to talk to; nobody would even notice his absence. Especially his wife.

They'd been married almost two weeks now and he still had yet to push her out of her shell. He'd come close a few times, but he hadn't yet succeeded. Perhaps he could do that tonight.

A groom was waiting for him by the stables and he gladly handed the reins to the shivering man and walked briskly to the house.

"Rather chilly out, isn't it?" Alex Banks, Liberty's cousin and the baron's oldest son, said as he walked up the front steps.

"Freezing," Paul concurred. "Is everyone inside?"

Alex nodded. "Just a word of caution, Paul, Liberty's madder'n a wet hen," he warned.

Paul had met Alex at the same time he'd met Liberty and the rest of her family. He was a good man, if not a little unusual. Alex was extremely smart but often missed some of the most obvious things. It wasn't that he meant to be obtuse, he just couldn't help it. He sometimes used words and phrases that made people second guess his intelligence, but Paul assumed he probably did it on purpose. In society, the poor man had somehow been termed Arid Alex due to his calm, unexciting personality and his scandal free past.

"Is she now?" Paul asked with a slight grin.

"Yes," Alex said, nodding and then pushed his spectacles up when they slipped down his nose a bit.

Paul's hand immediately went to his own spectacles and readjusted them. He had no idea why he did so, there was nothing wrong with them; but when a spectacle wearer sees another spectacle wearer adjust his, the need to adjust one's own spectacles becomes irresistible and he soon finds his own hand fiddling with his spectacles. It was quite an oddity really, kind of like how yawns seem to be contagious.

"Hmm, well, I've never seen a wet hen, I admit. Perhaps after I go upstairs, I'll see how one behaves," Paul said, walking inside.

He'd never say it to Alex, but he was actually a little worried walking into the dining room. Though he'd tried several times to get her in a dander, he didn't want her in a temper here. He'd done all his agitation in private where he thought he'd be able to handle her better. Who knew what might happen if she got angry here. Or maybe, he thought with a smile, there was nothing to worry about. In the past, she'd never taken her wrath out on him in front of an audience if she could help it.

"Thank goodness, we can finally start eating," declared Brooke as soon as Paul walked into the room.

"I'm sorry, Brooke. If I had known my absence was going to cause an expectant mother to starve, I would have been here sooner," he teased. Why were they waiting for him?

"She's not starving," Andrew said with a snort. "She's been snacking on that tart she brought with her in her reticule."

"That and filching biscuits when she thinks nobody's looking," Madison chimed in.

Brooke sent them both a mock scowl.

Paul took the empty seat next to Liberty. "Where have you been?" she asked testily then tried to force a smile to her lips to try to soften her words.

"Out," he said evenly.

"Out?" she repeated quietly, making extra effort to keep her voice low. "Did they not have clocks where you were?"

"No," he said, shaking his head. He could hear her grinding her teeth. He hadn't meant to be late and keep everyone waiting on him. He hadn't even known he was late. "What time is it?" he asked of no one in particular.

"Don't you own a pocket watch like all other men?" Liberty asked him sharply.

"It's broken," he said simply, shifting his gaze to the baron as he opened his watch.

"It's three o'clock," Baron Watson said earnestly before shoving his watch back into his pocket.

Paul had never been so late in his life. He was supposed to have been there at one. It was two hours past and they had waited all that time. "Once again, I'm sorry," he said to the whole room.

With the exception of his wife, everyone mumbled something

about it being of no importance.

The food was then served and several conversations started, none of which included either Liberty or Paul.

Halfway through the meal, Paul decided he'd paid for his sin enough and said, "Liberty, I said I was sorry. I lost track of the time. I apologize that I made everyone wait."

"It's all right," she said archly. "I understand that I, your wife, am not important enough for you to remember."

"I didn't forget you," he ground out. "I lost track of the time. Those are two very different things."

She flicked her wrist dismissively. "So you say."

Life was too short to argue with one's wife during a family luncheon, Paul concluded before turning to make conversation with his other dinner companions. He found conversation with them was far more entertaining.

After their meal, the men went to the baron's study to talk while the ladies went to "embroider or something" in the drawing room.

The decision for the split came about after Carolina suggested they all play parlor games. Her suggestion was met by an extreme amount of groaning, mostly from the men. Which, thankfully, led to John being the men's saving grace by suggesting, "Why don't the ladies go embroider or something and the gentlemen will go discuss science." His proposition was met by just as much groaning as the parlor games idea had been, but this time by those of the female persuasion.

Paul, Alex, the baron, and Andrew, however, were all so loud voicing their agreement with John, it was hard to know who said what exactly, but the general consensus among the men was that it was an excellent idea.

Of course there were a few scowls and a disappointed groan or two from the five women as the men walked away.

"Are things always this way between you two?" Andrew asked as soon as the door shut.

Paul smiled and leaned his shoulder against the window. "No."

"You know you two are very fascinating to watch," Alex said, taking a seat behind his father's desk. He started to shuffle through some papers on the desk and smiled brightly when he found what he'd been looking for. "Almost as fascinating as a pair of hedgehogs I've been watching mate down by the pasture."

"Excuse me," Paul said, blinking.

"I said, you two are quite fascinating."

"Yes, I heard that part, but what does that have to do with hedgehogs?"

"Not hedgehogs in general. Just when they're mating," Alex said to clarify.

Paul stared at him. Why on earth was this man comparing the fight he'd had with his wife to hedgehog mating patterns?

"See," Alex started, excitedly. "When the male hedgehog wants to mate with the female he—"

"That's quite enough, son," Alex's father said. "I don't believe it's wise to continue this vein of conversation with the young lady's father present." He cast a pointed look at John.

"Or me," Andrew muttered.

Paul would have muttered the same thing if he'd been Andrew.

"In that case, forget I said anything about Paul and Liberty," Alex said thoughtfully. "Now about the hedgehogs down by the pasture—"

"Alex," Andrew said gently.

"Yes?"

"Stop talking."

Alex groaned. "What's the big deal? We're all men here. It's not like any of us aren't familiar with the activity."

"That may be, but we're not all interested in the mating habits of hedgehogs," Andrew said flatly.

Alex blinked at him. "Why not? They're very interesting creatures."

"Be that as it may, nobody has the desire to talk about their mating habits just now," Andrew countered.

Last year, Alex had told Paul that he and Andrew had gone to Cambridge together and had been friends for the nearly ten years since. Only a true friend of Alex's could get away with speaking to him that way. If anyone else had, it would have been perceived as cruel. That was one reason he admired Andrew, he didn't care that Alex had some unusual tendencies, he just learned to work around them.

"But that's why we came to the study," Alex pointed out. "To escape Aunt Carolina making us play charades and to talk about science."

"Exactly, we're going to speak about science," Andrew agreed. "chemistry to be exact, specifically the combustible elements of Paul and Liberty's marriage, not the mating habits of hedgehogs."

"Well said," the equally scientific-minded baron said.

"I couldn't agree more," John said. "Now, son, tell me how things are progressing between you and Liberty."

"Not so well," Paul admitted. Since when did men get together in small groups to discuss their relationship issues? This was uncomfortable. The only reason he'd even bothered to answer John's question was because, even though they were talking about his daughter, he and John had become close and he respected him a great deal. Most of the time anyway. He still wasn't sure he respected or admired how John manipulated him into marrying Liberty.

"John, cover your ears," the baron said, causing panic to rise in Paul's chest. "How are things in the bedchamber?"

"What was that you were saying about those hedgehogs, Alex?" Paul asked hastily, trying to divert the room's attention from him and his red face. The details of the intimate relations between him and his wife were not up for discussion, even if there weren't any to discuss.

Alex smiled at his interest. "Well, the male hedgehog will sniff —"

"Stuff it, son," his father said abruptly, startling them all.

"I think I had better go soon," Paul said, looking out the window. There were several dark clouds outside threatening to burst at any moment.

"Not so fast," Andrew said. "Do you remember the day in my

study?"

"Oh, you mean the day I found out, unbeknownst to me, my newly established engagement had already been announced two days prior in the paper, and John was hiding in your storage closet? Yes, I remember that day very well," Paul said sarcastically.

"You did that?" the baron asked his brother, his lips twitching in amusement.

"Yes," John said, looking slightly embarrassed.

His brother clapped him on the shoulder. "Well done. I don't think I'd have the brass to do something like that. You're a braver man than I. Well, except the part about hiding in the closet. A bit cowardly, eh, John?"

"No, not at all. Trust me, you don't want to be in the room when that man's in a temper," John said, pointing a finger at Paul.

"Oh, is that why you matched him with Liberty? She has a devil of a temper," his brother said, shaking his head. Then as an afterthought, as if remembering he was in the presence of two ministers, he muttered, "Sorry. Forgive my language."

Paul rolled his eyes. The baron's use of the word devil hadn't bothered him one bit. On more than one occasion he'd said the same and had actually gone so far as to compare Liberty to the devil. Although, that had always been in his head, he'd never had the nerve to voice it aloud, especially in her father's presence.

"I see you apologize for your language, but not for calling my daughter a devil," John said smartly.

"Tell me, John, can anyone in this room deny it?" his brother countered. When nobody spoke, he said, "I see I've made my point."

"That's not true," Paul said at last, eliciting four curious stares with his statement. "I've noticed that she hasn't been quite the same foul-tempered creature in the past few weeks that she was before."

His statement was met by total silence. They were all probably suffering a small case of shock at his defense of Liberty.

"Today was the first time she'd stayed irritated with me longer than just a few minutes," he explained.

"Was this the first time you'd done something to give her reason to become irritated?" Alex asked, looking at Paul as if he were collecting information for a science experiment.

"No," Paul said quietly.

"That doesn't make sense," Alex said, shaking his head. "Is there any consistency to your actions that spark her temper?"

"What?" Paul asked, slightly confused.

"What's happened the past few weeks that made her angry?" Alex asked.

"Well, I…" he trailed off, there was no way he was going to tell them about the chemise incident, "…I…umm…used her first name," he finally said.

Four sets of eyes impaled him with their stares. He assumed they would have all taken his side and thought that was as ridiculous as he did. But John surprised him by saying, "Son, I've never doubted your intelligence before, but have you met my daughter?"

Paul was a bit taken aback and looked to the other three for support. But all three of them looked at him with identical faces that said, "Paul, you're an idiot."

"You do know that Liberty eats, sleeps, and breathes propriety, don't you?" John said flatly. "I've never seen anyone enjoy it so much. But for some unknown reason, she does. It's her life."

All three of the other men nodded their wholehearted agreement.

They were wrong. He may not know Liberty that well, but he knew they had to be wrong. Nobody enjoyed propriety. "That's not true," he said hoarsely. "If she cared so much for propriety, she wouldn't have a 'devil of a temper' as you so kindly put it."

"That's what makes Liberty a hard case study," Alex said thoughtfully. "She has a few extreme inconsistencies."

Paul scowled at him, suddenly feeling very defensive of Liberty. His wife was not a scientific experiment on display for everyone to pick apart. "What's wrong with calling her Liberty, anyway? You all do."

"I'm her father," John said.

"I'm her uncle," the baron told him.

"I'm her cousin," Alex put in.

"I'm her brother...in-law," Andrew added.

"Well, I'm her husband, which means my relationship trumps all of yours," Paul said triumphantly.

"That doesn't matter," John said, shaking his head. "It's perfectly acceptable, encouraged even, to address your spouse formally. You should know that."

"Well, it shouldn't be," Paul said, irritated. He crossed his arms defensively.

Andrew sent him a sympathetic look. "Have you given anymore thought to our discussion a few weeks ago?" he asked, tapping his teeth.

Paul's eyebrows furrowed in confusion. What on earth was Andrew talking about?

Andrew stretched his lips into an overdone smile.

"Oh. Actually, I have gotten her to smile, but only because she was truly angry and I suggested a way for her to ease her aggression."

Nobody said anything.

"Not that," Paul snapped, rolling his eyes. Get a group of men together and all they can do is think about sex. "I told her to pretend the beans on her plate were my head. She smiled for fifteen minutes straight while she stabbed every single one of those beans with so much force it caused the table to shake and the dishes to clatter."

All four men howled with laughter when he did his impression of what she looked like holding her fork and stabbing it down on her plate.

"Stop! Stop!" John bellowed, bent over holding his stomach. "I don't think my heart can take much more."

"Is that the only time?" Andrew asked, wiping his eyes.

"Yes," Paul said, nodding. "Sad, isn't it? The only time she's smiled in the past two weeks was when she was pretending to cause bodily harm to her husband."

"Have you tried to get her to smile?" Andrew asked.

"No," he said honestly. He thought the key to Liberty was to nettle her enough that she'd drop her act, and then he'd work on getting her to smile. He had no idea how to deal with the brittle person she'd become recently. At least if she were full of fire and fury, he might be able to get a genuine emotion out of her.

"You do know St. Valentine's Day is within the week, don't you?" Andrew asked as if that fact was of grave importance.

"What does that have to do with anything?" Alex, the only unmarried man in the room, asked.

"Everything," Andrew, John, and the baron said in unison.

"Don't bungle this one, boy," the baron muttered, "or you'll be paying for it for the rest of your life."

"Amen," John said vehemently. When all eyes turned to him, he said, "I may not know from personal experience like Edward here, but I've seen enough happy—and unhappy—couples in my day to know the truth of Edward's statement."

Paul nodded. He'd only given a girl a gift on St. Valentine's Day one time and that was more than eight years ago. Good thing he had a few days to think about something for her.

"You could buy her a book on etiquette. That's guaranteed to bring a smile to her face," Alex suggested helpfully.

"Don't," Andrew countered.

Paul shook his head. "I hadn't planned on it. She's read too many as it is."

"You have no idea," John said with a shudder. "When we loaded all her books up yesterday, I almost passed out when I started to think about how much of my salary was spent on books about manners."

"You wouldn't by any chance be willing to take all those back to London with you, would you?" Paul asked, beseeching John with his glance.

"No, sir," John said, not in the least bit apologetically. "I've already dropped them off at your house."

"Wonderful," Paul muttered.

"Just think, they'll serve as great reading material when you can't sleep at night," Andrew suggested with a grin.

"Perhaps you'd like a few, then?"

"I wouldn't do that," John said sternly.

"What?" Paul and Andrew asked at the same time.

"Separate them. Liberty has gone through great pains to catalog each and every book. She'll notice if some are missing," John said, trying to keep a straight face.

"You cannot be serious," Paul exclaimed, his eyes boring into John's.

"I'm not," he answered, giving an unapologetic shrug.

"Damn, John, you've got one weird offspring there," his brother said.

John's head swung around to face his brother. "And you don't?" he retorted, his eyes flickering to Alex.

Edward's gaze drifted to Alex who was rereading his notes on hedgehog mating. "Touché."

Just then the door swung open and the five ladies walked in. "What have you all been talking about?" Brooke demanded of no one in particular as soon as she was across the threshold.

"Nothing that any of you'd care to hear about, darling," Andrew said, brushing a kiss on the top of his wife's head.

"Try us," Liberty said pertly, pursing her lips and letting her gaze fall on each of the men. When she got to Paul, he flashed her a smile and said, "Nothing so interesting," he raised one shoulder in a lopsided shrug, "just the mating habits of hedgehogs."

Chapter 13

"Just how dimwitted do you think I am?" Liberty demanded, placing her hands on her hips and twisting her lips. "I don't pretend to know your mind, Mr. Grimes, but even I hadn't thought you capable of stooping so low."

"And how low would that be, Liberty?" he drawled.

She ignored his use of her given name. "So low you'd make up a ridiculous lie about the…the…" she waved her hand vaguely, her face flaming red, "habits of hedgehogs. As if I would believe such a thing. Who in his right mind would even care about such a thing?" she said with a sniff.

Madison walked up to her and placed a gentle hand on her arm. "Dearest, you might want to be careful what you say," she murmured softly with a pointed glance at Alex.

She sighed. "Even Alex has no interest in *that*."

"I wouldn't be so sure," Madison returned quietly.

Liberty's eyes flew to where Alex sat behind his father's desk rigid as a statue, clutching a fistful of papers. She walked across the room and thought she was going to die of mortification when she grabbed the papers from Alex's vice-like grip and saw right before her very eyes a detailed description of the mating habits between hedgehogs. "Oh, I'm so sorry, Alex," she said sincerely. "I didn't mean… Oh, please forgive me."

"It's all right," Alex said quickly, his bright red, embarrassed face belying his words.

"Perhaps we should be going," her irritating husband intoned.

She wanted to disagree, but embarrassment made her want to flee the scene.

If the tension in the baron's study wasn't bad enough, the hostility in the carriage was. Paul had to ride back in the carriage with her, because it looked like it might storm soon and he deemed it too dangerous to ride his horse when there was a chance of lightening.

"How dare you make a fool of me that way!" Liberty burst out once they were out of the drive.

"Whatever do you mean?" Paul asked testily.

She glared at him. "All day today, you've made a fool of me."

"Since all you've done is rephrased your accusation, allow me to rephrase, as well: how?"

Liberty had been angry before, but now she was borderline furious. Not only had he made her look bad in front of her family, he was now purposely playing like he had no idea what she was talking about. "You made me look bad in front of my family."

"I did no such thing," he countered irritably. "You did that all on your own."

Rage built in her chest. "No I didn't," she hissed. "You purposely provoked me and made me look bad."

"Nobody told you to insult Alex. Your problem is that you're always ready to believe the worst of me."

"That's not true."

"Isn't it?" He leaned closer to her bringing his face mere inches from hers. His nostrils flared and his eyes looked as hard as emeralds. His stare was hot, intent, and undoubtedly full of a challenge.

She'd never seen him look thus, and she knew she'd given him ample opportunity before now. For some reason, he was just as angry if not angrier than her. Good. They could have their fight now. She was tired of pretending to be some docile creature, not that she'd done a great job of it so far, but the game was up. The rage she felt inside her was similar to an inferno, and she was about to boil over.

"No," she said haughtily, "I've not always thought the worst of you. The problem lies with you. You repeatedly provide me with opportunities to think poorly of you."

Paul snorted at her words. "Is that so?" he asked, his voice hard as steel. "Tell me, the first night we were introduced, what did I do that made you take an instant dislike to me?"

She didn't even have to think about that. "You insisted I call you by your Christian name," she said primly.

Twisting his lips, he fixed his gaze on a sconce across the carriage. "The reason you dislike me so much is because I asked you to call me Paul?" His voice was full of disbelief.

"Well, no," she said, causing his head to snap back in her direction. "That's why I took an instant dislike to you. But the reason I continued to dislike you has to do with your pompous attitude."

"Excuse me?" he snapped. "I have never been pompous a day in my life."

"Oh, yes, you have," she replied, with a sharp bob of her head. "Not the very next day you were."

His lips twisted into something that would pass for a sneer. "Madam, if you refer to the set down I handed you after you criticized your sister, then you're thinking is more skewed than I thought possible."

"You had no call to say those things to me," she said sharply. She'd never let him—or anyone—know how much his words had hurt her that day. She'd always worried she'd never marry, and when he said she was well on her way to becoming a spinster, to her, that was as good as confirming her own worst nightmare.

"And if you remember correctly," he said through clenched teeth, "I apologized to you and your exact response was, 'apology not accepted'."

Releasing a pent up breath, she shook her head. "You only apologized because you were afraid of losing my father's friendship. It had nothing to do with any feelings of remorse."

"Maybe so," he allowed quietly. "To be honest, it's been a long time. I don't remember exactly what I was thinking. However, I do know that I approached you to apologize on my own. I was not goaded into it by your father."

"I know," she admitted. She knew he'd come to her on his own. She'd been so overcome with feelings when he'd approached her, the most prominent being anger, she'd rejected his apology and sent him away with a flea in his ear.

"Liberty," Paul said, breaking into her thoughts. "I have no wish to discuss the past with you. Unless you want to tell me the real reason you harbor ill feelings against me, that is." He gave her a look that was meant to encourage her to divulge her secrets, but she remained quiet. With a sigh he said, "Since the two of us discussing the past seems to be as productive as trying to win a foot race with your ankles tied together, please tell me what has set you off today."

"You!" All the anger that had been, for the most part, banked came flooding back with great momentum.

"How helpful an explanation you offer," he mused. "Care to elaborate?" His voice was light, but his facial expression hadn't changed. It was painfully clear he was in a temper, and a foul one at that.

"You were late," she said impatiently.

Paul's teeth ground together so hard, she wouldn't be surprised if soon he started spitting dust on the floor. "I apologized for that. I didn't expect anyone to wait on me."

"Why were you late?"

He crossed his arms across his chest defensively. "I told you, I lost track of time."

"Flimsy excuse. Try again," she said archly like she was a governess and he was a misbehaving child.

"I don't have to answer to you," he snapped. "I've apologized for being late. There's nothing more for it."

Now it was her turn to grind her teeth. "There was no reason for you to be late. If you were a normal man—and I've learned in the past few weeks you're not—you'd carry a pocket watch with you. But since you haven't an ounce of normalcy or sanity, I shouldn't have expected so much from you."

"I told you, it's broken," he bellowed so loudly she was certain he could be heard all the way to London.

"That's not my fault."

He looked like he might say something further, but instead he leaned back and pressed his head against the squabs, raking his fingers through his hair.

She wanted to yell at him again. She wanted to tear him to shreds. She was angry he'd been late. She was angry he'd teased and goaded her into making herself look bad in front of her family. She was angry that he'd made a joke out of her. But if she were honest with herself, she'd have to admit she was angriest because he'd forgotten her. Twice.

He'd forgotten about her this morning when he neglected to bring her water for a bath and had left with only a one line note telling her he'd see her at her uncle's. Then, he'd forgotten her again when he was two hours late arriving at her uncle's. And, as petty as it might sound, she was hurt.

Chapter 14

The next few days were nothing if not hazy. Liberty enjoyed spending time with Elizabeth. She could not have picked a better person to act as a companion to. She and Elizabeth got along better than she'd gotten along with anyone in recent weeks.

The dowager countess was friendly albeit blunt. Liberty nearly jumped with surprise the first time she'd heard Elizabeth refer to Mrs. Whitaker, one of the women in her village, as a "crotchety old biddy whose drawers are too tight for her own comfort".

Liberty agreed that Mrs. Whitaker was a crotchety old biddy, but she didn't know, nor did she want to know, the state of anyone's drawers. Nonetheless, Liberty was still stunned to hear Elizabeth utter such a remark. "You will get used to it," Elizabeth told her. "Despite my title, I've been on the fringes of society my whole life. Therefore, saying whatever pops into my head— whether nice or not—is my privilege."

Though Liberty didn't know the entirety of Elizabeth's situation, she was soon informed of enough of it to render Elizabeth's declaration valid. She was also told enough things about Mrs. Whitaker to take Elizabeth's assessment of her as gospel truth.

Mrs. Whitaker, Liberty was quickly learning, was one of the most vicious creatures in the country and the jest about her drawers being pinched too tight was the nicest thing Elizabeth had to say about her.

During their visits, Elizabeth treated her as an equal and within only a few days she'd known she'd made a friend she'd be able to turn to for life. That felt good considering she had so few to start with.

Mrs. Jenkins, the leader of the sewing circle, was extremely nice, somewhat bossy and slightly overbearing all at the same time.

She conducted her sewing group like a small factory. She'd tell everyone what they needed to make and supervise their stitches. Liberty wasn't the greatest seamstress, but she seemed to pass Mrs. Jenkins inspection.

The only negative about the sewing circle was the gossip that flew around the room. Much to her dismay, Mrs. Whitaker was self-appointed as second-in-command of the sewing circle. But instead of supervising the sewing, she was the ringleader of the gossip loom.

Nobody could weave gossip like Mrs. Whitaker. Thankfully Liberty hadn't learned this the hard way. She took notice of the other women in the room and the way Mrs. Whitaker interrogated them as if she were an investigator for the Watch. When she got to her, Liberty put on her best bland expression and said, "I haven't been in the district long enough to know anything about anyone."

Her words were true enough. But that wasn't the real reason she'd not wanted to gossip. She'd learned long ago what gossip can do to a person and decided she'd never gossip or give people a reason to gossip about her.

So far she'd had a little trouble with the second part; an excellent example of this would be Paul. But she'd firmly held onto her vow not to gossip.

Bringing food to the sick and elderly was not a bad way to pass her days, either. She always felt good about it afterwards—no matter how many miniatures she'd had to feign interest in.

The only activity she was still uncertain about was helping the illiterate learn to read. Most of the pupils were children, but there were a few adults. Helping them read was not the part she didn't like. In fact, she enjoyed the expressions of pure joy when they were finally able to read and write their names, no matter if they were five or thirty-five.

There was a special little boy that was about six or seven named Seth that had taken a very strong liking to her. Though he struggled with his goal to learn to read, he always had a bright smile and adored Liberty in a way she'd never imagined. If she didn't know better, she'd think the boy had a *tendre* for her. It didn't bother her that he clung to her skirts and was always trying to be near her. She found him quite enchanting and couldn't help smiling every time he did. She'd even gone so far as to stay and play games with him while he waited for his habitually late mother.

The part that was unsettling to her was that the meetings were conducted above the local tavern and there always seemed to be many drunken men hanging about when she arrived. Though she'd only gone a few times, she knew this was something she could expect every week.

At night, she'd occupy her time with organizing or reading her books. Since their fight in the carriage last week, she'd barely seen Paul. He didn't speak to her when they took breakfast together. Instead, he'd hold a newspaper in front of his face and only drag his eyes away from it when he went to refill his coffee from the carafe. Typically he was gone for lunch. As for dinner, that meal would be considered tolerable at best. He'd insisted they take their evening meal in the formal dining room now. He barely spoke to her during dinner, and when he did, he'd address her as "Mrs. Grimes". Then, after the meal, he'd vanish. He'd lock himself in his study or, if she was already there reading one of her books, would retire to his room.

Any trace of the man she'd seen before was virtually gone. He'd turned into the perfect coldblooded English gentleman. As much as she thought she'd like him better this way, she soon learned she was wrong. In a cruel twist of fate, she now realized that being married to a man who lived by the rules was actually quite boring.

Feeling restless due to her current bout of insomnia, Liberty slipped on her dressing robe and decided to grab a book from the library. She knew she should have just brought it up with her, but recently she'd been losing books. As silly as it sounded, the books were literally disappearing right off her nightstand. Well, they weren't disappearing exactly. She knew they couldn't magically vanish. That's just what she'd like to think was happening. The truth was she had a suspicion Mrs. Siddons was stealing them. That was the only explanation she could fathom for why the books she'd leave in her room were disappearing. She'd considered bringing it up with her husband but thought he'd laugh or say something demeaning to her for accusing his servant of stealing.

At the bottom of the stairs, she noticed there was a little sliver of light coming from under the door to Paul's study, which just so happened to be the same room as the library. Nervously, she bit her lower lip and contemplated if she should go in or not. It had been nearly a week since they'd quarreled, surely he wasn't still upset. She wasn't. Why should he be?

At the same time, she'd always heard her father say Paul had a mighty temper. Until last week, she'd never really seen it, and truthfully she had no idea if he held grudges.

Stiffening her spine and deciding if he behaved poorly, she'd spout Bible verses at him, she slowly opened up the door so not to make a sound.

The tableau waiting for her behind the door was the last thing she'd ever expected to see, and not because her husband was clad in only his trousers and shirtsleeves.

***

"What do you think you're doing, Mr. Grimes?"

Paul whipped his head in the direction of the doorway so fast his neck hurt.

He knew if she ever caught him doing this, she'd be angry. He'd just hoped she'd never find out. But she just had, and his belief that she'd be angry was not necessarily wrong. However, it might be more accurate to describe her as enraged or livid or infuriated, or perhaps a lethal combination of all three. Actually, come to think of it, nothing could describe the emotion that filled her face. She'd once expressed interest in seeing a part of him separated from the rest of his body, and, at the moment, he thought that very thing just might be about to happen.

"I should ask you the same thing," he countered. "What are you doing in *my* study?" He'd long ago realized answering a question with a question was an excellent way to defend oneself. He just hoped that would prove true this time. There really was no good way to explain his way out of why there were three of her etiquette books on fire in the hearth or why there was another one in his hand, waiting to be pitched in.

"I've come to get one of *my* books," she retorted, stalking across the room to grab the book from his hand.

His hand tightened around the book he held. She wasn't getting it without a fight. "You don't need these," he said more calmly than he felt. He was boiling with rage. He'd been boiling with it for almost a week now, ever since the day of that horrid family affair at the baron's house to be precise.

"Yes, I do," she snapped, tugging harder on the book he held. "Give it to me," she ground out. The tears in her eyes were on the verge of spilling over.

Her tears didn't bother him one bit. If they'd been shed about something—just about anything—else, he'd soften, but over etiquette books? No. "No," he said, yanking the book from her grasp and flinging it into the fire.

The fire was too large for her to have any chance of recovering the book and a sob caught in her throat as she stood in silent horror, watching the flames engulf it. "How could you do this?" she sobbed, swiping at the tears that coursed down her reddened cheeks. "You are a monster!"

"No, I'm not," Paul said flatly.

"Yes, you are. Only an unfeeling monster could do such a thing," she yelled the best she could through her sobs.

Paul just stared at her. He'd been burning etiquette books every night since her father dropped them off. That night he'd come home to find her parents had dropped off five hundred twenty-three books belonging to Liberty. Of those five hundred twenty-three books, five hundred nineteen were about etiquette, manners, or some nonsense related to behaving. It was infuriating. Poor John had likely spent hundreds of pounds on all that rubbish. Good thing the majority of them were treatises and not real leather bound books. "You're wrong," he said when her loud sobs had quieted down a few decibels.

"No, I'm not wrong," she said with conviction. "Those were mine. You had no right to touch them. And not only did you touch them, you've destroyed them. Why?"

Wrapping his fingers around her wrists, he forced her to face him. "Why do you want them?"

"Because they're mine," she cried.

"That's not good enough," he said, shaking his head.

Liberty tried to pull her trembling hands from his grasp, but his strong fingers tightened their hold on her delicate wrists. "Those books are important to me," she said, glancing at the shelves where she'd lined them all up only a few short days ago.

"Why are they so important?" he demanded, resisting the urge to let her go and light that whole bookshelf on fire.

Her glossy hazel eyes met his. "Because…because…they were helping me to get a husband," she said on a sob.

Abruptly his hands relinquished her wrists. "Well, you don't need them and their invaluable information now. You've got me," he mocked, jabbing his index finger at his chest.

"It's not the same. You're nothing like the husband I wanted."

"Not to worry, you're not exactly the wife I pictured, either," Paul retorted, taking a fraction of pride in seeing her blanch at his words. But the feeling was short-lived when only a second later, shame washed over him. By saying those words, he'd proven her earlier accusation of him true. "I'm sorry," he said in a softer tone. "That was cruel and I shouldn't have said it."

"Don't apologize," she snapped. "You meant it. I know you did. It's written all over your face."

No point in arguing with that. He'd meant it; he just shouldn't have said it. "Still, I shouldn't—"

"Don't," she repeated sharply, cutting him off. She stalked over to where his Theology and Latin books lined a shelf and started grabbing as many as she could hold.

"What are you doing?" he demanded, coming up right behind her and snatching books out of her arms.

"I'm sure you'll recognize it in a moment," she said, tightening her grip on the three volumes she'd managed to hold onto.

Paul put his arm around her, catching her at the waist and

hauling her back up against his solid chest. "Don't even think about it," he breathed in her ear.

"Let me go," she screamed, trying to stomp on his booted foot with her bare heel.

His embrace tightened. "Put the books down and I'll let you go," he said savagely in her ear.

"No," she replied fiercely, attempting to squirm from his hold. "You burned my books; it's only fair I get to burn yours."

"It's not about being fair," he spat. "Those books are worthless. They serve no purpose."

She snorted. "You'd be the one to think so," she retorted, her voice full of pity.

"Name me one thing those books are good for," he said, trying to hold her writhing body still.

"I already told you," she ground out bitterly.

Paul pulled her down to the floor and maneuvered his body so he was lying almost directly on top of her, trapping her on the floor. "You told me they were to help you catch a husband. And as I pointed out, you've caught one. Why do you think you still need them?"

"I just do," she choked, pushing at his immovable chest.

He took hold of her hands and pushed them away. "What is so valuable in those books that would make you behave this way?"

"You wouldn't understand," she snapped. "Nobody understands."

"Try me," he growled.

"You don't know what it's like to grow up in my sister's shadows," she cried. More tears rolled down her cheeks. It almost looked like there were two streams flowing from her eyes.

"Don't I?" he mocked. He of all people knew what it was like to grow up knowing he'd always be inferior. He wasn't heir to a title, his brother was.

"No," she exclaimed. "You're handsome. You don't know what it's like to be plain. Unlike my sisters, who have nice hair, pretty faces and beautiful teeth, I have unremarkable hair, ordinary eyes and crooked teeth. There is nothing special about me.

Therefore," she said, trying to wiggle out from under his body, "I studied propriety as a way to make up for what I lack in beauty. There, I've told you everything. Are you happy now?"

"That's why you don't smile," he mused in disbelief. He rested his body's weight on his forearms and stared down at her. She may not be a raving beauty like her sisters, but she was nowhere near as ugly as she thought herself to be.

She scowled at him. "You're not very quick, are you, Mr. Grimes."

"I guess not," he returned with a rueful smile.

"Care to share those thoughts?" she asked a minute later when he hadn't yet wiped the giant grin from his face.

He brought his hand up and brushed back a lock of her hair that had fallen across her forehead. "Nothing really," he said casually, "just what I'm going to get you for St. Valentine's Day."

"Don't bother. There's nothing you could give me that I could possibly want."

"Not even a book?" Paul asked, getting on his knees and offering her his hand to help pull her up. She was hesitant to take his hand, so with a shrug he stood up and watched her scramble to her feet.

"No," she said. "Well, wait, unless the book is *Proper Manners for the Proper Lady* or," she walked to the bookshelf and started scanning the titles, "*The English Wife*, or *Mrs. Sadie's Rules for Young Ladies,* or…" her fingers trailed more spines and she let out a strangled cry. "How many have you burned?"

Paul shrugged. "Thirty. Perhaps a few more," he said casually.

Her eyes flew to his. "You burned thirty of my books tonight?" Her voice rang with rage mixed with torment.

"No. I've burned about five or so a night since they arrived."

"You what?" she burst out. "Have you been stealing them off my nightstand?"

"No," he said, shaking his head. "That would be Mrs. Siddons. She doesn't like things out of place."

Liberty glared at him. "Has she been joining you for your nightly ritual?"

"No. It's been a solo pursuit, I'm afraid," he answered with an exaggerated sigh. "But if you'd like to join me," he suggested excitedly, walking over to the books and grabbing half a dozen treatises from the end. "It's an excellent way to relieve tension."

"I can think of better ways to relieve tension." She grabbed one of the bigger volumes near her and threw it at him, clipping him in the shoulder.

"I'm sorry you did that," he said, throwing all the books that were in his hands into the fire at one time.

Her eyes went wide and she let out a suppressed cry of frustration and rage. Grabbing another book, she took aim again and flung it at him. But this time he ducked and she missed altogether.

Paul leaned down and picked up the tome that was meant for his head. He blinked and tried not to laugh when he saw the title and the name of the author. "Hmm, I do wonder what Miss Bea Haven has to say about hurling books at one's husband in *Please Your Husband, Please Yourself?*" He'd flipped through only a few pages when Liberty's hands grabbed onto the book.

"Let go," she said slowly, trying with all her might to keep her hold on the book. "Please."

"Why?"

"Because I happen to like this one," she admitted solemnly.

Paul scoffed. "I'm not letting it go. If I do, you'll tell me you just so happen to like all of them for some idiotic reason or another. Into the fire it goes!"

"Please," she repeated, her fingers slipping off the edge when he gave it a yank. "I...this one...it's different."

"How so?" he inquired. He was about to let it fly into the fire, but to hear her reason, he could wait a second.

"I bought that one based solely on the author's name," she said testily.

A grin split his face. "So then you *do* have a sense of humor. Very well, you may keep this one." He handed the book back to her.

Her fingers snatched it from his palm and instinctively she

brought it to her chest.

"But as for the rest of these," he said, gesturing to all the other books on the shelves, "they're not so lucky." He started grabbing handfuls of pamphlets and treatises and tossing them into the fire.

"No!" she screamed, dropping the book she held on his desk before running to him and latching onto his arm.

Paul shook off her grasp. "Sorry, they need to go and nobody wants them. I asked at the lending library two days ago. They don't want them. There's nothing else to do with them." He shrugged. "It's a shame to waste your father's money this way, or to carelessly throw away paper, but at least we'll stay warm tonight." He shot her a quick smile as he tossed more books into the fire.

She stared at him. Her face was a mixture of distress and anger. Her lower lip quivered and tears ran down her cheeks. And yet, at the same exact time, her eyes told him her hatred for him was stronger now than ever before. "If you hate me so much, why not just ask me to leave? I would have gone if you'd only asked. But to stoop to *this*," she said, waving a shaky hand at the fire where even more of her precious books were currently being used in place of firewood.

Paul stopped throwing books into the flames and looked at her. "Lib—Mrs. Grimes," he began softly, "is that what you think? You think I did this because I want you to leave?"

"Yes! Why else would you be doing this? Why else would you do any of the things you've done to me since we married?"

Paul fought the urge to put his arms around her and comfort her. She thought he'd done all those things to get her to leave? That was completely the opposite of what he'd been trying to do. But how could he explain that to her? How could he tell her that he wanted the woman he'd met last spring? The one who had chatted without taking a second to breathe during dinner. The one he'd watched from across the room as she'd given comfort to her sister after she'd been thrown over for one of the most unpleasant chits in Society. Where was that woman? He'd liked her that night. He may not have done a very good job of showing it. But he was a man, for goodness' sake, what did she expect?

Seeing she was still waiting for an answer, he told her the truth, "I did those things because I wanted to break down your defenses. Ever since we married, you've been acting as docile as a lamb. I don't like it." He let out a deep breath. "I thought if I could provoke you, you'd break out of your little act."

"You burned my books because you intentionally wanted to vex me?" Her eyes grew huge and twin red flags stained her cheeks. "Congratulations, Mr. Grimes, you succeeded."

"I didn't burn your books because I wanted to annoy you. I did that because I wanted you to stop obsessing over propriety. It's not you," he bellowed back.

"Well, excuse me if it disappoints you that I was trying not to disappoint you," she said with a sniff. Then before he could respond, she fled the room.

Paul stared at the door she'd just exited through. He had no idea what she'd meant by that last cryptic statement. With a sigh, he took a seat. He was too exhausted to keep throwing books into the fire. If she hadn't come in when she did, he would have stopped at five like he had every other night. But when she came into the room, she'd somehow stirred the fire of his temper.

Each night he'd randomly selected five books and tossed them in. He hated having to look at them each time he came into the room. More than that though, he hated what they'd done to Liberty. Surely if it weren't for those blasted books, she wouldn't live her life like a crusty old bat.

He got up and walked to the hearth where the fire was still roaring. Grabbing the poker sitting to the right of the hearth, he started to bank the fire. He knew she'd find out eventually that he'd disposed of her books. He was just hoping it would be a few months in the future. Perhaps after she'd loosened up a bit, and preferably by him telling her, not by her walking into the room and witnessing it. Oh well, nothing for it now, he told himself. As funny as the situation wasn't, he couldn't help but smile when he thought about how she'd gone to the shelf and known exactly which books he'd burned. So much for his random selections.

With the fire banked, he walked to the door, picking up her

forgotten book on the way out. Tomorrow he'd make up for it, he promised himself. She may be hesitant to smile now, but he'd take care of that little problem tomorrow. As for tonight, he'd go to bed knowing she was upstairs thinking him an ass.

Chapter 15

"He is such an ass," Liberty ranted to Elizabeth as soon as she walked into her drawing room the next day.

"Really, dear? Tell me about it. I've always been quite fascinated with equines," Elizabeth said sweetly, pouring a cup of tea.

Liberty couldn't help the wobbly smile that took her lips. "Unfortunately, he's not of the four-legged variety."

Elizabeth smiled at her warmly. "I was afraid of that. Would you care to talk about it?"

"I shouldn't," Liberty said solemnly before taking a sip of her tea.

"Bah! We all do things we shouldn't." She fluffed a pillow and shoved it behind her back. "I'm in ready position. Complain away, my dear."

"He burned my books," Liberty said testily.

Elizabeth blinked at her. "Your books?"

"My books," Liberty repeated, nodding her head in confirmation.

"Why?" Elizabeth asked carefully.

Liberty blinked back tears. "Because he hates me."

"That's not true," Elizabeth protested. "I may not be an expert when it comes to men, but even I can recognize that he doesn't hate you."

"Well, he certainly doesn't love me," Liberty retorted carelessly.

Elizabeth's blue eyes lowered and she bit her lower lip as if she were choosing her next words with extra care. "Did you expect him to?" she said at last.

Liberty nearly choked on her tea. She hadn't *expected* him to love her. She hadn't even expected him to *like* her. But it surely wouldn't have been unwelcome if he had. "No, I suppose not," she said quietly.

Since there was nothing else to say on the subject, the two of them spoke nary a word about men for the rest of the day.

The night before, she'd been so distraught over Paul throwing all of her books into the fire, she'd cried herself to sleep. But now, after nearly an entire day to get over his heartless actions, her shock and anger were giving way to thoughts of revenge.

She knew she shouldn't want to take revenge on him. It was wrong. And, she reminded herself, it was revenge that had gotten her married to him in the first place. What would happen to her now if her plans went awry again? That was the one bright spot in a foiled revenge. She was already married to him. How could it possibly get worse?

Tonight, she told herself, after dinner she'd wait for him to go into his study, then she'd go look around his room to get ideas. Revenge was best done when planned out a bit. Obviously last time she hadn't planned it out well enough. This time she'd have to plan better.

Dinner was awkward, but no more awkward than it had been in the past. It was just a different kind of awkward.

Her husband sat at his end of the table staring at her, drumming his long, blunt-tipped fingers on the wooden table. She'd never seen him do that and she had to resist the urge to laugh at his nervous habit. The only reason it was possible to resist was because she knew he had something up his sleeve, but unbeknownst to him, she had no intention to comply.

That morning he'd given a note to Mrs. Siddons to give to her while she was in her bath. There was no seal, but she knew who it was from. She half expected there to be words of apology or something of the like. Instead, it told her that after dinner he'd like to see her in his study. She groaned. He'd mentioned to her last night he was going to buy her a book for St. Valentine's Day. He could toss it into the fire for all she cared. She wasn't joining him in his study so he could give her whatever paltry book he'd bought for her.

It was about time for dessert. Liberty almost groaned with disappointment when she realized it was trifle, her favorite. Tearing her eyes away from the tempting trifle, she announced, "I'm not feeling well. I think I shall retire for the evening."

Paul's eyes narrowed. "I'm sorry to hear that," he murmured and went back to his food.

Her room was a bit cold and she noticed the fire was barely going. Not wanting to call Paul to help her with her fire, she bared her teeth, pulled off her gloves and got a fire going.

She'd have to spend a while up in her room before she could go raid his. There was no reason to be cold while waiting.

She walked behind her dressing screen and started to remove her gown when a sharp knock rattled the door.

***

There were no two ways about it, Paul was nervous. He'd never been good at impressing those of the female persuasion before, and even though Liberty was his wife, that didn't make things any easier.

Until the night before, he'd still been unsure what he'd give her. Perhaps her barging into the room where he was burning her books was the best thing that could have happened. But he still felt uncomfortable about the display he was about to put on for her.

Last night she'd said she didn't want anything from him and he quite believed her. In fact, if it wasn't for his own selfish motives, he would have treated today like any other day and let her interpret that however she liked.

He'd anticipated Liberty might want to leave during dinner so he had asked Mrs. Siddons to make all her favorite dishes. Now looking at her untouched trifle, he realized that either she didn't like trifle as much as Mrs. Siddons thought, or she was so angry with him even the temptation of trifle couldn't make her finish dinner.

He reached over and grabbed her dessert. A nicer man would bring this up to his "sick" wife, but he wasn't in the mood to play her games.

A giant spoonful was heading for his mouth when he abruptly

slammed down the spoon, sending some of the trifle onto the table. Better save the trifle, it might actually help him in his quest tonight, he thought, getting up from the table.

A quick stop in his study to remove his strangulating cravat and grab a few things then he was on his way up to her room. If she thought to escape him by pretending to be sick, then she thought wrong.

He knocked on the door and waited precisely three seconds before swinging it open. He'd seen her wearing absolutely nothing before, whatever she had on just now should be adequate.

"Get out," she shrieked from behind the dressing screen.

Paul put the things he'd been holding down on a credenza that was positioned by the wall. "I'm here to see to the welfare of my sickly wife," he said, crossing his arms.

"I'm fine," she ground out, making quite a lot of noise behind that screen.

"Are you sure about that? Would you like a hand?"

"No," she exclaimed. "I do not require any help other than you leaving."

"In that case, I'll wait for you while you take off your gown," he said, taking a seat on a spindly chair in the corner.

"I'm not taking it off."

The rustling noises behind the screen sounding more agitated. "Then what are you doing?"

"I'm putting it on."

"You came up here just to change gowns?" he asked, deliberately being obtuse. "Do you have an assignation with someone?"

"No. I'm putting it back on because *you* invited yourself in here. And, because *you* are not leaving. And, because I don't want *you* to see me without it."

"I see," he said, drawing out his words. "You don't need to worry about offending my sensibilities, Mrs. Grimes. I've seen you in far less than whatever you have on just now."

A slipper flew in his direction from over the top of the screen.

"Just last night I saw you in your dressing robe," he drawled, leaning backwards in his chair.

This time a bejeweled slipper with a heel flew over the screen.

Paul chuckled. "Would you like me to continue to recount to you all the states of undress I've seen you in?"

"I've seen you undressed, too."

"Yes, I know," he conceded, getting up from the chair and walking to her wardrobe. "Do you want to see me that way again?"

"No!" she exclaimed, accidentally ripping a seam in her fabric presumably because of her frustration.

"I think you do," he teased, grabbing a simple frock from her wardrobe.

Liberty nearly grunted in frustration. "I have no such interest."

"Then prove it," Paul shot back, tossing her the frock he'd just pulled out of her wardrobe. "You have exactly two minutes to get that on and be out here. After that, for every fifteen seconds you make me wait, I'll remove an article of my clothing." He laughed at her frustrated noises as she tried to get her old gown off. "Oh, one more thing, I'll not be starting with my shoes, either."

He walked to the vanity where a clock was positioned in the back corner and watched as the second hand ticked off one hundred twenty seconds. "Your time's up," he called then waited another fifteen seconds before tossing his coat over the screen.

"Don't take anything else off," she squealed from behind the screen.

"Are you dressed?" he asked, unbuttoning his waistcoat.

"No, but—"

"No 'buts', Mrs. Grimes, you're late. And as you know, I prefer to be in my shirtsleeves anyway." He tossed his waistcoat over the screen.

"Stop! I'm dressed," she exclaimed, coming around the corner of the screen.

His fingers froze on the buttons of his shirt. "All right," he said hoarsely. His mouth had suddenly gone dry at the sight of her. That simple frock he thought he'd grabbed was not so simple after all. The blue silk clung to her womanly curves, leaving almost nothing to the imagination. The bodice swooped low showing off the tops of her plump breasts. Tearing his gaze away from her chest, he gestured to the bed. "Why don't you sit down?" His voice sounded uneven and he began to have doubts he'd be able to get through this.

Liberty took a seat and stared at him with hard eyes. "All right, Mr. Grimes, you win." She sighed, held out her hand and wiggled her fingers. "Just give me the book so you can be on your way."

Ah, the book. Good. He'd almost forgotten his purpose. "You'll get the book. But first I have something else for you," he said, flashing her a quick smile.

He walked over to the satchel he'd brought up with him. He pulled out several old cravats and placed them on the table. Next, he brought out a spool of silver wire in one hand and gold in the other. He placed the wire by the cravats then pulled out a handful of metal tools. With a clang, Paul put the tools down and picked up a poorly wrapped bundle.

"Now, Mrs. Grimes," he said as evenly as he could. He hated calling her that. He only did it in an effort to please her, even though it drove him insane in the process. "It has come to my attention that you *do* possess a sense of humor, but you choose not to smile."

She rolled her eyes.

"Well, m'dear, I have the perfect solution to your predicament. I shall fix your teeth," he exclaimed excitedly and beamed at her.

Liberty stared at him unblinking. "You sir, are an imbecile. There's nothing you can do to fix my teeth."

"So you agree there's nothing wrong with them, then?" he asked, his eyes searching her face.

"I didn't say that. I said there's nothing *you* can do to fix them."

"I beg to differ," he drawled. "If you'll sit down for a second." He waved his hand in a motion meant to stay her. "Very good. All right, the way I see it—and I could be wrong, so I'll need to have a better look at your snappers before I can know for sure—it seems that it's only your front tooth that's out of line."

Her face grew red and she pursed her lips. "If you're going to make fun of me, you may leave right now."

"I'm not making fun of you. And I'm certainly not leaving," he said, his voice making it clear he was brooking no argument on the subject. "Now, as I was saying. I think if I were to take a piece of wire—either silver or gold, your choice—and wrap it around that misaligned tooth, then wrap more wire around some of the ones that are next to it, the tooth might be forced to join its brothers in line."

Liberty looked at him like he was a simpleton. "And tell me, Mr. Grimes, just how is that tooth going to be forced to 'join its brothers in line'?"

"Good question, Mrs. Grimes," he said thoughtfully. "However, I anticipated that concern and believe every so often I'll have to replace the wires with tighter ones."

"So you're saying you want to wrap wire around my front teeth and a few others and then every so often tighten this wire somehow in hopes of straightening out my front tooth?" she asked slowly, in a way a person might speak to a two-year-old.

"Yes, exactly," he said, nodding his head as if he were the smartest man in existence. "Either I'll replace the wire with shorter ones, causing your teeth to have to shift on their own. Or I'll just grab the end of the wire with these," he held up a tool that had a v-shaped handle that when squeezed made its long pointy ends come together, "and give it a jerk, then clip the extra off with a pair of scissors." He shrugged. "We'll have to work out the maintenance later. Right now I'm just telling you my idea."

"Mr. Grimes, you never cease to amaze me," Liberty said sarcastically, shaking her head. "Every time I think you've said or done the stupidest thing imaginable, you always find a way to outdo yourself. The idea that anyone would put wires around their teeth in order to straighten them is beyond laughable."

"I thought you might say that," he said with a shrug. "That's why I have a second option." He picked up a tool that was similar to the first. The difference was the handles were a bit thicker and the end had two giant pinchers on it. He held it up and showed it to her. "The smithy I bought this from called this thing a pair of pliers. But you know what? I don't really like that name, so I think we'll refer to it as the yankers instead. Sit back down. Good girl. Now, this plan is much simpler. Instead of months—or years—of tightening wires, I'll just take the yankers and yank that offending tooth out right here and now and be done with this whole business."

She looked at him dumbfounded. "Umm...don't you think you might have overlooked one tiny detail?" she asked, her lips twitching. When he merely raised his eyebrows in question, she exclaimed, "That will leave a huge hole!"

"Oh, right," he said, trying to be obtuse again. "And would that be worse than a crooked tooth?"

"Yes," she cried with exasperation.

"Hmm, I guess that does pose a problem," he said easily, rolling his eyes up to stare at the ceiling for a few seconds before meeting hers again. "Unless, you would like to use this," he suggested, reaching into his pocket and pulling out a little piece of wood that was about a half inch wide, two inches long and a quarter inch thick.

"Oh my goodness," Liberty said, burying her head in her hands and shaking with laughter. "You cannot be serious! A wooden tooth?"

"What's wrong with that?" he asked, feigning offense. "They are actually quite popular. In fact, that George Washington fellow had a whole set of them. You've heard of him before, haven't you?" He smiled at her when she looked up and scowled at him. "I know it's a bit big now, but we can resize it." He went to where some of the other tools were on the table. "I have a chisel we can use if need be. We can make it shorter or take some of the width off. We can also get some paint and paint it to match your other teeth if you'd like."

"That won't be necessary," she choked out.

"Are you certain? I've brought all the necessary equipment to do the whole procedure right now." He waved vaguely toward all the items on the table. "I've got cravats to tie you down, two clamps to keep your mouth open, the mallet to hammer in the new tooth, and of course the yankers to pull the old one out."

She scowled at him and he grinned back at her again. He grabbed the atrociously wrapped book and walked over to where she was sitting on the bed. "May I join you?" he asked quietly. Seeing her hesitation, he said, "I'll just grab this chair."

"No, you don't have to," Liberty said belatedly, scooting over.

Paul already had the chair moved over and was about to sit in it when she moved over, making room for him. "Are you sure?"

She nodded.

"Can we agree there is nothing wrong with your teeth?" he asked after he sat down on the bed next to her.

She looked away and stared at a little crack in the wall. "Does it matter?" she mumbled.

"It matters a great deal," Paul said softly, putting his fingers under her chin and turning her face toward his. "It's the reason you don't smile."

"Why do you care?" she asked, her voice catching in the middle of her question.

"Because I like it when you smile," he said simply. "I'll admit I've only seen a handful actually meant for me, but I've seen enough to know I like it."

She shook her head. "I still don't understand what that has to do with anything," she said quietly.

Paul's face heated up as he handed her the bundle. "Sorry, the wrapping's a bit messy. After I opened it to make a few modifications, I couldn't get it back the way Mr. Calahan had it," he murmured as she untied the twine.

She eyed him askance as she pulled off the wrapping. "What is it?" she asked a moment later as she leafed through a book full of lined pages that had different dates written on the top of each page.

Taking the book from her, he flipped it closed and pointed to the front cover where he'd taken a heated piece of metal and scratched out her full name, *Liberty Ellis Grimes*, in the best script he could; then around it, he'd done his best to draw a box with scrolling edges and a few swooping designs. It was nothing too fancy, just enough to make it personal, and perhaps let her know he did care for her a little. "I've never been good at this sort of thing," he admitted, silently praying he wouldn't die of embarrassment on the spot. He ran his fingers through his sandy blond hair and gave it a tug before bringing his hand back down to his lap. "I think you need to smile more. So I bought you a journal of sorts. I thought if you were to record every time you smiled, you might realize how little you do it and decide to do it more often."

"I see," she said, appearing more confused than before.

This was a bad idea. Now she probably thought he was besotted with her. He was about two seconds away from grabbing the book back and hiding in his study for the rest of the night. But what good would that do? She still wouldn't smile, except when she remembered what a fool he'd made of himself yet again. He had to turn this around.

"Here's the deal," he said in a sharper voice than he intended. "Every page has a date on it. It starts with today and goes until February thirteenth next year. The one, two and three you see on each of the pages," he pointed to one of the pages that had a one on the first line, then a two written a few lines down and a three a few lines after that, "are so you can write in three incidents during the day that made you smile. Therefore, each and every day you must find three things that make you smile and record them."

"And who are you to say what I must do?" she demanded. "Maybe I don't want to smile."

"I don't care," he said fiercely, although he cared very much that she didn't want to smile. "You'll find three things about which to smile each day and record them."

"And if I don't?" she challenged.

"I think you will," he said with a slow smile.

"You're awfully confident, aren't you," she countered. "What makes you so sure I'll do what you want? How do you know I'm not going to toss it into the fire like you did with my books last night?"

Paul got up and strolled to the other side of the room where he'd left his satchel. "Because the fate of this book," he pulled her "favorite" propriety book out of his bag, "depends on the fate of that book," he said, pointing to the book she held in her hand. "If that book goes into the fire, then so does your misbehavin' book."

"It's Miss Bea Haven," she corrected through clenched teeth. "All right, I promise not to throw it into the fire. Now give me my book back."

"No. That's not good enough. I'll let you have it back after I know you're doing what you're supposed to."

"And how are you going to determine that?"

"By reading your entries, of course," he said with a wink.

"And how will you know if I make things up?" she asked tartly.

Paul shrugged again. "I won't. But I don't care because I'm sure you'll smile about it later that night when you think you got away with tricking me."

"You're absurd."

"That may be," he allowed. "But either way, I think you'll do it. You don't want anything to happen to Miss Bea, do you?" He tossed her propriety book into the air, letting it do a flip before catching it.

"I suppose you had better toss that book into the fire," she said, sounding resigned and pointing to the book he was holding.

His eyes shot to hers. "Why?"

"Because there's no way I can do this. It's time for bed and I just now got the book. It appears that I've already missed a whole day's worth of entries," she said, her voice sounding a bit sarcastic.

"Nice try," Paul said, stepping closer to her. "But I know for a fact that you've met your quota for the day."

"And how would you know that?" she asked, narrowing her eyes.

"First, I know you smiled when you were laughing at me while I was suggesting ways to fix your tooth. Second, I caught a glimpse of you smiling when you walked out of the dining room, thinking you were pulling one over on me. And third, when I told you that you could have your misbehavin' book back." He smiled

112

at her, daring her to deny his charges.

"I did not smile when you brought out Miss Bea Haven's book," she countered, crossing her arms defensively.

"Then what would you call it?"

"I don't know, maybe a smirk. But it certainly was not a smile," she said defiantly.

He shook his head. "Fine. I bet you smiled when I tossed my clothing over the screen," he teased and waggled his eyebrows suggestively.

She glowered at him. "Absolutely not," she declared, shaking her head for emphasis.

"All right," he conceded. "But we agree on the other two incidents?"

She nodded.

His smile turned wolfish. "Then, I guess that just means I need to stay until I can make you smile again."

"Th—that won't be necessary," she stammered.

Paul brought his free hand up to her face and tilted her head up so he could look into her eyes. His thumb rubbed a light caress on her soft cheek, causing her lips to part slightly. He watched as her pink tongue peeked out and moistened her lips. He slowly ran his long fingers along the edge of her jaw. Looking at her thus, he could actually see a very attractive woman. A woman who let society's dictums and her own foolish notions control her. If she'd learn to let go of all that and relax, she would be very beautiful indeed.

Paul leaned his head down, closing the space between them. Then, before he could stop himself, he gently pressed his lips to hers. Her lips felt soft and lush under his. He stayed there for just a brief few seconds, but it was enough to know that she'd enjoyed the kiss as much as he had.

He pulled back and looked at her face. Her traitorous lips were having the hardest time not curving into a smile. He was tempted to point out that she'd just smiled again. But decided to act the role of a gentleman just this once and said, "I know just the thing to put a smile on your face."

Her eyes flew open and two patches of pink spread across her cheeks. She opened her mouth to speak—some scathing retort, if he had to guess—but he cut her off by putting a finger to her lips. "I brought you something else," he said simply before walking across the room and grabbing the trifle he'd hidden from her view. He walked back across the room to her and handed her the dish. "Perhaps this will help."

She took the dish from his hand, her fingers brushing his as she did so. "Thank you," she murmured, favoring him with a small, shy smile.

"You're welcome."

She looked down at the trifle, then back at his face. "Did you eat some of it?" she asked blandly, her lips twitching.

"Not exactly," he confessed, "but not for lack of wanting to."

She looked like she wanted to ask him where the missing spoonful was; fortunately, she didn't. Instead, she just eyed him skeptically and took a big bite.

"I should be going," he announced abruptly, walking away to pack up his things. "Don't forget to make your entries."

Paul walked numbly out of her room and down the stairs. He knew she'd laugh at him. He'd actually hoped she would. That was half the reason he'd concocted the whole scheme and gone through with it. What he hadn't counted on was kissing her. He still couldn't describe what had possessed him to do so. Perhaps it was that blue silk gown and how it exposed the tops of her luscious breasts and clung to her curvy body, tempting him to look at what he wasn't allowed to have. Or perhaps it had to do with the expression on her face at the time. She'd been completely relaxed and still. He'd only seen her that way once before: the day of her accident. The only reason he'd seen her that way then was because she was unconscious. Or perhaps he'd kissed her because as much as he'd tried to deny it to himself, he was becoming besotted with her.

Just acknowledging the thought made his body tense. If she were to ever discover his true feelings and realize how much power she held over him, he'd be in deep trouble.

Chapter 16

Liberty was utterly confused as she stared at the door her husband had just gone through. The man changed moods more often than she changed drawers. One minute he was doing something nice, and the next he was barking out orders. He was definitely a mystery.

She scribbled her entries into the journal. Not because she wanted to please him, but because she wanted to ensure the safety of her favorite (and last) propriety book, or at least that's the reason she told her herself while scribbling down her entries. This morning she'd snuck into his study to grab her books and hide them before he could destroy them. Unfortunately, once she'd opened the door, she'd soon discovered he'd already destroyed the rest.

Thinking on it now only served to remind her of her new mission. Perhaps she'd find something of his to heartlessly destroy. Searching his room tonight wasn't possible, but perhaps tomorrow before she left to go tutor above the tavern.

The next week passed with no opportunities for Liberty to search his room or study, but she hadn't forgotten her plan. Each night she'd remind herself of it when he came in dressed only in his shirtsleeves with his top button undone and scanned her made up journal entries. As he perused her fiction, she'd bite her cheek so she wouldn't crack a smile at the expressions on his face and simultaneously plan when she'd look around his room.

During that week, she'd discovered he was right about something, and it almost killed her to admit as much. He'd said she would smile when she pulled one over on him, and undeniably, she did. Each night when he left her room after reading the nonsense she'd made up, she'd bury her face in her pillow to muffle her laughter as she thought about his facial expressions while he read the rubbish she'd written. He was right about something else, too. She rarely smiled.

Perhaps he was right about yet another thing when he'd said she let her insecurity surrounding her teeth get the better of her more than she realized. Maybe knowing they weren't perfect and having been criticized for them *was* the reason she didn't smile. She'd told him as much that night in his study but hadn't really believed it herself until now.

Sighing, she pushed her thoughts aside and snuggled more deeply into the pillow. Tomorrow was a new day. Perhaps it was time she took her task seriously. Truly, what would it hurt if she smiled more? And tomorrow would be a good time to start. Tomorrow was her day to help the literacy group which, despite the leering, drunken men, had become her favorite new pursuit since coming to live here, thus providing an excellent opportunity for her to smile.

The next morning she once again had difficulty getting into her husband's room. Why did the man suddenly decide that the kitchen was no longer a suitable bathing room, she wondered a tad irritably when she stood outside the door for the eighth morning in a row and heard the distinct sounds of a person bathing. Oh well, there was always the afternoon.

They ate their morning meal together in silence, only saying the obligatory lines of greeting and departure. That's how it had been all week. He seemed to be avoiding her, except when he came to her room to bring her water for her morning bath or read her entries. Other than that, it would seem the man ceased to exist.

Liberty rode in her carriage to Gray's Tavern the same way she did every week. However, unlike the previous weeks, she was greeted by Mrs. Jones, the director of the organization, as soon as she stepped out of her carriage.

"I have exciting news," Mrs. Jones exclaimed, clapping her hands together. "New literature has been donated. Someone donated literally hundreds of books to our group. Isn't that great?"

"Yes," Liberty replied, matching Mrs. Jones' level of excitement. "Do you know who?"

Mrs. Jones shook her head. "No."

Liberty nodded. "You didn't talk to them when they dropped the books off?"

A strange look came over Mrs. Jones' face before she said, "Actually, the books were not given to us directly from the donator. They were originally given to Mrs. Weslen's group, but she didn't want them. She said they were droll and boring and that her students had no interest in them."

"Oh."

Mrs. Jones shook her head. "If you ask me, a book is a book and a free book is the best kind."

"That is true," Liberty agreed. "Let's go have a look at them."

Together they made their way upstairs, and when Liberty saw the stacks of books on the table, she almost fainted on the spot. Paul had donated her propriety books to her literacy group! Why? She thought he'd destroyed them. She didn't know whether to be happy or upset. She suddenly found herself fighting off embarrassment when Mrs. Jones said, "I don't know who would have so many books about manners in their personal library, but as I said, a free book is the best kind."

Liberty mumbled something that could pass as an agreement.

"This was with the books when they were left for Mrs. Weslen." Mrs. Jones handed her a slip of paper.

Liberty's hands trembled as she grabbed the piece of paper that she knew would contain a message from her husband.

I hope the books bring about a smile.

The words seemed quite simple. Of course, Mrs. Weslen and Mrs. Jones probably just took it at face value. Liberty knew that wasn't the intent. He'd written that sentence specifically for her, although, for the life of her, she couldn't fathom why he'd left the books with the wrong organization.

Once the students were assembled and seated, Mrs. Jones made the announcement about the donation of the new reading material to the group while Liberty and the other volunteers handed out the books.

She couldn't stop her smile when she handed some of her favorite volumes to the students. She'd never tell them the books were hers of course, but she couldn't deny the pleasure it gave her to use them for a good cause rather than as a replacement for firewood.

Her pleasure came to an abrupt halt, however, when one of the men spoke up. "These books are about manners. Who reads books about manners?" he said, flinging one of her most expensive volumes on the floor, causing a loud echo.

"Hear, hear," said another. "The title of mine is *A Dinner Party with the Gently Bred*. Hell, if I was to go to a dinner party, I ain't gonna eat my bread gently."

A round of laughter erupted at his ridiculous joke.

"Listen to this," cut in a twenty-something woman who Liberty could have sworn was a prostitute at one time. "'If a gentleman touches the hem of your skirt be sure to gently, but firmly, tug the skirt from his grasp without letting any part of your body touch his or exposing yourself to his view.' If all he wanted to do was touch the hem of my skirt, I'd be disappointed. Then, I'd firmly grab my skirt and reposition it making sure to give him a peek of what he *could* have had."

Another round of weak laughter broke out before Mrs. Jones quieted everyone down. "Very good, students. Your reading skills have improved greatly in the past few months."

Liberty shook her head. She couldn't blame them for making jokes about the books. To some—all right, most—the books were just a bunch of nonsense, and she couldn't fault them for thinking so.

"All right," Liberty said. "Perhaps for those of you who can read the print well enough to make jests about it, you should work on your writing skills by rewriting the passages so they read how you think they ought."

"Splendid idea, Mrs. Grimes," Mrs. Jones said. "How about if everyone works on that for an hour, then we'll have some volunteers read them to the class."

There were a few giggles, sighs and groans, but all the older ones complied while Liberty made her way over to join the group of small children who still needed help learning to read.

After being begged and pleaded with, Liberty took a seat on the floor with the little urchins. They passed one of the volumes around, each child trying to tackle reading one to two sentences before passing it on to the next child in the circle.

"This book is boring," one of the little girls declared after the book had made one complete pass around the circle.

"Yeah," another agreed. "Why would anyone buy this book?"

"Or write it?" a dirty little redheaded boy asked with a yawn.

"Because it helps people to know how to behave," Liberty supplied, feeling a bit defensive having to explain about her favorite hobby to a group of mocking children.

"Do people get taken to the woodshed when they don't follow what's in this book?" a little boy who always wore tattered clothes asked.

Liberty looked at him curiously. "No. Why?"

The boy shrugged. "Father always takes me to the woodshed when my mum tells him I didn't behave," he said as a shadow that spoke of many trips to the woodshed with his "father", who was actually his grandfather, crossed his face

"Well, if that were the case, both of my older sisters would have spent half of the past six years in the woodshed," Liberty said dryly, causing all the children to giggle.

"But not you, right, Mrs. Grimes?" Seth asked hopefully.

Liberty blushed. "Well, maybe a few times," she told her favorite student as she remembered all the unladylike encounters she'd had with Paul.

"But not as much as your sisters, huh?" he asked to clarify she was indeed the angel he had built her up to be in his mind.

"Exactly so."

The boy gave her a wide grin and scooted a bit closer to her side.

After a few more of the children read sentences from *Cordial Encounters with Crotchety Countesses,* it was time to listen to the rewrites of her books. Liberty warned herself she probably wasn't going to like what she heard, but willed herself not to let it show.

Even after she'd steeled herself for more crude remarks, she was pleasantly surprised when a good portion of the students had actually taken the task somewhat seriously.

The first woman to read was a buxom blonde who was well known for her straightforward approach to life. "Mine read, 'One should never use a gentleman's given name without his permission, and never in public.' I think it should read, 'One should use whatever name the gentleman asked you to call him by, otherwise, it's just plain rude.'"

There were a few claps and snickers, but Liberty didn't pay attention to them. Instead, she thought of Paul. How many times had he asked her to call him by his given name? More than she could count. Perhaps it was time she started. She could no longer deny she thought of him as "Paul". What would be so bad about calling him by his Christian name anyway?

Lost in her thoughts, she missed the next few. Then she saw a volunteer named Richard stand up.

Richard was a burly man who had a coarse way with words. "Whoever wrote my book must have the personality of a piece of rope because they wrote, 'Always be polite, never speak unless spoken to, and always say something cordial and diplomatic'. I don't like that. Instead, I think it should read, 'If someone's rude, ignore them. Speak if you have something to say, and if it angers someone, who gives a hang? You are who you are, and if someone can't accept it, then you sure as h—'"

"Well done, Richard," Mrs. Jones said excitedly, looking like she was going to burst with pride at the fact these people had actually written so many words. Especially since Richard didn't say anything offensive until the end, and even then she'd been able to cut him off before he'd gotten too exuberant.

Liberty, on the other hand, just shook her head. No need to correct their misconceptions. None of these people were likely to dine, or even associate for that matter, with nobility, so why bother to explain the necessity for the rules they would never understand?

Mrs. Jones collected the books and the adults and older children took their leave. Liberty approached the small group of younger children to wait with them until their mothers arrived.

When she'd married Paul, she'd acknowledged that she'd never have children. She'd had no desire to be intimate with him and it seemed that he shared the feeling, for he'd never even tried to visit her bed. Even when she'd been in nothing but a towel in front of him, he hadn't looked interested in anything more than teasing her by dangling the chemise just outside of her grip. His eyes held none of the love and desire she'd seen in Andrew's when he looked at her sister.

Oh well, she thought, taking a seat by the children. If she couldn't have her own children, at least she'd have a niece or nephew to dote on in a few months, and until then, she could enjoy being around these children.

She sat with them and told them stories of America and the scrapes she and her sisters got into as children. She always left off any details that showed her in an unsavory light, of course. These children idolized her, no need to ruin that.

One by one, mothers came to pick up their children until it was just Liberty and Seth. It wasn't unusual for Seth to be there longer than the others. His mother worked down the street and sometimes she had a hard time getting away from her duties in order to come get him. Neither Seth nor Liberty seemed to mind though. They'd make up adventure stories or play war with little tin soldiers he brought with him. Last week, she'd even let him talk her into a sword fight with two wooden broom sticks.

She feared if someone walked in on them while she engaging in such activities, she'd be made into the laughing stock of the village. But somewhere along the way, she'd begun to learn there was more to life than following the rules and doing everything perfectly. As Paul so bluntly pointed out, she already had a husband. And that husband never took her to social events so why did it still matter so much to be all prim and proper? At home, she tried her best to behave herself and keep calm so not to disappoint her husband or father any further than she already had.

But there was no harm in letting her hair down and having fun while nobody was around.

Today Seth wanted to hear stories about the Indians he'd heard lived in America. Liberty obliged and told him everything she knew about Indians, which wasn't much, but the young boy found it fascinating all the same. Finding a few broken quills and an abandoned scarf, Liberty fashioned a headdress for him to wear around the room.

She smiled a smile borne of pure joy when she placed it on his head and he started running around the room patting his hand over his open mouth in an attempt to do the Indian war cry she'd shown him. He settled down for a minute but only to think up names for the two of them. "I'll be Chief Learn-to-read and you can be Read-a-lot," he said with a grin.

Liberty didn't particularly love the names, but it was better than she could have come up with. There was nothing in this world that would make her want to ruin the boy's joy, even if it meant suffering for a half hour with a ridiculous Indian name.

He ran around the room and jumped over small hurdles yelping and making masculine noises, occasionally saying, "Don't worry Read-a-lot, Chief Learn-to-read will save you!"

This would most certainly be a true entry in her journal tonight, and knowing Paul, he wouldn't even bat an eyelash at the tale. He might or might not believe her, but compared to some of the other stories she'd made up, this was actually rather mild.

Seth came to an abrupt stop in front of her. "Read-a-lot," he said with wide eyes.

"Yes?"

"How am I to protect you without a bow and arrow?" he asked very seriously.

"Ugh," she stammered. What did she do now? She wasn't going to give him a weapon, real or pretend. She had to draw the line *somewhere*.

His eyes lit up. "Forget the bow and arrow. I want a tomahawk!"

"No!" she exclaimed. That was even worse. "I don't have the

material to help you make a bow and arrow. Why don't you just use your imagination?" Though she didn't like the idea of violence, at least an imaginary weapon was better than a real one.

With a shrug, Chief Learn-to-read went back on the warpath in an effort to save her. He was jumping around and making so much noise neither of them heard his mother enter until he spotted her standing by the door and shouted, "Duck, Read-a-lot, it's the enemy, Milky Mum." He then pretended to shoot an imaginary arrow in his mother's direction.

As if on cue, the woman waited three seconds then brought her hands up to her chest pretending there was a wound there, then she gave a wounded squeal, rolled her head back and sank to the floor.

"Bravo, Milky Mum," Chief Learn-to-read cheered.

Liberty clapped her hands at the performance and went over to see if the woman needed help getting up off the floor.

"I'm all right, there's no need to help me," Seth's mother assured her. "He really likes you, you know." After Liberty shot her a quizzical look, the other woman clarified, "Seth. He enjoys coming to see you. He talks about you all week and gets so excited on the days he gets to come see you."

Liberty smiled at both Seth and his mother. As far as she knew, nobody enjoyed seeing her, except maybe the back of her as she was leaving a room. "I enjoy seeing him, too. Our time together is my favorite time of my week," she said truthfully.

"I'm glad to hear that. I must admit I was a bit surprised when I heard you volunteered. I mean, Paul is a very nice man and all, but even I didn't expect him to allow his wife to tutor the illegitimate."

"You mean the illiterate," Liberty corrected, scanning the woman's beautiful face. She had to admit Seth's mother was a very beautiful woman. She had raven hair, blue eyes, porcelain skin, red lips and a very curvaceous figure.

"Yes, well, that too, I suppose," the other woman said, with a dim smile.

Liberty eyed her askance. This woman might be gorgeous, but

she didn't seem very smart. Surely she knew the difference between illiterate and illegitimate.

"You did read the sign, didn't you?" the dark haired woman asked skeptically.

Liberty nodded. Of course she'd read the sign. That's how she knew there was a need to help the *illiterates* of the village learn to read.

"So then you knew you were helping the illegitimate learn to read," the other woman clarified.

Liberty sighed. Did she need to explain the difference between illiterate and illegitimate to this woman? Perhaps so. "Ma'am, I volunteered to help those who are unable to read learn to do so. Right now they would be termed as *illiterate,* but soon they should be *literate.*" She hoped by emphasizing "illiterate" and "literate", she'd get her point across without having to spell out for this poor woman the difference between illiterate and illegitimate.

The woman tucked a lock of black hair behind her ear and nodded. "Seth, gather your things. It's time to go." Turning back to Liberty, she said, "Ma'am, I mean you no disrespect, but perhaps you should reread the sign downstairs."

Rolling her eyes, Liberty marched down the stairs and to the front door of the tavern where the sign was posted. Squinting her eyes, she reread the sign:

NEEDED: Volunteers to help the illegitimate learn to read. Meetings held upstairs Tuesday mornings at 10 a.m.

"Oh, no," she breathed right before she dropped to the floor the same way Seth's mother had when she'd pretended to be shot by the arrow.

Chapter 17

"There you go," Seth's mother said to Liberty, helping her settle into an empty booth and sliding a glass of water into her hands.

"Thank you," she murmured, picking up the glass. She brought it to her lips and took a deep swallow. What was she going to do now? Society would shun her if they knew she was involved with a group that helped those born on the wrong side of the blanket learn to read. She tried not to laugh when she thought of how surprised everyone would be when they learned of her recent activities. Being caught playing games with a little boy paled in comparison to associating with a group of illegitimate illiterates. Yet, as disapproving as everyone else might be about this, Liberty felt a sudden urge to ignore Society's dictums. These were people, granted they were bastards, but that wasn't their fault. So why should they be denied the ability to read? They hadn't created their bastardy. Why should they be punished for it?

"You really didn't know," the other woman said, breaking into Liberty's thoughts. When she merely nodded, the woman added, "Nobody would fault you if you stopped volunteering, you know?"

Liberty nodded again. Did she have to stop coming? Nobody of any consequence would ever know. That wasn't true. Brooke and Andrew didn't live that far away, they'd probably find out, in time. She doubted either of them would actually care though. He might be an earl and she a countess, but she'd never met two people who cared less about others' opinions. That just left Paul. What would he think? Would he want her to stop? He obviously hadn't found out yet because he'd delivered those books to the wrong literacy group. Would he disapprove? Would this hurt his reputation with his church? Last year, when he'd sought Papa out for guidance, he'd said he already had a problem. Even after being married to him for nearly a month, Liberty still had yet to discover what that was. Would this make his existing troubles worse?

"Do you want to talk about what you're thinking?" Seth's mother asked, once again breaking into her thoughts.

"I just don't know what my husband is going to say," Liberty admitted, worrying the sleeve of her best red day dress.

The other woman waved her hand dismissively. "Paul won't care. I imagine if you tell him you've been coming here for a month without even knowing you were teaching a room full of bastards, he'd laugh."

Liberty's eyes went wide. She doubted Paul would find it funny in the least. He'd probably mock her mercilessly about it. That, or go out of his way to find a way to make her suffer. She'd always heard he had a temper but doubted she'd seen it at its worst —yet. The two times she'd seen him upset, she hadn't really thought it was *that* bad; nor did it seem to last long. Her father made it sound like it was preferable to endure the Devil's wrath over Paul's. She didn't truly believe that though, he always seemed to soften after a few minutes.

This could do it though. This could be the one final thing that would make him snap. "I don't share your opinion. I think he might be angry with me."

"Paul?" she said, shaking her head. "No. He'll think it's funny. I promise."

"Why do you keep calling him by his Christian name?" Liberty asked, truly interested in the woman's answer. It was no secret who she was married to, but why did this woman talk about him as if she knew him intimately. She should be calling him Mr. Grimes.

"My name is Lucy Whitaker; I grew up working in his family's dairy."

Liberty nodded. It felt rather intimidating to be sitting across the table from a gorgeous woman who knew her husband better than she did. "You've known him your whole life then?"

"No, not all our lives, just most of them," Lucy said with a laugh. "I was six and he was seven when we met. I used to play with him and his brother, Sam. The three of us got into all sorts of trouble together."

The wistful smile on Lucy's face told Liberty that their punishments had been well worth the scrapes they'd gotten into. "It's hard to imagine Paul getting into *any* trouble," Liberty said lightly.

"Oh, he did. He got into more than any of us. Not that that says a lot. We all got into more trouble than you could possibly imagine. Paul just always seemed to be the one who got caught." She shook her head. "He always took my side against Sam. See, Sam was three years older than me and didn't want me to join their games, but Paul insisted I could. Then they'd argue and sometimes start tackling each other to the ground."

Liberty chuckled. Paul seemed like a very relaxed type person. Picturing him fighting seemed nearly impossible.

"We had our good times together," Lucy said lightly. "When we were a bit older, I was maybe ten or so, Sam wanted to build a tree house for boys only, but Paul said he'd only help build it if I could go into it, too. Sam was unhappy about this, but he agreed to Paul's rules because he needed Paul's help to build it. Paul was always much better with tools than Sam could ever hope to be. It just comes naturally to him. Anyway, all summer we worked on building it. When it was finally done, we decided to sleep in it.

"None of our parents would allow it, so we all decided to sneak out. When the night finally came, we waited until two hours past our bedtimes and snuck out. Of course, Sam was disappointed when he saw I'd come, but there was no way I was going home. He said if I wanted to stay, I could as long as Paul slept in the middle because he didn't want to have to sleep near me. That was fine with me because I didn't want to be next to him, either.

"An hour later, a storm moved in and the thunder and lightning shook the boards while the rain came in through the cracks and soaked all of us to the skin. We were all cold and afraid. Sam tried to talk Paul into going back home and leaving me there alone. Thankfully, Paul always had the bigger heart of the two and said no. He offered to walk me to my house, but I was too terrified to walk across the field to my house. Finally, Sam couldn't take it any longer and he went home. I wondered if Paul would go home too because he was only eleven and was probably just as terrified as I was. But he didn't. He stayed with me all night. He told me every joke and story he could think of to distract me from the weather.

"The next morning, he mixed up some concoction, pitch or something, and smeared it in all the cracks. He said if it stormed again while we were playing in it, at least now we wouldn't get wet."

"And did you?" Liberty couldn't help but ask.

"No. But we never stayed the night in there again though, either," she said laughingly. "I caught a fever from that night and when their parents found out, both Paul and Sam had to play indoors for as many days as I was abed. To hear them tell it, you'd think they were made to suffer unfairly. I think Paul even remarked he would rather have had a fever than been well and stuck in the house for two weeks." She gave a shrug and twisted her glass of water.

Liberty smiled. There was obviously more to her husband than she knew. She should have known he had a tender spot for those in need of his help. Her family had described in detail how he'd taken care of her when she'd fallen through the ice. He'd probably saved her life, and he didn't even like her. Imagine what he would have done if he did like her. Most likely he would have stayed with her through her ailment. A shiver ran down her spine. Would she have allowed him to? At the time? Definitely not. But now? Yes, she decided, now she wouldn't be so opposed to his company. "I see the three of you remained friends," she said just to say something.

Lucy choked on her water. "No. Not at all. The three of us barely speak. That Paul and I live in the same area is pure coincidence. And not a happy one, I assure you."

"Oh?" Liberty questioned. What could have happened that made the three of them have a falling out? Even if Sam didn't want to play with a little girl when he was a boy, didn't mean they couldn't have become friends later. And why did this woman speak so highly of Paul one minute and then say it wasn't a good thing they lived so close? What happened?

Lucy bit her bottom lip and fidgeted in her chair. "Has Paul ever mentioned me?"

"No," Liberty said, shaking her head. Sensing that the woman really didn't want to tell her what happened, she added, "Lucy, Paul and I—we're not close. We've never spoken of our childhoods so please don't take offense that he's never mentioned you. It's my fault, really. I'm not the easiest person for him to talk to." While she hoped that made the other woman feel free to open up, Liberty realized it didn't shed a good light on herself.

Releasing a breath, Lucy said, "When I was seventeen, Paul asked me to marry him."

Liberty's jaw dropped.

"And, um, as you know, I refused," Lucy said flatly.

Liberty's eyes almost bulged out of her head, although she didn't know why. Of course, Lucy had declined. If she'd accepted, then *she'd* be Mrs. Paul Grimes, not Liberty.

Lucy sighed. "As I said, we grew up together on his family's estate. My father worked in the dairy and when I was fourteen, I started working there, too. Paul never seemed to take notice that I was a servant. He was always trying to see me and get me out of work. He paid me marked attention and was always bringing me things that he either made or spent his allowance to buy. Simple things really, ribbons, handkerchiefs, a bonnet, trinkets he carved out of wood, just little things.

"This went on for a few years and when I was seventeen, his brother inherited and Paul decided it was time to make his own way in life. He told me he loved me and asked me to marry me. I knew his words were true, he really did love me. But I had my sights set on Sam. See, though Sam didn't like being around me as a child, he later changed his opinion.

"Anyhow, six months before Paul proposed to me, Sam had started secretly coming to see me. He'd talk of love and marriage. And being the foolish girl that I was, I believed him. I believed he would marry me and make me his viscountess. Knowing I'd have a better life as a viscountess than as a vicar's wife, I refused Paul's offer of marriage."

Liberty stared at the woman. She couldn't believe it. Seth made a noise and she shifted her eyes to him before nearly jumping in shock. Now that she looked at him, really looked at him, she could see a lot of similarities between Paul and Seth. She'd always just assumed Seth's mother and father were just another local married couple that didn't attend church. But now...

Her blood roared in her ears and she stared at the boy. It couldn't be. Paul couldn't have a by-blow. Lucy refused his offer of marriage; surely they hadn't shared a bed. But why else would Seth look exactly like Paul? Maybe he was Sam's. He had to be. Though she'd never seen Sam to know if he and Paul looked similar, she had to believe Seth was Sam's.

As if she'd read Liberty's thoughts, Lucy said, "He's Sam's, don't worry."

Relieved, Liberty nodded. "I'm sorry; it's just that he looks so much like him. I mean, the green eyes, sandy blond hair and even his smile..." she trailed off, staring at the boy.

"Yes," Lucy agreed. "I imagine when you and Paul have a little boy he will look much the same. All the Grimes boys do."

Liberty nodded even though she felt a pang of remorse. She would never have a handsome little boy with moss green eyes, blonde hair and wide smiles. Actually, she'd never have a little boy at all. "What happened with Sam?" Then, as if she remembered her manners, she hastened to add, "If you don't mind my asking?"

Lucy flicked her hand. "I don't mind. After Paul ran off to pursue his life in the ministry, I found out I was expecting. When I told Sam, he shrugged it off and told me my employment was terminated. I tried to appeal to Paul and begged him to take me back, but he wouldn't because he was upset that I'd pushed him aside for a title. A few weeks later, I got a message saying I was to report to Sussex to work as a dairymaid for some friend of his. Grateful to have any type of employment, I went. I stayed there until about two years ago; when the friend died and his disgusting pig of a cousin took over.

"I wrote to my father and explained the situation. Obviously, he couldn't get me a job working for the dairy at Sam's, however, he was able to persuade his brother and his brother's wife to help me. Actually, I believe you're familiar with my aunt, Eunice Whitaker? By the scowl on your face, I surmise you know her well," she said laughingly. "Don't mind her. She's just an old bat that likes to stir up trouble. After I arrived, she told the whole village Seth was Paul's. I told her to stop because it wasn't true, but she seems bent on defaming the poor man."

"I see," Liberty said slowly. That was probably the trouble that Paul had been having when he came to see her father. If that was the situation, that was a problem, indeed; no minister could possibly have credibility as a man of God if he had a by-blow especially when the child in question lived in the same district. "Why?" she asked at last.

"I have no idea," Lucy admitted. "At first, I thought it was because she truly believed it. She knew Paul had been sweet on me. But I've told her repeatedly that Sam is Seth's father. Sometimes I think he's the reason she allowed me to come live here. I didn't know he was here, but she did and never said anything to me before I came. I have no idea who she was trying to punish more, him or me." She shrugged. "It really doesn't matter since neither of us goes out of our way to speak to the other."

Liberty felt numb. Lucy claimed Seth wasn't Paul's and she honestly believed her. But was it possible the whole area believed Mrs. Whitaker? There was only one way to find out. "Lucy, has your aunt really told everyone?"

"Yes," Lucy said. "Personally, I'm rather surprised you hadn't heard this already. Now that I think about it though, I shouldn't be surprised. If you'd known, surely you wouldn't have been so accepting of Seth. I just assumed you knew the whole truth…"

"I do now, thank you," she said sincerely.

"You're welcome. I just hope you won't hold it against Seth and me," Lucy said timidly.

"No, not at all," Liberty assured her. "I would be proud to call you a friend. As a friend, I must be honest with you. I'm not sure if

I'll be able to continue to come here or not. Please don't take it personally."

"Of course not," Lucy said with a smile.

Liberty had a lot to contemplate on the way home. A lot of new developments had come to light today. She'd learned Paul truly did have a good heart. If he hadn't, he wouldn't have stood up to his brother or stayed in a tree house during a storm with a scared girl. Nor would he have found her work after she'd rejected him. He'd practically done the same with her. How many times had she treated him poorly, only to have him turn around and pretend it never happened? He'd never tried to seek retaliation against her for all the things she'd done to him. And she knew better than anyone, she'd given him plenty of reasons to.

She shook her head. He was a good man. A good man that found himself in a lot of bad situations, that is. How could she help him? He'd never ask for her help, and he probably didn't want it. But he deserved it. It was the least she could do for him. What could she do to help him gain his credibility back with his congregation? There weren't very many of them as it was, probably because a majority of them no longer attended due to the rumors. Tomorrow was her day with Elizabeth. She would ask her opinion. Elizabeth wasn't a stranger to gossip. She'd have good advice, Liberty was sure of it.

Chapter 18

Paul had tried his best to avoid Liberty over the past week. He'd spent more time locked in his room or study than was good for a body. But it was the only way he could avoid her. After she'd leave to go do whatever she did for the day, he'd emerge, go take care of errands, and then go fishing until it was time for dinner. These days, fishing seemed to be the only thing that took his mind off his troubles. Out by the creek, he could toss his fly into the water and worry about nothing but whether or not a fish would bite.

There was a slight tug on his line. He set the hook and reeled in his catch. Taking a minute to admire the beauty of the fish and remove the hook, he knelt by the water and let the fish go. He glanced at the sky and figured it was time to go back. He still lacked a working watch, so he wasn't positive, but he didn't want to be late and make Liberty wait for him again. She'd be furious. He smiled. Maybe he should toss his line out again. He still hadn't been able to break down that line of defense she'd put in place since they married, not that he'd been trying this past week. He'd hoped if he backed off, she'd come around.

Grabbing his gear so not to agitate Her Majesty, Queen Liberty Grimes, Paul walked back to the house to wash up before dinner. He changed quickly and was walking to the dining room when he heard voices coming from his open study.

"So, you're my brother's wife?" he heard Sam say to Liberty who had her hands behind her back.

"That's correct," she returned stiffly, not meeting his eyes.

Odd that Liberty was so rigid around Sam. Besides the fact that ladies generally giggled and blushed in the Sam's presence, Paul honestly thought he was the only one to provoke such an adverse reaction in Liberty.

"I must say I'm not surprised," Sam said, shaking his head.

Liberty looked like she wanted to chew him up and spit him out. "What is that supposed to mean, Lord Bonnington?" Her voice was strained, almost like she was trying to keep a tight rein on her true emotions.

"Nothing," he said with a nonchalant shrug. "It's just you're rather homely, that's all. But I wouldn't expect anything less from Paul. He never could get a pretty girl," Sam added with a jeering laugh.

Paul wanted to vault into the room and punch his brother for his rude remark, but before he could move, Liberty put him in his place. "There's more to a woman than her looks. Perhaps you'd know that if you did your thinking with the head that's attached to your shoulders."

Paul fought the impulse to laugh. He'd never imagined she was capable of saying such a thing, much less thinking it. For a girl who didn't even know what a man's privates were called only a few weeks ago, she surely surprised him with that remark. Although, it shouldn't have. Last spring, she'd made a comment to him using the word bullocks. At the time, and even now, he'd just assumed she'd overhead a man use the word and didn't know what it actually meant or implied. But where had she picked up the words she'd just said to Sam, he wondered with a frown. He'd have to ask her tonight when he went to her room.

"Is that the way of it, then?" Sam replied with a sneer. "Are you just some common whore he knocked up and felt obligated to marry?"

Liberty gasped as Paul rushed into the room. "That's enough!" he shouted at his brother. "That was uncalled for. Apologize to Liberty, now," he demanded, completely forgetting to address her formally.

Sam laughed. "I see you didn't deny the charge," he said, glancing at Liberty's ample bosom.

"You know as well as I do that it's false. If I wouldn't have a whore when I was sixteen, what makes you think I would have one now? Now apologize," Paul demanded, shooting Liberty an

135

apologetic look for what he'd just revealed.

His brother shook his head. "From what I understand, the problem lay with you that night, brother."

Paul ground his teeth. "Perhaps so. Unlike you, bawdy house diseases don't excite me the way you think they ought."

Sam shrugged. "Whatever you need to tell yourself."

Turning to his wife, Paul said, "Perhaps you'd be more comfortable waiting in the dining room." He noticed she looked past his shoulder as she nodded. After she was gone, he crossed his arms and looked his older brother straight in the eye. "Why are you here? What do you want from me now?"

"Is that how you greet family these days?" Sam asked with a sneer.

"No. Only you. But then again, since you're the only family, close or otherwise, I've got that's still alive, then I guess the answer would be yes," he said mockingly.

"That woman must be good in the dark if you married her. I couldn't imagine leaving a single bedroom candle burning," he said with a shudder. His smile disappeared and his head snapped hard to the right as Paul's fist connected with his jaw sending a loud cracking noise echoing through the air.

"That's my wife you're talking about," Paul barked. "You may be my brother and share the same blood, but I have more loyalty to a snake than I do to you."

Sam rubbed his red and swelling jaw. Then he brought his hand away from the side of his face and looked at the blood from his busted lip that was now on his fingers. He wiped them on his shirt while curling his bleeding lip inside his mouth and sucking off the fresh blood. "I see you still have a stake lodged permanently in your arse. Very well, I shall be on my way," his brother said tersely before stalking out of the room and presumably out of the house.

Paul raked his hand through his hair, ruining the brushing job he'd just done in his room. He walked to the dining room and sat in his place at the far end of the table. To his mind, the seat was far too distant from his wife's, especially tonight. "I'm sorry, Lib—

Mrs. Grimes. My brother is…er…I really don't know how to describe him. He's not a very good man. Please don't take offense to what he said about you."

She stared at her plate. "Please, let's not talk about it," she said softly.

"Very well," he agreed. Perhaps tonight when he read her book, he could explain that he didn't find her unattractive.

The rest of the meal was quieter than normal. Liberty stared at her plate; and try as he might, there was nothing he could think of to say to her.

After dinner was finished, Paul reached for Liberty's wrist as she was walking by him to leave the room. "Are you ready for me to read your entries now, or do you need more time?"

"I'm almost ready," she said evenly. "I was working on it in your study when your brother arrived. I just need another couple of minutes, please."

Paul nodded. "If you don't mind, I'll work on some papers for a bit in there while you finish up."

Together, they walked to his study. Like every other day, he was rather curious about her entries. He'd known she'd make up wild stories when he gave her the book. He'd have been disappointed if she didn't. Since she didn't like to act like herself in real life, at least she could on paper even if that meant fabricating fictitious scenarios and trying to pass them off as the truth. He shook his head. Some of the stories were so ridiculous even his wild imagination couldn't have thought them up. Mrs. Whitaker wouldn't be mending a pair of her husband's drawers at the sewing circle if her life depended on it. Nor would Andrew's mother tell her about the trials of dressing little boys. Now that he thought about it, that one wasn't so far-fetched. He may only know a little about Elizabeth, but he knew enough to know she'd talk of just about anything. However, the one about strange bodily noises and corresponding smells emanating from Mrs. Baker's pew at church last week was doubtful—but humorous all the same. Perhaps one day, she'd learn it took much less time and energy to write a simple, true sentence than it did to concoct a wild tale.

As usual, Paul removed his coat, cravat, and waistcoat and unbuttoned a few buttons before he sat down and dug out one of the notebooks he used to write down his sermon ideas. Likely, Liberty disapproved of his habit of discarding half his clothes after dinner, but she'd never voiced her complaint. Even if she had, he wouldn't have stopped. Life was too short to be formal all the time, especially when he was by himself in his own study.

He sat in his chair and tried to stay focused on what he was doing in order to let Liberty finish her work. His eyes wouldn't behave, and more than once, he caught himself watching Liberty as she wrote. Sam was wrong. She wasn't homely in the least. She may not be as gorgeous as some, but she was still pretty in her own regard. She normally wore her hair in the same bun she wore now, but he'd seen it down when he'd brought her water in the morning. Her hair was long and flowing with slight waves. When she was relaxed, her face looked sweet, almost fragile even. Her lips were full and when she smiled, they curved up in a way that sent an uneasy tendril of warmth spinning in his stomach. Despite her slightly crooked teeth, her true smile was breathtaking. It lit her eyes and changed her face in a way that made it impossible for him to look away.

"I'm done," she said, startling him a bit.

Paul cleared his throat. "That didn't take long."

She shrugged. "As I said, I had been working on it when I was so rudely interrupted by your brother."

He nodded and took the book from her hands. His eyes scanned her first entry and he felt the urge to laugh.

1. Was given an Indian name, Read-a-lot, by young Chief Learn-to-read, then watched him run around the room squawking like he was on the warpath until he shot his poor defenseless mother in order to save me.

Paul glanced up at her. She was biting her lip and looking at the bookcase beyond his left shoulder. He turned his eyes back to the paper.

2. New reading material arrived for the literacy group.

He'd been wondering when, or if, he'd see that entry. At first, he'd thought she might come home and be in a temper about it. Then, when she'd neither severed his head from his body nor written about it, he'd assumed Mrs. Weslen had disposed of the books with the assumption that nobody would want to learn to read from such a boring primer. He didn't look at her again before skipping down to the number three. A few sentences were scrolled with a line scratched through them. Reading them carefully, he could tell she'd written some wild tale about watching Mrs. Siddons chase a chicken around the yard until she slipped in a puddle and fell in the mud. Now *that* was a falsehood if he'd ever read one.

Looking a little farther down on the page, he saw she had written another number three and what she'd written brought a smile to his own face.

3. Watched from the hall as Paul punched his wretched brother in the face.

His heart squeezed in his chest. "Why did you use my Christian name?" he asked, pleased that finally, after all this time, she'd referred to him as Paul.

Flippantly, Liberty answered, "Someone told me it was rude not to call a person by what they've asked you to."

Paul chuckled. "Wise person," he mused. "Does this mean I may call you Liberty?"

She took a deep breath. He could see she was warring with the decision. "If you must."

"Liberty," he said, catching her attention. "You do know why I hit him, don't you?"

"Because he insulted you," she said flatly.

"No. Because he insulted *you*," he corrected, getting up from his chair and coming to stand in front of her. He leaned back on the edge of his desk and crossed his arms casually. "Liberty, look at me. The things he said to you were purposely cruel. He's angry with me, and he said those things to provoke me. Do you understand? They're not true."

She looked at him curiously before shaking her head. "They are true. I'm not attractive. I know that. He only spoke the truth."

"No he didn't," Paul countered, his voice full of conviction. He took her hands in his. "You are a very attractive young lady."

She shook her head again. "No, I'm not."

"Yes. You. Are." Each word its own sentence, final.

She looked at him disbelievingly. "You must be the only one to think so."

"Who cares if I am?" he countered flippantly then his tone turned serious. "I'm your husband. I'm the only one who matters."

"Thank you," she said, after a few minutes of staring at him as if she didn't quite believe the words that had tumbled from his mouth.

"You're welcome. Now, on a less serious note, I have a question for you." He looked at her to see her nod her agreement for him to ask his question. "Where did you learn that set down you leveled on Sam?"

Her face turned crimson. "You heard that?"

"Yes."

"Oh." She lowered her gaze to where his hands were still holding hers. "I...um...I heard Elizabeth say something to that effect once about the man who runs the bookshop."

"Do you know what it means?" he asked, although he could tell by the look on her face, she had absolutely no idea.

Still blushing, she said, "I imagine it has to do with a man's..." she trailed off and sent a pointed glance toward his waist. Her blush suggested she was more embarrassed to try to guess at the right term again in his presence rather than the actual topic.

"You're correct," he said softly. Then, before he could stop himself, he gave her a wolfish grin and said, "Would you like me to explain it to you?"

***

Liberty's face flamed and her eyes widened. But her reaction was not wholly due to his words. That devastating smile on his lips coupled with the way his thumbs were stroking the back of her knuckles were causing a stir of emotion she'd only felt one other time: when he'd kissed her last week.

She moistened her lips. "No. I think I have a good enough idea." She had a good memory and she definitely remembered what she'd seen two months ago. She may be a virgin who didn't even know the proper name for such parts, but she could puzzle it out well enough to have a fairly accurate idea. Now, if only he'd stop tenderly stroking her hand, she could catch her breath and escape before she entertained further thoughts of her building desire for this man.

"Very well," he said. His grin vanished and it was hard to tell if he looked disappointed or relieved. "You do know that you can talk to me about anything, don't you?"

"I truly don't need it explained to me," she protested, pulling her hands away from his searing grasp.

Paul flicked his wrist dismissively. "I'm not talking about that anymore. I just wanted to let you know that anytime you want to talk about absolutely anything, you're welcome to come to me."

Touched, Liberty said, "Thank you. I shall keep that in mind."

"Please do. We may not have the same closeness that your sister and Andrew share, but I'm your husband and I would like you to feel comfortable talking to me. It doesn't matter what it's about. All right?"

"All right," she agreed. Thinking this was a good time to leave before she said or did something to embarrass herself, like ask if he wished they were as close as Brooke and Andrew, she grabbed her journal and quill and walked out the door.

She walked down the hallway and was about to step onto the first stair when the sight of Paul's open room caught her eye. She'd decided before dinner that she wasn't going to retaliate against him for burning her books. Yes, it had hurt to see them catch fire. And yes, she had believed he had done it with malicious intent. But now, more than a week later, she was having a hard time hanging onto her anger about it. Anyway, it wouldn't solve anything to purposely hurt him because he'd hurt her. He knew what he'd done had hurt her, ruining something of his wasn't going to bring her books back. Harmless retaliation was one thing, but she was learning heartlessness was quite another. And he didn't deserve that.

Seeing his bedchamber door open and knowing he was tucked away in his study for a while, she couldn't resist the urge to go inside and take a look around. She hardly knew the stranger she was living with. What better way to find out more about him than to see his room, she convinced herself as she tiptoed to the open room. She was only going to have a quick peek, nothing more. After casting a quick glance back down the hall to the closed door of his study, she hurried past the threshold.

His room was much larger than hers. The bed was at least twice the size and with the hard angles and sharp edges carved into the wood, it gave off the image of pure masculinity. Both his counterpane and pillows were royal blue. A small blue square throw pillow with gold fringe around the edges sat in the middle of the bed.

A scuffed up wardrobe was in the far corner by the window. The right door to the wardrobe was slightly ajar. Liberty peeked inside and let her eyes roam over his neatly pressed clothes. With shaky hands, she grabbed the knobs on one of the drawers at the bottom. Inside, the drawer was filled with neck cloths. Closing it carefully, she debated whether she wanted to see what was in the other drawer. After only a few seconds hesitation, she grabbed the knobs and pulled it open to find rolled up stockings and several pairs of his neatly folded drawers. She quickly shut the drawer with an abrupt snap and turned her eyes to see what was on the back wall. Ah, the vanity table. That would be a safe place to look around.

She noticed his pitcher had a slight crack in the handle and she frowned when she ran her finger along the edge of the basin and felt the rough edge that was pitted with chips. Her attention was then caught by his shiny shaving razor sitting on top of the strop. Just behind his shaving supplies was a small circular mirror and next to that was a little white dish. Curiosity piqued, she pulled the dish closer.

Two cravat pins, one emerald and the other ruby, winked at her from the dish. Right next to them, was a flat circular object. Her slender fingers plucked up the disc. As soon as it was in her hand she realized what it was: his pocket watch. She turned it over and saw a crest she recognized but couldn't place. He'd told her the day he was late arriving to the luncheon at Alex's that his pocket watch was broken, but she hadn't believed him. Actually, she'd been willing to believe the worst of him ever since the first time they'd met and, after knowing her for a whole fifteen seconds, he'd asked her to call him by his Christian name and bored her all through dinner. There was only one way to know for sure if he'd been lying to her that day, or if perhaps, as usual, she'd been too hard on him.

Holding the bottom with one hand, she used the other to work the clasp. She soon found there was no need to have bothered with the clasp. It wasn't latched. Flipping the lid open, she let out a gasp. He had not been lying. The watch was beyond broken. It was in complete disrepair. Not only did the clasp not fit together any longer, the hinge was out of alignment, and the lid literally came off when she flipped it open. But the most startling and convincing proof was right there on the watch face. The glass was not only cracked, it was shattered. Behind it, she could see the second hand wasn't ticking. Having seen men wind their watches before, she knew it was possible it might work if she wound the stem. She highly doubted it though and didn't want to even try for fear of making it worse.

She lightly ran her thumb over shards of glass that were barely held in place and wondered what he'd done that caused his watch to break. Had he fallen from a horse with it in his pocket? Had he accidentally stepped on it? Had he dropped it on the hardwood floor?

Suddenly, the blood drained from her face and her heart

started pounding so hard she thought it was going to burst out of her chest as she realized exactly what had happened. He hadn't dropped it on the hardwood floor, *she* had. She knew she'd seen that crest before and now she knew where. The night she'd stolen into his room and taken his clothes, his watch had been on top of the towel that was on the stool. Afraid she'd make a noise and draw his attention if she put it back down after she'd grabbed the towel, she'd just kept it in her arms along with his towel and clothes. Then, when she'd so carelessly thrown everything across the room, the watch had gone, too. It must have been at the bottom if it hit hard enough to break this badly.

Why hadn't he ever said anything? The watch clearly was a family heirloom; it had to have been important to him. The answer to her unspoken question came to her quickly enough. He hadn't said anything to her because there was nothing to say. She wouldn't have been able to do anything about it. Furthermore, he probably doubted she'd even care. And he'd been right to assume such, she admitted to herself. Her previous actions toward him had been as he'd once accurately described, cold and callous. He had no reason to believe she'd have felt any remorse for her actions.

But why hadn't he fixed it? He'd been late, or close to it, so many times in the past few months it was obviously creating a problem for him not to have it working.

An idea formed in her brain, and a small smile took her trembling lips. She could fix it for him. She'd been saving all the money she'd gotten from working as a companion. It wasn't much, but perhaps it would be enough so she could fix his watch and give it back to him as a way to make amends.

With a plan in place, she quickly slipped the watch into her bodice and fled the room.

Chapter 19

"I need to ask you for advice," Liberty said as she swung open the door to the drawing room of Elizabeth's cottage.

"While I'd love to be of assistance, I doubt it was me from whom you were seeking advice," drawled a deep baritone voice across the room.

Snapping her head in the direction from which the familiar voice had come, Liberty saw Benjamin Collins, Duke of Gateway, lounging on a settee and basking in the sunlight streaming through the window. "Oh, I'm sorry, Your Grace. I've become quite friendly with Elizabeth and she was expecting me today. I'm a bit early. Perhaps I shall come back later."

Gateway shrugged his shoulders. "She'll be right back. She went to retrieve something from another room."

Liberty nodded. "All right, I'll wait." She took a seat on another settee and stared at the toe of her slipper as it made lazy figure eights on the carpet in front of her.

"What kind of advice do you plan to ask Lizzie for, Mrs. Grimes?" Gateway asked curiously.

Her head snapped up at his question. He was the last person she wanted to tell about Paul's problem having to contend with his brother's by-blow being rumored to be his. Gateway was a snake. He'd spread the rumor far and wide without a thought to Paul or his future. In fact, he'd probably do it gladly and add a few extra details, too. Last spring, he'd tried to create a scandal to shame her family. If he still had that goal in mind, he'd surely use this as ammunition.

Swallowing a lump in her throat, she tried to think of something to tell him. When the deafening silence was broken by a chime from the clock that hung right behind her as it struck the hour mark, Liberty remembered that Paul's watch just so happened to be in her reticule. "Actually, you might be a better person to ask," she said with a weak smile. She reached into her reticule and withdrew the broken watch. "I fear I dropped my husband's watch on the floor. I would like to get it repaired."

Gateway held his hand out to her. Liberty suppressed a groan as she stood up and walked over to hand it to him.

Sitting up, he opened it and let out a low whistle. "Wow, you really bungled this one."

She bit her lip and waited for him to finish his appraisal of the ruined timepiece.

"Dropped this on the floor, did you? Looks more like you slammed it," he said, twisting the stem.

Liberty shifted her gaze to the floor causing Gateway to shake his head and chuckle. Clearly there was no way she could deny what she'd done.

The duke grabbed a rubbish bin that was under the table at the end of the settee then banged the watch upside down on his palm. When all the glass fell out, he dumped it into the bin.

"Stop!" Liberty squealed, trying to grab the watch from him.

Gateway pulled the hand that held the watch out of her reach. "It's already broken. It's not going to make a bit of difference if the glass is there or not. I just want to touch the hands to see if they can spin."

"What difference does that make?" Liberty demanded. "Just spin that stem." She pointed to the stem she knew was used to set the time.

"I already did," Gateway explained, piercing her with his cool blue eyes. "It didn't move the hands. But if I can move the hands by touching them, then there's hope the gears aren't bent."

She had a vague idea what gears were. He obviously had a better idea since he seemed to know what he was doing. Her eyes left where his hands were working on Paul's watch and traveled to his face. Something was different. She hadn't seen Gateway for some time, but there was definitely something different about his face. She just couldn't put her finger on it. Her eyes roved up and down his face several times before she registered what was altered.

It was his nose. It looked different. Not a lot, just enough to catch notice.

"You just now noticed that," Gateway said roughly, making her realize she'd spoken her thoughts out loud.

"I'm sorry, Your Grace. I didn't mean to say that," she said, embarrassed.

Gateway gave her a slim smile. "A nose for a nose," he said simply.

"Pardon?"

"My nose, I broke Townson's more than ten years ago, and he broke mine in return. Took him a long time to get around to it," he muttered, still toying with the watch.

"Was it after he married Brooke?" Liberty heard herself ask without prior thought.

"Yes, the next day, in fact."

"I see," she said slowly. "You two got into a fight about him not shaming her and sending us home."

"No. Actually, I think the punches were thrown because I said some rather insulting things about her." He flashed her a wry smile. "You're in luck, the hands spin. The watch isn't as hopeless as it first looked. I know a jeweler in London who could fix this easily enough. It might take a few days and it won't be cheap."

She'd wanted to ask him if he still was trying to bring her family shame and why he'd even wanted to in the first place, but his announcement of knowing someone who could fix the watch erased all previous thoughts. "Wonderful!" She jumped up and scurried to the writing desk in the corner of the room. Pulling out a piece of parchment and grabbing a quill, she turned to face the duke. "What's the man's name and address?"

"Mr. Holler. I don't know his address," he said, closing the watch the best he could. "He's on High Street, next to Miles Bakery. He's pretty easy to find. However, you'll not get an appointment."

"And, why not?"

Gateway chuckled. "He only does business with titled gentlemen."

Liberty fought to keep a sound of frustration from escaping her lips.

"I'll tell you what. I'm on my way back to London today. How about if I have it done for you?"

She bit her lip. Could she trust him? Just because he'd been nice to her today, didn't mean he'd do the right thing. But why wouldn't he, she argued with herself. There was nothing for him to gain by keeping it.

As if sensing her inner struggle, Gateway said, "I see you don't trust me. And, you're right not to. Hmm. How about if I give you something of mine to hold onto until I bring this back?"

"All right," Liberty agreed. "What do you have with you?"

He dug into his pockets. "I'd give you my own pocket watch, but I fear I'll need it," he said, laying the contents of his pockets all over the table and making all sorts of noise as he did so. The man had all kinds of odds and ends in there. He carried a knife, a watch, a vast array of coins, a few keys, a deck of cards and several other things she couldn't even identify. "Ah, what about this?" he asked, holding up a little black box.

Liberty walked across the room. "What is it?"

"Open it," he answered simply, shoving all his things back into his pockets.

Slowly, her fingers opened the black velvet box and her eyes almost popped out when she saw the prize that was resting inside. "I can't hold onto this," she said with nervous excitement.

"Why not?" he asked in a tone so casual one might think they were discussing something as trivial as the weather and not an expensive piece of jewelry.

"Because, first of all, it's most clearly a betrothal ring and I am not your intended. And second, the value far surpasses Paul's watch." Though she was verbally refusing to keep the ring, she couldn't take her eyes off of it. The center stone was a large, round diamond and two sapphires were positioned on either side of it. The ring wasn't fashioned from the typical yellow gold. Instead it was silver or, perhaps, white gold. All along the band was an intricate design of soft swirls and swoops.

"Mr. Grimes might place the same value on his watch that I place on that ring: priceless."

"Are you getting betrothed?" she asked, closing the box.

"I hope," he said easily, but his face didn't look so sure. "I was bringing it to London to get the setting fixed. If you look closely, you'll see one of the prongs is broken."

"If you're planning to get engaged, don't you think you'll need this back soon?" she asked, extending the box in his direction.

He pushed her hand back. "You hold onto it. I'm not planning to ask for a while. I have plenty of time to get it fixed."

"Are you sure? Don't you think the young lady in question will mind that her ring was in my possession for a while?"

He shrugged. "I don't think she'll mind. And if she does, I'll just make it clear the ring was still mine at the time."

"Thank you," she said quietly, tucking the ring into her reticule. "Please let me know how much it costs to fix the watch. I insist on paying."

"And I insist on it, too. My generosity doesn't extend that far," he told her evenly, slipping Paul's watch into his pocket.

Gateway spent the rest of the day with Liberty and Elizabeth. Elizabeth vaguely explained that the two of them were close and had a common family tie, but Liberty got the impression she didn't wish to discuss it, so she kept her questions to herself.

That night as she dressed for bed, she had only one regret about the day: she hadn't been able to ask Elizabeth's advice regarding Paul's reputation. Reminding herself that Gateway was going to London and wouldn't likely be at Elizabeth's two days hence, she decided she'd ask Elizabeth then.

She crawled into bed, pulled up the covers and felt satisfied that at least one of her two goals was as good as accomplished.

Chapter 20

Liberty wanted to pull her hair out when she was awakened by sun streaming through the window, signaling the start of a new day. It wasn't that she had a desire to sleep the day away. It was that she dreaded the miserable Mrs. Whitaker and her dratted gossip circle. And just her luck, today the circle was meeting at her house, which meant she couldn't beg off like she wanted to. The sewing itself didn't bother her one bit, she actually liked that part, it was the company that was miserable.

Gritting her teeth, she got up and bathed. She dressed in a pink day dress and went down to breakfast. Paul was already waiting for her. They exchanged pleasantries and ate while she prattled on about slipper heel repairs. Ever since she'd taken—or stolen, if one wanted to be blunt—his watch, she'd been nervous around him and had begun to incessantly talk, so he couldn't ask her questions. So far, it had been working; she just hoped Gateway could get the watch back to her soon.

In between inane comments, she inhaled her food in the most unladylike fashion and excused herself to go wait in her room until it was time for the ladies to arrive.

Bored, she started to read one of the books Elizabeth had loaned her. Stretching out on her bed, she read and read until she was startled out of her reading trance by the distant sound of a horse whinny. She glanced at the clock on her credenza and sprang to her feet when she saw she was twenty minutes late to host the sewing circle. Why hadn't Mrs. Siddons alerted her?

Dismissing the thought, she flew down the stairs and dashed in the direction of the drawing room. Slowing her steps as she got closer so not to appear discomposed, she heard the waspish voice of Mrs. Whitaker, "Perhaps she's fled now that she knows about his scandalous past."

"His scandalous past?" Mrs. Vase said dubiously. "She's no angel, either. Didn't you read the article in the *Daily News* about her trying to seduce him?"

Liberty's heart started to pound. These women had known about that this whole time?

"Seems to me she doesn't have what it takes to carry it off," a young woman who was falsely named Miss Prudence Sweet piped in. "So many other women have been successful."

"Surely you don't wonder why she was unsuccessful." Mrs. Whitaker replied. "It's because she doesn't have what it takes to get a man interested. She's as plain as the side of a stable. Any man would struggle having to bed her."

Willing herself to stay calm because it would only make matters worse if she didn't, Liberty reasoned it was best to confront the group straight on rather than run back upstairs as she wanted. She took the final steps that brought her into the room. She quickly noticed Mrs. Jenkins wasn't present—which accounted for the gossip. That didn't matter though. She was not going to take this, and in her own home, no less. "Hasn't anyone ever told you it's rude to talk about your hostess behind her back?" she asked as evenly as she could. "Furthermore," she said, ignoring their shocked gasps. "My private life with Mr. Grimes isn't any of your concern." She sent each of them an accusing look.

"Perhaps then, you should tell your husband not to make a private thing so public," Mrs. Whitaker said sharply.

Stung, Liberty turned her gaze to the older woman and said, "I was not aware my husband spoke of our private life to you. Are you two great friends, then?"

Mrs. Whitaker snorted. "Hardly; and no, your husband doesn't speak about his private life with you. He doesn't have to. It seems he has had a 'private life' with plenty of women 'round here."

"You had better check your facts, madam," Liberty snapped coldly, surprising herself she'd spoken out that way.

"And you better get checked for the pox," Mrs. Whitaker snapped back. "That husband of yours has more bastards than any man I've ever heard of. At least a dozen that I know of, and who knows how many he has stashed somewhere we don't know about."

A dozen? Did she really just say a dozen? "That's not true," Liberty protested hotly, shooting her a cold stare. Inside, she felt her world crumbling around her ears. Was it possible there were so many? Lucy had said Sam was the Seth's father, but what of the others? Could Sam have fathered that many, or had a few of them been Paul's? He's a vicar, she reminded herself. He didn't have any by-blows. He couldn't. Could he?

"I assure you, it's true," Mrs. Vase said, breaking into Liberty's thoughts. "That man might hide behind the cloth, but we're all sinners. And that man's sins litter the countryside."

"I don't believe it," Liberty said defensively, crossing her arms.

"Of course not," Mrs. Whitaker said, clucking her tongue. "No woman wants to believe her husband has an addiction to fleshy pleasures."

"Nor does any woman want to acknowledge she can't keep her husband satisfied," Mrs. Vase added smugly.

Not for the first time in her life, Liberty wished she could hold her breath, make a wish, and magically be transported just about anywhere else. "I'd like you all to leave now," she said through clenched teeth.

"With pleasure," Mrs. Whitaker said as she sprang off the settee.

Liberty cast her an icy glare, not wanting to respond to her comment.

"You, madam, are very naïve," Mrs. Lewis said, entering the conversation for the first time.

"She's right. Perhaps when you see poor Mrs. Whitaker's niece, Lucy, in town, you should ask her about her son," Miss Sweet said before casting 'poor Mrs. Whitaker' an apologetic glance.

"Paul isn't Seth's father, Sam is," Liberty burst out before she knew what she was saying.

"You two talked?" Mrs. Whitaker asked sharply. "It's not

every woman who talks to her husband's mistresses, you know. But then again, I wouldn't expect anything more from you."

"She had to inspect the competition," Mrs. Vase taunted cruelly.

"I was not 'inspecting the competition' as you suggest. She approached me and explained the situation," Liberty said coolly.

"Did she now?" Mrs. Whitaker asked acidly.

"Yes, she did. She said Sam was the father and that *you're* the one who insists otherwise. However, I'm inclined to believe her over you since she was present at the conception, not you."

Mrs. Whitaker harrumphed and said, "Of course she told you that, he paid her to."

"Excuse me?" Liberty squeaked.

"Once we're gone, perhaps you should go check your husband's ledger and see just how many he's supporting," Mrs. Vase said with a cackle.

"Be sure to look for Clare Goode, Sarah Forrest and Diane Rivers," Mrs. Lewis said haughtily, standing up with Mrs. Whitaker.

"And don't forget Mary Osborn, Michelle Thomas and Glenda Smythe," added Mrs. Whitaker airily.

"We could be here all day naming names, ladies. Just let her put the pieces together on her own," Mrs. Vase said, gathering her sewing materials.

Liberty stepped back against the wall next to the doorjamb and waited for the women to leave. There was nothing else she wanted to say. She may not have always thought great things about Paul, but she'd been wrong. He was a good man and he deserved better than to be talked about this way. Unfortunately, when she'd tried to intervene, she'd only made it worse. The best she could do now was to wait quietly until they left.

Once all the gossipmongers were gone, Liberty went to Paul's study. Angry tears that had formed at their words were now streaming down her face. How could anyone be so heartless as to insult a woman's husband in her presence? She sniffled and swiped at the tears on her cheeks. She'd thought it was bad when Lucy mentioned everyone believed Seth to be Paul's son; but to know some people thought he had a dozen by-blows was horrible. How had she been living with him in this village so long and never heard a word of it before, she wondered. She rolled her eyes when the obvious answer popped into her head. Besides the sewing circle, she wasn't involved with a lot of gossips.

At church, no one dared to gossip to her. Elizabeth, for all her sharp remarks and crude language, refused to speak about anything she didn't know to be fact. The old and sick people she brought meals to likely hadn't heard of it before, and if they had, they wouldn't want to tell Liberty for fear she wouldn't visit them again. As for the illegitimate illiterates, it was likely they also feared she'd stop helping.

She sighed. Mrs. Vase suggested she could check Paul's ledger and see records of his payments to these women. Her confidence high, she leapt off her seat and went to the shelf where Paul kept his ledgers.

Mrs. Vase was right about one thing: if Paul had fathered any children, he'd pay to support them. But that didn't matter because Mrs. Vase was wrong and these dozen illegitimate children she'd spoken of didn't exist. She had to be wrong, Liberty convinced herself, strengthening her resolve as she reached the shelf with the ledgers. His ledger would be the greatest piece of evidence she'd have in proving Paul hadn't fathered any illegitimate children. And when she found there were no entries showing money being paid to women, she'd shove it in Mrs. Vase's face and make her apologize. Surely, all those women would acknowledge the truth after Liberty presented it to them.

Plucking down the ledger farthest to the right, Liberty hugged it close and headed to his desk. She opened the book and realized it started in 1812, last year. No matter. If Mrs. Vase were to be believed, he'd have been supporting those women at the time.

She ran her fingers down the entries, scanning over different household expenditures. Her eyes flew to the right out of curiosity when she saw the words "salary" on one line and "deposit" on the next. Ever since they'd married, she'd been curious as to how much he earned. It obviously couldn't be that high if he still hadn't felt the need to give her an allowance. She scowled when she ran her finger along the line for his salary and saw there was a relatively impressive number. She hadn't realized that vicars made two hundred fifty pounds a month. Not that it was a fortune, but it was enough that he could have spared a bit for her allowance, she thought with a hint of annoyance.

Moving to the next line, her breath caught when she read the amount on the line for his mysterious deposit. "A thousand pounds," she squeaked, shaking her head. "You'd think with that kind of money he could afford to give me *some*." Perhaps it was a one-time thing, she told herself. But when she quickly flipped the page, and the next, and the next, she realized it was not a one-time thing, but a monthly thing. "What a beast!"

Deciding she'd definitely confront him about this later, she went back to the business of checking his account books for illegitimate children. Her fingers skimmed down the page as her eyes quickly read the words. She nearly reached the bottom of the page when her heart sank.

On the third to the last entry was a series of initials: LW, MO, CG, MT, RT, LC...her eyes looked away. She couldn't force herself to keep reading. She recognized some of those initials from what the sewing ladies had told her. Fighting a new wave of angry tears, she forced her eyes to look back at the list. Making her watering eyes focus and her trembling finger to meet the page, she slowly counted the pairs of initials. Each time, touching them to make sure they were real, and counted. "One, two, three," she said softly under her breath. When she reached the end, she sighed, "Fourteen."

He had fourteen illegitimate children! She could hardly believe her eyes. Slamming the book shut, she haphazardly replaced it and fled to the comfort of her room, where her roiling stomach gave over to nausea and she sat sick and trembling on the edge of her bed.

Chapter 21

Paul swung down off Stallion, his stallion, as he approached the stable. Holding onto the bridle, he led Stallion into his stall for the night. After a quick brush down, he grabbed the contents from inside his saddlebag that was hanging on a post before heading to the house.

Liberty had been avoiding him ever since she'd met Sam two days ago. He was sure of it. Since that night, she'd dominated the conversation every time they'd spoken. Which, in and of itself, wasn't a bad thing, but the things she had chosen to talk about were things he was absolutely certain she didn't have any more interest in than he did. Perhaps he should try talking to her again. A slow smile spread across his lips. The last time they'd talked about her conversation with Sam, he'd almost kissed her again.

Her face had looked so beautiful when she looked up at him after he'd grasped her hands. He'd even taken delight in the shiver he felt run through her hands when he started to stroke her knuckles. Then, emboldened by her reaction, he'd opened his mouth and ruined it all by asking if she wanted an explanation. She hadn't pulled her hands away immediately, so he kept stroking them while he talked, but he knew she'd never let him kiss her after what he'd said. Ever since then, she'd been colder and more elusive than before.

With a sigh, he reached his hand into his pocket for the umpteenth time in the past two days only to feel lint. That was another thing he'd lost that day, his watch. He thought he'd put it on his vanity when he'd changed after fishing, but it was nowhere to be found. To no avail, he'd spent the better part of yesterday searching the creek bank for it. Oh well, it had to turn up eventually; nobody around here would have any use for a broken watch. Even he'd found less sentimental value in it now that it was broken. But that had more to do with who had broken it, and why, not necessarily the watch itself.

Thoughts of his watch gave way to worry when he saw Mrs. Siddons come outside to greet him. "Mr. Grimes, Mr. Grimes," she shouted, running in his direction.

"Is everything all right?"

"It's Mrs. Grimes. She's sick something awful, sir," she exclaimed as she impatiently tried to hurry Paul into the house.

"What do you mean?" he asked cautiously. She'd been fine just last night. What happened?

"She has some sort of stomach ailment, sir," the housekeeper said with conviction. "She's been shooting the cat all day."

Paul's eyes widened. No matter that he'd never heard Mrs. Siddons talk this way before, he was more worried about what it meant. How had Liberty suddenly gotten so violently ill that she was casting up her accounts? "Is she in her room?" he asked hoarsely.

"Yes," Mrs. Siddons said, moving out of the way so he could go up the stairs.

Outside her room, he knocked on the door and when he didn't hear a reply, he slowly opened it.

Liberty was asleep in her bed. Her flowing hair was tossed over her pillows and she still wore her day dress. Her skin was whiter than his whitest handkerchief and the skin around her eyes looked puffy and slightly red. He walked up to her bed and slowly sank down onto the mattress. When she stirred, he asked, "How are you feeling?"

Her eyelids snapped open, revealing two bloodshot hazel eyes. "Go away, please," she said at last. Her eyes closed tightly and her hands clenched into fists. A moment later, a fat tear squeezed through her eyelids.

Using the pad of his index finger, Paul wiped the tear away. What would make her cry? Was she embarrassed that he was seeing her when she was sick and vulnerable? He got up as gently as he could so not to shake the bed and walked down to the end of the bed where her covers were pooled by her bare feet. He gingerly grabbed one of her ankles and lifted it off the covers. While his hands still held her foot, he gently massaged it. He pressed his thumbs into the bottom of her foot and moved them in a rhythmic, circular pattern moving from her heel to her arch to her toes and then back again. When he was finished with her first foot, he put it back down and tucked it under the covers before grabbing the other and doing the same.

When he was done rubbing her feet and had tucked them both under the counterpane, he grabbed the counterpane and dragged it up to her chin. Settling it around her neck, he reached up and swept back the unruly hank of hair that had fallen into Liberty's face before leaning down and brushing a kiss on her cheek and whispering, "I hope you feel better soon."

***

His kiss was her undoing. As soon as Paul left the room, the tears started all over again. How could he be so kind and compassionate to her and yet be such a scoundrel at the same time?

When she'd finally cried what she hoped was her last tear, it was well after midnight and she was well and truly sick. She'd never been given to tears as much as she had since marrying him. It seemed he was able to stir emotions in her easier than a cook stirring a pot of soup. What gave him this power? How was it that he could control her emotions so thoroughly?

She fell asleep pondering the reasons and when she woke up the following day, she was no closer to her answer than she was the day before.

Today was Friday, her day with Elizabeth. There was no way she could go spend the day with Andrew's mother in her current state. She rolled over and resettled herself in the pillows. She'd just wait for Mrs. Siddons to come up and ask her to send Elizabeth a note making her excuses.

The following week passed quicker than any week in her life. She stayed abed for seven days straight. And then on the eighth, she got an annoyed visitor.

"Liberty Grimes," Elizabeth said, bursting past a startled Mrs. Siddons. "If you have no intention of acting as my companion anymore, I would at least appreciate the courtesy of you telling me to my face."

Liberty shook her head. "I'm sorry, Elizabeth. I've been sick. Truly, I have."

Elizabeth eyed her askance. "Fatigue?"

Liberty nodded.

"Nausea?"

Liberty nodded.

"Are you hungry?"

Liberty nodded.

"Been crying a lot recently?"

Liberty nodded.

Elizabeth smiled knowingly at her. "In the family way, eh?"

"No!" Liberty shouted, coming to her feet. "That is, no," she said, much softer this time.

"No?" Elizabeth asked, cocking her brow the same way her son was prone to do.

"No," she said firmly, crawling out of bed. "It's not possible," she mumbled after she sat up. "Paul and I, well, we…um….we have an in- name-only marriage."

"Ah," Elizabeth said as understanding dawned. "Sometimes, I wish that was the way of mine. But, then I remember I wouldn't have had my son."

Liberty stared at Elizabeth. The woman could be so blunt sometimes.

"It was a beastly experience," she said, waving her hand. "Thank goodness, I only suffered the travesty once." She shuddered. "Some women, like your sister, seem to enjoy the activity, but I did not."

"Perhaps it depends on the partner," Liberty offered weakly. She knew Brooke loved Andrew more than most wives love their husbands, and the love was most clearly returned. Maybe that was why they both enjoyed bedroom activities so well.

"Of that," Elizabeth said, her voice full of conviction, "I have no doubt. My husband was atrocious. That and he had no great affection for me."

"Exactly so," Liberty agreed, wanting this uncomfortable conversation to end soon.

"The man treated me like I was a broodmare and he was the stallion only doing the deed to achieve his goal: an heir." The hint of disgust in her voice spoke volumes about how much she detested her late husband. "I doubt he even knew how to treat a lady in the bedroom. Brooke should be thankful that, even for all of his peccadilloes, at least Andrew learned to treat a wife better than a tavern wench."

"Peccadilloes?" Liberty repeated in confusion.

"You know, the wild oats that all young men seem so interested in sowing before settling down. While we women are expected to be sweet and innocent when we marry, men are supposed to have had past sins and a lot of experience," she explained with a wink.

Liberty's face burned. What would Elizabeth think if she knew just how extensively Paul had sown his oats?

"I can just be thankful Andrew didn't give me any bastard grandchildren," she continued without seeming to sense Liberty's unease. "I must confess, being a bastard myself, I don't know that I could have not gone to see them."

Liberty's jaw almost hit the floor.

"Which part shocked you?" Elizabeth asked, her eyes twinkling with laughter.

"Both," she said, ashamed she'd been so obvious.

"At least we can be thankful that one of those two situations was avoided," Elizabeth said, coming to sit by Liberty. "You don't look sick, you know?"

"I was," she said weakly, looking at her hands.

"And now?" Elizabeth asked, a hundred questions in her eyes.

Liberty looked at her friend. She could trust Elizabeth with anything. She'd proven to be a great friend to her these past few weeks. Taking a deep breath, she said, "Apparently Paul wasn't quite as responsible as Andrew."

Understanding lit Elizabeth's eyes. "So you've found out your husband has a bastard and you're embarrassed," she mused, her voice not condemning or unkind.

Liberty nodded. "Actually, there's more than one," she said numbly.

"How many?" Elizabeth asked, rubbing her hand up and down Liberty's back in a motherly way.

"Fourteen," she mumbled.

Elizabeth's hand paused for a split-second before continuing on its trek down Liberty's back. "Did I hear you correctly? Did you say four?"

"No," Liberty answered, shaking her head. "Four*teen*."

"Oh. Perhaps it's best you have a marriage of convenience," she added dryly a minute later.

Liberty smiled at Elizabeth's jest. "I just cannot face him. That's why I've been holing myself up in my room."

"I understand."

"He comes several times a day and tries to talk to me, but I just can't bear to look at him. He tries to be sweet by fluffing my pillows or rubbing my back and he brings me flowers and books. And all I can do is wonder if this is how he seduced all those other women. As soon as he leaves, I pull the petals off the flowers and shove the books under my bed." A new wave of tears started to form and she tried to stave them off. She didn't want Elizabeth to bear witness to her fit of vapors. But the inevitable happened anyway, and a few tears slipped out.

Elizabeth wrapped her in a hug.

"I'm sorry I've become a watering pot," she said, swiping at the offending tears.

"It's all right," Elizabeth assured her. "In light of this unsettling news, I doubt this will be of any comfort." She withdrew Paul's pocket watch from her reticule.

Liberty's traitorous hand reached out and picked it up. She struggled for a few minutes to snap it open, noting that the latch was most definitely fixed. When she finally got it to flip open, she was also pleased to find the hinge worked and the lid stayed on.

She looked at the face and watched in awe as the second hand ticked off the seconds, and the minute hand followed suit once the second hand reached the top. She flipped the lid closed and ran her thumb over the gemstones and crest that was etched on the top. "Tell His Grace thank you for me when you take his ring back to him," she said, gulping past the new round of emotion that was tearing through her. She'd wanted this watch to make amends for their past, and now she couldn't give it to him without feeling there was still a wedge between them.

She stood up to go get Gateway's ring when Elizabeth's gentle hand encircled her wrist. "Why don't you tell him yourself," she said with a smile.

"He's not here, is he?"

"No. But he'll be at my cottage tomorrow and so will you."

"Oh," Liberty said dumbly. Apparently, Elizabeth wasn't going to let her wallow in self-pity any longer.

"Now, pack your things. You're coming to stay with me," Elizabeth said authoritatively.

Liberty smiled. She wasn't going to argue with that pronouncement. It seemed like a good idea to her.

She quickly packed up her things and scribbled a note to Paul informing him of her new living arrangements.

***

Another week later

"We have to do something," Brooke said to her husband as she brushed her long brown hair.

"Do something?" he echoed, coming up behind her and taking the brush from her.

"Yes, about Liberty and Paul. She cannot live out the rest of her days in your mother's cottage," she said as he gently pulled the brush through her hair.

"No," Andrew agreed, setting the brush down. "But I don't think it's our place to get involved, Brooke."

She looked into his dark blue eyes, searching their depths for a simple signal of understanding. He knew as well as she did that something was not right between the two. Liberty hadn't said a word, good or bad, about the man since she'd arrived. That alone was worrisome. In the past, she hadn't given a second thought before flaying him with her words—no matter who was present, including the poor man himself.

"I know you don't want to get involved, but we need to," she urged.

"No, we don't," Andrew said with conviction. "What he needs to do is introduce her to St. Peter." He pressed his chest to his wife's and ran a large hand up and down her back, gently pressing her more firmly against him.

"St. Peter?" she asked, twisting her lips in confusion. "What good is telling her about a dead saint going to do? They're not even Catholic, Andrew."

Andrew clucked his tongue. "Not that St. Peter, my dear."

She looked at him even more confused than before. "What are you talking about?" she asked, exasperation filling her voice.

His eyes full of amusement, he smiled at her and said, "You've been introduced before, but if you need another introduction, I'd be happy to oblige."

Thirty minutes later, a breathless Brooke opened her eyes and met her husband's loving blue eyes as he propped himself up on his elbows to look at his wife's face. "Yes, she definitely needs to meet St. Peter. He is the answer to all their problems."

"I tried to tell you," he said, dropping a kiss on her forehead.

She shook her head, smiling. "Unless you want to go into his study and tell him he needs to exercise his husbandly rights, I suggest we do something else," she said, pushing some of his black hair off his brow.

Andrew groaned. "All right, you win."

"Good. Here's what I'm thinking…"

Chapter 22

Paul read her note for what must have been the thousandth time in the past fortnight. She'd as good as left him, he thought sourly. And the worst part was he had no idea why. Her note had been nothing if not vague. He read it again.

Going to recover at Elizabeth's.

What type of disease had overtaken her that she felt the need to vacate their home and take up permanent residence with Elizabeth? He'd gone to see her every day just as he'd done when she was still at home. But every time he went, he was informed she wasn't well enough to allow visitors. He hadn't believed that for a second. He'd been a minister long enough to know doctors typically informed the family of the bad news, if there was any. No doctor had contacted him about bad news. He even doubted she was sick in the first place, because he'd never seen a single doctor's bill. He may be a vicar and she his wife, but no doctor was going to accept an extra prayer in their favor as payment.

He'd graciously accepted the excuses made by the timid maid that answered the door. At first, he didn't want to get her into trouble with her employer by pushing past her and searching the house for his wife. But after the third day, he accepted her flimsy excuse because he was afraid he might throttle Liberty when he did find her.

Paul brought his elbow to the table, made a fist and rested his head against it. Closing his eyes, he sighed. Did it even matter if she was gone? Even when she'd been here, he hadn't broken down all of her defenses. He'd come close a few times just to have them reconstructed even stronger. As long as he lived, he'd never understand women.

Perhaps it was better this way, he decided. Without her here, he didn't have to put a tight rein on his feelings when he saw or heard her. Ever since the night he'd kissed her in her room, he'd been more guarded around her. The realization that he was besotted with her and she may never share the feeling was painful enough. If he let her any closer to him, she could have the ability to devastate him.

But out of sight didn't necessarily mean out of mind. No, not at all. He'd thought about her every day. He'd tried to evaluate every aspect of their relationship. He'd long ago realized she hadn't liked him from the start. However, the feeling wasn't mutual. Not at first, anyway. That came the next day.

He knew without question he hadn't carried a torch for her before they married. And the more time he thought about it, the more he decided his feelings had developed during the first few days they were married. All the things he'd done to get a response from her were done not only because he couldn't take the brittle façade she'd presented, but because he wanted to know and see the real her. This realization rocked him to the core.

He wanted her to smile because she was happy, not because she was coerced into it. He wanted her to say what she wanted not because he couldn't stand her acting as obedient as a trained animal, but because he wanted to hear what she had to say. He wanted the real woman hidden under all the rules and expectations. He wanted to meet the woman John claimed had a heart of gold. He hadn't believed it when John had said it, but he believed it now.

She'd stepped into so many positions since becoming his wife and he never doubted for a minute her charitable works were her superficial way of doing what she thought was expected of her. She wanted to do them. She may not have enjoyed the women in the sewing circle—who would?—but she'd suffered their painful company to make things for others. She'd taken food to the cranky old shut-ins, and they'd done nothing but praise her kindness whenever he went to check on them. She'd volunteered to help illiterate students learn to read. And when she wasn't doing those things, she was either with him at his church or acting as a companion for Elizabeth. Contrary to what he initially believed, he now knew there wasn't a selfish bone in her body.

And yet for all his musings, he still didn't have an answer. What had he done to drive her away this time? Sure, he'd been guarded around her. But he hadn't done anything to purposely push her way. Perhaps he should just ask her. Now that was a brilliant idea. Tomorrow he would find her and ask what he'd done. As painful as it was to see her everyday knowing she held no regard for him, it was far less painful than not seeing her at all. Perhaps it was time to think of earnestly trying to woo her. He'd dismissed the idea initially because he wasn't keen on her, nor she on him. Now, for some reason, the idea didn't seem so wretched.

Mrs. Siddons stomped into his room and he started. "Forgive me, I was woolgathering," he said with a smile.

"'Tis quite all right, Mr. Grimes. I have a message, just delivered," she said, tossing a folded missive onto his desk.

Fingers shaking, he quickly picked up the missive and broke the seal. He gave a dismissing nod to Mrs. Siddons who had taken to treating him coldly since Liberty's departure. He unfolded the paper and read the message.

Paul,
It appears I need another favor. Can you meet me at my townhouse tomorrow about noon? I promise this favor will be nowhere near as demanding as the last.
John

Paul groaned. He had no desire to go to London to see John. Likely, the whole family had heard about the separation by now, and he had no wish to discuss the details with any of them.

***

Paul looked at the clothes laid out on the bed, then swung his gaze back to John. "You want me to do *what*?" he asked in disbelief.

John shrugged. "It's nothing really. Just go to the ball, dance a few dances with her, and take her for a stroll in the gardens. It couldn't be simpler. You'll have a good time."

"Except you're forgetting one thing: she's not my wife," Paul said irritably. He could not believe he'd been dragged to London to attend a pre-Season masquerade ball thrown by Brooke and asked to entertain one of Liberty's cousins. He should be home trying to woo his wife. "Why not get Alex to do it?"

"Alex?" John echoed, rolling his eyes. "Are you insane? He'd either bore her with 'fascinating' details from his latest science circular or shock her with information about the mating habits of his equines. He won't do. As for your complaint about her not being your wife, perhaps I should ask you where your wife is currently residing," he said shrewdly, his clear blue eyes daring Paul to lie about the state of their relationship.

"You know very well where she is," Paul responded angrily, crossing his arms. The realization that she'd still rather be anywhere other than with him felt like a knife to the heart. And knowing her family knew all about it, only made him sourer about the whole situation.

"Yes. She's ill and *you're* not taking care of her, are you?" John asked coldly.

"No," he agreed. "But not for any lack of trying on my part. I've taken care of her before when she needed it." He knew his words sounded bitter, but he couldn't care enough to change his tone.

"I know," John conceded softly.

"I even have Mrs. Siddons there to help her with a bath this time," Paul said wryly, uncrossing his arms and falling into a chair. "I just don't understand what she finds so offensive about me. I honestly thought we'd been making good progress. Then one day, she just closed up tighter than a clam; and a week later she disappeared." He shook his head.

"So then take a break. Just for this one night. Go out and have a good time. Go dance with this young woman and talk to her until midnight. Forget your problems with Liberty. Have a good time," the older man urged again, picking up the clothes. "Nobody will recognize you in this costume. Besides, we'll change your name.

You can be 'Mr. Daltry'. Come now, Paul. Please do me this one last favor."

Paul eyed him warily. Would it really be this "one last favor" or would there be another one day? Did it really even matter? John had helped him more times than he could count. What was one more favor? "All right," he agreed. "However, I want it noted this is the last one."

"Agreed."

Paul stood up and with an inaudible mumble, he dressed for the masquerade. John had left nothing out when considering his disguise. By the time he finished dressing and looked in the mirror, he hardly recognized himself. The black walnut oil in his hair had turned it so dark brown it bordered on black. The fake mustache served to harden his facial appearance and make him appear older. The rest of his costume was a bit awkward, but he wouldn't have expected anything less from John.

He was dressed head to toe in black. He wore only a shirt, trousers and leather boots. Tied around his neck, he wore a ridiculous black cape. A small, and thankfully dull, rapier lay across the bed, still waiting for him to slide it into the sheath that was attached to his belt. He considered leaving that part of his costume here, but knew John would question him about it and he didn't relish the idea of trying to talk his way out of wearing it. So with a sigh, he picked it up and slipped it into its sheath.

After another quick glance in the mirror to satisfy himself that nobody would recognize him in this ridiculous costume, he went downstairs to wait for John and Carolina.

To his surprise, they were both already in the drawing room waiting for him. "Oh, you look dashing," Carolina cooed, coming over to straighten his cape. "Allison will fall in love with you on the spot."

Panic momentarily swelled in Paul's chest. "Let's hope not," he remarked, thinking of the bitter irony. His own wife had known him for nearly a year and despised him, and yet, Carolina seemed absolutely certain his wife's cousin would fall in love with him at first sight.

John coughed and patted his chest. "Right you are. Perhaps you should leave your spectacles here," he suggested, reaching up to Paul's face to remove his spectacles for him. "Oh, stop that scowling, boy. Tonight you are Mr. Daltry, Knight Swathed in Black; and Mr. Daltry does not wear these."

Paul groaned. Without his spectacles, he was hopeless. He could see large things, but for the life of him he couldn't read or make out fine details. With how dark ballrooms typically were, it was going to be nearly impossible to get through the night without incident.

"Oh, do you know how to imitate a Welch accent?" Carolina asked, a hopeful expression on her face.

"No, ma'am. How about if I try to drop my voice an octave or two? Will that do?" He suppressed the urge to roll his eyes when she nodded enthusiastically. He'd never tell her, but he was glad she'd mentioned that. It wouldn't do for someone to recognize his voice. Not that he really thought that was possible, but one could never be too careful.

For some reason Paul couldn't understand, they rode in the carriage to the Townson's residence. They were only a few blocks away and it would have made more sense to walk. His suggestion was met with a simple, "It's not fashionable," and he knew better than to argue with that.

They walked in and made their greetings to the hosts. Paul was rather shocked to see a recognizably increasing Lady Townson acting as hostess. Even he knew it wasn't customary for an increasing woman to be in town taking part in social events. Yet, Brooke was Brooke, and he knew as well as anyone, she would do whatever she pleased. At least she was able to wear a costume that disguised her state. Her husband, on the other hand, was a very lucky man who appeared to have escaped the trap of wearing a costume.

John introduced him as Mr. Daltry to Brooke and Andrew who accepted it with not a hint of disbelief or question in their eyes. "And this," Brooke said, grabbing hold of the arm of the young woman who was dressed as a queen and standing behind her, "is

Miss Allison Ellis. She's my cousin."

"How do you do, Miss Ellis?" Paul asked with a slight bow, making sure not to injure himself or anyone else with his wayward sheathed rapier. He remembered Liberty's middle name was Ellis, it must have been a family name, he decided.

"Very well, thank you, Mr. Daltry," she said with a curtsy.

"Miss Ellis has just arrived from America and this is her first ball," Brooke explained.

"Is that so?" Paul said evenly. Was it his imagination or had Miss Ellis winced both times Brooke said her name? He couldn't see much in this dim room, but he was almost certain she'd winced.

"Actually, Mr. Daltry," John cut in smoothly. "I know it might appear presumptuous on my part, but would you be willing to keep my niece company this evening?"

No, Paul wanted to say, *I wouldn't. I'd rather be with my wife. You remember her, don't you? You ought to, she's your daughter!* But he couldn't say that, he'd already agreed to go through with this nonsense. "It would be my pleasure," he said smoothly, offering Miss Ellis his arm.

"Excellent!" Carolina chirped with a staccato clap. "As her official co-chaperone, I give my consent for her to waltz."

"Waltz?" Paul echoed. The only time he'd ever waltzed was with his dancing master. He couldn't possibly have his first public waltz be while he was wearing a disguise and dancing with his wife's cousin.

"Yes, a waltz," Brooke chimed in. "Allison has been looking forward to it since she arrived. I believe the orchestra will be playing one next."

Paul looked at Miss Ellis. He couldn't see her very well without his spectacles. Her face looked blurred, but he could see she shared the same beauty as her cousins. Best of all, he could tell she was smiling; and it was directed straight at him.

He led her to the floor where partners were indeed preparing for a waltz. "I must confess I haven't waltzed in a long time. I hope you don't value your toes," he jested.

"Not to worry, Mr. Daltry. I have the most uncomfortably hard slippers on tonight," she informed him. Then she peeked up at him from under her lashes and added slyly, "They also have a heel, and I am not above retaliation."

Paul chuckled. "Ah, now I know where it comes from."

"What's that?" she asked curiously.

He shrugged. "I always wondered where the Banks sisters got their vengeful streak," he said lightly, "and now I know. It's from Carolina's side."

"Are you acquainted with them, then?" she asked after they'd started to dance.

"Not well," he said to cover his slip. It wouldn't do for him to reveal too much after all the pains he'd gone through to disguise himself so Liberty would never know of this.

"Are you counting, Mr. Daltry?" she asked laughingly after a moment.

"I'm afraid you've caught me, Miss Ellis," he said sheepishly. He'd definitely been counting. And it wasn't for the reason she'd thought. Ever since he'd taken her in his arms, his blood started pumping so quickly he could hardly stand it. Perhaps it was because he was afraid of someone finding out his identity, which would cause more problems than he'd like to consider. Or maybe it was because for some strange reason he liked the way she felt in his arms. The way her hands were touching his shoulder and hand felt like twin branding irons on his skin. The silk of her crimson gown brushed his leg with every move, which only added to his excitement. An excitement he should not be feeling. So to stave off the excitement, he'd focused on counting.

"It's all right," she said softly. "If you don't wish to waltz, I won't hold it against you."

"Are you certain?" he asked, relieved. "Perhaps we could take a tour of the veranda?"

"That would be most excellent."

***

Thank goodness that was over. Liberty thought her body was going to catch fire with all the sparks he was sending through her merely by touching her. Only one man had ever been able to cause those types of sensations before, Paul. She bit her lip. Paul would be appalled to know where she was tonight. He still thought she was with Elizabeth recovering from her "illness".

She hadn't wanted to come tonight, she reminded herself again. However, yesterday when Brooke approached her about needing a favor, Liberty couldn't refuse. She'd been hesitant when Brooke explained the favor was to help one of Andrew's friends, a shy Mr. Daltry, feel more at ease in a London ballroom. Bemused, she'd asked Brooke why on earth she'd been chosen for this mission. Brooke ignored her questions and protests, claiming there was no one else to do this. For obvious reasons, Madison was not a good candidate, but surely Brooke knew someone else to do this.

After much cajoling, Liberty agreed. Brooke acted so excited at her agreement and waxed for thirty minutes about how much fun Liberty was going to have while Liberty just rolled her eyes and shook her head. Helping a shy stranger acquaint himself with the social scene of the ballroom did not sound like her idea of an evening's entertainment. Yet, now she realized she may have been wrong.

She looked up at the devastatingly handsome Mr. Daltry. Where had he been when she'd first come to London, she wondered, taking a seat on a bench. Mr. Daltry tried to join her, but his sword kept banging into the bench. She tried unsuccessfully not to laugh at his situation. "Having trouble?" she teased.

He flashed her a quick smile. "Indeed. I believe the man who picked out this costume has a wicked sense of humor."

His smile made her heart skip a beat. It was nothing less than a full out grin. Averting her gaze, she said, "Perhaps you should just take it off." His eyes went wide and she realized she'd inadvertently just suggested he take off his whole costume instead of just the sword. "I meant the sword," she said to clarify, blushing.

He chuckled. It was a low, rich sound that sent shivers to her toes. "Fine suggestion, but I think I'll leave it on for now," he said, twisting the sword in a way that allowed him to sit down. "I would have left it off altogether, but I feared your uncle would have complained. He's the one who picked this ridiculous outfit."

She laughed, causing all the curls Brooke's hairdresser put into her hair to shake. "I believe it. I didn't pick mine, either," she said, gesturing to herself. Brooke and Mama had taken it upon themselves to pick her costume. Since she'd arrived this morning, they'd been fighting over who was going to be her chaperone and she'd suggested they could be co-chaperones, not that there was such a thing, but it made them happy enough.

She would have argued with their costume choice if not for their fierce determination mixed with her fear of being discovered. Instead, she ignored the little voice inside her that was screaming, "Do not put that ghastly costume on!" and put it on anyway. There was nothing Liberty liked about the costume, except maybe the color of the dress. It was a dark crimson red and had white lace stitched around the edges. The bodice plunged a bit too low, revealing more of her bosom than she liked. There was a gold chord that was woven in and out of different loops on the bodice then formed a bow that rested right in the middle of her breasts. If the low swoop wasn't enough to draw a man's attention there, the bow would do it, except she had yet to catch Mr. Daltry's gaze drift there.

She shifted again and felt her headpiece shift. She hadn't a clue what the thing was called. All she knew was it was ugly and heavy. It looked like a giant pillow that formed a semicircle and rested right on the crown of her head. At least her curls had turned out well, Liberty thought with a sigh. Brooke's hairdresser worked for more than two hours to get her hair just right. And she had to admit, she'd done a great job with the curls.

"Well, it looks very pretty on you, Miss Ellis," he told her, making her blush and cringe at the same time. "Forgive me, I didn't mean to be so forward." His voice was quiet and he made a move as if he were about to get up.

"No, no. It's not what you said," Liberty rushed to assure him, laying her hands on his arms to stay him.

He looked at her as though she was fit for bedlam.

"That is to say, it's not your fault exactly. See, I hate my name," she explained and felt him relax.

He still stared at her as though she'd lost her mind, but at least his body had relaxed and he wasn't in a rush to depart her company. She couldn't explain why she was relieved that he'd relaxed and was still sitting next to her. "If you stay, I shall tell you a secret," she said, hoping he'd be more likely to stay if he knew she was about to reveal something personal, and perhaps vulnerable, about herself. "I have this great-grandmother that wasn't so great," she said with a bitter smile. "Great-Grandma Ellis we all called her. Anyway, the woman was nothing but a sour faced, hateful old windbag. She went around criticizing the whole family. She'd always look for flaws and when she found one, she'd publicly ridicule the person for it. I remember a specific birthday dinner I attended where she criticized poor Liberty about her crooked teeth the entire time." She abruptly stopped herself and dropped her eyes to stare at her fisted hands. She didn't dare look at Mr. Daltry for fear he'd see right through her disguise and she'd be exposed. Though she didn't recognize Mr. Daltry, she couldn't be sure he didn't know Paul. Thinking she better say *something* and quick, she hastened to add, "Anyway, I just prefer not to be called 'Miss Ellis' because it reminds me of her and I'd rather not think of her."

"All right," he agreed. His voice sounded uneven and held a hint of a sharper edge than it had a minute ago. Turning to favor her with another grin, he said, "We shall never speak of her again. Instead, I shall call you, Miss…?"

Mrs. Grimes, she wanted to say proudly. She'd been thinking a lot about Paul recently. After many heart-felt conversations with Elizabeth, she'd decided she would ask him the truth. Not only did she think as his wife she deserved that, but she'd missed him more in the past two weeks than she could have predicted. Somewhere during that fortnight, she'd discovered she truly cared for him, and even if he would never feel the same way for her, she at least wanted to know if there was even a sliver of a chance he might. Earlier today, she'd decided after this folly with Mr. Daltry was over, she'd go see him. But for now, she needed to play her role.

"Allison. You may call me Allison," she said at last.

"Allison," he repeated. "You may call me Tom."

Was it her imagination, or did he slightly hesitate before he said his name? "If you'd prefer I not call you Tom, I can still call you Mr. Daltry," she offered, knowing she probably would anyway. She had no business calling another man by his Christian name, especially after all the trouble Paul had gone through to get her to use his.

He smiled. "No, no. It's fine."

She looked at him curiously. "All right, Tom," she said nervously with a half-smile. She'd said it only to please him so he wouldn't call her "Miss Ellis" again.

"Your accent is quite pronounced," he said, leaning back on the bench.

Oh drat. Brooke and Mama had insisted she feign a strong American accent so not to be recognized. Perhaps she was overdoing it a bit. "Yes, well, I just arrived. Perhaps it will take a while for it to fade." She flashed him a hopeful smile which he returned.

His gaze locked with hers for a moment and she noticed he had the most stunning green eyes. They were beautiful. Paul's eyes were green, too, she thought with a pang of guilt as she tore her eyes away. She shouldn't be thinking of this man's eyes. And she really shouldn't be enjoying his company nearly as much as she was.

"She has a lot of admirers," Mr. Daltry said, startling her.

Liberty followed his gaze to where Madison was surrounded by a gaggle of gentlemen tripping over themselves while trying to vie for her attention. "She always did," Liberty said numbly.

"Hmm, I always got the impression she was shy."

"Not at all, quite the opposite actually," Liberty said, shaking her head. "Back home the men flocked to her like flies to honey. Every man of our acquaintance danced attendance on her. But her downfall was her soft spot for Robbie Swift. She fancied herself in love with him and he told her he felt the same. Yet, I doubt he did because he courted her for five *years* before ruthlessly throwing her over in order to marry another."

"I see," he said, nodding.

"The last time I saw her, she was still dreaming about what might have been," she said, shaking her head.

"Do you not approve of daydreaming, then?" he asked, looking at her curiously.

Startled, she met his curious eyes. "No, well, yes. I mean, my reaction wasn't because I disagree with daydreaming exactly. It was the reaction I have every time I think of that varmint and how he ruined her life. She is better off without him in her life, even if it causes her to daydream. Of which, I must confess," she lowered her gaze, "I haven't always been the most understanding."

"Haven't you?" The question was spoken with more than just his lips. His whole face seemed to be asking her the question, and she couldn't lie.

Taking a deep breath, she said, "Sadly, no. I've been far more critical of her than anyone else." He turned his face away so quickly she wasn't able to gauge his expression, but she knew he couldn't possibly think very highly of her after this revelation. "If you'd like, I can arrange a dance with her for you," she offered, trying to end the uncomfortable tension by ending this conversation entirely.

"No."

"Are you sure? She won't mind that you count," she countered, trying to sound encouraging.

"No, I'd rather not go back in there and dance with her. I'd rather stay here and dance with you," he said with a smile that made her bones melt and her breath catch.

Chapter 23

Paul stood up and pulled her into his arms. The orchestra had just begun playing the first strains of another waltz. He forced himself to calm down and think clearly. His blood was pumping faster than it had last time they'd danced together. But this time, it wasn't for the same reason. This time, he was angry. This was Liberty in his arms, not some cousin. She probably didn't even have a cousin named Allison Ellis. Why had she come to a ball to meet with another gentleman? Even if her parents had set it up where she was only meeting with him, it still hurt that she'd come in the first place. He wanted to drag her from this veranda and demand an explanation but not before having some fun at her expense first.

Holding her closer than was proper and hoping to scandalize her by doing so, he waltzed her around the veranda, ending up in an even darker, more secluded spot.

"Perhaps we should go back in," she said, a hint of anxiety in her voice.

Good. He wanted her to be anxious thinking a man other than her husband was taking her off to a dark corner where he could ravish her and nobody would hear a thing. Where was the woman that cared so much for propriety that she'd have a fit at the mere suggestion of leaving the ballroom? He knew her propriety obsession hadn't been an act; she'd had five hundred nineteen books on the subject when they'd married.

"No," he said silkily, shaking his head, "I'd rather stay right here. With you."

Her face turned a fetching bright red. "Well, umm…" She cleared her throat and stepped on his foot. "Sorry," she murmured. "It's just that dancing out here with me won't help you."

"Help me?" he questioned, searching her eyes.

She bit her lip and looked away. "With your problem."

"My problem?" he echoed.

She bit her lip harder now. His hand left her waist and went up to her face. With the pad of his thumb, he pulled her lower lip free of her teeth's brutal grasp. Startled, she abruptly jerked her head up to look directly into his eyes. She swallowed and he used the pad of his thumb to brush the teeth marks that were left on her lip, while his fingers glided along the rigid edge of her jaw. She closed her eyes and leaned into his hand.

"My problem?" he prompted.

Her eyes flew open and she colored again. "Umm, Brooke told me you were painfully shy and asked if I would acquaint you with the ballroom, so to speak."

"I see," he said unevenly. She'd just revealed that Brooke was a part of this. Why? More importantly, why had Liberty eagerly agreed to her plan? Had she known who he was? "And you have a wealth of experience navigating London ballrooms?"

"Not really. I've only been in a few ballrooms in New York," she said evasively. "I actually refused, at first. I reminded her of my limited ability to help you. Then, she started begging and pleading, and at one point I thought she was going to twist my arm —quite literally. Finally, after hearing her prattle on and on for the better part of four hours, I agreed."

Paul felt his anger ebb slightly. She'd been tricked into this just as he had. She hadn't come here tonight looking for his replacement after all. "I see. However, I do wonder about one thing," he mused aloud.

"Which is?"

"It seems you're stuck helping a shy fellow like me. What is she going to do for you in return?" He flashed her a shy smile then moved his hand back to her waist and gave her a tight squeeze. Though his anger had dimmed, his blood was still thrumming through his veins. Perhaps it hadn't only been his anger making his blood course a few minutes ago.

"Oh, actually, she promised not to retaliate against me in our next game of charades," she said with a laugh.

"Pardon?"

"I once played a game of charades and embarrassed her in front of a gentleman. Badly. Anyway, in exchange for my helping you, she agreed not to do the same to me," she explained.

"I see. And do you believe she'll keep her word?" he asked, pulling her a touch closer.

"I have no doubt she will. She won't like what will happen to her if she doesn't," she said with a laugh.

"Right, you believe in retaliation," he said playfully.

"Yes, I do," she retorted.

"Even if it's against someone you love?"

"Especially then," she answered, her lips twitching. "Where do you think I learned it from?"

He grinned. "And do you think she'll keep her promise?"

"Of course," she said with a bright smile. "I made her put it into writing."

He chuckled. "You're very clever. But what if she reneges?"

"Oh, she won't," she said with a giggle.

He pulled her a little closer to him and gave her waist another encouraging squeeze. "You seem rather certain."

"I am. She also signed something acknowledging that if she reneged, I'd pretend to get drunk and expose her biggest secrets next time she hosted a house party."

He let out a bark of laughter and she playfully swatted his arm.

"Shhh. You'll draw attention to us," she said, putting her pink-tipped index finger to her smiling lips.

"And would that be a bad thing?" he asked, scanning her face for a better answer than her lips would give.

"There could be a scandal," she said, biting her lip again.

Once again, he freed her lip then rubbed his fingertip across it to sooth the pain before grabbing her waist again. "Would that be so bad?"

"Yes," she squeaked, trying to break out of his grasp.

He tightened his hold so she couldn't flee. "Wouldn't it likely lead to marriage?"

"Uh...umm..." she stammered, looking anywhere but at him

as she struggled to get loose.

"You do know if a single man and woman are connected in a scandal of this nature, they'll be forced to marry?" he asked easily, feeling his heartbeat pick up. What would she say to that?

"I know that," she snapped, her eyes flashing fire.

"And would that be such a bad thing, Allison?" He'd deliberately used her fake name to catch her off guard.

Her eyes shot to his. "I can't," she said with a slight hitch in her voice.

Not sure if her voice faltered because she was uneasy in his tight grasp or because she'd want to marry him if she were able, he decided to press her further. "And, why not?"

"Because, I'm already married."

Chapter 24

Liberty felt Mr. Daltry's racing heart beat in time with hers as he hugged her close. Who would have guessed that revealing she was already married could elicit such a reaction? Unless, of course, he took that to mean it left her free to engage in a torrid affair with him! That would be the only reason for his sudden reaction.

Pulling back out of his hold, Liberty stepped back and looked in his general direction. It was so dark on this part of the veranda that she could hardly see anything more than the outline of his form. At least where he was standing, he could see her because of the moonlight, but he was covered in darkness from the shadows.

"Just because I'm married, does not mean I'm free to be your lover," she spat. She brought her hand up and rested it on her thudding heart. The man was a scoundrel of the worst sort. He knew just how to hold and touch her to get her blood to simmer.

"I have no such interest," he confided. "Although, I am flattered you thought I did. I had no idea I held such appeal."

She stiffened her spine. "I assure you, you do not," she said as waspishly as she could manage.

"Are you satisfied with your husband, then?" he asked, curiosity evident in his voice.

Her lower lip trembled on its own accord and she bit down on the inside of her mouth to keep it still. "Uh…yes," she lied.

He chuckled. "Spoken like a woman in love. Say, is he here tonight?"

Her eyes widened. "N-no, he's n-not h-here," she stammered, fidgeting with the laces on her sleeve.

"Pity, I would have liked to introduce myself to the poor sod, so he'd know who was waltzing in the dark with his wife."

She gasped. "You're nothing but a…a…cold-hearted man," she burst out.

He chuckled at her ridiculous statement. "Is that so? I just thought the man ought to know who's dancing with his wife, that's all. If you were my wife, I wouldn't let you out of my sight if I could help it."

Her eyes flew up to his face. "Truly?" For some reason, his answer meant a lot to her.

"Yes," he said unevenly before clearing his throat. "But that's not important. Where's your husband tonight, madam?"

"At home, I think," she said dully.

"You don't know?" he asked, stepping closer and grabbing her hand.

"No." She shook her head and licked her lips when his warm thumb started rubbing soft strokes on the back of her hand.

"Where else do you think he might be?" His body so close, she could feel the heat radiating from him.

She closed her eyes to squeeze in the tears that had formed. "With another woman," she whispered at last.

Mr. Daltry's hand tightened, creating an almost painful vice. She would have tried to take her hand from his, but oddly enough his painful grasp felt as good as balm on an open wound. He seemed just as upset that her husband had paramours as she was; and for some reason his angry feelings were refreshing.

He relaxed his grip and brought her hand to his lips, placing a warm, searing kiss on the spot where he'd almost left a bruise with his thumb. "Forgive me," he murmured. "Do you mind if we have a change of plans for the evening?"

Her eyes went wide with shock and she tried to pull her hand from his. "If you think just because my husband is unfaithful that I intend to be as well, you are about to be greatly disappointed," she said fiercely, grabbing her skirts and trying to scurry off.

His hand grabbed her just above the elbow. "That's not what I meant. I intended to offer you some advice, nothing more."

She stopped struggling and turned to face him. They were both bathed in moonlight now and she could see his face. Her eyes searched his face the best they could in the dim evening light. "Advice?"

"Yes, advice. Being a man myself, I think I can offer you some advice about your husband," he offered.

Her heart leapt. Although she'd already made up her mind she was going to go to Paul as soon as she got home, it couldn't hurt to listen to what this man had to say. After all, Elizabeth was the only other person who knew everything, and though she meant well, her marriage could never have been considered a success. She knew she could trust Mr. Daltry, she didn't know why, she just could. She swallowed a lump in her throat as she realized exactly what she was going to be revealing to a perfect stranger. With a single nod in his direction, she led him to Brooke's private sitting room.

***

Paul was full of nervous excitement as she led him through her sister's townhouse. Putting aside his jealous feelings that she'd willingly take a stranger to a poorly lit private room, he focused on *why* she was taking him there. She thought he was having affairs? Where had she gotten that crazy notion? He was home every single night for dinner. He was there in the morning to bring up her precious bathwater so she didn't have to go to the kitchen. What on earth had given her the idea he'd been unfaithful?

Taking a seat on the end of one settee, Liberty waved her hand and said, "Make yourself comfortable. If you'd prefer a chair, just bring over the one from the secretary in the corner."

Paul gave her a quick smile as he unhooked his sword and untied the cape. When he was done disassembling his costume, he sat down right next to her. She cast him a wary look and tried to scoot away, but there was nowhere to go. "What exactly were you supposed to be anyway?"

"'Mr. Daltry, Knight Swathed in Black'," he said, quoting her father.

"No shining armor left at the costume shop?" she teased.

"I have no idea. As I said earlier, it was picked out for me. I must confess, your dislike for it rivals my own." He flashed her a smile. "But we're not here to talk about my costume."

"Right," she agreed, looking down to where the nail of her right index finger was digging into the nail bed of her thumb. "On the way up, I thought perhaps I should give you some background information about my marriage."

He closed his eyes so she wouldn't see him roll them. He didn't want to hear everything; he just wanted to know why she suspected him of cheating. "Very well," he said slowly.

"When we were initially introduced by my father, we both immediately took a strong dislike for each other," she said uneasily, shifting her weight on the settee.

Perhaps he did want to hear everything. "What do you mean?" He truly wanted to know, too. She'd told him it was because of his request she not address him formally, but he hadn't fully believed that.

"Well," she paused to bite her lip and shift again. "Before we were introduced, I saw him across the drawing room and thought he was rather handsome." A slow blush crawled over her face.

Paul put his head down to hide his grin. He still didn't know why her family had set this whole thing up, but right now he could kiss them for it. Without having to beat it out of her, he was about to know the answers to all his questions with unabashed honesty.

"But then we were introduced, and I discovered a handsome face doesn't make up for a lack of personality," she said, causing his grin to vanish as his short-lived glee came to an abrupt end.

"What do you mean?" he asked again.

She shrugged. "He was a conversational bore."

"A bore?" he asked, astonished. They'd just met. Did she expect him to regale her with tales of his boyhood or something?

"Yes, a bore."

He stared at her in disbelief. His great sin was that she thought him boring? "Pardon me, but being a man and not fully understanding the situation, could you please explain what constitutes a bore?"

"He barely spoke to me," she said with a sniff.

"Did you give him a chance?" he retorted. He remembered the night she was talking about very well. And unless he'd suffered a brain fever he didn't know about since then, he'd swear *she* talked so much *he* couldn't get a word in if he'd tried. She'd talked about everything from the voyage from New York to the origins of her and her sister's names to some prank her sister had pulled on her involving a toad. She'd even gone so far as to tell him the details of her sister's courtship with the man that was now her husband.

She sent him an icy glare. "What makes you think I didn't?"

"Perhaps you were distracted by his dashing looks and started to prattle," he suggested with a wink. When she lowered her head and looked down at the floor in embarrassment, he let out a bark of laughter. "That's what happened, isn't it?"

"Partially," she admitted.

He shot her a grin. "My, my, this gets more interesting by the moment."

"If you're going to mock me, you may leave," she said defiantly, crossing her arms across her chest defensively.

"Not at all. Pray continue," he said, crossing his ankles and leaning back.

She relaxed her body, but continued to stare at the floor. "All right, I admit I talk overmuch when I'm nervous, and he made me undeniably nervous. But I was also irritated. See, when we were introduced, he immediately asked me to call him by his Christian name."

Paul studied his boots a moment before asking, "And why did that bother you?" He already knew her answer, but thought Mr. Daltry would ask to be polite.

"Because it's not proper," she insisted.

Turning to face her, he reached his fingers under her chin and tipped it up so that she faced him. "And do you always do what's proper?" he asked quietly.

She swallowed. "No," she breathed. "Not anymore."

"And what changed that? Your faithless husband?" he asked bitterly, letting go of her face.

"As a matter of fact, yes," she told him, holding his gaze.

"Really," he drawled, crossing his arms across his chest.

"Really," she confirmed.

"And how did the bounder accomplish that?"

"I couldn't say," she said unevenly. "He just did."

"I see," he said dubiously. "So are you telling me that you act improper around him, or is it just me?"

She looked away from his face, which told him she'd understood his question. "Both," she said.

"Just with the two of us, then?" he asked, searching her face the best he could in the dark room with no spectacles, hoping, nay praying, she'd say yes. He didn't think he'd be able to hear her acknowledge she'd misbehaved with another. Even if she thought "Mr. Daltry" was Mr. Daltry and not him, he could accept that, but he couldn't stand the idea there had been another.

"Yes," she answered, looking chastised.

"Look at me," he said, running a slow finger up and down her cheek. "You still haven't told me why you suspect your husband of infidelity. But I want you to know that you've done nothing with me of which to be ashamed."

She nodded her agreement even though she looked doubtful.

Bringing his other hand up to her face, he cupped her chin and leaned as close as he dared to her. She smelled of lilacs and her plump, moist lips were calling to him. Lowering his lashes so he could shamelessly stare at them, he said in a husky voice, "Your husband doesn't deserve you."

Her lips parted in surprise and he could no longer control his own. Leaning in another inch, his lips collided with hers, sending sparks of heat straight to his groin. Her lips responded to his and a low, sweet groan escaped her lips. Encouraged, he ran his tongue back and forth across her bottom lip. He licked the corner, and she opened to him. He reveled in the taste of her. She tasted sweet and minty. He swept his tongue along one cheek, then to the other. Crossing back between the two, he ran his tongue along her teeth, going slowly, not wanting to miss the one in the front that was misaligned. He groaned when he reached it. There was no doubt, this was Liberty. His wife. The woman who hid her insecurities behind a cloak of propriety.

Abruptly, two cold hands grabbed his and pulled them off of her face. She jerked her face back and looked at him uneasily. "I can't. I'm sorry. It's not right," she panted, pressing her fingers to her flushed cheeks.

Perhaps he should tell her the truth, he thought. But not until she told him why she suspected him of adultery. He shook his head in disbelief. What would make her think such a thing? Would she believe him if he told her he was just as virginal as she was? Truth be known, he didn't want to do that, either. No man, even a man in his position, wanted to admit to such a thing.

"It is I who should be sorry," he said at last, adjusting himself next to her on the settee.

"No, I'm just as responsible. I responded to your advances all on my own accord."

He smiled at her. "Very well. Now, are you ready to tell me about your husband's indiscretions?"

"I suppose. Although I left a lot out," she said, frowning. "Be warned, this isn't a pretty story. If you ask questions, it might lead to other not-so-pretty revelations."

"I'm listening," he said with a grin.

"All right. I found proof that an illegitimate child exists," she said tactfully.

Paul's gut clenched. Had someone told her about Sam's illegitimate brood? "And did he tell you himself this was his child?" he asked carefully.

"No," she admitted softly. "I know it sounds awful, but it's not just one. I have reason to suspect there are more."

He sucked in his breath. She'd heard and he hadn't been the one to tell her. He was a fool. He should have told her. How bad could it be though? Lucy was the only one still living close by and she had no qualms telling anyone who Seth's father was. He'd managed to find employment elsewhere for all the others as quickly as possible. How many of those could have heard about? Cautiously, he asked, "How many?"

She looked at him with such sad eyes, he'd swear he'd just had an arrow shot into his heart. Finally, she took a deep breath and said, "Fourteen."

Chapter 25

Paul felt as if there was a shortage of air in the room. If not for the hard hand whacking him on the back, he'd think he'd just died from shock. Fourteen? *Fourteen?* Is that how many of Sam's brats he was supporting these days. And how on earth did Liberty know? He'd gotten in the habit of writing down a long string of initials in the ledger, not even wanting to count the pairs to know how many there were. Then he'd send a set amount to his solicitor who divided it between them. It wasn't much, just enough to support the children, about fifteen pounds each per month. Perhaps he needed to increase the monthly amount. "Are you certain?" he asked weakly.

"Yes," she said solemnly after she was convinced he could breathe without her further assistance. "A little over three weeks ago, some ladies had come over to sew and I overheard them talking badly about my husband while I was out of the room. I came in and jumped to his defense. But instead of apologizing as individuals living in a well-behaved society should, they continued to gossip about him. One thing led to another and I was informed my husband had a slew of illegitimate children. I didn't believe them. But, then one of them told me to check the ledger and I'd discover the truth. Thinking to clear my husband of the gossip, I did just that." She choked back her sobs and wiped her eyes. "That's when I found a long list of fourteen pairs of initials. I recognized a few of the initials from the names the women had told me."

His emotions were warring inside of him. He couldn't deny he'd felt joy when she said she'd defended him. But knowing she'd had cause to defend him, ate him up. Those harpies had no business spreading lies to his wife. But he couldn't fault them completely, he should have told her. But when? They hadn't exactly been getting along for most of their marriage; and this was not a topic you bring up over a casual dinner.

No wonder she'd left him. She thought he was like Sam, addicted to sex. She must have assumed since she wasn't warming his bed, some other woman was. Bile rose in his throat. Swallowing, he picked up Liberty's trembling body and hauled her on his lap, pressing her head into his solid chest. Sobs wracked her body and he carefully rubbed her back to calm her down. "Shh," he whispered into her hair. He should reveal himself now and ease her worries. But first, he wanted to see her smile at him just once more.

Tucking a tendril of stray hair behind her ear, he brushed the tears off her cheeks and waited for her to look at him. "You should look at the positive in this situation," he said with a smile.

"You mean I should be thankful he's proven to be so virile," she said blandly.

"Sure; but that wasn't what I was going to say," he said. "I was—"

"Good," she said, cutting him off from finishing his previous sentence. "I have no desire to go to bed with him."

His jaw clamped together, "Why not?" he asked, tightly. If he had it his way, he'd reveal his identity, explain about Sam and be hauling her off to the nearest bed in the next fifteen minutes.

"Why?" she echoed. "You cannot seriously think after he's been with so many women that I'd actually let him touch me with his...his..." she trailed off, waving her hand wildly.

"Wedding tackle," he supplied with a roguish grin.

"What?" she asked with a shaky laugh.

"Wedding tackle," he repeated with a shrug. "It's just one of the many names for a man's privates."

"Men name their body parts?" she asked, perturbed.

He chuckled at her naivety. "No, well, maybe, I don't know." He shook his head to clear the thought. "What I meant was, there is the scientific name and then there are...er...less than scientific names."

"Less than scientific?" she said dubiously.

"Right," he agreed. "Most men call it their rod, tool, pole, unit, piece, member or something along those lines," he didn't want to get *too* graphic with her, and wisely chose to leave off some of the coarser terms, "but some, myself included, use different terms when in mixed company." He winked at her blushing face. "Wedding tackle, privates, package, equipment, pizzle, t—,"

"Pizzle?" she repeated, a slight giggle bubbling from her lips.

"Yes, pizzle," he said in mock irritation. "It's an older word with German origins."

"Oh, well, I'd never heard it before, that's all."

"And do you typically spend time trying to learn slang terms for a man's genitals?" he asked, trying not to laugh. He knew the answer to that as well as she did.

"No," she blustered. "Actually, I've heard more from you than anyone else."

"Even your husband?" he asked casually.

She looked up at him again with that sad, dull look in her eyes that ate at his heart. "Yes. The night before I married, my sister and mother tried to explain what would happen. And for as much as they fought over who would get the honor, neither of them were very informative. The only thing I learned was that he was going to touch me with it. They didn't say exactly where, nor what the thing was called. The only term I'd ever heard for it was earlier that night when my other sister called it a 'love musket'. When I asked my husband if he planned to touch me with his 'love musket', I thought he was going to die of laughter while I died of mortification."

He tried not to laugh again. "I'm sure he didn't mean to embarrass you," he assured her unevenly, then turned his head to hide his grin.

"Oh, you can laugh," she said lightly, flashing him a smile. "But if you want a real laugh at my expense, I must tell you another story. But first, you must promise not to tell anyone. Ever. I'm serious. This is far worse than anything I've told you so far."

"All right," he agreed, wrapping his arms around her and pulling her closer to his chest.

She looked up at him with questions in her eyes, but still didn't make a move to get off of his lap. "When I first married, I joined a few charitable organizations. One of which was to help both children and adults learn to read. I thought it was odd that the meeting was located above the local tavern but didn't let that stop me. Anyway, every Tuesday I went to the meeting, walking right by the sign, mind you. Every Tuesday, I'd stay later than everyone else because there was this little boy whose mother was always late to collect him, and we'd play all sorts of wild games while we waited for her.

"Then, one day when she came to get him, she praised how nice it was that my husband allowed me to help the illegitimate learn to read. Thinking she had her terms confused, I tried to correct her and explain the difference between illegitimate and illiterate.

"After five minutes of arguing with her, I ran down the stairs to grab the sign and show her. I swooned when I read that sign. The sign itself did indeed advertise for volunteers to help the *illegitimate* learn to read."

Paul couldn't stop his laughter as he thought what her face must have looked like when she reread that sign. "It seems you might not be as literate as you thought," he teased when his laughter ceased.

"Indeed not," she agreed, with a wide smile.

"Do you plan to go back?" he asked.

She shrugged. "I honestly don't know. It will depend on how my husband handles it. I haven't told him yet, and I don't know if I'll be able to screw up the courage to do so. It wouldn't be very advantageous for his work if I continue," she explained.

"I see. Can I ask you something personal?"

"Sir, we've discussed my husband's affairs, names for men's private parts and the fact that I was unknowingly tutoring illegitimate illiterates, what could possibly be more personal?" she said, resting her head against his heart.

His heart would have squeezed at her gesture if he hadn't been so jealous of himself. She'd never talked so freely or acted so tenderly with him, but with a stranger, all restraints were down. It was heartbreaking. He cleared his throat and said in a husky voice, "I can think of many things more personal than that." He winked at her when she pulled away and gasped. "But what I wanted to ask you is if you honestly think your husband would put his work above you and your interests?" he asked, pulling her back to him.

She turned her head up to face him and wet her lips with the tip of her pink tongue. "I don't know, probably."

He stiffened. She really thought he cared more for his position than for her. Sure he loved to preach, but it wasn't as if his reputation wasn't already in the privy. Her helping illegitimate illiterates learn to read wouldn't harm him one bit. Even if his reputation was pristine, he wouldn't stop her. "Why?" he asked hoarsely.

She shrugged. "Maybe he wouldn't. I truly don't know. But I'm afraid to tell him, all the same."

"He's not cruel to you, is he?"

"No, not really," she admitted. "I mean, we've had our moments, but who hasn't? I'd be afraid to disappoint him, that's all."

"Disappoint him?" he repeated, hating the way the words tasted bitter on his tongue.

"Yes. Before we were married, it was explained to me that I was lucky he'd have me and I needed to be on my best behavior— always. Otherwise, I'd disappoint him and he'd send me away," she said unevenly.

He felt like he'd been punched in the gut. In a fit of anger, he'd told John he'd send her back to America with them if she gave him fits. And in turn, she'd erected the wall of ice around her heart all because of his careless words. Choking back his own waves of emotion, he sought to comfort her. He pulled her as tightly to him as he could and kissed the top of her head before resting his cheek on the crown of her head, knocking her hairpiece askew. He felt her silent tears wetting his shirt, and it was almost his undoing. Not trusting his voice, he moved his left hand to rub small circles on her back, while his right held her face firmly against his chest, massaging her scalp with the ends of his fingers.

After a few minutes, he whispered soft and low, "You couldn't be a disappointment if you tried." He meant it, too.

"That's not what Papa said," she told him, wiping her nose on the handkerchief she'd found on the inside of his shirt pocket.

"*What?*" he hollered, making her jump.

"I needed a handkerchief, and it was right there. I'm sorry. Just wait a minute and I'll get you a new one."

"No, don't bother," he said, squeezing her to him. "I don't give a hang about the handkerchief. I want to know what your father said to you."

Her hazel eyes went wide at his demand. "Nothing that wasn't true," she mumbled at last. "He told me once that I was a disappointment."

"When? Why?" he demanded, anger seeping into his voice. What had she done that had been so bad John would feel she deserved those hateful words?

"Before I married, my husband and I were caught in a *very* scandalous situation that was of my making. That night, he told me I was a disappointment."

Paul wordlessly nodded. He remembered that night very vividly. He'd gone into John's study and waited for her to join them. The whole time he'd answered John's uncomfortable questions and silently hoped John wouldn't demand marriage. However, if he'd known Liberty was going to be treated so badly after he left, he might have offered for her just to save her the pain of her father's cruel words.

"Let me see if I have this right," he said, his voice sounded like gravel in his throat. "You've been afraid to do the things you want around your husband because your father said he was disappointed in you, and you didn't want to disappoint your husband and be sent away?"

She nodded.

He exhaled sharply. He'd never been as angry with John as he was right now. Not even when he'd learned John duped him into what he thought would be a miserable existence until they put him in the ground, compared to this. But Liberty didn't need to hear angry words about her father, she needed soothing words. Words that would help her understand that John hadn't meant what he'd said. For as furious as he was with the man, he knew John hadn't meant it and he'd be disappointed in himself if he knew how Liberty had reacted to his words.

Bringing his hand up to the back of her head, he grabbed a curl and twisted it around his finger. Her hair was so soft, he thought as he let the hair go and watched the curl spring back to her head. "I'm personally not a father," he said truthfully, "but I believe I've had enough experience with matters of the heart to tell you that he didn't mean what he said."

She looked up at him with her doe eyes and asked, "Who?"

"Both of them," he said hoarsely. "From what I understand, you and your husband didn't have a good start before your engagement. Perhaps his words were said because he was just as uneasy as you about entering into a marriage with someone who didn't hold him in any esteem." That was true enough.

"I suppose you're right," she acknowledged, cocking her head in contemplation. "Actually, that makes a lot of sense. If I remember my father's words correctly, he just said that if my husband didn't think we suited after six months, he'd return me to my parents." She twisted her lips into a mock sneer.

He might have said something similar to that, but he knew in his heart now—and maybe even then—there was nothing she could do that would make him send her away. Leaning forward, he pressed a soft kiss against her sneering lips, hoping they'd curl into a smile for him when he pulled back. And just like magic, they curved in an upward direction. He pushed another tendril of hair from her forehead and allowed his hand to linger at her temple for a moment before he pushed it behind her ear.

"Now, as for your father, I honestly think his words were just spoken in anger and had no significance attached." At least they had better be or John was going to find himself at the far end of a dueling field after Paul called him out. She didn't look convinced. "Think about this, you've done or said things that weren't thought out before, haven't you? That's all his words were. I think he may have been overwrought about the scandalous situation he happened upon and didn't think before he spoke."

She looked up at him with a twinkle in her eye. "You're rather smart, you know?"

He grinned. "Thank you." Here she'd just told him he was smart, and all he could do was string two words together. What a dolt.

"Your wife will be one lucky lady," she continued, oblivious to his somewhat incoherent state.

"You really think so?" he asked unevenly.

"Yes. I really do."

"Will you promise me two things?" he asked nervously. He was ready to end this charade and reveal who he was. It was time to be honest, get everything out in the open, and then take her home to be his wife in every way.

"Anything," she said breathlessly.

He looked down at her and stared into her beautiful eyes for one more peaceful minute. He knew once the words were out, it was possible—nay, probable—she'd be furious. Exhaling deeply, he said, "When you see your husband again, try to be understanding of what he tells you about those fourteen urchins."

"All right," she said with a gulp. "Second?"

"Second, promise me you'll be yourself, no matter who you're with." He waited for her to respond before he ripped off his mustache and revealed the ruse. But she never responded. Not with words anyway. Instead, she rendered him breathless once more when her hands grabbed his cheeks and pulled his lips to hers in a blood pumping, groin hardening, soul searing kiss.

Chapter 26

Liberty had no idea why his words sparked such a reaction in her, but they did. And now she was powerless to stop herself from kissing him. This man intrigued her and elicited feelings in her she'd never even known existed and kissing him again seemed inevitable. His soft lips moved on top of hers, making her groan with pleasure.

She was a wanton and this proved it. She'd only kissed two men in her life, Tom Daltry, the stranger in black, and her secretive husband, Paul. A pang of guilt stabbed her heart as she remembered her husband. They may not be a love match, but he was her husband and she owed it to him not to kiss strange men in moonlit rooms.

Pulling back, she looked up at this handsome stranger. How was it she felt more comfortable with him than she did with anyone in the world? He'd held her without making demands. He'd listened to her drone on and on about nonsense he probably could care less about. When he'd spoken, he'd been genuine, not critical of her about anything. He didn't act scandalized about her actions; instead, he seemed to take them in stride and make a joke. Perhaps that was because she'd conveniently left out some of the worst details. But did it matter? He hadn't been judgmental of her at all.

"Sorry," she said with a sultry smile when she realized he was staring at her. "You said to be myself, and I must admit that I'd been holding that back for a while."

"It's all right. I'm sure I'll survive the shock," he teased, but his voice sounded gravelly and uneven.

She smiled. "I sure hope so," she said, tracing his soft lips with her fingertips.

His hand came up and he started stroking the back of her wrist with one lone finger. His movements were slow and sure with no set pattern. Her fingers stilled on his lips as her body trembled from his scorching touch. He kissed the fingers that she held at his mouth. First, all at the same time, then he took her wrist and held it still while he kissed each fingertip separately. He lowered her hand and bent his head to her parted lips before taking them again.

Mr. Daltry's kisses had been gentle and coaxing before, but this time it was different, demanding. He clasped her face between his hands, using his thumbs to stroke her cheeks as his mouth plundered hers. Liberty's hands came up around his neck and sank into his thick, black hair. Twirling her fingers into the soft mass, she let out a gasp when his tongue touched hers.

She felt herself being lowered backwards on the settee and offered no protest to his machinations. Leaving his hair, she moved her hands to his face. She was in awe of how soft and smooth the skin over such a hard ridge could be as she traced the edges of his cheekbones. He pulled back and she blinked up at him. He looked just as unsure as she felt. He pulled his hands away and went to sit back up. Feeling bereft at the absence of his hands, she grabbed his wrists. "Don't go," she pleaded. "Stay. Touch me."

His eyes went wide and she thought he'd refuse and walk away. But he didn't. He only swallowed hard and asked, "Where?"

She brought his hands to the hard plane in the center of her chest. "Anywhere. Everywhere."

He groaned and seemed to need no more encouragement. His hands started to do a slow and thorough investigation of the top of her chest. His fingers left a searing trail as they traveled along her collarbone and the top of her sternum. Becoming bolder, he leaned down and dropped hot, searing kisses along the same paths his fingers had just taken. She shivered in delight when he placed an openmouthed kissed on her chest just above that atrocious gold bow.

His eyes flickered up to her in a silent question, and she lowered her lashes in response, hoping he'd understand. She shivered again when his fingers pulled the ends of the chord, destroying the bow and loosening her bodice. His hands worked the laces, loosening them as he went. Then, his hands traveled away from the center of her bodice and took hold of the shoulder straps. Very slowly, he pushed her right strap to the edge of her shoulder, kissing each quarter-inch of skin he exposed along the way. When the strap had fallen loose, he kissed her bare shoulder and back to his starting place, this time with an open mouth. She gasped when he dipped his tongue into the hollow right above her collarbone before repeating the tantalizing process on the other side.

When he'd gotten her left sleeve down and had kissed the top of her chest until she thought she'd go insane if he didn't stop, he looked up at her. "Open your eyes," he whispered. When she complied, he swallowed and quietly asked, "Are you sure?"

She scanned his taut face. He looked to be struggling with her decision just as much as she was. When she saw his eyes, her mind relaxed and she knew what she wanted. She'd seen that look before. That was the look of hunger and desire. She'd seen it many times, just never directed at her. That was the difference. This man desired *her*. No one else, just her; and though she knew she shouldn't, she desired him, too. "Yes," she whispered back.

His lashes lowered and his shaky hands pulled her bodice apart. With how low the bodice on her dress was cut, she hadn't been able to wear a chemise, only her corset, which was now exposed to Mr. Daltry's hungry gaze. She swallowed as he put his left elbow next to her head and rested his head onto his fisted hand, looking straight at her chest. He moved his free hand up to her chest and lightly skimmed the planes and slopes with the ends of his fingers.

He shifted his gaze to her, though she couldn't see it through her closed eyes, she could feel it. He then used his fingertips to trace the outline of left breast, followed by the right, causing them both to swell with anticipation.

She knew she should be embarrassed. She was as good as topless with a stranger in her sister's sitting room. Yet, she wasn't. Not with him. She just couldn't be.

His hand moved to the edge of the cup on her corset and she held her breath when it slipped inside and squeezed her tender breast. She felt her nipple tauten against his palm and turned her head to the side in pleasure at the sensation of his rough palm chafing her.

"Can we loosen this?" he asked, his voice uneven and his breathing ragged.

"In the back," she whispered, "just pull the string at the top." She arched up so he could reach under her and untie the string that would loosen her stays.

He untied the string and the cups fell loose, exposing her breasts to his consuming gaze. "You're so beautiful," he rasped, bringing his hand back to her naked breast.

"I'm sure you say that to all your lovers," she blurted.

"Never," he said, shaking his head. "Only you."

He said something else, but she didn't hear it, she couldn't hear anything when he was sending waves of pleasure through her body like this. He continued to shape her left breast with firm and tender squeezes while he bent his head to the breast closest to him and feathered kisses on her skin, causing it to tingle. Holding her nipple between his thumb and index finger, he gave it a light squeeze while his lips placed a gentle kiss on her other pebbled peak. She sighed and arched her back in pleasure.

His hand spread to cup her swollen breast while his mouth continued its wicked exploration of the other. His lips parted over the tip of her breast before covering it. She cried out in pleasure when his tongue flicked then circled the rigid peak. His hand left her breast and moved to the center of her chest where he used one of his long, blunt-tipped fingers to move as if spelling out a message while his mouth continued laving her.

His mouth released her breast and blew a small puff of warm air over the tip, making her shiver. "Would you do it again?" she asked when she was sure he was looking at her. It was hard to see anything anymore now that the moon had slipped behind a group of trees.

His chest rumbled as he chuckled. "If it's what the lady wishes, I shall be happy to comply." Then he bent his head to her other breast.

"I didn't mean that," she said with a pleasure-induced sigh.

He released her and moved his head up to look at her. "Did I mistake your pleasure?" he asked, his voice hoarse, unsure.

"No, not at all," she assured him, reaching up to stroke his silky hair. "I liked it very much. But I missed the letters you wrote. Would you do it again, please?"

"Oh." He shook his head and swallowed audibly. "No. I'm sorry," he said before he turned his head to the side and planted a searing kiss in her palm.

Disappointment at never knowing the identity of those elusive letters cut through the haze of lust and desire that had surrounded her, but a door slamming not so far away, made it shatter. Eyes wide, she asked, "Did you hear something?"

She felt his head nod against her hand. "I think it came from the room right next to us. Whose room is that?"

Panic seized her chest. "Brooke and Andrew's," she said quickly, not caring she had referred to her brother-in-law so informally in Mr. Daltry's presence.

"That door connects the two rooms, doesn't it?" he said, pointing at a door in the middle of the wall that ran adjacent to her sister's room.

She gulped then nodded. The muffled sounds of voices could be heard through the wall. The very real possibility that someone could come walking through that door and find them at any minute terrified her. "We have to get out of here," she whispered, trying to scramble from his grasp.

"All right," he said, helping her to her feet. "How do I get out of the house?"

"Leave this room and go to the right. Walk down to the end of the hall, then go left and go down the servants' stairs. At the bottom, there'll be a back door on the right," she said, trying to bring her dress up.

"Do you need any help," he asked, grabbing his cloak.

"Can you do my corset?" she asked hopefully.

"This might shock you, but I'm not all that familiar with ladies clothing," he said sheepishly. "I suppose I just have to retie it. Hold on a second, and I'll try." He grabbed the loose strings on the back of her corset and started trying to tie it.

She smiled at his confession. "And here I thought all men knew how women's clothing worked."

"No, most are more concerned with getting a woman out of her gown, not so much with getting her back into it," he said, tying the strings.

"And are you only interested in getting a woman out?"

"Would I be tying up your corset if that were the case?" he asked, taking a step back to look at his handiwork.

"No, I suppose not. You didn't do it right, I'm afraid." She turned around to show him that when she pulled up her bodice, she couldn't get it to close because her corset wasn't tight enough and her breasts were too big.

"Here," he said, grabbing his cape. "Drape this around yourself and walk to your room"

She grabbed the cape and tried to cover up the best she could with it. It was useless though. With her shoulder straps stuck in the middle of her upper arms and not budging when she tried to yank them up, she had limited mobility. When she'd tried to maneuver the cape in a way to get the cloth to just rest on her shoulders, it would fall down because it was too heavy, and expose her barely covered breasts and gaping bodice. After the third attempt, she let it slide to the floor and mumbled, "I suppose I'll just have to go like this. Hopefully, nobody will see me."

Holding his sword and picking up his cape, he walked with her to the door that led to the hallway. He handed her his sword and cape and said, "Hold these. Which room is yours?"

"Wh—what are you planning to do?" she asked cautiously as she watched him peek his head out the door to see if there was anyone in the hallway.

"What does it look like? I'm going to carry you. Now, which room is yours?"

She swallowed a nervous bubble that had formed in her throat and said, "Second door on the left."

"Very well." He nodded and reached an arm around her

shoulder and one around her knees, then scooped her up. Once he got her settled in his arms, he whispered, "Use the cape to cover up anything you don't want seen."

Without a second's hesitation, she brought the cape all the way up to the top of her head to cover her face as well as her gaping bodice. "I think they'll still recognize you," he said in a low tone, his chest rumbling with a low chuckle.

She lowered the cloak down from her face. "What do you mean?"

He glanced at her feet. "The bottom of your dress and slippers are still exposed. They'll know you're a woman, not some parcel for delivery."

"That's all right. They won't know my identity. They'll just think I'm some doxy you found at the ball," she said, flashing him a smile then covering her head again.

Slipping quietly from the room, he carried her down to hers. While his strong hands held her tightly to him, her ear rested against his heart and listened to its strong and steady beat as it sounded in time with his sure steps.

Once they crossed the threshold of her room, he paused for a moment before carrying her to the bed. Gently placing her on the bed, he took a few steps back and she instantly missed the heat of his large body. Lowering the cape, her eyes were drawn to the fire that was already blazing in the hearth. Mr. Daltry stood next to it with his hands in his pockets, looking rather serious. "I should go now," he said after a minute.

She bit her lip and looked away. "Could you help me out of my dress?" she whispered.

***

Paul fisted his hands inside his pockets. She was going to allow a stranger to undress her? "I don't think that's wise," he replied with a calm he didn't feel.

She looked at him innocently. "Please. I can't get it off myself and I'd be embarrassed to go find someone else to help me."

Paul closed his eyes. Was she so innocent and naïve that she didn't understand how her suggestion might be interpreted? Had she asked any other man, he would have taken it as an opportunity to have his way with her. Did she not realize that? Or did she just not care? Bile rose in his throat again. He knew his wife didn't hold him in high esteem, but tonight proved she likely held him in no esteem at all.

"Please," she repeated weakly.

"Fine," he agreed savagely. "But I'm only undoing the fastenings to help it come off, then I'm turning around while you take it off." Turning around? Did he really just say that? He should have said "leaving".

She stood up and came to stand in front of him. His fingers went to work on all the little ties and clasps that held her gown and corset in place. His moves were quick and methodical, not wanting to offer her any tenderness or love as he went about his work. Taking care not to touch or look at any exposed skin, he undid the last tie and walked away to go stand in front of her vanity while she scurried behind her screen.

His hand reached into his pocket again and felt the slip of paper he'd seen lying on Liberty's bed addressed to the two of them. Good thing she'd had that cape over her eyes or she might have seen it and the whole thing would have been exposed. It was too late now to expose his role. If he did, there would be no way she'd forgive him. It would be better to just follow his original plan of going to fetch her from Elizabeth's in a few days and trying to woo her, although now that would be nearly impossible. She might come to like him well enough as himself, but she'd always have her night of passion with the mysterious Tom Daltry. He clenched his fist tighter and crumpled the note.

Stepping closer to the vanity, his eyes caught on a familiar object: her journal. She'd taken it to Elizabeth's? He would have thought she'd left it since she was obviously very upset with him when she left. Why would she want to take something he'd given her? Quickly, he flipped it open and thumbed through to look at the dates. His fingers stopped and a chill ran through him when he reached a date from last week and noticed there were entries. He flipped a few more pages and saw more entries. There were entries for every single day since she'd been gone. He wanted to read them. He wanted to know what or who had gotten her to smile. The entries had to be true. She'd had no reason to write nonsense since he wasn't there to read them. His hopes lifted slightly. Maybe there was a chance for him.

Hearing her coming from behind the screen, he quickly shut the book and turned to face her. He'd seen her countless times in her nightrail since they'd married and he'd started bringing up her bath water each morning. But this time, it was different. The way she stood in front of the fire in her paper thin nightrail made his blood simmer. His gaze swept her from the top of her head to the pink ends of her toes that were poking out the bottom. Desire thrummed through him and he had to look away. He had no right to take her innocence. He may be her husband, but she didn't know that. Perhaps he was wrong to kiss and caress her in the other room. Here, in this room, he'd do the right thing and keep his hands to himself.

The awkward silence was broken when he heard her pad over to her window. "It looks like everyone's gone home," she said softly.

"Yes, I assumed as much when we heard your cousin and her husband go into their room," he said evenly.

"Oh," she said, blinking owlishly. "I wonder what time it is."

He scanned the room for a clock and didn't see one. Finally, he shrugged and said, "Early morning, I expect. I don't know the exact time as I haven't a watch."

Her eyes lit up. "I do." She rushed over to where he stood and started digging in her reticule.

Paul couldn't stop himself from inhaling her scent once more while she stood next to him. "I didn't realize women carried watches in their reticules," he said inanely to distract himself from her.

She laughed. "Most pin them on their bodice, actually. However, I left that one at home and the one I have with me isn't the kind one pins to their clothing," she said as she pulled out a golden pocket watch with a long gold chain.

His eyes were trained on her delicate fingers as they turned it over to undo the latch. But before she could get it open, his eyes locked on the crest that was engraved on the top and his heartbeat escalated. He hadn't lost his watch after all. She'd taken it. Why? "Where did you get that," he asked raggedly, turning his head so she would see his face and ask why he was so interested.

"It's his," she said simply without seeming to recognize his stiff posture.

Her fingers continued to fruitlessly work the fastening and he rolled his eyes. Did she not realize that it didn't even work? Losing his patience at her failure to get the blasted thing open, he jerked it from her hands. "Be careful with that," she snapped. "It cost me six weeks worth of wages to get it fixed."

His fingers stilled. "Fixed?"

"Yes, fixed," she said, turning her head away. "As it turns out, I…uh…inadvertently broke it."

"I see," he drawled.

She rolled her eyes. "I doubt it. To quote the Duke of Gateway, I bungled it badly. Anyway, he helped me find a jeweler who was able to repair it. I almost fainted when I saw the bill."

His stomach lurched. "Did Gateway pay it for you?" he asked with a sharp edge to his voice. Was she involved with the duke romantically? Had that led him to agree to pay her jeweler's bill?

"No," she said, grabbing the watch back. She fiddled with the latch again and finally got it to open. "He only tried to pay for the chain since it was he who asked the jeweler to add it, but I refused. I wanted to pay for everything, even if it cost me six weeks of wages."

"Wages?" he echoed irritably. "Is that how you refer to the generous allowance your husband graciously bestows upon you?"

"No. I mean wages as I work for my pin money. My husband has never seen fit to give me an allowance."

"What do you mean?" he asked, trying to keep his voice even despite the irritation that was coursing through him. He'd arranged for her to have more money each month than she could possibly spend.

"I meant exactly what I said. I don't get an allowance. For some reason, my husband didn't see fit to give me one, so I started working as a companion," she said defiantly.

He blinked at her. That's why she was working as a companion? More importantly, where was the money he'd set up for her to have? He remembered creating an account for her at the local bank in Bath the morning after they'd married. They were supposed to draw on his account from London each month and send her a notice of her funds. Why hadn't that happened? He'd have to sort that out first thing tomorrow, he told himself. Shaking his head, he softly asked, "Why didn't you say anything to him?" He hoped she didn't realize that she'd never mentioned to him that she hadn't asked her husband about it.

She shrugged. "I didn't wish to argue with him."

"You mean because you were afraid if you asked for an allowance, he'd send you away?" he asked, understanding the situation better.

She ran her fingers up and down the gold chain and nodded. "I heard Papa say he'd had to add my sister's dowry to mine in order for him to agree to marry me," she said as a single tear rolled down her cheek.

Wiping the tear away with the pad of his thumb, he lowered his voice and softly said, "I'm sorry. I would have married you without a dowry." His words were completely honest. Too bad she didn't know who it was that was really saying them.

She smiled a watery smile at him and his heart squeezed. "That is very sweet of you. You're a good man."

"You care for him, don't you?" he asked before he could stop himself. He didn't need her to admit to loving him. But if she cared for him, even a little, he knew they stood a chance together.

She shifted her gaze to his open watch, then back to his eyes. "Yes. I think so," she said before swallowing. "A wise woman pointed out to me a few days ago that I must, or else I would have given his watch back to him when I had the chance, instead of carrying it around with me."

He smiled at her as his heart nearly burst out of his chest.

Elizabeth was a wise woman indeed. He wanted to pull her into his arms and reveal his identity now more than ever. But the fear he'd ruin everything if he did, kept him from acting. "Well, the watch turned out beautifully," he told her honestly. "Your husband is a lucky man to have you, even if he hasn't realized it yet." The last words added only to keep up the disguise. He'd realized long ago he was a lucky man.

"Thank you. Mr. Holler did a beautiful job, didn't he? I'm just glad the duke had agreed to help me. Apparently, Mr. Holler was the only one who could fix some of the pieces and he only does work for titled gentlemen." She rolled her eyes.

"I should go," he said abruptly. "I hope everything works out well for you and your husband. Be sure you tell him that you care for him, you might be surprised what he'll say in return."

"I doubt it," she said, waving her hand dismissively. "But, thank you for everything."

"Everything?" he repeated, feeling his elation slip.

"Yes, everything, but mostly for talking to me and being a friend," she said sweetly.

Not sure what to say, he just nodded and said, "You're welcome."

He walked across the room and was almost to the door when she came up behind him and grabbed his wrist. "Wait. You didn't tell me why I should be thankful so many women have been intimate with my husband."

He looked at her curiously. "What?" What had made her think of *that?*

"Earlier, you said I should be thankful my husband had had so many mistresses, and then you got sidetracked talking about men's parts." Her face flushed and her gaze dropped to his chest.

"Oh, that," he said, not sure if she'd even see the humor in it now. "I was just going to make a jest really." When she looked at him as though she expected him to tell her, he said, "I was just going to say at least now you know that *someone* doesn't find him boring."

"Oh." A simple smile took her lips. "I've already discovered that."

He bent down and brushed a kiss on her lips and whispered, "Goodnight."

"Goodnight."

Chapter 27

Walking from her room was the hardest thing he'd ever done, but he couldn't stay. He'd let things go too far for that. Now, he'd have to play the oblivious husband and wait for her to come to him. He could still go fetch her from Elizabeth's, he supposed, but for some selfish reason, he wanted her to be the one to come to him.

He walked down the stairs and wasn't surprised at all to see Liberty's family anxiously waiting in the parlor. When he'd carried Liberty down the hall to her room, both John and Andrew had seen him from where they were talking at the end of the hall, presumably debating what happened with him and Liberty. Paul had given a terse shake of his head, hoping they'd understand his silent message. He doubted they had, which explained why they were waiting for him.

Not wanting to reveal his private life to them, he simply told them he'd figured out who "Allison" was within five minutes, but she'd never discovered his identity and he'd prefer to keep it that way. John opened his mouth to ask questions, but Andrew took pity on Paul by kindly reminded John that Liberty was Paul's wife and the best thing was for Paul to handle it from here on out by himself. Thankfully, John accepted this and let him be.

The next morning he leeched the color from his hair and went to his bank in London to straighten out the mystery regarding Liberty's allowance. After speaking to three employees, it was discovered his signature was missing from a release form. He scribbled his name and left feeling slightly better about the money situation.

With no other business to take care of in London, he mounted his horse and rode in the direction of home. He made a quick stop at Elizabeth's. He knew he'd be denied entry, but he wanted to put in an appearance nonetheless.

He tried his hardest not to crack a smile when the maid described Liberty as a lifeless limp lily that needed to rest. He'd felt the urge to play the role of the worried husband and demand to see her, especially when the maid thought to deter him by mentioning she was currently being bathed. Instead, he left his well wishes and went to his house to face an irritated Mrs. Siddons.

Ignoring her and her disapproving looks, he went fishing in the creek. He hoped Liberty would be there by the time he came back. Disappointment flooded him when he came in and realized she wasn't there. He reminded himself it had only been one day and that she may have stayed in London with Brooke for a day or two.

The next day he went about his business, constantly wondering if she'd be there when he got home, and was disappointed again to find she wasn't.

Late that night, Paul awoke to the sound of loud pounding on the front door. Throwing his dressing robe on, he ran to the front door to see what the racket was. Opening the door revealed a liveried messenger. He recognized the livery right away and snatched the note from the man's fingers.

He scanned the content. Twice. The words could not be correct, he told himself. He looked up at the messenger who looked just as unsettled as Paul, telling him there was no mistake, the words were correct. He dismissed the servant, went to his study to write a missive of his own, dressed and saddled his horse. It was going to be a long night.

***

Liberty spent the past two days thinking of what she'd tell Paul when she saw him next. She wanted to tell him she cared for him, loved him even. But how would he react when she told him about her night with Mr. Daltry? Would he discount her love when he heard what she'd done? She couldn't keep this from him. He had a right to know. If there was any chance for their relationship, she'd have to tell him.

Feeling nauseous at remembering how shamelessly she'd

acted that night, she tapped on the roof and asked the coachman to pull the carriage over. A few minutes later, she felt well enough to continue her journey.

Brooke and Andrew had returned to Rockhurst the day after the ball and threatened to drag her along and deposit her on Paul's doorstep. She'd refused and insisted she'd stay with Mama and Papa because she wanted to meet some of the gentlemen that were calling on Madison. That was only partially true, and they all knew it. Fortunately, they hadn't said anything to her, but she had a feeling they knew what happened with Mr. Daltry the night before.

Mama and Papa graciously allowed her to stay and she met several nice gentlemen. Then after two days, Papa all but threw her out, telling her she needed to go home to her husband. She supposed he was right, and she'd never know how Paul would react if she didn't go. So now she found herself in a carriage less than a mile from Bath, feeling sicker by the minute.

When the carriage came to a halt in front of the familiar cottage, Liberty breathed a sigh of relief, followed by a nervous cry when the front door opened. Taking a deep breath, she made her way to the carriage door and descended once the coachman placed the stairs in front. She kept her eyes down, locked on her slippers as she descended, praying he wouldn't see her transgressions in her eyes when he looked at her. From the bottom of the stairs, she looked up and blinked to see a fitful Mrs. Siddons clutching a piece of paper as if it were a bank note for a thousand pounds.

"Mrs. Siddons," Liberty greeted, thankful she'd have some support until she had to face Paul.

"Ma'am, I got some bad news, I'm afraid," Mrs. Siddons said solemnly.

"Bad news?" she echoed. "Is it Paul? Is he all right?" Her voice bordered on hysterical and she didn't even care.

"I believe so, ma'am," she said, holding out the letter. "The details are in the letter, I imagine. The house was empty when I got here this morning. I found this in the kitchen."

Liberty snatched the letter from her grasp and broke the wax seal. With shaky fingers, she unfolded the missive and read the lines.

Liberty,
I'm in Cornwall at my brother's estate. Please come join me.
Paul

"He's rather evasive, isn't he?" she said with a frown.

Mrs. Siddons, being the ever dutiful servant, had already packed Liberty's remaining clothes and had them loaded into Paul's carriage before she'd even arrived. With nothing holding her back, she dismissed her father's coachman to return the coach to London and climbed into Paul's carriage to begin her journey to Cornwall.

She'd never been there before and was certain that if the circumstances were different she'd enjoy the journey more.

It was the dead of night by the time she reached a far off estate on the outer stretches of Cornwall. There were neither torches burning, nor anyone outside to greet them. The coachman bade her to wait in the coach while he went to the stables. She gladly complied and fell asleep waiting for him to come back for her.

She didn't know how long she slept before she heard a noise that half startled her awake followed by two strong arms lifting her up. The arms felt like strong bands as they firmly held against a warm chest. He carried her out of the carriage and into a dark house. She heard boot heels clank on the floor with each step and she snuggled closer to him. He felt good. Solid. Not sure if she was dreaming, she refused to open her eyes, too afraid she'd wake up only to find herself back in the carriage lying against the squabs. This dream was too good to wake up from.

When she did wake the following morning, she found herself clad in only her chemise alone in a room she'd never seen before. Pulling the covers up to her neck, she took in her surroundings.

The sparsely decorated room was bigger than half the cottage she lived in with Paul. The furnishings were curiously elegant for a man as harsh as the viscount. She got out of the bed and walked to where her belongings were waiting for her across the room. Her trunk was placed to the right of the wardrobe and her reticule was resting on top. She opened the wardrobe and her nose was assailed by the scent of fresh cedar. Not sure how long they planned to stay, she decided not to unpack and make use of the wardrobe.

She walked around the room, opening drawers, peeking in cabinets, inspecting the furniture, all in an effort to delay the inevitable. Looking at the clock, she sighed. She could wait no longer. It was time to talk to Paul.

Finding a dress that didn't require a corset, therefore, making it possible for her to put it on unassisted, she dressed. While she was dressing, she thought of what she'd say to Paul. He'd most likely be waiting for her in the breakfast room. She frowned. Was the breakfast room of his brother's estate the best place to have this conversation? No, she decided with a shake of her head. Perhaps she should wait until they went back home. That would be the better time. That way he could rant and rave at her all he wanted without having an audience.

Resigned to her choice, she opened the door and walked down the long hall. Not sure which way to go, she picked a direction and started walking. She stopped every few feet to view the portraits that hung on the walls. They were mostly of landscapes during a storm. One had lightening striking a tree in the middle of a field. Another was of a ship in the middle of the ocean during a heavy rain storm. Farther down the wall was a painting of a horse and rider riding through the forest during a lightning storm. A shiver ran up her spine at the image.

At the end of the hall, was a stairwell with a servant standing at the top. "Excuse me, can you tell me where the breakfast room is?" she asked the impeccably dressed man.

"You must be Mrs. Grimes. I'm Ludwig," he said with a low bow. "I was asked to show you around. I apologize for not greeting you earlier."

Ludwig took her to the breakfast room where she ate a magnificent breakfast in complete solitude. After the meal, Ludwig took her for a tour. He showed her where some of the common rooms were located and explained the routine around the estate. She was still curious as to why she was here in the first place and wanted to ask him where Paul was so she could ask him, but before she could, he led her to the portrait gallery and told her to look around, and he'd catch up with her later.

Frowning, she turned to the portraits. There were so many she could hardly see any empty wall. She scanned the faces and read the plaques on the bottom so she'd know their names. She walked from one end to the other until she got to two teenage boys holding rapiers and froze. Without having to look at the plaque, she knew it was Paul and his brother. She smiled at the different expressions on their faces. Sam had a wild grin and Paul looked terrified. She would be, too, she supposed, if her attacker looked so giddy about it.

Farther down, she saw a more recent picture of Sam. His hat was askew, shirt half buttoned, one side of his shirt untucked from his breeches and a smug look on his face. It seemed like he enjoyed making a mockery of his title and position. She shook her head at his idiocy and looked at the last portrait on the wall. It was of Paul. He was riding his stallion. He was in his shirtsleeves with the top button undone, the way she'd seen him so many times when he was relaxing in his study or when he'd come to her room to read her entries. His hair was whipping in the wind and his face was split with the biggest grin she'd ever seen. He looked truly happy.

Staring at the portrait so intently, she didn't hear footsteps coming up behind her and nearly jumped out of her skin when a voice said, "That was painted just last spring."

Her body froze in place. This was it. The time had come for her to see her husband for the first time since she'd left. She slowly turned around and swallowed when she looked at his sandy haired, clean-shaven appearance. He looked just the opposite of Mr. Daltry, yet for some reason, she found him just as handsome. She shook her head to clear her thoughts. "You looked like you were enjoying the ride," she said easily, gesturing to the portrait.

"I suppose I was. Thankfully the artist was good enough that I only had to keep my face like that for thirty minutes while he made the outline. Any longer than that, and I'd probably refuse to ever smile again," he admitted with a quick grin. "I see you've recovered nicely from your illness."

She flushed. "Yes, thank you," she said, looking at the floor.

"Would you care to go for a walk?" he asked, offering her his arm.

"I'd be delighted." She slipped her hand through his proffered arm.

He flashed another quick smile before leading her down the hall. "Did Ludwig show you about, then?" he asked, steering her into a dimly lit hallway.

She was about to answer when suddenly he brought his hand up to cover where hers was holding onto his sleeve and gave her hand a light squeeze, sending a thrill of excitement up her arm. "Not here," she said abruptly.

He looked at her, cocking his head. "You mean he didn't take you here?"

"Right," she agreed, slightly flustered. Why was his touch affecting her so? Was she such a wanton it didn't matter whose hands were on her? She'd react this way to anyone's touch?

"Do you ride?"

"No," she said, shaking her head. "Brooke and Madison do, but I never learned."

"Pity, that" he said, twisting his lips. "Would you like to learn?"

"Of course," she readily agreed.

He looked down and grinned at her. "Excellent."

She tore her gaze away from his. She'd promised Mr. Daltry she'd be herself, and for the past few days she had. Hopefully Paul wouldn't be annoyed by her unabashed excitement. This was her. She wasn't holding anything back anymore.

Outside, there was a chestnut mare saddled and ready. "She's beautiful. What's her name?" she asked, coming up beside the beast.

"Horse."

"Did you think of that all on your own?" she teased, putting her foot in his cupped hands.

He boosted her up and helped her get settled. "Actually, I did. My brother wanted to name her something else. Something entirely unsuitable, I might add."

She wondered what it had been. If Paul had been Mr. Daltry, she would have asked. Her face heated up thinking of the scandalous things they'd talked about. His soft chuckle brought her back to reality.

"Your fetching blush suggests you're thinking up all sorts of naughty possibilities. However, I can assure you, you'll never guess," he said, flashing her a wolfish grin.

"Then you shall have to inform me," she said, holding the reins a bit too tight.

He shook his head. "No. Believe it or not, there are things even I won't say. And if I were the kind to say such filth, I wouldn't say it in front of you."

"And why not?" she demanded haughtily.

"Because I'd hate to offend your sensibilities by shocking you," he said, still grinning. "By the way, you're holding the reins too tight. Relax your hold. That's better."

"Your excuse won't wash with me. I know lots of shocking things," she returned pertly.

He snorted. "Like what?" He grabbed onto Horse's bridle and started walking her forward.

"Like all sorts of dirty slang for a man's pizzle," she said, hoping he wouldn't turn around and catch her blushing.

He stopped walking, but didn't turn around. "Finally puzzle that out, did you?"

"Yes, no thanks to you," she retorted after he started walking again.

"I would have told you if you'd asked. You never did. And when I offered, you refused and fled the room soon after." Silence engulfed them, broken only when Paul made an unusual sound with his mouth and mused, "Who did tell you, I wonder."

Heat flooded her cheeks. This had not been a good

conversation to start. She'd wanted him to confide whatever secret he was keeping from her and thought he'd tell her if she exposed that she wasn't as innocent as he thought. Apparently she was wrong. "A friend," she said at last.

"A friend?" he repeated bitterly, sending nervous chills up her spine.

"Yes, a friend," she confirmed.

He pulled on Horse's bridle and she turned slightly to start walking toward a not so distant stream. "Why Miss Live-by-the-rules Liberty, I must say I'm rather surprised you would choose a friend who'd discuss such things; or even think abou them, for that matter."

Irritation at his words caused her lips to twist into a sneer. "There are many things you don't know about me."

"Of that, I am quite certain," he said dryly, guiding the horse around a knot of trees and shrubs. "You hardly see fit to share anything about yourself with me." His last sentence was barely louder than a whisper and caused her heart to squeeze at the raw emotion exposed in his words. He'd wanted to know her and she'd purposely been distant.

"What would you like to know?" she asked, ready to make a new start.

"There are many things I'd like to know. But first, I'd like to know if you'd care to have a picnic with me," he asked, leading Horse around one final tree to where a picnic had been laid out and was waiting for them.

"You planned this?" she asked, dumbfounded.

"Not at all," he said, shaking his head earnestly. "About an hour ago, I was walking from that gazebo over there," he pointed to a white gazebo a hundred yards away, "after having my daily devotions and I happened upon a couple of young lovers in the midst of a tryst. Scandalized, I preached to them until they abandoned their wicked activities, begged me to baptize them in the stream and went along their merry way. Then, I thought what a shame it would be to let their food go to waste and came to see if you would like to indulge in the act of gluttony with me."

She couldn't control the giggle that overtook her. "I would be happy to be a glutton with you. Although, I must admit, I had no idea you had such a sense of humor," she said, wrapping her arms around his neck as he put his hands on her waist to help her off the horse.

"Didn't you?" he murmured in her ear, his warm breath fanning her ear. "Perhaps there are many things you don't know about me, either." He led her to the blanket and unloaded the basket while she sat down on the blanket and watched the ripples in the stream.

Placing her hands on the ground behind her, she reclined and tilted her face toward the sun. It was a rather warm day for the middle of March, she mused as the sun heated her face. Feeling daring, she brought one hand up untied her bonnet, and tossed it down next to her. "What did you pack for us?" she asked casually.

"Nothing," he said, pulling out a wheel of cheese. "But I have it on the best authority that Sweets sent some of her famous shredded chicken sandwiches."

"Sweets?" she repeated with a small giggle.

"Also known as Cook," he said, coming to sit next to her. He'd stripped to his shirtsleeves and had undone his top button. He sat with his knees up and his arms resting across them. "That's just what we call her. Sadly, I don't remember all of the story, but I'll tell you what I can remember. When I was three, I liked to go help her make biscuits and other treats in the kitchen. One day, I told her I loved her and thought she was sweeter than any baked sweet ever could be." He put his head down and shook it, undeniably embarrassed. "Thank goodness, I don't remember saying that to her. However, even though I don't remember it, both Sweets and my mother thought it was the most darling thing ever, and from that day forward, everyone always called her Sweets."

She laughed. "You'll have to make biscuits for us sometime, then," she said, favoring him with a smile.

"Oh, you don't want me to, I assure you," he told her, grabbing a sandwich and handing it to her. "I've tried, on a few occasions, to make them myself. They were so bad a stray dog I found in Bath wouldn't eat them."

She stripped off her gloves before unwrapping the sandwich and taking a bite. "These are good. Do you think she'd write the recipe down for Mrs. Siddons?" she asked before sinking her teeth into the sandwich again.

"Probably," he mumbled as he inhaled his sandwich.

They finished their picnic and Liberty was helping to put the glasses away when Paul put his hands on her waist and hauled her to her feet. "You don't have to do that, I'll get it."

"No; you got it out. I'll put it away."

He shook his head. "If you want to you can, but I was wondering if you might want to do something else instead."

"All right," she said curiously. He was being extremely nice to her today and she couldn't understand why. Not that he'd been especially mean to her in the past, but today it felt like he was going out of his way to be overly friendly and it caused the guilt of what she'd done with Mr. Daltry to increase tenfold.

"Do you remember the day I was late to Alex's?" he asked.

"Of course."

"Well, you asked where I was that day and I said out. Do you remember that?"

"Yes," she said, breaking eye contact. "You said your watch was broken and you lost track of time while you were out." This would have been a perfect time to give him his watch back. If only she'd brought it with her.

He nodded. "Yes, that's true. But I didn't say anything just now about my watch. I asked if you remember that I told you I was out."

"Yes," she said, looking back to his face. "You said you were out, but never said what you were doing." She pulled her wrist from his fingers as if she'd been burned. Had he been with another woman that day?

"Would you like to know what I was doing?"

"I—I don't know," she stammered. She knew he'd been with other women, but she wasn't sure she wanted to hear him admit it, especially after they'd had such a good morning so far.

He smiled at her. "How about if I tell you anyway? I was fishing."

"Fishing?" she repeated, astonished. "Do you do that often?"

He nodded. "As often as I can. It's my favorite pastime. I usually go in the afternoon after I've taken care of all my responsibilities with the church."

"I see."

"I brought my equipment with me today and I thought I'd teach you, if you'd like."

She couldn't have been more surprised if he *had* confessed to an affair. "I would like that very much," she said simply, watching as a grin bent his lips.

He walked over to where a smaller basket was sitting closer to the stream. He lifted the lid and pulled out a little box. She walked over to stand next to him as he pointed at the objects inside and said, "These are called flies. They're made from bits of animal hair and bird feathers wrapped around a hook and made to look like an insect." He took a couple out and placed them on his bare palm then held it up for her to see the different flies. "As you can see, some turned out better than others. The one on the far right, for example; it would be a perfect mayfly except I didn't wrap the thread tight enough and some of the hair has come loose."

"You made them?" she asked, picking one up to inspect it more closely.

"Of course. A fisherman is only as good as his tackle," he told her, putting all but one fly back into the box. He put the fly box back and grabbed what looked like a giant spool of thread. "This is called the reel and the string you see wrapped around is called the line," he said, holding it up so she could see it. He frowned. "There seems to be a tangle in it. Say, why don't you grab my rod while I work out this knot?"

"Excuse me?" she exclaimed in shock. He wanted her to grab his *rod*?

He looked up with wide and innocent eyes. "Grab my pole while I finish untangling this."

Her eyes went even wider. She hoped she'd misheard him the

first time, but apparently she hadn't. The rude man had brought her out here with the intent to do unspeakable things. Well, that did not mean she had to let him. She crossed her arms and stared at him while he picked at the knot.

"Or just stand there and watch me," he grumbled, tugging on the line.

Angry heat crept up her face and she bit the inside of her cheek. Her gaze dropped to just below his waist and she swallowed. Slowly she uncrossed one of her arms and extended her hand in the direction of his waist. Her fingers were just scant inches from him when suddenly his fingers closed around her wrist, staying her hand. Her eyes flew to his. "What are you doing?" he asked hoarsely.

Her face flamed with embarrassment and she moistened her lips. "You said to grab your rod."

"Oh, for goodness' sakes, Liberty," he burst out, "I meant my fishing rod. Look to your left. Do you see that long skinny pole leaning against the tree there? That's what I was talking about, not my privates. It seems you have willies on the brain today."

Mortification overtook her. "I'm sorry, I—"

"Don't worry about it," he said, cutting her off. "You didn't realize I wasn't talking metaphorically. It's all right. Would you please go grab my *fishing* rod?"

Without responding, she walked over to the tree, snatched the pole and walked back over to him. "Here," she said, resting it against his shoulder.

"Thank you," he said, picking up his rod and attaching the reel.

"You're welcome. Once again I'm sorry about..." she trailed off and looked at his hands as they twisted little metal objects on the rod.

"It's all right," he assured her. "Although, I must say, it's good to know you're so eager to touch me there," he teased.

She shook her head. "I wasn't willing at first," she countered cheekily. "It was only after I decided you'd never ask me to do so again when I was done with you that I reached forward."

He threw his head back and laughed. "Is that so? I knew you were a bloodthirsty one."

"Yes, I am," she confirmed with a smile.

"Never fear, now that I know that, I shall not ask you to touch me there," he told her with a smile. "However, I would like you to grab onto the end of this." He held the rod out to her and she grabbed the handle.

"Now what do I do?"

"First, you wait a minute while I finish tying the fly onto the line." He quickly tied the line around the hook eye. "Done. Now, we go fish with it." He led her closer to the stream and stood behind her before covering her hands with his. "First you have to pull out a good bit of line, like so. Then you cast. To do that you put your right hand here and you loosely hold onto the line with your left. Exactly so. All right. Now, you're going to bring it straight up in the air and then snap it forward. Very good. Now, do it again. Don't go so far back. You want to keep your wrist straight and stop when your forearm meets your upper arm." He released her and stood back to watch.

"Like this?" she asked, demonstrating what she thought to be proper form.

"Close," he said, covering her hands with his again. "You're bending your wrist. Keep it straight." His body being so close to hers made hers hum with awareness. There was no mistaking the sheer masculinity of him.

"Is this better?" she asked, pulling the rod back again.

"Perfect. Now this time, do that three times and on the third time, snap it almost all the way to the water and loosen your grip on the line enough that it flies out."

She looked at him curiously before trying to do what he just said. She pulled her arm back as he instructed three times then she let go of her line, and watched with a frown as her line just fell into a pool of circles at her feet. "I don't think I did it right."

"That's not your fault," he assured her, taking the rod from her and pulling the line back in. "It's difficult to explain. I'll show you instead." He grabbed the pole and crooked his left index finger around the line. "All right, you bring it back and snap it forward. Each time you need to allow some of the line to escape. Like so." He demonstrated twice. "Then on the third time, you'll want to loosen your hold almost completely to allow even more line to escape as you bring your rod tip almost to the water." He started over and showed her a complete cast. "Then when the fly is in the water, you move the line over a bit and hold it loosely with your right index finger under the rod while using your left hand to pull in the line."

"Why are you pulling it in so jerkily?"

"Actually, I'm not pulling it in just yet. I'm making small jerking movements with the line so the fly on the end moves under the water. See, the goal is to fool the fish into thinking there's a bug for him to eat. So you have to jerk the line to move the fly to fool the fish," he explained with a smile. "It sounds confusing, but it's really not." He started to pull the line in, letting it collect into a mass on the ground. "Here, why don't you give it another go?" He handed her the rod and stepped back.

She tried to cast a few more times. Each time she got slightly better, but that wasn't saying much. "I don't think I can do this," she said, admitting defeat and offering him his rod back.

"Nonsense," he said, pushing her hand away. He walked behind her and covered her hands again. "You just started. You'll get it. I'll help you this time," he murmured in her ear, sending sparks of excitement skidding down her spine. He was *so* close.

Together they cast and the fly landed right in the middle of a shadowed weed bed. "Did I do something wrong?" she asked tentatively.

"No, not at all. We want it there. That's where the fish are," he said, pressing his body closer to hers and helping her work the line.

"Oh." Was it just her or did the weather just heat up ten degrees? Being nestled against Paul's hard body made her blood race with excitement.

A second later there was a soft tug on the line. Not sure what to do, her eyes went wide and her hands tightened their hold on the line and pole. "Relax," he murmured. "You caught a fish. Now you need to set the hook. Slightly pull up on the rod. All right, now reel him in."

She was too excited to comply and heard Paul chuckle in her ear. "He's so ugly he's cute," she said when they finally brought the fish out of the water.

"Now that's a compliment if I ever heard one," he remarked, reaching into the fish's mouth to dislodge the hook. "Do you want to put him back?"

"What do I do? Just fling him in?"

Paul's eyes went wide and he shook his head. "You could, I suppose. Most do. But it's best if you don't. It shocks the fish when you do that."

"Oh, sorry."

"No need. What you do is hold the fish like this," he placed the fish in the palm of his hand and brought his fingers and thumb up to hold it firmly in between, "then you walk to the edge of the water and lower him in. Be sure to hold onto him until he's fully submerged. Then let go and he'll take off."

She twisted her lips and looked at their squirming catch. "I don't know if I can hold onto that wiggly thing," she admitted.

"You'll be fine. Just hold him tightly so he doesn't break free," he encouraged, transferring the fish to her hand.

She'd never felt anything so slimy in her life and was rethinking her decision to discard her gloves before they ate. Even if the gloves would have been ruined, her hands wouldn't feel so disgusting. "He's so wiggly, I think I'm about to drop him," she panicked.

"He'll live. I've had a few that have wiggled from my grasp before. You shouldn't drop him on purpose, mind you, but if you do, he'll be fine," he assured her as she nervously walked to the edge of the water.

"Is this good?" she asked, holding the fish in the water.

"Yes. Now let him go."

She watched the fish swim away and couldn't stop from grinning like a simpleton. "That was really exciting. Does it always feel so exciting to catch a fish?"

"I think so," he said with a smile. "Would you like your own rod?"

"Uh...I don't think I'm good enough."

He flashed her a smile. "That's not a problem. You'll get it. Then we can go together. When we get home, I'll make you your own."

"You make your own rods, too?" she marveled, impressed.

"Of course. Though I must admit, I had to buy the reel. Even I'm not that talented," he confided, his eyes sparkling with mirth. "We should go back in now. I have some business to attend."

"All right," she agreed, hiding her disappointment. She didn't want to go in and be left to her own devices.

Chapter 28

Liberty sat in her room staring out the window. She had to tell Paul. He deserved to know everything. Was it possible he cared for her? He'd spent time with her without intentionally vexing her. And if she were forced to admit it, she'd say he'd even been quite entertaining.

She'd forgotten to ask him how long they'd be staying and why they were here in the first place, she thought while absentmindedly chewing the inside of her mouth in contemplation. No matter. She'd just enjoy their time together here then tell him the truth when they went home. At least they'd have some fun together, before she ruined it.

A knock at the door brought her into the present. She went to the door and opened it to see Ludwig standing on the other side. "Your presence is required downstairs," he said with a bow.

"All right," she said slowly. "Do you know what Paul wants?"

"It's not Master Paul requesting to see you. It is I who thinks you should come down. We have guests. And seeing as there is no longer a mistress to the house, I thought you should act as hostess."

Liberty tried not to scowl. She didn't want to play hostess in a house that she was unfamiliar with to guests she didn't even know. "Very well. I shall be down momentarily," she said before shutting the door.

Checking her hair and grabbing a shawl, she went down the stairs. Turning the corner to the hall that led to the drawing room, Liberty caught sight of Paul's broad back. She smiled. At least he'd be in there with her. Almost to the door, she heard a young child call, "Pa! Pa!" She peeked around the corner just in time to see a little urchin run across the room straight into Paul's open arms. Her heart missed a beat. And not in a good way, either. She stood frozen in place as Paul hoisted one of his illegitimate children up onto his shoulders.

When she was able to tear her eyes away, she noticed there was a beautiful woman sitting on the settee on the far side of the room. The woman was too far away to see Liberty where she stood in the shadows outside the door. Anyway, her eyes were locked on Paul playing with their son. Numbly, Liberty looked back to father and son, trying to pick out some characteristic of the little boy that wasn't consistent with Paul's. She couldn't find any. Just as Lucy had told her, Grimes males bred true. She was going to be sick seeing Paul playing the father role. He would have made a great father to their children, she thought with a pang of remorse.

"So will there be another little sandy haired, green eyed boy in the near future, Paul?" the woman asked shrilly.

Paul shook his head. "She died."

Liberty's eyes were about to bulge out of her head. Who was dead? He better not be suggesting *she* was dead, or he'd soon find himself in that state.

"I can't say I'm sorry to hear that," the shrill woman said rather rudely.

Paul frowned at her. "That's not very nice."

The woman shrugged. "It may not be nice, but it's the truth. What of you? I heard you just married. Is your wife breeding?"

Lowering the boy from his shoulders, Paul joined him on the floor. They sat with their backs to Liberty, giving a side profile to the other woman. "No. It's a complicated situation where she's concerned," he said softly at last.

Liberty swallowed. Although she didn't like him talking of their relationship with others, she was grateful he hadn't implied she was the dead woman.

"Complicated?" the strange woman repeated with a laugh. "You mean she denies you." She repositioned herself on the sofa, leaning forward to let the bodice of her dress fall open and expose the swell of her plump breasts. "Perhaps I can be of comfort. I know as well as you do that the nights can be long and lonely without someone to share them with; and don't deny there's only so much comfort a man can find on his own."

Liberty vaguely understood the woman's last sentence, and she understood enough of her words to know she'd just witnessed a woman proposition Paul. And it hurt. It felt like the wind had been knocked out of her as she stood there and waited for his next words.

But he didn't respond; not to her anyway. He leaned over to open a cabinet and pulled out a little box of tin soldiers and lined them up on the floor. "Do you know how to play with tin soldiers?" he asked the boy.

"You sent him a set at Christmas. Why, I'll never understand," the boy's mother said, shaking her head.

Paul turned his head to her sharply. "Every boy needs a set of tin soldiers. Sam and I played with them. Why can't he?"

She waved her hand dismissively and leaned back. "I don't care that he has them. I understand you sent Lucy's boy a set, too.'

"Yes. I did," he acknowledged stiffly. "The two of you compare what I send your boys?"

"No, no," she laughed. "I just happened to see her and Seth a few weeks back. And while we were visiting, her boy talked for more than thirty minutes about how some woman who's teaching him to read played with his tin soldiers with him."

The blood drained from Liberty's face. What if this woman mentioned her name to Paul? How would he react when he found out that she'd unknowingly been interacting with his illegitimate son? Peeking to look at Paul, she noticed he wore a broad grin on his handsome face.

"My, don't you look happy," the woman mused.

"I am. I'm just glad he enjoyed them, that's all," he said, then made fighting noises associated with the weapon the soldier in his fingers carried.

The woman rolled her eyes. "You have a soft spot for him. Just like you do for Lucy," she said in a knowing tone.

"That's not true," he countered. "I had feelings for Lucy when we were younger, but not any longer."

"Oh really?" she said with a tone full of doubt. "You were madly in love with her. You even told her so right before you proposed."

His head snapped up. "You knew of that?"

"Of course I did. We've known each other a long time. She tells anyone who will listen about how you loved her and all the wonderful attributes you possess." Her words sounded careless and flippant, but Liberty knew there was something more.

Paul scowled at her. "Did she also mention why she refused me? Hmm? Did she tell you that my love was only good enough for her when it benefited her? Or when it came time to make a decision, she preferred to take a chance dancing to Sam's tune because he possessed a title and I didn't?" His words were harsh and bitter, but most of all, full of hurt. Lucy had hurt him badly, indeed.

The woman brought her thumb to her lip and chewed on her nail for a minute. "Are you saying you love your wife, then?" she asked softly.

Liberty didn't want to hear his answer. She knew he'd say no, and for as much as she despised him for his legion of children and his adulterous ways, she couldn't bear to hear him say he didn't love her. Rushing in the door, she startled them both by saying, "Good afternoon. Sorry to keep you waiting." She looked to Paul whose facial expression looked like that of a little boy getting caught skipping his lessons.

The woman stood up and turned a curious eye to Liberty. Belatedly, Paul scrambled to his feet and cleared his throat. "This is my wife, Liberty. Liberty, this is Evelyn Long, and this, is her son, Billy," he said, picking Billy up.

"Nice to meet you both," she said smoothly, looking at Miss Long.

A tea tray Liberty never ordered mysteriously appeared, and feeling more awkward than ever before, she poured their tea. Once they were all served, she couldn't find it in herself to strike up a conversation. After an hour of uncomfortable silence broken only by little Billy's playing, Miss Long made her excuses and scooped Billy up to leave. Paul walked Evelyn out while Liberty picked up the tea service to put it back on the tray.

Not wanting to be alone with Paul when he returned, she left the room and walked past them as they continued to talk in low tones by the door. They'd obviously not seen her and she had no interest in what they were talking about, or so she told herself as she climbed the stairs.

She spent the next hour in her room sorting out her feelings. She wanted to give their marriage a chance, but every time they made progress something would come up and ruin it. Today wasn't the first time she'd felt his presence so keenly and enjoyed being around him. She'd felt the same way before she'd left to go stay with Elizabeth. These were not new sensations. In fact, her body had responded to him ever since they'd married. But just like the heat and desire weren't new, neither were the problems. The man was a born seducer, she thought with a sigh. There was no other way to explain why he could affect her and so many others that way.

Hungry, she changed into a black velvet gown and went down to the dining room for dinner. She didn't want to eat with him, but she did want to eat. Perhaps with others present, it wouldn't be so uncomfortable, she reminded herself. This was his brother's house, after all. Though she hadn't encountered him yet, she assumed she'd see him at dinner. And even if he was a nasty sort, he would be a welcome addition to the dining company.

The dining room was quite full. So full it almost resembled a house party of sorts. She found it odd when she was directed to fill the seat as hostess. And she nearly gaped in astonishment when she looked down the long, long table and saw Paul occupying the host's seat.

Dinner was a delightful blur. She'd been seated near some of Paul's close relatives who felt the need to regale her with humorous tales of Sam and Paul's childhood. She had to admit most of them were hysterically funny and all were highly entertaining.

After dinner, she led the ladies to the drawing room where they all gossiped and she pretended to listen while studying the carpet. When the men joined them, she was surprised to notice everyone was dressed in black. Funny she hadn't noticed that before. Perhaps she only noticed it now because everyone was talking very somberly and nobody suggested they play parlor games.

Curious, but not knowing anyone well enough to inquire, she waited until a handful of people started to take their leave before approaching Paul. "Why are they all here?"

"They're guests. Don't worry, they've all been here before and can find their way to their rooms," he assured her.

"All right," she said slowly. "How much longer are they going to loiter in the drawing room?"

"I don't know," he admitted. Glancing at the clock on the far wall, he said, "It's nearly ten now. At ten, I'll kindly remind everyone we follow country hours. Likely, they'll take my meaning and go to bed then."

As he had promised, at ten Paul made the announcement and not ten minutes later everyone was tucked off to their rooms. Liberty wanted to play the part of hostess the best she could and waited until the last person had taken their leave of the drawing room before she turned to leave. "Oh, I thought you'd left already," she said to Paul who was blocking her path.

"Not yet," he said, shaking his head. "I thought I'd escort you to your room."

"All right," she agreed, taking his arm.

"Thank you for acting as hostess tonight," he said as they climbed the stairs.

"It was nothing really," she said dismissively. "Although, I do wonder why we're even here?"

They'd arrived outside of her room and he looked down at her. "Do you mind if I come in with you?"

Awareness shot through her body and her blood rushed through her veins. Did she dare let him in? If she did, would he think it was an open invitation to her bed? An invitation she wasn't ready to extend yet. Biting her lip, she shook her head. "No. Whatever you have to say, you need to say it here," she said in a small voice.

He smiled. "Are you sure? If you'd like, I can help you with your gown."

Her cheeks heated in anger. Was that how he did it? He'd offer to help a woman with her gown and then seduce her from there. She sent up a prayer of thanks for Mr. Daltry and his words of caution. If not for his comment about men only wanting to get women out of their clothes, she might have allowed Paul the Seducer into her room. "No, thank you. I don't need any help with my gown," she said hotly.

His eyes held a new gleam. "Do you ever?" he asked, cocking his head to the side.

A shameful blush stained her cheeks as she remembered just a few nights ago she'd let a strange man into her room to help her disrobe. "Sometimes," she whispered, "But not tonight."

"I see," he said quietly. "In that case, how about if we meet tomorrow at ten in the upstairs library. I think there are some things we need to discuss."

She swallowed. "We do?"

"Yes," he said, nodding. He brought his hands up to frame her face and cup her chin.

The tender gesture caused her breath to catch and she couldn't look away. His eyes spoke volumes of secrets he needed to reveal and she wanted to hear every single one. She nodded. "Ten, then," she agreed, staring at him.

"Goodnight," he said, releasing her face abruptly.

Shocked, she couldn't form a reply and watched as he walked across the hall to his room and slipped inside.

***

Liberty slept fitfully that night. He'd said they had a lot to talk about and she agreed. To be quite frank, the reason they were at his brother's house was the least of it. She was going to demand to know about all the other women and extract a promise from him that he'd stay faithful before she told him her feelings. Thanks to Elizabeth and Mr. Daltry, she'd realized she loved him. She couldn't tell him though. He wouldn't want her love. But perhaps if he knew she cared for him, he'd be willing to have a real marriage with her, one with friendship and trust and children. Yes, children. She wanted children. She wanted Paul's children. She wanted to see him play tin soldiers on the carpet of the drawing room with their children.

Sunlight filled the room and Liberty sprang from bed. A quick glance at the clock reminded her she needed to slow down. She still had nearly three hours to fill before her meeting with Paul.

Trying to pass the time, she leisurely dressed and attended her *toilette* before joining a group of rowdy men in the breakfast room.

Filling her plate and taking an empty seat next to Paul, she wondered what they were all talking about. A minute later, she realized they were reliving all their childhood antics. Again. She rolled her eyes. Really, how many times did they need to discuss whose hind end got sunburned from swimming naked in a creek from sunup 'til dusk? And as for the horse eating a pail of prunes, she could live without hearing those details again. But her husband seemed to enjoy listening to their stories, so she'd listen, too— even if they made her squirm.

Halfway through breakfast, a serious looking bespectacled man with a grim face and carrying a large black satchel came into the room. The room silenced at once and the man scanned the table until his eyes landed on Paul. "Mr. Grimes, I have some good news for you. Can you attend me in the hallway?"

Paul jumped up as if he'd been expecting to see the man and followed him out of the room.

Liberty looked around at the other men, an unspoken question printed on her face.

Lloyd, one of Paul's more colorful cousins, leaned over and in a stage whisper said, "I think we all know where Paul will be sleeping tonight."

Heat flooded Liberty's face as all the other men started to laugh.

"Perhaps tonight we'll all retire at nine to give him some extra time," another cousin, Peter, suggested with a wink in her direction, causing another eruption of laughter.

"Don't worry," Lloyd said in Liberty's direction, "once he gets his heir, he won't be so demanding."

"His heir?" Liberty repeated uncertainly. "What are you talking about?"

"Yes, his heir," Peter confirmed, but explained nothing further.

"Paul doesn't require an heir."

"He does now," David, a more serious cousin, informed her. "With Sam having no male issue, his wife dead and his carriage accident last week, Paul's role as heir has just been given a violent shove from meaningless to serious."

"Wh-what?" she stammered.

"Congratulations," Lloyd said. "You're now a crucial part of keeping the Bonnington title in the Grimes family."

She still didn't understand exactly what they were saying. The words male issue, dead, carriage accident and heir swirled around in her head, but she couldn't make sense of any of it. "But the man just said he had 'good news'."

"Of course he did," Peter acknowledged. "It is good news for a second son to find out no one stands between them and the title they've grown up knowing they'd never have."

Liberty's eyes widened in shock and partial understanding. "You mean—"

"What this nodcock means, is that Paul's just been given a direct path to the title. And you, my dear, are now as a good as a viscountess. Congratulations, you married well," David said, giving her a mock toast with his glass.

The blood rushed from her head. She wiped her clammy hands on her skirt and stammered through an excuse before leaving the table and running up to her room, shutting the door and sinking to the floor in despair.

He'd only wanted to meet with her because he was about to be made viscount and he needed an heir. That was the only reason he was being nice to her. And fool that she was, she'd fallen more in love with him. Not that it mattered anyway. She could never even tell him that she cared about him without him being suspicious. He'd think she was only saying it because he had a title. He'd think her no better than Lucy.

Chapter 29

Paul was furious. It had been four days since Liberty mysteriously vanished. If not for the fact that she'd taken his carriage along with his trusted coachman and he still had a responsibility to arrange for the funeral, he would have run her down as soon as he realized she was gone. This is what he got for abandoning his plan of letting her come to him and trying to woo her.

Finally after three days, he received a missive from Brooke that made his anger escalate to new heights.

Brooke had been brief and rather evasive in her letter. But he'd gleaned that Liberty was at Rockhurst and was demanding to be told the whereabouts of one Mr. Thomas Daltry. Just reading the words made him bitter. Just as he was about to tell her he loved her and explain everything, she'd run off to her lover. Brooke further tried to explain that she'd told Liberty Mr. Daltry wasn't the solution; but Liberty had threatened that if Brooke didn't produce Mr. Daltry in the flesh, she'd go to London and search for him. Therefore, Paul discarded his spectacles, put oil in his hair, slapped on a fake mustache, dressed in the black clothes from the other night (adding a waistcoat and coat for good measure) and was currently riding to Rockhurst.

He'd considered going to her as himself and demanding to know what was going on in that foolish head of hers. Sometimes, he'd swear she had rocks for brains. Yet, in the end, he decided he'd have better luck if "Mr. Daltry" talked some sense into her first. But there was no mistaking his irritation about going through with it.

He arrived at Rockhurst and was greeted by her entire family —literally. John, Carolina, Brooke, Andrew, Madison, even the baron and Alex were there.

"Don't you think you're missing something?" John asked solemnly, holding up a rapier and cape.

Paul sneered at him. "Sir, I don't think you want me to bring a weapon with me. At this point, I cannot guarantee I wouldn't use it."

John's eyes went wide and he hid the rapier behind his back. "Point taken."

"Thank you. Now where is she?"

"She's upstairs. Third door on the right," Brooke told him.

He nodded his thanks and stared at her for a minute. Her eyes had a sparkle he couldn't place in them. That was of no importance, she wasn't the one he'd come for.

Not bothering to knock on the door, he swung it open and walked inside. He abruptly halted when he realized he'd entered her bedroom. She sat on her bed wearing a green muslin day dress looking down at her toes as they dug into the carpet.

Thinking she hadn't heard him enter, he cleared his throat and startled her. Her eyes flew to his and she sprang off the bed, jamming her stocking-clad feet into her slippers before offering him a weak greeting. "Sorry. You caught me off guard. Brooke was supposed to have you wait in the drawing room."

"It's fine. We'll talk here," he said tightly, remembering to lower his voice.

She looked around. "Very well. We've been alone in a bedroom before," she said cheekily, taking a seat on the bed. She patted the space next to her.

"I'll stand, thank you."

She frowned. "That's just as well, I suppose."

"As charmed as I am that you felt the need to speak to me again, I must ask why it was necessary," he said as evenly as he could. He needed to stay calm and act nice if he was going to be able to convince her to go back to "her husband".

"Things didn't work out," she said evasively, not meeting his eyes.

"It's only been a week," he pointed out, trying not to grind his teeth. They'd only been together one day of that week; and try as he might to present her several opportunities to talk to him, she hadn't taken the bait.

She bit her lip and turned her face to survey the empty space next to his head. "I lied to you last week," she said with a slight hitch in her voice.

"Oh, you're husband doesn't have fourteen by-blows, then?" he teased.

She laughed. "That's not what I lied about. I'm not from America. I mean, I am. But I've been living in England for almost a year now."

"I already knew that," he said dismissively. "What importance does that have?"

"Because my husband is English," she explained as if that mattered a great deal. "Wait. How did you know that already?"

He flashed her a wry smile. "You're not exactly the best at keeping up a pretense."

"What do you mean?" she demanded in mock outrage.

"Oh, calm down," he said, shaking his head. "You told on yourself when you mentioned your relationship with the duke. No newcomer to England could have made that connection *and* had a ducal crested watch fixed in a matter of two days." That was true enough. If he hadn't already known, that would have raised his suspicions.

"Oh," she said, pink touching her cheeks. "I told Brooke I'd be no good at her game," she grumbled. "Well then, I'll tell you the rest of my secrets. I'm not Brooke's cousin Allison, I'm her sister, Liberty."

"Now that we have that established, what's going on with your husband? How has it all turned to dust in a matter of a week?"

"Right," she said sadly. "As it turns out, I've ruined everything."

He sighed. "You mean because of what happened between us the other night?"

"No," she said, shaking her head sadly. "I've waited too long to tell him how I feel and now it's too late."

He walked to the bed and sat down beside her. "What do you

mean?"

She tucked a stray lock of hair behind her ear and swallowed before turning to face him. "I mean that it's too late. If I tell him now, he'll not believe me. He'll think I experienced a change of heart because of his good fortune."

"His good fortune?" he echoed. Nobody had informed him of any good fortune.

"He's to inherit a title," she clarified.

Oh. That *good* fortune. "Do you care about a title, then?" he asked softy. His heart hammered in his chest waiting for her answer.

"No," she burst out in a slightly hysterical tone. "Haven't you been listening, you dolt? I don't care one whit about his title. But he'll think I do."

"Why do you think that?" he asked, resisting the urge to wrap his arms around her.

"Do you remember the woman who pointed out to me that I was tutoring illegitimate illiterates?" she asked, brushing a tear from her cheek?

He nodded. "Yes. The mother of the little boy you played games with."

"She also told me that my husband used to be madly in love with her until she threw him over for his brother because his brother had a title. She said she'd later realized her mistake, but it was too late and he wouldn't take her back."

He couldn't argue with that. Lucy had hurt him when she'd refused him due to his lack of title. But *he* later realized that if he had indeed loved her, he would have taken her back when she wrote to him. Instead, he realized it had only been an infatuation and had helped her the best he could. But playing the part of Mr. Daltry, he couldn't explain that to Liberty just now. "Perhaps you should just tell him and see what he says," he suggested.

She rolled her eyes. "You seem to have a lot of faith in the two of us."

"I do," he acknowledged. "I think you'd both benefit greatly from a candid conversation."

She frowned at him. "You would," she said sarcastically.

He scuffed his boot on the floor. "You don't?"

"I don't know," she said, shrugging. "I was going to talk to him after our last conversation. But then when I got home, he was gone to Cornwall because his brother was in an accident of some sort. A carriage I think. Anyway, I couldn't talk to him there where someone could overhear. Especially if I were to tell him about you, which I fully intended to do.

"Then he wanted to meet with me privately. He said we had a lot to talk about. I thought he might explain about his brood of children because I'd caught him entertaining one of his mistresses and their child. But then, before our meeting he got called away for some 'good news'." She let out a deep exhale before continuing her rambling. "After he was gone, his cousins—who I'd just learned were there for his brother's funeral—started commenting about how I married well and didn't know it, and I was as good as a viscountess now. A few even made crass comments about how they'd all retire early that night so my husband could start working on his heir."

Paul's jaw clenched. As irritated as he was with her for always running from him and never confronting her problems, he was equally irritated with his cousins. They should have had more sense than to say those remarks to her. "Is that why you came here?" he asked hoarsely.

"Yes," she whispered, burying her head in his chest and wrapping her arms around his neck

His arms came up around her, pulling her even closer to his body. "Shh. It will work out," he whispered against her hair.

"No, it won't," she cried fiercely, choking back a sob.

"Yes, it will," he assured her, stroking her back.

She shook her head. "I don't think you understand," she said, pulling her head back from his chest and lowering her hands to his shoulders. "I cannot tell him my feelings because he'll throw my love for him back in my face."

"Love?" he repeated, shocked. She loved him? Him as in Paul Grimes?

She groaned then closed her eyes and let out a deep breath. When she opened them again, she turned her head and nodded. "Yes, love. I love him. But he doesn't love me. He's nice enough to me, but he doesn't love me."

"Do you think your husband so callous to spurn you for loving him?" he questioned, very interested in her answer.

"Well, no," she admitted. "He's not cruel or anything. But I've no doubt he'll think I only love him for his title and since he can't exactly abandon me, he'll use my love against me."

"I beg your pardon?" he said sharply, pulling her hands off his person. "You just said he's not cruel, but what you just suggested he'll do when you inform him of your feelings sounds rather cruel to me. So which is it, madam, do you love your husband or do you find him to be some sort of nasty brute?"

"You misunderstand me," she interrupted hastily. "He won't spurn me right away because I'm his wife and he needs me to secure his heir. But that's all he'll see me as, a broodmare."

"I don't think you know his character very well if you think that of him," he said as she playfully pushed him backwards on the bed and came to rest her head on his heart.

She brought her right hand up to rest on his stomach and he felt a coil of desire form directly under the spot she touched. "Perhaps I don't," she confessed, pulling his shirt free of his trousers.

He didn't say anything. He couldn't say anything. Her fingers worked loose the buttons of his waistcoat and laid it open, along with his coat. She brought her hand back to his stomach and traced lazy figure eights over the top of his shirt. Even through two layers of linen, her touch made his blood race. He should end this and leave before things went too far. Her hand reached under his shirt and his blood chilled. "You didn't invite me here to use me as a replacement for your husband, did you?" he asked raggedly.

"A replacement?" she asked, her fingers skimming his bare abs.

"Yes. So you don't have to be his broodmare, as you so delicately put it." His hand grabbed her wrist to still her wandering fingers. "I will not be used in that way."

"Are you saying you'd bed me under different circumstances, then?" she asked with a teasing smile.

"Yes," he answered honestly. He'd bed her tonight if she wished it. Who was he trying to fool, he'd bed her ten minutes after she walked through the door to their home. He was planning on it. She couldn't get there soon enough in his mind.

"Well, too bad for you, this broodmare plans to do right by her husband," she said, breaking free of his grasp on her wrist and letting her fingers twirl the coarse hair that ran down the middle of his stomach.

"Good. I think you'd break the heart of that besotted sap you call a husband if you gave him a cuckoo," he teased as he closed his eyes again and let her touch him. He shouldn't let her continue. He needed to end the conversation and go home to wait for her to come to the real him. And yet, for as much as he knew he should stop her, he just couldn't. It was the first time she'd ever touched him and he was too lost reveling in her touch to care she thought he was another man.

She laughed. "Paul's not besotted."

"Yes, he is," he countered with a harsh laugh. "Only a besotted man would give his wife such a gift for St. Valentine's Day. All the rest just buy them a bauble or trinket."

Her hand stilled and she lifted her head off his chest and favored him with a curious glance. "How did you know about that?"

"I saw it. It was laying on your vanity and I flipped through it while you were changing." A lock of hair had fallen loose of her bun and his hand came up to push it behind her ear.

She put her head back on his chest. "He's a good man," she admitted after a minute.

"Promise me you'll work it out this time. Don't run away from him anymore," he said, bringing his hand up to caress her arm just above her elbow.

"I promise," she whispered. Silence filled the room for a few minutes as they lay there with their hearts beating in time with each other. "You know what's funny," she said, breaking the quiet.

"Hmm."

"You've hair in the same place as my husband," she said, tugging on a tuft of hair near his navel.

"Most men do," he said, chuckling. "But how would you know, anyway? I thought you had a marriage of convenience?"

"Yes, that's true, but I've seen him naked before," she confided with a laugh. "It may have been only once, but I remember the details quite well."

"Oh really," he drawled, trying not to grin at her revelation.

"Oh yes," she laughed. "I even remember he has a scar right," her hand slipped into the waistband of his trousers so fast he couldn't react in time to stop her, "here." Just as she ran her slender finger over his left hipbone in the direction of his groin, her eyes went wide and he knew instantly he'd pressed his luck too far, and now the game was over.

Chapter 30

"Drop! Your! Pants!" Liberty demanded angrily as she pulled her hand from his trousers and stood up. Her voice was so loud she'd even hurt her own ears.

"Pardon?" he said in feigned innocence, standing up.

"You heard me" she yelled, a little softer, but not much. "Drop your pants."

"No."

She shrugged. "Fine, don't."

He crossed his arms defiantly and stared at her. "Fine, I won't."

Anger and mortification swelled up inside her. How could he do this to her? How could he play her a fool this way? She walked up to his defiant form, grabbed the corner of his fake mustache and yanked it off, taking pleasure watching him wince in pain. "Get out!" she yelled, pointing toward the door. "Get out of my room and stay out of my life."

"No," he said, shaking his head. "You made a promise. I intend to hold you to it."

"You can't hold me to anything, you filthy liar," she snapped, moving to the door. She tried to open the door to flee the room, but it was locked. She pounded on the door with her palm, trying to get someone's attention. "Brooklyn, this isn't funny. Open the door this instant."

"Sorry, Liberty," came Brooke's muffled voice. "I'm not unlocking the door until you two have worked it out."

"We have," Liberty said.

"Is that so?" her sister taunted, irritating Liberty all the more.

"Yes," she said through clenched teeth.

"Really?"

"Yes, really. Now let me out."

"Not until I know you two have worked it out and I am well on my way to being an aunt."

Liberty rolled her eyes. "That will *not* be happening."

"Yes, well, usually asking a man nicely to drop his pants, or just undoing them for him, is a better approach."

"And just how long have you been standing there."

"I walked up as you were pounding the door. But I heard you yelling for him to drop his pants all the way downstairs. You were so loud I daresay the whole shire heard."

Heat crept up her neck and she turned to face her snickering husband. "Think that's funny, do you?" she asked coldly. "Well, rest assured, dear husband, it was the only time you'll ever be issued such an invitation by me."

He shrugged. "It wasn't much of an invitation," he retorted.

"Nonetheless, you'll never hear me say those words to you again."

"I don't think you have much room to be angry," he drawled. "You were the one caught sticking your hand down another man's trousers."

Oh, he wanted to play that card, did he? "I don't know why you even care," she replied angrily. "That's nothing compared to your multitude of sins!"

"To what do you refer?" he asked sarcastically. "The fourteen illegitimate children you seem to think I possess?"

She snorted. "You know as well as I do they exist. Don't deny it."

"I don't deny their existence," he said firmly. "However, I deny they're mine. They're Sam's."

"Yes, they're Sam's and that's why *you're* paying for them. Right, I forgot, the younger, untitled and considerably less wealthy brother always pays to support his older, titled and wealthy brother's illegitimate children," she mocked, rolling her eyes. "You know, I think you use Sam as your excuse for everything bad that happens to you. Fourteen illegitimate children, the reason you couldn't get Lucy to marry you, and now for me discovering your identity because of that scar. Sam, Sam, Sam; he's the reason for all three. It's just too bad, now that he's gone, you can't use him as a scapegoat anymore."

"Hold it right there, madam," he bellowed. "First and foremost, Sam is still alive. His wife died in the accident, not Sam. However, yes, as his heir, I am now next in line and will inherit upon his death due to his current and future lack of male issue. As for those fourteen children I support, they are all his. Some men are addicted to cards or alcohol or horse races, but Sam is addicted to pleasures of the flesh. I pay their support for the same reason you tutor the illiterate illegitimates, or whatever it is you call them, in a little room above the tavern each week. Because *we* both know *they* can't help the circumstances of their birth."

"That may be true," she acknowledged softly. How was it he knew her so well? "However, that does not prove you're not the father."

"Doesn't it?" he said, rocking back on his heels.

"No," she exclaimed. "I admit even I have a hard time believing you capable of the time and energy to produce that many children. And I'll even accept that a few truly aren't yours, but I doubt they're all his. Take Billy, for example; I was there when he called you 'Pa'. If that's not proof, I don't know what is."

Paul closed his eyes and shook his head. "Did it occur to you that perhaps at only eighteen months of age, Billy cannot say 'Paul'? And calling me 'Pa' is as close as he can get? Goodness, Liberty, give me a little more credit than that. No man who has illegitimate children allows them to call him by a fatherly sort of name."

"Then why were they even there?" she countered, trying to deflect the valid point he'd made about the little boy calling him 'Pa'.

"I don't know," he said with an annoyed shrug. "Ludwig told me they were waiting and I knew I couldn't ignore them in hopes of them leaving. When I walked into the room there was no way I could ignore the little boy. He doesn't deserve that. I only played with him to be friendly, not because he's mine; and certainly not because I entertain any sort of romantic notions about Evelyn."

"Fine," she allowed. He'd made convincing arguments that even she couldn't doubt where Billy was concerned. She also still believed Lucy's claim about Seth. "That clears you of two. What of the others?"

"They're not mine, either," he said, his voice hard and cold. "If you need more proof, I'll take you to see all fourteen of their mothers and you can ask them who they bedded. But it would be far easier if you just took my word for it."

"Your word," she mocked, casting him a dubious look. "Your word means nothing to me. You lied and tricked me." She couldn't control the sob that rose up in her throat.

"I acknowledge I deceived you," he said quietly. Then his eyes lit with anger and his voice grew hard. "But I've given you no other cause to doubt my word."

"Does that matter?" she burst out. "Why did you set out to do this? Did you want to have your fun at my expense, is that what it was?" She could feel the tears building behind her eyes as she remembered just how much she'd exposed to him. It hadn't been so bad to tell him those things when she thought him a stranger, but now to realize the person she was talking about was the person she was talking to made everything seem all the more mortifying.

"No, I didn't," he said softly, scuffing his boot on the floor. "Actually, I didn't go to the ball that night knowing you'd be there. Your father sent me a note asking me to come to London. When I arrived, he begged, pleaded and nearly twisted my arm," he paused to flash her a smile at his use of her own words, "to get me to go to the ball to help his niece, Allison Ellis. He claimed she was just in from New York and he wanted me to help her get acquainted with the ballroom. I grumbled about it and eventually gave in because he promised it would be the last time he'd asked for a favor." He ran his hand through his hair. "However, unlike you, I didn't get that promise in writing," he added ruefully.

"You'll learn," she said automatically. Then her eyes went wide when she realized she'd just given him a false glimmer of hope that things would work out. "I mean, in the future, when dealing with people. You'll learn to get a written agreement..." she trailed off and shook her head. If about nothing else, she knew he was telling the truth about being tricked into meeting her at the ball. Her family—specifically Brooke—had a knack for involving herself in other people's business.

He grinned and nodded slowly. "I see," he drawled.

"No, you don't," she snapped. "There is no chance at a future for us."

"Why?" he snapped back. "Because all of your false assumptions about me?

"No. I now have plenty of true ones to add to the list," she said pertly. "To start with, you should have told me your identity as soon as you learned mine."

"I was about to," he admitted sharply, "and then a second later you accused me of adultery."

"Well, if the boot fits," she said sarcastically.

"Well, the boot doesn't fit," he retorted angrily through clenched teeth. "I've kept my marriage vows. Unlike you, who seemed nearly willing to cuckold me with a stranger."

"Oh, congratulations! You've managed to keep your pants up for two months," she yelled sarcastically with a huff, ignoring his unflattering remark.

"Back to that, are we? I'll have you know, I've had just as much bed play as you have," he said, his face turning red.

"If you think I'll believe that, you're cracked," she said sardonically. "You seemed awfully skilled a few nights ago." She swallowed a lump in her throat and felt the heat of embarrassment flood her cheeks.

"I'm glad you think so, darling," he drawled tauntingly. "However, your body is the only one I've ever touched. As for my reaction, it was based solely on desire and instinct, not some practiced skill learned in a brothel."

She gasped and reached up to slap him, but he caught her wrist. "Let go of me, you vile, despicable man." She tried to pull her hand away, but his grasp was too firm.

"No. Now you listen here. You accuse me of infidelity, and yet, you're the one who sneaks off to dark places with strangers and lets them kiss and caress you." His voice was sharp, but his eyes were sharper.

A wave of shame washed over her. "As it turns out, you weren't a stranger after all, were you?" she shot back. "And you were just as involved in everything as I was."

"Yes, I was," he admitted coldly. "But *you* didn't know who I was. At least I knew who I was kissing and caressing in the dark."

Another wave of shame came over her. "No, I didn't. I didn't know him then and I don't know him now." She took a ragged breath. "I thought I did, but as it turns out, I didn't; more the fool I."

"You're not a fool, Liberty. Naïve, perhaps, but not a fool," he said gently.

"Yes, I am. I didn't even recognize my own husband at a ball," she said lamely, feeling deflated.

"I didn't recognize you right away, either," he allowed. "People typically believe what they're told they see. You only tipped me off with your overdone accent. I knew 'Ellis' was one of your mother's family names. Which would mean, like your mother, anyone from her side of the family, would have a southern accent, not one from New York. Then, you confirmed it when you mentioned Madison's daydreaming and how critical you were about it."

She fought to keep from grunting in dismay. Of course *he'd* picked up on that. He'd once eavesdropped on her most condemning conversation with Madison about that habit. "That was a good ten minutes before I said I suspected you of infidelity, why didn't you say something then?"

He smiled. "I wanted to dance with you."

"You already had."

He shook his head. "That may be true, but I didn't get to enjoy it. I was dancing with who I thought to be my wife's cousin and my body was reacting in a way that should be reserved for my wife. That's why I was counting. I needed a distraction. After I realized who you were, I wanted you in my arms again."

"But you waltzed me into a dark corner. Why? Why not reveal

your identity to me and take me to the ballroom?" she asked, confused.

He dropped his gaze to his boots. "I suspected you already knew who I was and I wanted to teach you a lesson so you wouldn't pull a trick like that again. But then I realized you'd been duped the same way I had. I would have told you then, except you openly accused me of being unfaithful to you."

"All right, so after I explained that, why did you continue to lie to me?" she asked sharply, crossing her arms.

He exhaled a pent-up breath. "I don't know. I should have told you, but I couldn't force myself to. I liked talking to you and holding you. And even if you were painting the real me in a very unfavorable light, I wanted to be with you."

"You mean you liked touching me inappropriately and discussing bawdy topics?" she asked with a smile.

"Of course, I did."

Her smile dimmed. "Wait a minute. Earlier you practically admitted to being a virgin, but that night you rattled off a whole list of words you said you used for your privates in mixed company." She cast him a sharp look that relayed an unspoken message of: "I don't know what to believe of you."

"That's simple," he said easily. "You're the only company, mixed or otherwise, I've ever talked that way in front of. For some reason, you embolden me." He shrugged and cast her a simple smile. "When I'm around you, I do and say things I'd never imagine saying in front of others. In a way, Brooke had it right when she claimed I was shy. I am, but not with you. As you already know, I've made an idiot of myself more times than not in your presence."

Her smile returned. "But why did you let it go so far?"

"You mean why did I kiss and touch you?"

She nodded weakly.

"You're my wife, Liberty. It's no secret I desire you that way. I wanted to kiss and touch you. And, as selfish as it sounds, when you kissed me, all thoughts of telling the truth fled because I wanted whatever you were offering; even if it was meant for another man." His voice cracked on the last sentence and Liberty felt her heart break.

"I'm sorry," she said, truly meaning it. She'd always been the model of all that was prim and proper, and in a moment of weakness, she'd given into lust and allowed liberties to a man she didn't know. "I didn't do that with the intention of hurting you," she whispered.

"I know," he whispered back, taking a seat on her bed.

She ached to join him, wrap him in her arms and feel his strong arms come around her and pull her close. Instead, she settled for sitting next to him. "Can we talk honestly? No lies, no barriers?" she asked quietly.

"I'd like that," he said softly, taking her hand in his.

"Why did you stop?" she asked quietly. "It's no secret I enjoyed your touches. Why didn't you take my virtue?"

"It wouldn't have been fair to the two, or should I say three," he winked at her, "of us. You would have thought you'd given your innocence to a stranger and I wouldn't be able to correct your assumption. Not to mention that I, as your husband and Mr. Daltry, would have found myself in the awkward situation of trying to shoot myself from both ends of a dueling field." He sent her a grin. "Truly, Liberty, I wanted you. But if I couldn't have you as my true self, then I'd rather not have you at all."

"Why didn't you reveal yourself when we went to my room?" she asked, biting her lip.

"Are you cracked?" he teased. "There was a rapier in there. I've no doubt you would have gladly finished the job Sam started."

She laughed. "I noticed you didn't bring it today."

"No. But not for fear you'd use it on me," he replied, giving her hand a light squeeze.

She gave a mock gasp. "And you say I'm bloodthirsty. All right, why did you come today?"

"I didn't want to," he confided, rubbing her knuckles with his thumb. "I came because I thought I'd have better luck talking sense into you as your trusted, mysterious confidant than as your dull, skirt-chasing husband."

She swallowed a lump in her throat. "All right, I understand. All is forgiven about the masquerade. However, I'd like some other explanations."

He brought her hand to his lips and kissed her knuckles. "Ask away."

The sensations his body was creating in hers made it hard for her to think. All the questions faded so much she couldn't even remember any she'd previously wanted to ask. Finally, she asked, "Why are you a vicar?"

He laughed. "You mean why do I stay on even though everyone thinks I'm Seth's father? At first, I panicked and tried to stem the gossip. But, I soon realized that short of having Lucy announce the truth in front of everyone, the problem wasn't going to go away. I knew that would hurt her more than it would help, so when she offered, I told her no. Then I tried to get transferred, but there were no openings. So I stayed on and watched my congregation fall apart. A few months later, I met your father, he suggested I should go visit the families that had left and let them get to know my character."

"That's why they've been coming back?" she asked, then "Oh, no, they'll all leave when they find out what I've been doing."

"You mean with your illegitimate illiterates?" he asked with a lazy smile and a shrug. "Who cares? If someone has a problem with that, I'll quit."

"But you can't," she protested.

He intertwined his fingers with hers. "Money isn't a concern any longer," he said with a shrug. "My grandfather, the duke who gave me the watch, left all his money and investments for me in a trust. On my next birthday, all the money is mine."

"Oh," she said simply. "And when is your birthday?"

"Soon."

"It had better not be tomorrow," she said only half-jokingly.

"It's not," he assured her. "It's the day after."

She looked at him horrified. "You're having me on," she said laughingly after a minute. "That silly grin of yours only comes out when you're teasing."

"So I am," he acknowledged. "My birthday is at the beginning of next month. I'll be five and twenty on the first of April."

She looked at him skeptically. "You're serious, aren't you?"

"Unfortunately, yes," he said solemnly. "However, I'll be the one with the last laugh this year when I receive more than one hundred fifty thousand pounds worth of investments."

"So you really didn't need my dowry?" she said dumbly.

"No." He shook his head and smiled at her. "Last January, I started getting the monthly dividends from my grandfather's investments. That money alone is enough money to support us." He gave her a tight squeeze. "Speaking of which," he said abruptly, his voice turning rather serious. "I never intended for you to have to work."

"That's all right. I like being Elizabeth's companion. I don't think of it as work," she said with a smile.

"Nonetheless, I intended for you to have an allowance. Apparently, I forgot to sign something. Anyway, the money is in Bath, waiting to be spent."

"Thank you," she said as he let go of her hand and slipped his arm around her shoulders. "One last thing; if Sam's not dead, why did the doctor, or whoever that was, say there was good news and your cousins say I'm as good as viscountess? Can't he just remarry?"

"Yes, he can," Paul said, nodding. "But that's not the good news the *solicitor* was speaking of."

"What do you mean?" she asked, furrowing her brow.

"Sam won't be having any more children," he said simply. "The solicitor knows I support Sam's brood. The good news was that there wouldn't be anymore. Sam *can't* have anymore," he further explained after he caught sight of her blank stare.

"Why not?" she asked innocently.

He pulled her onto his lap. "All his parts aren't in operating condition anymore," he told her with a grimace.

"Oh," she said, turning pink.

"So now, Mrs. Grimes, it depends on us to continue the family line," he said with an exaggerated sigh.

She swatted him on the arm. "So you do want a broodmare," she teased in mock indignation.

"No," he said quietly. "I want you."

"Oh, Paul, I'm so sorry," she said, wiping a tear from the corner of her eye. "I'm sorry for the way I've treated you all this time."

"I don't want to talk about the past. I forgive you for everything, including the bit with 'Mr. Daltry'," he said with a smile that didn't reach his eyes.

"I didn't intend to hurt you," she said, her voice cracking and lips quivering. "I j-just wanted to b-be wanted."

"I do want you," he said raggedly, pulling her closer to him. "I do want you."

"Did you mean everything you said when you were 'Mr. Daltry'?" she asked uneasily.

"You mean the parts about wanting you for you and marrying you without a dowry?" he asked as if he'd read her mind.

"Yes," she whispered.

"Absolutely," he said without hesitation. "Your father may think he tricked and bribed me, but he didn't. I wouldn't have married you if I hadn't wanted to. I just didn't know at the time that I wanted to."

She shook her head and ran her fingers in mindless patterns on his chest. "What did you write on my chest that night?"

"Isn't that obvious?" he asked, reaching up and pulling a pin from her hair. "I wrote 'I love you'. When you asked me to do it again, I didn't dare."

"I love you, too," she said, wrapping her arms around his neck and bringing her face close to his.

"I know," he said before pressing his lips to hers. "Liberty," he said raggedly, breaking their kiss. "I want to make you my wife."

"I already am," she giggled, pressing her lips back to his.

Pulling back, he said, "No. I want to make you my wife in truth."

"Oh," she said, blushing. "Here? Now?"

"Yes, here," he said, standing her up.

"But, we can't," she said, shaking her head.

"Why not?" He pulled the last of the pins from her hair and released it into a thick wavy mass.

"It's my sister's house," she squealed as he started undoing the buttons at the top of her gown.

His hand stilled and he turned her to face him. "I think it would be all right, she all but gave us her blessing."

"Well," she said with an exaggerated sigh. "I suppose we'll have to get to it if we don't want to be locked in here for the rest of our lives."

"Just so," he agreed, bending to kiss her neck. "And, we have my family line to think of. I'd hate to see the title go to Lloyd."

She shuddered at the thought. "All right," she sighed, feigning playful resignation. "For the sake of duty, take me to bed."

He flashed her a grin. "Gladly."

Chapter 31

Paul drew back and whispered, "Liberty, as I said earlier, I'm not an expert in this area. You'll have to tell me what you do and don't like."

She flashed him a grin. "Well, sir, I *don't* like all these clothes, I think I'd like it very much if they vanished," she said, flicking her wrist.

"Yes, ma'am," he said with a mock salute. "I'll get right on it, ma'am" Then his lips took hers and he brought his fingers back up to the top of her gown to work the buttons.

Liberty returned his kiss, matching his movements. She brought her hands up to his face and ran her fingers along his smooth cheeks, tracing the outline of his cheekbones and jaw. "So smooth," she murmured against his mouth.

He leaned back and grinned. "Did the mustache make you itch, too?" he asked, bringing his hands to the front of her gown.

"No, not really, it kind of tickled, actually," she said with a smile, running her finger over his bare upper lip.

He grabbed the caps of her sleeves and reverently let his hands slide them over her shoulders. "You've beautiful shoulders," he murmured before leaning closer and kissing the flesh he'd just bared. His hands lowered her gown all the way to the floor and she felt so naked and exposed standing before him this way.

Her hands delved to the inside of his waistcoat and pushed it open. He shrugged out of it and let it fall to the floor along with his coat, forming a careless, forgotten heap. His mouth came to settle on her right shoulder, tenderly kissing a path to her neck. Her fingers went to work on his shirt, making quick work of the buttons as he started to kiss the sensitive skin behind her ear and absentmindedly toyed with the straps of her chemise with his fingers.

She gasped when he gently nipped her neck. Recovering, she started pulling his shirt off. With a growl, he broke away from her neck and allowed her to remove his shirt. Her eyes did a slow and thorough survey of his chest, mentally taking note of each contour. Nervously, she reached her fingers up to run them over his chest. Funny that she'd been so brave about touching him when she hadn't known who he was.

As if sensing her hesitation, Paul reached up and covered her hand, bringing it to rest on his chest. "Touch me," he rasped.

Slowly, she moved her hand from the spot he'd placed it. She ran her fingers over his muscled chest, stilling on top of his heart for a second. His hands came to rest on her shoulders, and he hooked his thumbs under the edge of her chemise straps. Bending to kiss her lips again, he groaned when she brought both hands to his chest and slowly trailed them down his torso to the top of his trousers.

Breaking their kiss, he lowered his head and scattered kisses on her chest above her chemise while his hands dropped lower to caress her breasts. Sighing at the sensation of his strong hands firmly shaping her, her fingers stilled on his buttons. His head lowered again and his mouth closed over the tip of her breast. She groaned and arched her back, offering him more of herself. His hands grabbed the hem of her chemise and lifted it up. Abruptly, his mouth left her breast and she whimpered at the loss of his closeness. She felt rather than saw his grin at her reaction and she blushed in embarrassment.

"No need to be embarrassed," he murmured. "I want you to enjoy it."

Her eyes flew to his. He was right; there was no need to be embarrassed. He was her husband. He wasn't going to mock her for enjoying his touches. He loved her.

As soon as her chemise was off, his mouth took hold of her aching nipple once again. Her hands flew to his hair. Twining her fingers in the back of his dyed locks, she held his head to her chest. His hands came to rest on her hips and slowly he walked her backward toward the bed. Laying her down atop the feather mattress, he kissed a trail of kisses from the top of her sternum to her navel. "You're so beautiful," he panted. "Did you know I thought so the night we met?"

She rolled her eyes and ran her palms up and down his thick arms. "Do you know where you go for lying?" she asked with a sweet smile.

He chuckled. "Of course. But, I'm not lying. The night we met, I saw you smile and I thought you were the most beautiful woman in the room," he said, his voice full of conviction. "I love to see you smile, Liberty."

"I know," she said honestly. "Only a besotted man makes an idiot of himself in front of his wife on St. Valentine's Day," she teased, brushing her knee against his arousal.

"Right," he said curtly. "I forgot. You've a curiosity for male parts."

She put her foot flat on his thigh and inched her toes in the direction of his waist. "Hmm?"

He stood up all the way and brought his hands to rest on his waistband. "Since you seem to remember my body so well, perhaps I shouldn't even bother taking off my trousers," he said, rolling his eyes up to look at the ceiling and twisting his lips as if he were in deep contemplation.

She repositioned herself on the bed so she was lying on her side with her head propped up on her hand. "Drop your pants," she demanded with a sultry smile.

His eyes went wide and he gasped. "And here I thought you'd never extend me the invitation again," he said, feigning shock.

"I didn't," she chirped. "It wasn't an invitation, it was a demand. Now, drop 'em."

"Or what?" he asked, grinning.

"Or I'll do it for you," she said sweetly.

He groaned. "As much as I'd love to have you do just that, you'd better not. It might be my undoing." Making quick work of his boots and trousers, Paul soon stood before her in all his naked glory. "Look your fill," he told her hoarsely. "I know I've been."

Liberty giggled. "You know, I have a hard time sometimes

remembering you're a vicar," she said laughingly. "You have a tendency to say some of the most shocking things."

"Only to you, Liberty," he returned. "As I said, you embolden me. I may be a man of God, but I'm still a man. I still get angry like a man and I still have the same desires of a man."

"Clearly," she remarked dryly with a pointed look at his rampant erection.

In a second, Paul was on the bed with Liberty. His hands traveled down her legs, taking her stockings with them. Carelessly, he threw them to the ground before starting to work on her drawers. When he had her free of her drawers, he brought both hands to her thighs and softly massaged her tender flesh, sending waves of excitement coursing through her body. Burying his head in the crook of her neck, he spread her thighs.

Her hands kneaded the hard muscles in his broad shoulders and back. His body shifted and came to rest between her legs, causing her to involuntarily stiffen. "Relax," he murmured into her neck. He slid his hand up her thigh until he reached the apex of her thighs. Slowly, his fingers started touching her soft flesh, causing a fresh wave of sparks to fly through her.

"I thought—"

He kissed her lips to silence her question. "Just let me touch you first." He slipped one of his thick fingers inside and she gasped.

She opened her mouth to ask if he knew what he was doing, but he silenced her again with a playful pinch on her bottom. Perhaps he did know after all, she thought a minute later when an intense pressure started building inside her. She shut her eyes and let the sensations created by his steady rhythm take hold. The pressure became too much and just as it threatened to overtake her, he stilled and withdrew.

On the verge of protesting his sudden absence, she felt him at her entrance again. This time he felt bigger, thicker. Awareness dawned. This was it. His eyes met hers and they locked gazes as he carefully pushed forward. Her body stretched and adjusted to his size, and she braced herself for what she knew was coming next.

With a murmured apology, a look of remorse, and a savage cry, Paul pushed forward past the last barrier between them, catching her startled cry with his mouth. His body stilled and he waited for her eyes to meet his. "There was no other way," he said raggedly.

"It's all right," she assured him, wiggling her hips to get more comfortable.

He groaned and lowered his head to rest next to hers for a second before he started moving in a steady rhythm. Instinctively, she started to respond by rocking her hips to match his movements, increasing her pleasure. Once again she felt herself on the verge of something she couldn't comprehend. Not wanting to miss it again, she closed her eyes and gave herself completely over to it. She was lost in her own pleasure and was barely aware of Paul's savage growl of release.

His body rested on top of hers for a minute before he rolled off, mumbling something about being too heavy. Laying her head on his chest, she stroked his sternum with one delicate finger.

"I love you, too," he said a second after she was done.

She looked up at him. "You're better at that than I am."

"No. You were just distracted when I did it to you, that's all," he pointed out.

"You'll just have to do it again sometime," she said, kissing his cheek.

"I will. Don't worry," he said, holding her close.

She idly twirled a curl of his chest hair. "I wonder if Brooke's unlocked the door yet."

"Who cares?" he asked, favoring her with a wolfish smile. "I've no plans to leave anytime soon. Do you?"

"Absolutely not, we have duties to fulfill in here," she teased, moving her hand down to his hip to trace the scar she'd longed to touch since the night she'd first seen him naked.

He laughed. "You can use that as an excuse to share my bed if you want. But I want to share yours for love. And I think you do, too," he said, giving her a gentle squeeze.

"It's true, I do," she said, snuggling closer. "I've hidden

behind duty and propriety for too long. I want to share your bed because I love you, Paul, not for any other reason."

Paul's large hand rubbed soothing strokes on her shoulders and she was about to close her eyes to go to sleep when her eye caught a little white ball on the floor. "What's that?" she asked, pointing to the ball.

Paul stopped rubbing her and looked to the ball beside his discarded trousers. "I believe that's a note," he said matter-of-factly. "The night of the ball it was lying on your bed and I snatched it up before you could see it and realize who I was."

"What does it say?" she asked, looking at him curiously.

"I don't know," he admitted. "I shoved it into my pocket and forgot all about it until now."

Not wasting another minute, she leapt from the bed and scooped up the ball of paper. Unfolding the note, she read it aloud, "'Dear Paul and Liberty, I thought you two needed a new start. Love, Brooke'."

"No post script from the others, begging us not to be angry with them?" Paul inquired with a smile.

"Actually, yes, except the three of them begged we not seek revenge by killing, maiming, or injuring any of them," she said, leading them both to laugh at their ridiculous pleas.

"She was right, you know," he commented a minute later when his laughter had subsided. "We did need a fresh start. For as much trouble as that masquerade caused, it led to a new beginning for us."

"Oh, Paul, I love you," Liberty said, tossing the paper on the floor.

"Come show me."

And she did.

Epilogue

July 1813

"Did Mama and Papa say when they're coming back?" Liberty asked her oldest sister as they sat in the perched look out of Brooke's ballroom.

Brooke shook her head. "I don't know." She turned to face her husband who was staring at the beautiful young lady dressed in blue and surrounded by far more gentlemen than any other young lady in the room. "Do you?"

"I imagine we all know the same thing," Andrew commented a moment later. "They'll be back in a few months."

Liberty nodded. A month after Brooke had given birth to little Nathan, her parents had gone back to America to tie up some loose ends. With two out of three of their daughters happily married in England, they'd decided to make England their permanent home as well.

"Don't worry," Paul murmured, breaking into her thoughts. "They'll be back in time."

She smiled at him. He was such a good husband to her and she knew he'd make a great father in a matter of months. "I know," she said, leaning against him.

"Well, *I* hope they make it back before a different kind of event altogether," Andrew put in. "It's not easy acting as Madison's guardian. I detest all the gentlemen buzzing around my house vying for her affection." He shuddered and curled his lip in disgust.

"Oh, stop," Brooke told her husband, giving him a playful shove. "She enjoys it, and I daresay she deserves to."

"Who's the favorite, then?" Paul asked as he glanced down at Madison who was surrounded by a dozen eligible gentlemen, most of whom were titled.

"I would say it is a three way tie between Chapman, Drury and Wray," Andrew said with a scowl. "Not that I dislike the men, mind you. I just don't like the responsibility."

Paul nodded. "Of the three, I'd say Drury. He's a decent sort."

"I agree," Brooke added. "He's titled. He's handsome. He's wealthy. And he's hopelessly in love with Madison. What more can a girl ask for?"

Liberty laughed. "My, my, Brooke, you talk about him like he's your suitor."

"Now, now," Andrew broke in. "Don't be putting ideas in her head. She's all mine." He wrapped his arm around his wife and pulled her tightly to him.

Liberty was about to make a flip return when suddenly she was silenced by Brooke's gasp. "What is *he* doing here?" she demanded of no one in particular.

"Who?" Liberty asked, craning her neck to see who Brooke was talking about. "Gateway?" she asked, when she saw Gateway standing in the back corner with his hands in his overstuffed pockets. "I told you, he came to London to find a wife this season."

"Poor girl," Andrew muttered.

Brooke sent her husband a sharp look. "No, not Gateway. Believe it or not, I invited him."

"You did?" the other three said in unison.

"Elizabeth asked me to," she said with a shrug. "She promised me he wouldn't cause trouble. Anyway, he is not the 'him' I was referring to. I was referring to *him!*"

Liberty's eyes followed the direction of Brooke's accusing finger and thought her heart was going to leap out of her chest when she saw the 'him' in question: *Robbie Swift.*

Liberty didn't realize she'd made an unladylike noise until she heard the other three laugh at her "unLibertylike behavior", as they'd all begun to refer to things she did that broke the rules of propriety.

"Is that the one you told me about?" Paul whispered in her ear.

"Yes," she confirmed aloud. "He's the bounder who stole her

heart, broke it, and served it back to her on a platter."

"That was quite an eloquent description," Paul stated.

"Well, it's true," Brooke said in her defense. Snapping her fingers, she turned to her husband and said, "Get over there and throw him out, Andrew."

"Why me?"

Brooke twisted her lips and gave him a bemused look. "Because you're the host. Because you're Madison's guardian." She moved close to whisper something in Andrew's ear Liberty and Paul couldn't have heard, no matter how hard they strained.

Andrew rolled his eyes. "All right, I'll go."

"I'll go with you," Paul said.

"Men," Brooke groaned after they'd departed.

"Tell me about it," Liberty muttered.

"Let's just hope they get that bounder out of here before Madison sees him," Brooke said, just as Paul and Andrew came into view walking across the crowded ballroom.

"Too late."

.

If you enjoyed *Liberty for Paul*, I would appreciate it if you would help others enjoy this book, too.

Lend it. This e-book is lending-enabled, so please, share it with a friend.

Recommend it. Please help other readers find this book by recommending it to friends, readers' groups and discussion boards.

Review it. Please tell other readers why you liked this book by reviewing it at one of the following websites: <u>Amazon</u> or <u>Goodreads</u>.

Other Books by Rose Gordon

BANKS BROTHERS' BRIDES

His Contract Bride—Lord Watson has always known that one day he'd marry Regina Harris. Unfortunately nobody thought to inform her of this; and when she finds that her "love match" was actually arranged by her father long ago in an effort to further his social standing, it falls to a science-loving, blunt-speaking baron to win her trust.

His Yankee Bride—John Banks has no idea what—or who—waits for him on the other side of the ocean... Carolina Ellis has longed to meet a man whom she can love, so when she glimpses such a man, she's determined to do whatever it takes to have him—Southern aristocracy be damned.

His Jilted Bride—Elijah Banks *cannot* sit still a moment longer as the gossip continues to fly about one of his childhood playmates, who just so happens to still be in her bridal chamber, waiting for her groom to arrive. Thinking to save her the public humiliation of being jilted at the altar, Elijah convinces her to run away with him, replacing one scandal with one far more forgiving. But when a secret she keeps is threatened to be exposed, it falls to Elijah to save her again by revealing a few of his own...

His Brother's Bride —Henry Banks had no idea his brother agreed to marry a fetching young lady until the day she shows up on his doorstep and presents the proof. To protect the Banks name and his new sister-in-law's feelings, Henry agrees to marry her only to discover this young lady's intentions were not so honorable and it wasn't really marriage she sought, but revenge on a member of the Banks family...

Coming July 2013
Celebrate America's independence with the:
OFFICER SERIES

(American Historicals based in Indian Territory mid-1800s)

The Officer and the Bostoner —A well-to-do lady traveling by stagecoach from her home in Boston to meet her fiance in Santa Fe finds herself stranded in a military fort when her stagecoach leaves without her. Given the choice to either temporarily marry an officer until her fiance can come rescue her or take her chances with the Indians, she marries the glib Captain Wes Tucker, who, unbeknownst to her, grew up in a wealthy Charleston family and despises everything she represents. But when it's time for her fiance to reclaim her and annul their marriage, will she still want to go with him, and more importantly, will Wes let her?

The Officer and the Southerner—Second Lt. Jack Walker doesn't always think ahead and when he decides to defy logic and send off for a mail-order bride, he might have left out only a few details about his life. When she arrives and realizes she's been fooled (again), this woman who's never really belonged, sees no other choice but to marry him anyway—however, she makes it perfectly clear: she'll be his lawfully wed, but she will *not* share his bed. Now Jack has to find a way to show his always skeptical bride that he is indeed trustworthy and that she does belong somewhere in the world: right here, with him.

The Officer and the Traveler—Captain Grayson Montgomery's mouth has landed him in trouble again! And this time it's not something a cleverly worded sentence and a handsome smile can fix. Having been informed he'll either have to marry or be demoted and sentenced to hard labor for the remainder of his tour, he proposes, only to discover those years of hard labor may have been the easier choice for his heart.

If you never want to miss a new release, click here to subscribe to her New Release list or visit Rose's website at www.rosegordon.net to subscribe and you'll be notified each time a new book becomes available.

GROOM SERIES

Four men are about to have their bachelor freedom snatched away as they become grooms...but finding the perfect woman may prove a bit more difficult than they originally thought.

Her Sudden Groom—The overly scientific, always respectable and socially awkward Alexander Banks has just been informed his name resides on a betrothal agreement right above the name of the worst chit in all of England. With a loophole that allows him to marry another without consequence before the thirtieth anniversary of his birth, he has only four weeks to find another woman and make her his wife.

Her Reluctant Groom—For the past thirteen years Marcus Sinclair, Earl Sinclair, has lived his life as a heavily scarred recluse, never dreaming the only woman he's ever wanted would love him back. But when it slips out that she does, he doubts her love for his scarred body and past can be real. For truly, how can a woman love a man whose injuries were caused when he once tried to declare himself to her sister?

Her Secondhand Groom—Widower Patrick Ramsey, Viscount Drakely, fell in love and married at eighteen only to be devastated by losing her as she bore his third daughter. Now, as his girls are getting older he realizes they need a mother—and a governess. Not able to decide between the two which they need more, he marries an ordinary young lady from the local village in hopes she can suit both roles. But this ordinary young lady isn't so ordinary after all, and he'll either have to take a chance and risk his heart once more or wind up alone forever.

Her Imperfect Groom—Sir Wallace Benedict has never been good with the fairer sex and in the bottom drawer of his bureau he has the scandal sheet clippings to prove it. But this thrice-jilted baronet has just discovered the right lady for him was well-worth waiting for. The only trouble is, with multiple former love interests plaguing him at every chance possible, he must find clever ways to avoid them and simultaneously steal the attention—and affections—of the the one lady he's sure is a perfect match for him and his imperfections.

Already Available--SCANDALOUS SISTERS SERIES

Intentions of the Earl—A penniless earl makes a pact to ruin an American hoyden, never suspecting for a moment he'll lose his heart along the way.

Liberty for Paul—A vicar's daughter who loves propriety almost as much as she hates the man her father is mentoring will go to any length she sees fit to see that improper man out the door and out of her life. But when she's forced to marry him, she'll learn there's a lot more to life, love and this man than she originally thought.

To Win His Wayward Wife —A gentleman who's spent the last five years pining for the love of his life will get his second chance. The only problem? She has no interest in him.

About the Author

USA Today Bestselling and Award Winning Author Rose Gordon writes unusually unusual historical romances that have been known to include scarred heroes, feisty heroines, marriage-producing scandals, far too much scheming, naughty literature and always a sweet happily-ever-after. When not escaping to another world via reading or writing a book, she spends her time chasing two young boys around the house, being hunted by wild animals, or sitting on the swing in the backyard where she has to use her arms as shields to deflect projectiles AKA: balls, water balloons, sticks, pinecones, and anything else one of her boys picks up to hurl at his brother who just happens to be hiding behind her.

She can be found on somewhere in cyberspace at:

http://www.rosegordon.net

or blogging about *something* inappropriate at:

http://rosesromanceramblings.wordpress.com

Rose would love to hear from her readers and you can e-mail her at rose.gordon@hotmail.com

You can also find her on Facebook, Goodreads, and Twitter.

If you never want to miss a new release, click here to subscribe to her New Release list or visit her website to subscribe and you'll be notified each time a new book becomes available.

CPSIA information can be obtained at www.ICGtesting.com
Printed in the USA
LVOW10s1615030614

388429LV00022B/1469/P